ESCAPING WHITSUNDAY

Escaping Whitsunday

E.A. STARK

Escaping Whitsunday

COPYRIGHT

DEDICATION

Thank you to my family for your unwavering support all these years.

Thank you to my dearest friends, Maria and Lida, for believing in me and being my first devoted readers.

Your encouragement and persistence gave me the courage to publish this story.

INTERACTIVE ELEMENT

For the past few years, we have lived through the pandemic, lockdowns, and travel restrictions. Unfortunately, our world has drastically changed.

To cope with life's stresses and strains, many have taken up hobbies to pass the time and escape this new reality. Thankfully, for some, reading has filled that gap. Whether you are looking for an adventure, crave suspense, enjoy a good mystery, or want to fall in love, the written word has been there through these difficult times to transport us away at a moment's notice.

When writing this story, I wanted to grant the reader an opportunity to explore the world from the comfort of their favorite nook, so I created a treasure hunt of sorts using the locations featured. For those looking to enhance their reading experience, embedded inside *Escaping Whitsunday*, you will notice DMS (Degrees, Minutes, Seconds) coordinates posted at the beginning of later chapters. Their purpose is to involve the reader in Eva Thompson's epic journey - this emotionally charged detour her life unexpectedly takes once she arrives on Hamilton Island. Hopefully, it will encourage you to follow along using one of many digital mapping applications available today. When you locate these markers, dig deeper. Look at the photos provided of the location, even the 360-degree views available. Doing this will immerse you in the scenes depicted because, in essence, each location is described as it truly exists. Not only is it an entertaining way to read, but educational as well. So often in our lifetime, we never stop and appreciate the world around us. The magnificence of it all. There is so much to be discovered.

Even though the planet is moving in a new direction, it doesn't mean we can't go on an adventure!

I hope you enjoy *Escaping Whitsunday.* It is a story filled with extraordinary destinations, experiences, intrigue, suspense, and heartfelt romance.

Happy reading!   E.A. Stark

PROLOGUE

Within seconds of the explosion, the house went deadly quiet. The widespread crackling of the fire consuming fuel is all I could hear. Dense smoke blanketed the second floor. Firmly holding a cloth tight to my face, desperate for air, eyes burning and watering profusely, I listened and waited. Were they gone? Was it over?

Amidst the eeriness, the hardwood unexpectedly creaked with the weight of heavy boots ascending the stairs. Deep down, I knew they'd fulfilled their mission. The love of my life was gone. Now, they were in search of me - the final thread. Alone in the darkness, I knew my life was about to end. Sadly, there was no escaping it now.

Inside a shallow closet, hidden behind a few unpacked boxes, trembling uncontrollably, I bowed my head in prayer, wondering if death would be the way some describe it - a peaceful departure while quietly disconnecting from this world before transitioning to the next. My heart hammered in my chest as the air around me thickened. It was hard to refrain from coughing, but there was no avoiding it. Struggling to stay quiet, gasping in the smallest of doses, I heard the boots inch closer and closer down the hall, then suddenly stop a few feet away. Afraid to make a sound, the slight breeze from the closet door drifted past my face, revealing the black barrel of a gun. With it, a red laser dot slowly crept across the void along the wall, prompting tears to flood my cheeks, giving way to paralyzing fear - selfishly reducing my lifespan to mere seconds. Time stood still when the ominous marker found me in its crosshairs. Courage fading sharply, the blood rushed from my limbs, leaving them lifeless and weak. My lungs ceased to function as the world ground to a halt.

BANG!!! BANG!!! BANG!!!

Flinching with each shot, producing an intensely prolonged gasp, I clutched my chest to halt the bleeding in a panicked state, focused on survival. My spirit frantically tried to evade the smoke and gunfire, death, and destruction. Somehow able to wipe the beads of sweat dripping from my brow with hands shaking incessantly, I scoured the room, gradually recognizing where I was. Body pulsating at a dangerous clip, the silence was almost deafening.

Out of the shadows, a familiar voice emerged to offer comfort. Safely in his arms, I clung tightly. A flick of the switch illuminated the bedside table lamp, bringing me out of the darkness and releasing me from the ongoing nightmare. The love of my life attempted to restore my body's natural rhythm as we've done so many times before. Our handlers say it could take several months or even years for the memories to stop haunting us in this way. If they ever will. Scars like this are not easily dismissed. Supposedly, it's part of the healing process - the body's ability to deal with the aftermath of trauma. Thankfully, through it all, I was not alone. He stood by me and will never leave.

Our life is very different from the future I envisioned years before, but that's because fate stepped in to correct my mistakes. My name was once Eva Thompson. This is how I vanished without a trace into a hidden world where no one exists - how I gave up everything to live a life with him.

| 1 |

Eighteen Months Earlier...

"Wake up, Eva. No rest for the weary," my peppy Italian roommate Antonia said as she passed the door of my room. "Come on! We can't be late."

Eyes barely open, I realized it was Monday. The hum of rush hour traffic and the odd siren and horn reminded me of the beloved city of New York. Reaching for my phone on the bedside table, struggling to focus, I glanced at the screen, mindful of today's date, and turned off the alarm. Aware that it's been exactly two months since my firm transferred us to the Beverly Hills office, I felt this tremendous sense of accomplishment. Still unable to fathom being granted this rare, once-in-a-lifetime opportunity, I rolled over in bed, realizing the milestone hadn't come without sacrifices. I'd given up a lot to be here, but it was a dream come true.

"Let's go, lazy bones!" Antonia shouted from her bedroom on the opposite side of our luxury apartment rental off Wilshire Boulevard.

"Okay! You do realize this is my sixteenth day straight, right?"

"What do you want? A medal?" she taunted, putting on her necklace, half-dressed, with hair still looking disheveled as she stood in the doorway. "Can I borrow your grey hair tie?"

Laughing at her sharp reply, I grabbed it off my bedside table and tossed it to her before opening the blinds. Greeted by the rising sun over the eastern hillside, my thoughts drifted to the population of Manhattan, already three hours into their workday. Among them was my fiancé, Scott. Being an early riser, I assumed he had already visited many of his development sites by now. Feeling distant but not at all homesick, a part of me did wonder why my heart wasn't missing him terribly these days. I mean, it had been a while since we'd seen each other, let alone talked.

"Perhaps I'm working way too much?" I mumbled, trying to find a reason for feeling this way. "Maybe it's time for a break?"

Closing my eyes, envisioning sun and sand, crystal blue waters, and utter tranquility, my spirit knew a real vacation was not remotely in the cards.

Moving into the bathroom to prepare for work, I muttered, "You knew this was a four-year project, and there would be no time off until it's done."

Immediately releasing a sad sigh, my problem-solving nature was determined to fit some relaxation time into my demanding weekly schedule. Missing the water views from my Chelsea apartment, close to the High Line and the Hudson, I figured visiting a beach somewhere along the Pacific Coast Highway would suffice for now.

Turning on the rain shower faucet, the sounds of the water falling helped bring the idea to life, but reality soon set in.

"Be realistic, Eva. It's day sixty, and you've only seen the ocean from the air," I concluded with an enormous amount of disappointment while staring at myself in the mirror.

Right on cue, Antonia walked by and shouted, "Gotta leave in thirty! Coffee's on!"

Usually thankful for her military-style nature since it complemented mine, the constant reminders annoyed me for some reason this morning. Accustomed to being alone since I was young, it had been challenging to have her around all the time.

While growing up, my sister and I were always expected to be independent and never rely on anyone. This is how our parents raised us – forever at arm's length. We were the product of our environment, parented by people who'd send their children to boarding school all year, then leave at the drop of a hat to tour the extravagant resorts of the south of France for five weeks every summer, leaving us behind.

Wrapped in a fluffy towel after my shower, swiping some shadow across my eyelids soon after, thoughts of my late grandparents came to mind. They were our saviors every year. Thankful to spend the summers at their oceanside home along Cooper's Beach in the Hamptons, I believe that if it weren't for them, my sister and I would have never felt loved. Each day of our vacation, we were greeted each morning with open arms, hugs, kisses, and excited expressions upon revealing what adventures they'd planned for us. At night, while getting tucked into bed, we always heard, 'I love you.' These three little words forever filled my relatively empty heart since that verbal bond between a parent and child never graced my mother and father's lips – even to this day, so many years later.

Standing in my closet, bringing my head out of the clouds, I tried to decide what to wear after mentally strolling down memory lane. Dressed in a white blouse, navy pencil skirt, blazer, and neutral pumps, I added the Hermes scarf Scott had bought me, boasting various shades of blue for a pop of color. Still confused about how women dressed for work in Beverly Hills, looking in the mirror, my suit seemed very corporate. Stauncher NYC than lively LA, I thought, if I ever get a moment to shop, I probably should. An outing, Antonia, would never pass up, I'm sure.

Briefcase in hand, fumbling around with my blueprint canisters and my shoulder bag, I set them on the table. Draping my blazer neatly over the back of the dining room chair next to the kitchen, I was thankful to have fifteen minutes to spare. Able to enjoy a morning coffee before heading out, my engagement ring happened to sparkle in the morning light. Thinking about Scott, I felt lucky to have him. Throughout life's many milestones and poorly orchestrated attempts to find Mr. Right, terribly heartbroken, disappointed, and frustrated, like many girls, I inevitably stopped hoping and wishing I'd ever meet the person everyone describes as 'the love of their life.'

Funny enough, that's when it happened. When I least expected, the guy of my dreams walked casually through the door of Gunther's hardware store. It was almost a year ago now. While getting an extra key cut for my new apartment, Scott arrived shortly after me, apparently searching for gorilla tape. Hard not to notice someone hastily walking by in such a hurry, I kept perusing the aisles, trying to avoid the intrusive noise of the key machine. Eventually, we ended up at the checkout at the same time. Scott stood in line impatiently as I paid. Sharply dressed in a tailored suit, looking perfectly polished, I offered him a nervous smile, then looked away, realizing a guy like that would never be interested in me anyway.

Yes, Scott Egan. Mr. tall, dark, and handsome. Towering 6'4", his light brown hair was perfectly coiffed, allowing him to effortlessly create his signature style with a simple pass of his hand. His sharp blue eyes seemed to mesmerize me as that radiant grin, centered amidst the professionally sculpted facial scruff, captured the attention of anyone standing in its wake. Scott had built his empire in commercial development and brought his family's business into the next century by transforming and refurbishing most of Manhattan in the past ten years. On the New York social scene, he was the bachelor every woman tried to impress. Something much easier said than done. Forever surrounded by powerful bachelorettes and divorcees, Scott had his pick of women, all vying for an ounce of attention.

Awkwardly exchanging glances while standing in line with tape in hand, he asked, "Excuse me. Have we met before?"

Recognizing him, thinking the line was rather lame, I replied, "No, I don't think we have," and confidently introduced myself with a firm handshake in a slightly smug way, which was highly uncharacteristic of me. "Hello. Eva Thompson. And you are?"

With a killer smile, he said in a charismatic tone, "Hi, Eva. Scott Egan. Nice to meet you." All the while shaking my hand, his eyes did not waver from mine for a second.

"Pleased to meet you, Scott..." I responded, quietly melting. My throat going bone dry.

Our conversation continued with some rather mundane weather-related commentary, each divulging we lived nearby. Not hesitating, he asked for my number, suggesting we have dinner sometime. Out of the blue, my legs weakened, and my hands shook while exchanging contact information. Stepping forward to pay for the tape he needed, I looked on in disbelief at what was happening.

In a rush, he said, "Well, I have to get going, but it was a pleasure meeting you, Eva. We'll talk soon, okay."

Bidding goodbye with a wave and a slight tilt of his head, he added a sexy smirk before leaving me breathlessly floating.

Later that day, I answered Scott's call as time stood still. In a reasonably forward way, he invited me to dinner the next night. Our first date led to a second, then a third. Eventually, it brought us to his romantic proposal four months later, perched high above the island of St. Lucia with the stunning oval diamond engagement ring proudly placed on my finger. Five months later, with wedding plans well underway, Scott and I met for dinner after work to discuss the once-in-a-lifetime project my firm offered me in California. Encouraging me to pursue the opportunity wholeheartedly, we agreed to delay the wedding until the project concluded. I felt so lucky to have a man who supported my career.

While sipping the last of my coffee, staring out the window into oblivion, I truly believed fate had intervened and brought us together. Despite a few challenges in our relationship, all in all, I knew he loved me. He wouldn't have agreed to us living on opposite ends of the country if our connection wasn't strong enough to survive the distance.

"Daydreaming again, are we?" Antonia snickered, standing in the foyer, waiting for me.

I smiled, knowing she was right.

"Ready to go?" she asked.

Nodding, I replied, "Yes. Ready."

Out the door, departing on schedule, locking up behind us, we drove along the iconic palm tree-lined Wilshire Boulevard, still getting used to the morning traffic flow. It wasn't long before we hopped on the highway to merge northeast to the 110 in our company-leased A5. With the sun shining brightly, its warmth filtered through the glass, making me wonder how hot the summer would be.

Exiting into a jungle of tall, modern skyscrapers, dubbed the Financial District, we maneuvered the many streets before carefully entering the gates of the construction site. Parked beside the foreman's trailer, I once again glanced up at my museum design renderings on the billboards lining the development. Grateful for every aspect of my life - there was no doubt this was the most significant accomplishment to date.

Guess not having a social life or any free time has its perks, I thought as I turned off the ignition.

"Ten minutes to spare. Perfect," Antonia said, hurrying along, grabbing her shoulder bag and briefcase from the back seat, hoping her boss, Mr. Heller, was running late and hadn't arrived yet.

About fifteen feet behind her, I tried to ignore the unwanted whistles and cat-calls flowing from the upper scaffolding, something we sadly were becoming increasingly numb to. It was now part of our daily life as women immersed in a man's world. Reaching the door of the trailer, we both went into a morning full of meetings and walkabouts.

While the day went on, there were times I did not know how to persevere through the next five months. That is when I decided to prioritize trips to the ocean – it seemed like the only way to refuel my soul enough to keep moving forward.

| 2 |

Absence Makes the Heart...

Thankfully, returning to the firm around two o'clock that afternoon, having suffered through a stressful marathon of structural discussions, Antonia and I went our separate ways as I closed my office door, ready to sit in a dustless chair. Sliding off my shoes and giving my poor feet a quick rub, I settled in for the rest of the day and quickly moved on to the next order of business.

Asked to join a conference call already in progress with my boss, Mr. Gavin, and other senior staff members, I dialed in to listen to the partners and the Project Lead. When asked to present my latest findings, I sometimes felt intimidated, like a little fish in a rather big pond. Guess that's how you pay your dues in this business. My grandfather used to say – *If you plan on moving up the ladder, learn what you can from whomever you can.* Easier said than done, being a woman in a male-infused environment. It seemed like I often had a lot to prove.

After almost an hour of banter going back and forth, the call was about to end. Mr. Gavin asked that I stay on the line for a moment, making me wonder why he needed to speak with me privately.

Beginning the one-on-one conversation, apart from requesting the veil fabrication updates, he also casually inquired, "So, Thompson, do you have any plans for your upcoming birthday this weekend?"

Surprised that he remembered, responding with slight hesitation, I said, "Umm, no, nothing planned. Might spend the day at the beach or a spa."

Acting in place of the father I technically never had, knowing how many hours I'd put in recently, Mr. Gavin quickly insisted, "You should take a few days off. Make it an extra-long weekend of sorts. God knows you've earned it."

"Thank you so much, Sir. I appreciate that. Think I might make a trip home to New York then. It's been two months since I've seen Scott. That might be a nice surprise for him."

"What you do with your time off is up to you, my dear. If you decide to visit New York, please enjoy the break," he added sincerely before signing off the call.

Taking me under his wing for the past couple of years and teaching me the ins and outs of the architectural design world, I felt a tremendous debt of gratitude for all the time and effort he kindly gave to help build my career. Without his guidance and insight, it probably wouldn't have progressed as quickly as it did. Unable to have children of their own with his beautiful wife, Sarah, I assumed our professional association filled that gap for him occasionally. We just seemed to share this unexplained father-daughter-like bond, something very unfamiliar since my father never spent any time with my sister and me over the years, citing that he was always too busy with work.

Breaking from those thoughts, I moved through the day and tackled every task assigned to me. Before tidying up my desk and leaving the office around 7:45 that evening, I successfully booked my airline ticket. Opting to keep the visit a secret, hoping Scott would be surprised by my unexpected romantic weekend rendezvous, a part of me wondered if seeing him would help rekindle things between us, knowing that over the past while we had disconnected.

I met up with Antonia on my way out. She looked mentally spent. She wasn't the same ball of energy I saw this morning. That increased the guilt level since I was about to tell her my plans for the weekend.

"You okay?" I asked with great concern.

"Yeah. Just tired. Heller drains the life out of me every day."

"Yes, he's pretty demanding. I don't know how you do it."

Laughing, she said, "Me either." Pausing, she slowly placed her baggage in the back seat.

While standing along the driver's side before getting into the car, I looked across the roof and said, "Umm, just wanted to let you know that I'm heading to New York this Thursday. I will be back Sunday."

"What? Really?" She seemed disappointed.

"Mr. Gavin authorized the weekend off. I really need to recharge. It'll be nice to see Scott, too, finally. The past month has been rough."

"Well, you know what they say? Absence makes the heart grow fonder. I'm sure it'll be like you never left once he sees you."

I got into the car and replied, "Let's see if this trip proves your theory because I believe out of sight, out of mind seems to fit my situation pretty well."

"Don't worry, Ev. Everything will be fine. You'll see."

Nervous, I hoped she was right.

| 3 |

Happy Birthday Weekend

Struggling to open my eyes early that Thursday morning, thankful to have the luxury of sleeping in an extra hour, Antonia stood outside my bedroom door, intent on waking me up.

"Well, I guess I should say Happy Birthday, my friend."

She looked so sad.

"Are you going to be okay while I'm gone?" I asked, overly concerned.

With an abundance of uncertainty, she forced out the words, "Yeah, of course. I'll be fine. Enjoy your visit. Have fun."

"Thank you. I'll call you when I land."

"Okay. Please send me updates along the way, too. I want to know all the details."

"Will do," I nodded, wishing she could have accompanied me.

Leaving for work moments later, I heard Antonia close the door behind her. Rolling out of bed, thinking about the trip, I wondered how Scott would react to my surprise visit. Strangely experiencing a rush of butterflies, every ounce of my being hoped the weekend would go well.

When I first arrived in California, it never seemed like Scott and I were miles apart. Recalling the days when we would speak on the phone and Skype regularly, it seems this is no longer the case. Our communications have dwindled to maybe a phone call once a week, but not one video call. Determined to pick up where we left off, a part of me contemplated whether the weekend would be weird or uncomfortable.

"Maybe I'm overthinking it," I whispered to myself. "Perhaps things need to play out naturally, letting the chips fall where they may. Not so calculated and controlled, which is usually the norm for me."

Excited to be on my way within the hour, I embedded the last of my toiletries into the carry-on suitcase with essentials for precisely four days. In minutes, my driver texted me that he was waiting downstairs.

Meeting the man outside our long-term residence hotel lobby, I offered him a pleasant "Good morning" as he commandeered my bag and opened the back passenger door without saying a word.

Quietly sitting in the rear seat of the black SUV on the way to the airport, not long after, I soon realized the guy greatly lacked in the personality department. Trying a few times to start a casual conversation, he promptly answered yes or no to my questions and continued staring straight ahead, somewhat annoyed.

Eventually, stopping underneath the Delta sign outside of Terminal 2, he revealed how much I owed him the second he shifted the vehicle into park. After paying the fare and setting my bag on the curb, I could tell he was ready to move along to his next passenger. It was apparent he didn't like his job very much. Then again, maybe he was just struggling with something personal. Who knows?

"Have a good day, Sir," I said, only to be ignored while he went about his business. Angered by that, turning around, I muttered, "Great..." while breaching the terminal's sliding doors. "Not exactly how I wanted the weekend to begin."

Maneuvering through the crowded check-in and security, I grabbed a toasted bagel and coffee across the hall from Gate 21, hoping things would improve after a rather cold start. About to enjoy my light breakfast in a less crowded corner, I sat down to watch ABC Eyewitness morning news as the story of Hollywood actor Anthony Morgan quickly caught my attention. The news anchor firmly stated with a sense of urgency,

Now to Breaking News out of Malibu, California. Sources have confirmed the disappearance of actor Anthony Morgan. ABC affiliates are reporting Mr. Morgan was last seen on Sunday evening before heading out fishing on his boat. He had planned to meet a friend later that evening, but never arrived. The star's family stated that Mr. Morgan's vessel did not return to his private boat slip in Marina Del Ray Harbor. Coast Guard officials were notified Monday afternoon, and a massive search and rescue operation has been underway over the past 48 hours. Those involved are hoping to find the actor safe and sound. We will update you as we receive more information on this developing story.

Taken by his picture in the top right-hand corner of the screen, looking so handsome, with a smile that would warm anyone's heart, I figured the movie star had probably run out of gas or wanted to have some time alone out of the public eye. Maybe he decided to park the boat in another marina, hoping to avoid the paparazzi. All in all, I believed he would turn up. The thought also crossed my mind that, just maybe, this whole thing was a planned publicity stunt created to promote his upcoming movie release.

"Never know?" I whispered under my breath. "After all, this is Hollywood. Anything's possible."

This is the first boarding call for all passengers on Delta Flight 562 with service to New York JFK. Please proceed to Gate 21 for check-in.

Hearing the voice of the Delta attendant, I finished my last bite of bagel. With a hint of excitement brewing, knowing I'd be back in Manhattan in five and a half hours, a spark ignited my spirit. Boarding the plane with ease, I found my seat and got settled.

"Let my Happy Birthday weekend begin," I said quietly, wondering what the next few days would bring.

| 4 |

The Big Surprise

After a peaceful coast-to-coast flight, I landed at JFK that evening. Hailing a cab, I was soon on my way to Midtown. Anticipation building, we drove along the Expressway in the bright yellow taxi, marveling at the beautifully lit city. I could hardly wait to see the expression on his face when I knocked on the door, and he'd open it to find me standing there. Would he hug me or swing me around? Maybe flood me with kisses? Those thoughts sent shivers down my spine.

Huh, I silently considered. I must have missed him, after all.

The driver stopped outside Scott's building. Not wasting any time, I paid him the fare.

"Thank you, Miss. You have a pleasant evening," he said in a strong Jersey accent.

Happy to hear that, I, in turn, replied, "You as well," before heading inside the lobby.

Waving to Gerald, the doorman, I said, "Hello!" on my way to the elevators.

Overwhelmingly anxious, fidgeting a little, I pressed the button as the doors slid open. Filled with positive vibes, it did not take long to hit the 34th floor. Slowly walking down the corridor, offering encouraging self-talk the entire way, I arrived at the entrance to his apartment.

"This was it," I mumbled. "The moment I'd been dreaming about all day."

Knocking twice, then a third time, with hands still shaking, there was a strong possibility that he was not even home yet. Proud of his work ethic, it quickly became apparent throughout our ten-month relationship that a developer's life could never be considered nine-to-five. That was something I had gotten used to and accepted.

Fumbling about inside my bag to find my phone, I decided to call and track him down.

Answering the third ring, he said, "Hey, Babe," in a deep, suave voice.

"Hi," I replied, almost unable to contain my eagerness.

"Is everything okay? You're calling earlier than usual," Scott asked, knowing we always spoke later in the evenings, given the time difference between Los Angeles and New York.

"Yes, everything is fine. Did you have a good day?" I responded, patiently waiting for his answer.

"Yeah, busy day, but that's not unusual."

Listening intently, I heard a crowd in the background. "So, where are you? Out for dinner with clients, then?"

"Yeah. I'm meeting with a couple of investors at Brushstroke. We will be wrapping up shortly. How about you?"

"Me? Well, I ended the day a little earlier. Looking forward to hopefully getting a good night's sleep. After all, I do deserve a break since it is my special day tomorrow," I hinted, trying to string Scott along.

"Aww, yes, the big birthday. What do you have planned?"

"Not quite sure if my idea will materialize just yet," I stated, gearing myself up to ask the next question. "Can you maybe join me for the weekend?"

"Oh, Eva. I would if I could. Work is too hectic right now, with the new project needing to be funded. You know how it is."

"That's alright…I understand."

Picking up on my disappointment, he replied, "Look, I'm sorry, Babe, but I need to go. Can I call you later? I should be home in about an hour and a half or so. These guys are getting ready to leave, and I need to drop by the office to pick up a few files I forgot."

"Sure, no problem. We'll talk later then."

"Okay, I'll call you back," he confirmed in a rush.

Upon ending our conversation, realizing that my key to his apartment was at my place, I knew I couldn't get there and back in time to surprise him.

Quickly descending to the lobby, I was lucky to catch Gerald moments before his shift ended. Explaining the situation, thankfully, he didn't mind letting me in. While the two of us returned to the 34th floor, I noticed Gerald seemed somewhat distant - not as talkative or jovial as he typically was. Believing the man was tired after his nine-hour day, I kept the conversation light.

Standing outside Scott's apartment again, he quickly unlocked it with the master key and instantly bid me goodnight. Thanking him, I turned on the lights and wheeled my suitcase inside as he walked down the corridor.

The door closed behind me. I immediately noticed Scott's housekeeper mustn't be coming by as often as she once did. The place was a disaster. Moving my suitcase into the front closet, I rolled up my sleeves, unsure where to start. Peering at my watch, I had exactly one hour to whip this place into shape.

About to pick up a week's worth of Wall Street Journals, gathering everything else off the coffee table in the living room, which included a few dishes, cups, and mugs with cappuccino stains in the bottom, I then came across a recent Cosmopolitan magazine. Wondering what it was doing here, I figured Scott's mother had visited and left it behind while checking up on him occasionally, since Cosmo was her mag of choice.

While filling the sink with water to soak the dishes and glassware before placing them in the dishwasher, I checked the powder room to see what damage he'd inflicted on it. Thankfully, it remained relatively untouched except for a hand towel resting beside the sink, which got returned to its holder.

As expected, I rounded the corner into the bedroom and found my next challenge - his messy, unmade bed. Remembering how often I'd done this in the past made me think this man could not make a bed to save his life. Carefully opening the room-darkening custom drapes to allow the city lights to filter through the sheers, I switched on one table lamp. Battling the complete disarray of sheets, wondering which way the comforter indeed went, I finally straightened it all up and casually tossed the decorative pillows to finish the task.

Veering into the master bath, gathering three slightly damp towels from off the floor, that pile got stuffed into the washer, hoping it wasn't too late to remove the mildew smell.

Ready to finish cleaning the vanity area, placing his toothbrushes in the holder, and tucking a hairbrush into the drawer, I wiped down the countertop. Straightening the mats and stepping back after cleaning the mirrors, I made sure I got every smudge.

Headed back to the kitchen, glancing at my watch - time was ticking. The dishes soaking in the sink soon found a spot in the dishwasher. Finished, I wiped down the counter, happy I was finally done. Dehydrated from the flight, opening the fridge to grab bottled water, I found a few resting beside a carton of almond milk on the top shelf.

"That's weird," I whispered.

Casually noting the expiry date, confirming the almond milk to be new, hesitating, I remembered Scott always hated the thought of me drinking the stuff. Then it hit me. Did Scott buy some knowing I was coming to visit? But how? Who would tell him?

Fluffing it off as a coincidence, I turned off all the lights with only ten minutes to spare. Swiftly stepping into the powder room to change into fresh, comfortable clothes, I washed my hands and fixed my makeup. That is when I heard Scott place his key in the lock. Excited that he was home, ready to swing open the door to surprise him, my heart pumped in my chest. It was hard to catch my breath.

Waiting for it to close behind him, I jumped out of the bathroom and shouted, "Surprise!!"

Frozen, stopping dead in my tracks, I could not move a muscle. There, standing in front of me, was Scott in the arms of a woman with long, dark hair, a half-open blouse, and a black skirt hiked up slightly to her thigh.

Unable to produce a single sound, I stared at the girl.

"Umm, Scott, what's going on?" she questioned as her eyes bounced back and forth between us. Instinctively flashing a hurt-filled expression, followed by one flaming with anger, I added, "Who is she?" Knowing full well what this was.

Stunned, he lowered his head and tightly squinted his eyes shut. He'd gotten caught, and there was no going back.

My sights hit the floor. Almost gasping for air, with my body caving and legs buckling, going numb, I gradually became conscious of the fact that everything I thought we had was an absolute lie. Without warning, the beautiful diamond ring on my finger unexpectedly swung around. Feeling its unwelcome presence, instantly taking it off, I threw it at him as hard as possible before grabbing my things from the closet and storming out the door.

Scott kept his distance while guiltily following me down the long corridor to the elevators, explaining himself poorly the entire way.

"She's my ex-girlfriend. I'm sorry. Eva, come on. I'm sorry. Please listen and let me explain."

Repeatedly pressing the down button, he stayed ten feet from me. Seconds later, when the doors opened, I stepped inside. Unfortunately, he followed.

"Get out! Get away from me! Now! I mean it!" I shouted in a bout of rage.

With little regard for my feelings, standing on the opposite side of the confined space, he continued the verbal torture as we began to move.

Holding me captive, Scott said with little remorse, "When you left, I was lonely. She came over one night, and I guess one thing led to another. It was just going to be until you got back."

Dumbfounded by his rationale, staring him down, I couldn't find the words to respond. Was he serious?

Without warning, my world began to implode in slow motion as the shock of it all inflicted incredible pain. My life with him was over. In an instant, it was all gone.

"I love you, Eva. Please don't go. I'm sorry. What I did was stupid. Please forgive me."

While pleading his case, our eyes never met once. Regrettably, despite what just happened, I caught myself still feeling love for him as a small piece of my heart wanted to forgive and forget. But this? This? No way. Absolutely not.

I tried my best to fight back the tears when the elevator opened on the bottom floor. Thankfully, Scott stayed, allowing me to depart without further conflict. Dragging my carry-on behind me, focusing forward, I did not look back. My heart was breaking.

That night, I eventually made it to my building, totally numb, dazed, and confused. While sitting on the floor, curled up tightly, late May showers fell against the wall of windows. The blurred view of the darkened sky resembled how my mind fought to foresee a future. Devastated, I stared out over the city for an unknown length of time, then pressed the button on my phone to see the numbers 12:01 a.m., reminding me of something.

"Happy Birthday, Eva," I whispered to myself… "What a way to celebrate turning 28…."

With streams of tears engulfing my face in an unstoppable flood, I surrendered to the agonizing heartbreak and rejection sustained and allowed every torrent of emotion to flow freely, hoping that eventually, I'd have nothing left to expel. That is when reality struck.

I am alone again. Where do I go from here? What do I live for now? Will anyone else ever tell me I love you?

| 5 |

The Aftermath

Inconceivably surviving the night, I woke to a dismal grey day. Spotting a blanket of low-hanging clouds, it wasn't long before I noticed the absence of my engagement ring. Flashes of what happened the night before confirmed it was real and not a bad dream. Alone, abandoned, and cast aside, I felt worthless. Grieving, it seemed a piece of me had died. The confidence I once had was now gone as doubt infiltrated every ounce of my being. Needing to face facts, somewhat in denial, I forced myself to disconnect from the life I once had. Expelling both sadness and anger, I cried as my body heaved. Pounding my fists into the bed, attempting to release these emotions, I suddenly stopped.

"He does not define you, Ev. He does not define you," I repeated in a moment of clarity. "He does not define you."

Abruptly rolling out of bed, wiping the tears from my face, I found it hard to produce every step towards the kitchen. In need of a strong cup of coffee, I robotically placed a pod in the machine, barely able to smell the aroma as it slowly seeped into the room. All I could do was focus on surviving the day. Faintly hearing my phone chime, afraid that Scott had sent me a message, I stared at the device. Silencing the ringer, assuming I'd receive many birthday wishes today, not looking at the screen, it took enormous strength to ignore each call, text, and email that started popping up.

My life has ended, I thought to myself, unable to stay positive. One moment changed everything. It's all gone.

Thankful I never told anyone else about my visit, I closed the blinds to darken the living room. With my mind in a muddle and the impact of what transpired remaining very intense, minutes blended into hours as my birthday weekend dwindled by slowly. Drowning in my thoughts, I had this dreadful need to spend the entire time isolated from the rest of the world.

But by Saturday evening, the anger intensified, making me feel a need to run away. Calling the airline to change my scheduled late afternoon flight to one leaving earlier in the morning, I was relieved to confirm a seat on Delta departing at 9:55 a.m.

Hardly able to sleep a wink that night, I finished packing my suitcase at four o'clock Sunday morning and called a cab just before five. While placing my bag at the front door, ready to depart, I caught a glimpse of my phone resting face down on the counter in the kitchen. Compelled to look at it, I caved and discovered countless texts from Scott embedded amongst the many birthday wishes I'd received. Ignoring them all, I decided it would be best to block his number and erase the messages he'd sent. At the last second, stupidly hesitating, I couldn't do it. Setting the device on the table by the door with my keys, I did not read anything from him in case the words pulled at my heartstrings.

After closing the apartment, knowing I wouldn't be back for a while, I sat at my drafting table by the window in the living room. Hoping and praying that I'd have the courage to travel back to Los Angeles today, I began texting Antonia and briefly shared with her what had happened. Despite the time difference, she immediately responded and supportively said she'd be waiting for me when I got back.

Moments later, hearing that my driver had arrived, I locked up and headed downstairs. Cautiously walking through the lobby of my building with sunglasses on to hide my swollen eyes, I thought Scott might be waiting for me to emerge since I hadn't responded to him. Approaching the limo parked along the curb, I sneaked through without further incident or drama, leaving the same way I arrived - secretly and undetected. Departing the city, looking back at the skyline I once treasured before passing through the Queens Midtown Tunnel, it seemed almost like it had betrayed me, too. After all these years, New York didn't feel like home for the first time.

Slowly shuffling through security at JFK in a zombie-like state, I spotted an empty seat near my departure gate. Knowing that in a few short hours, I'd be far away from New York somehow didn't make me sad or lonely. If anything, it seemed like a welcomed relief or anticipated escape. Turning my attention to the TV monitor positioned slightly to my left, I tried to follow the headlines on CNN to keep my mind from flooding back to thoughts of Scott and the horrible aftermath of a romantic getaway weekend gone wrong. Intently listening, getting caught up on the many political issues plaguing our country today, the tragic story of Anthony Morgan once again captivated my attention. The news anchor read the following statement with a heavy heart, repeating that the actor had disappeared off the Pacific Coast a few days before.

Now, after a grueling six-day search for the action star, Senior Officials of the Coast Guard have officially suspended their rescue operation for missing actor Anthony Morgan. The Captain stated that a person would not have survived in the cold waters off the coast for this long, and sadly, Mr. Morgan is presumed dead after finding his boat capsized yesterday in shark-infested waters about five miles off the coast of Malibu. The California Law Enforcement Agency has assumed the lead in the recovery phase of this operation. Captain Ben Walker, the Commander of the Coast Guard Sector, released this statement today - "All of us who have been dedicated to this search effort since last Sunday's tragic events offer our sincerest condolences to Mr. Morgan's family and friends. The Coast Guard and California Law Enforcement Agency have continuously searched for more than 144 hours, covering almost 14,000 square miles of water and 280 miles of shoreline. Only his severely damaged vessel has been located along with a few personal items." Lion Entertainment is now trying to regroup in light of this horrible tragedy, which took the life of one of their lead stars in the most recent film. Our thoughts and prayers are with his family during this difficult time.

The news then switched to a more unpredictable topic of impending war in the Middle East, allowing my mind to become engrossed by how that poor actor died, understanding that in his final hours, he was dreadfully alone, cold, and facing death head-on.

What a horrible way to go, I envisioned while sitting there. No money in the world can save you if your time is up. Pondering this upsetting news a bit further, I realized that there were indeed worse things in the world to suffer through than finding your fiancé with another woman. Drifting back to that devastating moment when I saw them standing together, my body unexpectedly froze as I relived every shocking detail in a series of flashes. That negative train of thought was interrupted by the boarding announcement echoing around the gate area, bringing me out of the darkness and into the light.

Making sure I hadn't left anything behind, I walked over to the check-in counter. Handing the lady my boarding pass and passport, she casually asked me to remove my sunglasses to verify that my photo matched my identity. Reluctantly pulling the glasses from my face, she looked into my eyes and gave me this overly sorrowful expression. Passed back the documents, the attendant gently tapped my arm to silently show her sympathy and support before I once again hid behind the dark lenses, hoping the other passengers hadn't seen the condition of my face. Continuing past her, I solemnly wandered down the ramp attached to the plane as an intense déjà vu caught me off guard. Strange how, just a few days prior, I felt so anxious and happy to board the flight to New York, and now, well, it seemed as though I was an entirely different person - damaged, scarred, hurt, and unavoidably lacking trust. How I wished that this tunnel were a time machine that could take me back to a simpler, less complicated place in my past, one not filled with so much pain and suffering, heartbreak, and loneliness.

In a blurred state of mind, flying high amongst the gloomy-looking clouds, leaving the dismal Manhattan skyline behind as we ascended into the air, I noticed raindrops gracefully hitting the plane window. Each created a different patterned line across the glass. My finger traced a few. It was a welcomed distraction that helped me relax and fall asleep.

Eventually, touching down in the land of sandy beaches and palm trees, I made my way to the front of the terminal to hail a cab. Proud to snag one on the first try, I jumped in and took a second to enjoy the warmth of the midday sun. Acutely aware of my posture, slouching horribly in the back seat, while checking my phone for messages, I noticed Scott had probably texted, emailed, and called at least one hundred times in the past six hours. Still not reading a single word, reminded that our relationship was over, I slipped the device into my bag, noticing the absence of my diamond ring again.

Mindful of my overall demeanor, I straightened my body and silently told myself, "This whole thing will not stop you from finishing what you started here. You can't let this ruin your professional focus. Don't let him do that to you, too."

When the taxi stopped along the curb in front of my rental in Beverly Hills, I saw Antonia outside, waiting for me. Sliding out of the back seat after paying the driver his money, she rushed over with open arms. Immediately, the tears flowed. She held on tightly.

"Come on," she said, wrapping one arm around me. "Let's get you inside."

Nodding my head, I agreed as she dragged my suitcase behind us.

For the next hour, Antonia listened to every horrid detail of my birthday weekend with a glass of wine in one hand and a tissue in the other. The flash of emotions from the past couple of days and the feeling of desertion were pretty unbearable. I still couldn't believe he had been cheating on me all this time.

"You can't let a man beat you down like this," she said firmly, not having had a high opinion of Scott from the beginning. "You are better than this. I know it hurts now, but imagine how bad it would have been if you had gotten married. Trust me, Eva. This is for the best."

Recognizing that I was tired and desperate for sleep, she respectfully left the room to prepare for work tomorrow. Not having any choice, I knew I should do the same. With my wine glass refilled, I looked out over the city, believing that diving back into my museum project would allow my mind to venture down a more positive path. Initially, it seemed almost impossible not to dwell on the painful event I'd endured. But with a list of tasks a mile long awaiting me tomorrow, I figured I'd take one day at a time and bravely soldier through.

Back in my room, needing closure, I located my journal in the side table drawer. Comfortable, with pillows resting against the headboard, I propped myself up and opened it for the first time in a long while. Not having to think, the pen started expelling everything onto the page. Word for word, I recorded every horrific detail. It seemed this process always helped me through troubling times in the past. If anything, by doing this, I hoped, at some point down the road, I could look back and happily say I survived one of the worst things any woman could ever encounter in her entire life.

Finally, tired enough, my head found a spot on the pillow late that night. The realization that this project was now the only thing worth clinging to boldly stood front and center as my only priority. In contrast, my personal life was floating somewhere in oblivion without a definitive direction or purpose.

Dark clouds descended upon me the next day. I felt destined to be alone. Had the universe abandoned me? Despite my faith dwindling, I hoped fate was waiting in the wings to send my life into a new and unexpected direction - somewhere surprising and unimaginable. Perhaps all I needed to do was be patient and wait.

| 6 |

The Healing Process

Over the next five months, my world changed drastically. Scott stopped his futile attempts to contact me, which made life a bit easier to manage since, in my mind, bluntly severing ties was indeed for the best. There was nothing more to say.

Antonia kept a close eye on me from morning until night. She was the only person I confided in. No one else, other than my sister, Ellie, knew the intricate details of what had happened.

At work, my peers noticed a difference in my overall demeanor. It wasn't as lively or welcoming, and I rarely smiled or laughed. Most of the time, I quietly kept to myself. Opting to work in my office with the door closed each day, I continued this uncharacteristic antisocial behavior. Many thought I'd become arrogant and self-centered. From what I understand, that was the rumor, apparently. If only they knew the truth. I was still grieving the relationship I'd lost, despite it being harmful and toxic, and my career was the only thing saving me from the aftermath haunting every minute of the day.

One lonely Friday evening, while Antonia was out on a date, some emotional healing settled in as I cuddled under a soft throw blanket on the couch. Watching the sun fade in the distance, met by rational thoughts surfacing, I wondered what might have happened if Scott and I had gotten married. Whether or not that woman would have kept lurking in the background? Had she been there all along, and I was too naïve to see it? Was he lying to me this entire time? So many questions did not have answers, and sadly, I'd probably never really know what went wrong. One thing that surprised me the most was how difficult it was to let go of my feelings for him. It left me very confused since the obvious thing to do was move on. Unfortunately, my heart was still pleading otherwise. Was it because I just hated being alone, or did I truly love and miss him? My Grandfather used to say *life is full of peaks and valleys. Every struggle shapes us into the person we are today.* Expecting this battle of emotions would smolder for a while longer, a piece of me hoped I'd eventually rise from the ashes as a much stronger version of myself. Deciding to press forward sporting a Cheshire cat smile, I began emitting a more optimistic disguise to benefit those around me, all while internalizing the battle to simply just exist.

| 7 |

Something Unforeseen

Midway through the seventh month onsite, the team worked night and day to finish the first phase of the construction before taking another short, well-earned break.

On Tuesday evening, I got home earlier than usual. Antonia had gone out to dinner with her new boyfriend, Carlo, so I had the place all to myself for a few hours. Happy for her, proud of everything we'd accomplished in the past while, I opened a bottle of red wine and poured a glass. Enjoying the peacefulness, I took a sip and went out onto the balcony, realizing that completing this phase of construction meant a return visit to New York was imminent. The firm had pushed for an in-person development assessment to discuss any changes requested by the client before proceeding to the next stage.

"Not sure if you're ready to go back, Ev," I mumbled at the thought of dealing with Scott and the excess fallout. "It's going to be like reliving that moment over again."

After my rare relaxing evening, feeling rested and energized, Antonia and I arrived at the office early the following morning. Unfortunately, our day began with the team being asked to meet in the boardroom for an emergency meeting once everyone was present and accounted for on-site.

One by one, the group gathered around the large table, some seated, others leaning against the walls with arms crossed.

Upon hearing all the whispers and chatter, Mr. Heller, the Senior Lead, asked, "Please, can I have your attention, everyone? The partners will join us virtually from New York in a few minutes."

When he said that, I knew this was going to be big. Something had happened. Something was wrong.

Everyone stayed quiet as the partners appeared on the screen mounted at the end of the room. I watched Mr. Gavin step forward to make an announcement.

"As you know, we've been having difficulty with the details surrounding the museum's unique exterior façade outlined in Phase II. Something many have coined – 'the veil." It has become an engineering nightmare over the past three weeks. The problem has prompted the firm to hire a team of specialized engineers to help resolve these complicated fabrication issues. To date, they have been unsuccessful in dealing with the company contracted to do the work. Look, the bottom line is - we know this can be done. We are searching for a new fabricator, so continue as normal until we know more. In the meantime, we will keep you posted on any progress or delays. Updates will be made available at the end of the week."

"Thank you, Mr. Gavin." Mr. Heller nodded before the partners disconnected. "Alright. Everyone back to work," he said as we filed out the door to go about our day.

In an instant, on the way to my office, I felt like I'd failed. The design I'd created had caused this.

Sitting at my desk moments later, frustrated, I scanned the blueprints for my museum. Deep in thought, my phone suddenly rang. Looking at the screen, I was surprised to see who it was.

"Hello, Mr. Gavin," I said, overly concerned. "I'm so very sorry for the trouble the veil…."

Before I could continue, he interrupted. "Ms. Thompson. This issue has nothing to do with your intricate design. It's the fault of the fabricator we've hired. They assured us that they were capable of producing what we needed. They failed. Not you. If we do not move forward with this company, there will be another to take its place." He sounded so calm and confident in his words. "The reason for my call is..." pausing, he took a breath and said, "Well, I noticed during the meeting that you looked stressed. I want to give you a heads up so this doesn't come as a surprise."

"Oh?" I stated, quite concerned.

"Keep this under your hat for the time being," he stated bluntly, adding, "Our client is talking about a possible lawsuit against the fabricator if they can't deliver on time. If this happens, construction will halt until the situation is resolved. Without the veil, we can not safely proceed with the interior completion. Like I said to the others, I'll keep you posted." Pausing again, he added with a hint of uncertainty, "On a personal note, I trust you are doing well?"

Not sure if he'd heard anything about my breakup with Scott, I decided to keep things professional.

"Yes. Everything is good here. I just hope we can move forward and resolve this issue."

He knew I had dodged his question.

Morphing back into boss mode, Mr. Gavin hesitated, then replied, "Happy to hear that. Don't worry. These kinds of things often happen on large-scale projects. We will see what the client decides. Take care, my dear. Chin up, okay."

"Thank you, Mr. Gavin. Will do."

Hanging up the phone, I immediately went into another meeting. My day continued with a growing number of tasks being added to my to-do list. Through it all, I tried my best not to let this entire situation bring me down.

| 8 |

The Interruption

That week, the fate of our project loomed over each of us. The last thing the team wanted was to be placed in limbo for the next six months to a year. Not surprisingly, this subject was the main topic of conversation amongst the team. We knew whatever decision the client and the partners made would inevitably affect almost every division working on the West Coast.

Walking into the office on Friday with rattled nerves, the staff got an email from Mr. Heller to meet in the boardroom again at nine o'clock.

Anxious to hear what was happening, sadly, as Mr. Gavin predicted, Mr. Heller stood at the head of the large table and confirmed, "I am sure all of you are concerned about the future of this project. Unfortunately, the dispute between the fabricator and the client has escalated. It is something we anticipated and expected. We wanted to confirm that a lawsuit has been filed." When the room erupted into whispers, Mr. Heller explained the firm's plans. "So, with that said, the partners are calling the team back to New York until further notice. Please clean your desks by the end of the day and pack up your apartments for checkout by Sunday morning. The firm will email you your travel arrangements in a few hours."

And just like that, the development was halted, effective immediately. The mood in the room fell into a gloomy state. Each person was left shell-shocked. I, too, felt the same despite being given inside information by Mr. Gavin. Following my co-workers as they returned to their desks, possible solutions to the veil issues passed through my mind. Thinking I would share them with Mr. Gavin upon my return, my heart went out to everyone around me while they gathered their things into bankers' boxes. For whatever reason, I felt responsible for uprooting the team.

| 9 |

The End Result

The next couple of days were challenging as we prepared to move our lives back to New York City. Antonia was not doing well with the news. It meant she'd have to endure a long-distance relationship with her boyfriend, Carlo. Sadly, she would be miles away from the one she loves tomorrow. Strange how I was in her shoes not long ago.

With our suitcases lined up at the front door before eleven Saturday morning, carry-on bags only half-packed, I went to sit on the balcony to soak up a little vitamin D and take a much-needed break. It was difficult to ignore the extreme disappointment and feelings of defeat and utter failure that weighed me down.

"Hard to believe it's the first week of November. Where has the time gone?" I said while sipping my coffee, looking at the clouds drifting by, trying to think of something uplifting.

My sister, Ellie, immediately came to mind. I texted her the news and revealed that I was returning home. She replied within seconds, expressing how much she missed me and that it would be nice to have me home.

Home? I thought to myself. Was it, really?

Part of me wondered if Los Angeles would be a suitable place to start over. The conditions here were favorable this time of year, unlike Manhattan, which would fall into parka weather shortly. Even though I didn't want to be away from my sister, at least I'd be less edgy not having to run into Scott anywhere, figuring then, it was worthy of consideration.

Like the Santa Ana winds wafting through Southern California, I drifted back to the problems lingering in my personal life. With thoughts of friends and family back home, I hoped they'd heard along the proverbial grapevine what had transpired with Scott. I wasn't interested in validating the details upon my return. When thinking further about his motive, only one conclusion made sense. Marrying me would have solidified relationships with several new clients and investors, eventually opening many doors for him in the future. My parents had countless connections worldwide, so uniting our two families was not only a personal decision but probably a business move as well.

| 10 |

Homebound

Waking bright and early on Sunday, I was overly exhausted and stressed. Slowly packing the last of my suitcases, it soon came time to leave and catch our flight to New York.

Departing the Beverly Hills apartment, thankful for its comforting refuge, standing in the entryway, Antonia and I paused and looked around the cold, stark space. Closing the door felt symbolic since it meant we were leaving this phase of life behind and moving forward to the next, even though we didn't know what direction that might entail.

Carlo was outside waiting for us when we emerged from the building, rolling our suitcases along. Helping us load everything in the SUV, I watched them share a tearful goodbye. Strange how when I left Scott to embark on this project, I was the one who cried, not him.

Running a little behind, needing to be on our way, we got into the airline limo. Part of me was prepared to go home and start over, while the other felt sad to leave California. Somehow comforting Antonia as she sobbed offered a distraction from an abundance of emotions I was trying to dismiss. Right now, above all else, she was more important. I had promised to be there for her the same way she was for me months prior.

With a heightened sense of anxiety and uncertainty, sitting at the gate within LAX, it was difficult to accept the crossroads my life had encountered. Being on the West Coast meant I didn't have to run into

Scott at any point, but back in New York, it was another story, as our paths would certainly cross here or there. Thoughts of finding a new apartment and starting fresh seemed to be the only solution to that. Wanting to pull out my phone and peruse a few rental websites for any places currently available, still considering the option to move to the West Coast, I happened to look over at Antonia. Sitting quietly, holding back tears, completely heartbroken, I put it away. Without saying a word, I inched over and touched her arm. With tearful eyes focused on her feet, the boarding announcement broke her stoic stare. Lining up with all the other passengers and making it onto the plane, we soon found our seats in the second row.

About two hours into the flight, she fell asleep after crying non-stop since the plane lifted off. Never in my lifetime had I missed anyone that much. It was hard to fathom. Flying high amongst the clouds, my mind now idle, thoughts of Scott resurfaced.

Like it was yesterday, I could hear him sincerely say that meeting me at the hardware store that day was coincidental, adding that he'd *just broken up with his girlfriend of nine years about three weeks before we met.* Assuming he would stay single for a while, he told me *I was a pleasant surprise.*

In hindsight, I should have known he was too good to be true. Scott had his choice of women and picked me. Given his socialite status and reputation, how did I ever think he could remain faithful? Why didn't I see it at the time?

Guess that's why they say love is blind, I concluded while looking about the plane. Disappointed in myself, desperately needing to break away from the internal torment, my fingers started flipping through Antonia's fashion magazine. I hoped the latest styles would keep my mind occupied and help me avoid speculating how my first week back would inevitably go.

| 11 |

Home Sweet Home

Safely landing in New York after a bumpy flight, sending Antonia on her way home, I reached the front of my building a while later in the lively, high-energy, darkened city. Graciously greeting my doorman, Eddie, while struggling to feel happy about returning home, his smile seemed to brighten things a bit.

Standing outside the door of my apartment, I suddenly stopped. Would it still encompass the pain from my last visit, or had that dissipated while I was gone? Visions of that fateful weekend unceasingly haunted me in waves. It seemed I'd be free of it from time to time, but without warning, the rejection, pain, and sadness would torment me again. Afraid to walk inside, I slowly opened it with my heart pounding. Sliding my hand over the light switch to my left, I noticed my sister Ellie had left floral arrangements on the tables and had freshened up the place. The smell was inviting and comforting. Not at all what I expected. Locking the door behind me, I rolled my suitcases towards the closet and left my keys in the bowl on the side table. Happy to take a deep breath, I felt a sense of relief and knew I would be okay.

That night, I settled in, so thankful that Ellie had also stocked the kitchen with a few staples and washed the bedding and towels. In a way, it was nice to be back, but regrettably, the space didn't feel the same. Something was missing. It didn't have that sense of warmth and serenity it once had. Perhaps it was the void of happiness I picked up on? Or was the sadness overriding it all?

Knowing I had to keep moving forward, I raised my head high and selected some warmer clothes to wear to work in the morning. While getting ready for bed, it was hard knowing Scott's apartment was a mere ten blocks from where I lived. When sliding under the covers, the thought crossed my mind: Was he still with that woman? Realizing it had almost been a year since we got engaged during that surprise St. Lucia vacation, fawned over by many, I shook off the sentiment.

Inevitably, thinking back to our luxurious Moon Sanctuary Suite, with a high-level balcony overlooking the Caribbean, boasting a view of the island's iconic pitons or volcanic spires, Scott got down on one knee and endearingly asked me to be his wife. Describing how captivated he was by *my grace and elegance*, saying how *perfectly I fit into his life*, the whole experience made me the happiest woman on earth at the time. Spending the very first night together, ever, was how I dreamed it should be until I woke in the morning and noticed Scott wasn't there. Leaving me a cold, instructional note on the desk requesting that I order him breakfast was not how I imagined this life-changing moment. Hungry and in desperate need of coffee, I called for room service. Being alone for two hours, I'd waited for him so we could have breakfast together. But another hour passed. Starting to eat my food, which was now cold, I heard him walk through the door as I finished my last bite. He casually kissed me on the forehead and said he was happy I got the note.

In hindsight, this was the first of many warning signs I should have detected but didn't. For the rest of the vacation, Scott had difficulty staying away from his phone. I can't help but think - was she ever on the other end of any of the countless phone calls he privately took?

On the last day there, he arranged for a seaplane to take us back to the airport. I thought that was a nice gesture since we would get a tour of the island from the air before catching our flight home. Remembering his comment, to this day, still makes me want to cry.

The faster we get to the airport, the faster we board the plane home to NYC. I can't wait to get back to work. This trip has been exhausting, he huffed.

It was as though he didn't want to relish our time alone. Nor did he enjoy it. Staring at him while he arrogantly ordered around the baggage handler once we landed adjacent to the main airport terminal, I tried to smooth things over with the kind gentleman. Apologizing for Scott's behavior, he again answered his phone and silently gave me a stern look for undermining him.

Throughout our first day in St. Lucia, Scott was warm, endearing, and doted on me, but he seemed non-existent and self-centered the rest of the time. Maybe because my parents treated each other this way, I thought this was normal. Looking back, I know I deserved better.

On the plane ride home, I constantly fidgeted with the beautiful diamond ring adorning my finger. Moving it from side to side, I hoped it would provide the answers I needed to my life's troubles. Glancing over at Scott, who had decided to sleep the entire flight, I assumed he did so to avoid further conversation with me. That is when I realized I didn't know the real Scott Egan. Both of us always worked and never spent blocks of time together. Even though I cared for him and could not imagine living apart, I often wondered if the St. Lucia trip was a blessing in disguise. Something I hadn't fully appreciated until now.

Landing in New York, when our trip ended, Scott dropped me off at my apartment.

Hugging me goodbye, he said, "Well, it looks like you have a wedding to plan."

"Guess so," I replied, slightly taken aback by the comment. Waving to him as he drove away, I immediately asked myself, "Doesn't he mean we have a wedding to plan?"

That left me speechless, believing I would eventually be the only one in this marriage. How wrong I was about that. It seemed there were three of us.

Angry for not speaking up at the time, feeling stupid and needy, closing my eyes tightly in disgust, I shook my head to break away from these destructive thoughts. Violently pounding the mattress with my fists, I hated myself.

"Why!" I shouted. "Why did you let him treat you like that? Seriously!"

Lying there in bed, fuming, I tried to calm down and focus on falling asleep so that I could get up for work the following day. I realized little memories like these would keep invading my life unless I chose to move on - something that would be easier said than done. How many other comments and situations would show themselves for what they truly were? How many times did I naively ignore the warning signs in a desperate attempt to feel loved?

| 12 |

Turning A Corner

Monday morning came faster than expected. Tired, having had a restless night's sleep, I woke to see the trees starting to change color along the Highline, which helped make me feel somewhat joyful. Loving the autumn season, the shades of red, orange, and yellow made me anticipate the views I'd experience later in the week when I'd reintroduce my usual Saturday morning walk. There was nothing like the beauty of Central Park in the fall.

While on the way to work around 7:30 a.m., I received an email from my boss, which the partners had provided him, outlining the current update on the museum's legal situation. Sighing while reading the latest news, I strolled along the elevated greenway to West 26th Street, knowing it wouldn't be a good day.

The elevator opened on the firm's 18th floor at precisely eight o'clock, and within ten minutes, I was sitting at my desk, powering up my computer. It was hard to settle in at first and find a new normal, but once I began responding to emails requiring a prompt reply, it seemed like, somehow, I had never left.

Finished tying up loose ends before eleven, I sat in my office with idle hands for the first time in almost nine years. Used to being busy, I hated having too much time to think. It was always destructive. Thankfully, Mr. Gavin requested my presence. The anticipation around that meeting helped keep my mind occupied for the next half hour. Moving down the hall to the executive offices, I arrived on time.

Greeting his secretary warmly, I said, "Hi, Lila. How are you?"

"Oh, Eva! I am doing quite well, thank you. Welcome back, dear," she said joyfully. "Go ahead in. He's expecting you."

"Thank you," I replied, stopping at the entrance to Mr. Gavin's office. Knocking gently, I heard him shout, "Come in!"

Swinging open the heavy door, I watched the handsome older man with grey hair happily walk around the enormous desk in the middle of the room.

Presenting a firm handshake, looking my way strangely, he said, "Great to have you back, Thompson. I know you're probably disappointed that they've suspended the project for the time being, but the construction is still scheduled to move forward as planned once both parties reach a court settlement. Hopefully, that will not take too long."

Attentively nodding at his comments, I didn't have that sparkle in my eyes or brightness to my face any longer. I think that had all but drained from me months prior.

Offered a seat in one of the guest chairs situated in front of his desk, Mr. Gavin returned to his library chair and sat down, casually leaning back in it. Pausing a moment, he wondered how he would phrase his next comment. Making sure it wasn't intrusive or wrongfully taken, given my noticeably apparent physical state of being, he cautiously remarked, "So, as you well know, word travels very fast on the streets of New York...."

The moment he said it, I knew which direction our conversation was heading. Speaking up to stop him from addressing the problem any further, I quickly interjected. "Mr. Gavin, I'm fine. The project was not affected by certain events in my personal life, and the client has been more than happy with the construction until this delay. Now that I've returned, I will continue regardless of what's transpired in the past few months. I assure you, I am fine."

Not entirely convinced, listening intently to what I had to say, he still felt the need to offer something positive anyway.

"What happened a while back is your business. I know that, but please understand I've also been through something similar many moons ago and have first-hand experience with what you are feeling. Returning to New York means addressing this problem head-on after sweeping it under the rug for a while. Are you ready to deal with that and continue working here? I think not."

Facing the floor, decoding his blunt observations, I knew he was right. I did need a break. I truly did. Right now, the best thing for me was to regroup and mentally focus my life in a new direction, but how could I do that? I needed to work to pay the bills.

Not saying a word, I just looked his way with a forced smile as his pointer finger moved tactfully along the crease of his lips while resting his elbow on the arm of the leather chair. Suddenly, as if reading me like a book, he outlined the terms of the firm's proposal.

"To reward the hard work and dedication shown on this project over the past seven months, the partners and I have offered you a month off with pay, since you will not be back on site until the lawsuit settles in court. Given the expected tight construction timeline, the next phase will probably push you to your limits. We thoroughly believe you deserve a break for working night and day without fail through some rather difficult circumstances. Upon returning from your time away, you will have a new office to walk into, along with that title on the door you've been chasing since you got here, although by then, you'll probably be heading back to LA to continue where you left off. How does that sound?"

Fighting back the tears, grateful for my career blessings, I said genuinely, "Thank you. Thank you, Mr. Gavin. I appreciate that very much."

With his finger pointed in my direction, inching forward, with both elbows sliding across the top of the desk, he quietly explained in a concerned, fatherly tone, "How many times have I told you to call me George, by the way?" Smiling, he added, "No matter. Remember, as of Monday, you are not to set foot in this office, young lady. Get out of this city. Go on an adventure. Make travel arrangements through Barbara, my travel agent. She books everything for the firm. I look forward to seeing you in exactly 30 days, my dearest Eva – refreshed and ready to continue making this company proud."

"Thank you. Yes, as of Monday, it is."

Tearing up while taking Barbara's business card from him, he offered a kind-hearted hug. I felt so appreciated. At least I had that in my professional life, since it didn't exist on the relationship side of things.

Bidding Lila goodbye, I walked past her, analyzing the state of my life now, how I wouldn't have it all. You know, the career, husband, house, and a family of my own, but surprisingly, there was still this ample appreciation for what little I did have left.

| 13 |

Have A Little Faith

That Friday, I learned Carlo had arrived in New York to surprise Antonia. She was thrilled to be reunited with him. Happy she wouldn't need me over the next few days, I left work a little earlier, relieved by how the week had gone by without incident. Ordering some Azuki Sushi on my way home, making sure to time the delivery just right, the plan was to reinstate my usual Friday evening ritual. It didn't take long to slip into some cozy clothes and turn on the pay-for-view movie channel after the food arrived.

"Okay, so what do I want to watch?" I asked out loud. "Comedy, romance, maybe an action film?" Scrolling through the options under the most popular selections, I found the movie The Lake House. By this time, I felt I could use a release of emotions - partly a good cry and a bit of reinforcement that true love did exist out there somewhere, wondering one day if it would find me because I had no intention of ever looking for it again. Pressing play, I cozied up on the sofa with a box of tissues.

In a moment of faith, when the movie ended, I gave up a little prayer, hoping to prompt that special someone to appear when least expected. Praying for him to love me with every ounce of his being, never want to spend a moment without me, and genuinely want to grow old together for as long as time granted, I asked that my broken heart and its many missing pieces would eventually mend. These thoughts left me feeling uncertain if I'd ever accept anyone into my newly resurrected life after everything that had happened. Knowing deep down, I deserved better; I longed for that one person to show up with a smile that would give me butterflies like the movie's last scene was able to provide for a few captivating minutes.

Falling asleep that night, feeling a glimmer of hope as I drifted off, convinced He heard my prayers, I believed that one day I'd find my true love, that one man meant for only me, knowing it was just a matter of when.

| 14 |

The Spontaneous Decision

Being a creature of habit, I got up early to venture out on my Saturday morning walk. It usually consisted of a visit to the coffee shop to grab a latte and a cab before being dropped off at Columbus Circle to embark on the long, much-needed stroll through Central Park to clear my head. Excited to see what colors awaited me on this crisp autumn sunny day, putting on the new running shoes I bought during the week, I slipped my cross-body bag over my head and placed my phone inside it before going out the door.

Departing the lobby, all bundled up in a scarf and feather-lite down jacket to greet much cooler weather, I suddenly froze as my heart raced. With legs buckling, I told myself to stay strong. There, to the left of my building, blocking my path, was Scott. Knowing my predictable nature, he was sure I'd be there, and of course, there would be no escape.

Not wanting to create a scene, I angrily clenched my teeth and said, "What do you want? Haven't you done enough? Just go and leave me alone."

Silently backing off, staring my way with his hands extended outward, he calmly tried to prompt a civilized conversation. "I just need to talk to you. Please, one minute. That's all I ask. Then I'll leave you alone, I promise."

"Well, we all know your promises aren't worth very much, so…" I bluntly acknowledged, crossing my arms firmly in front of me, with eyes glued to the sidewalk below.

A hint of frustration crept across his face. "May I continue?"

"What? What do you have to say?" I snapped, turning away, not allowing him to see tears developing.

"I wanted to apologize. I'm truly sorry, Eva. I am," he stated sincerely, burying his hands in his jacket pockets. "Umm, as you well know," he paused, snickering with a nervous half-smile, "My mother always tends to get what she wants. Sometimes, it comes across endearingly—other times, not so much. My whole life, she's demanded that I find someone who fits her mold. She wasn't accepting of my last girlfriend, obviously. Even though she and I were together for years, Mom finally gave me an ultimatum - something I couldn't ignore. I ended my relationship with Yolanda that week and decided to pursue things with you when we met a month later. Knowing she was so happy and supportive of us, I figured marrying you would be a good fit for the family. What I didn't plan on was falling in love in the process. Guess I didn't realize that at the time."

Amazed by this confident man standing before me, wearing his heart on his sleeve, I figured I would soon hear - *I made a mistake. I want you back.*

Taking a deep breath, he paused a second. With my heart unwittingly melting as his words resonated, he continued with what he felt compelled to say.

"I guess when I ran into Yolanda a few weeks after you left for California, I realized my feelings for her never faded. What I did was stupid and unforgivable, and, of course, there is a consequence for every action. This whole mess caused me to lose the one person I respect above all others. You are one of a kind, Eva, and I've always thought I was never good enough for you. You deserve someone far better than me...."

"Wait? What? What do you mean?"

"My mother warned me that Yolanda would never willingly give me up, no matter what happens. She figured she'd somehow find a way to inch back into my life." Hanging on his every word, I heard him say, "She's pregnant, Eva - five months." Pausing, he silently stood there, afraid of how I'd react.

The shock hit me full force, making me turn away and shake my head in disbelief.

Attempting to gain sympathy, he added, "That said, I have to do the right thing. I still love her - always have. I've asked her to marry me, Eva. I wanted to tell you that in person. Didn't want you to find out from anyone else."

Immediately, my hand went up, signaling that I'd heard enough. Placing my earbuds in my ears and pressing play on my iPhone, I began walking down the street towards the coffee shop, hearing him call out faintly in the distance, "Eva, I'm sorry!"

Amidst a sea of people, loneliness, rejection, and pain festered. Emotionally beaten and bruised, hating my life, I got the sudden urge to run. With it came a flood of anger. Speedily dodging pedestrians, moving from the sidewalk to the street, I passed by the coffee shop and continued until I reached Central Park.

How could I have been so wrong about someone? He didn't love me. Guess that answers my question. I was the rebound relationship that went too far. Reaching Columbus Circle, replaying Scott's confession, I knew there was no way I would ever recover from this. Figures. Just as I started to rebuild my life, he waltzed back in and shattered everything I'd worked so hard to repair. Where do I even begin to pick up the pieces? First, my relationship failed horribly; then, my museum project halted, and now this? Really? How could someone do this to a person he supposedly loves?

After passing the Maine Monument, my travels brought me to Bow Bridge overlooking the Lake. Surveying the patterned currents as the water flowed gracefully by, I watched the odd autumn leaf float here and there as the sun sparkled on the surface, lulling me into a mindless trance. In a muffled state of consciousness, bombarded by multitudes of questions cultivating in my head, my attention was diverted to the sound of laughter drifting from the end of the bridge. Observing a sharply dressed young couple facing each other, the man began sharing how much she meant to him, how his life was complete since they met, and how he would love her forever. With an array of emotions, getting down on one knee, ring box in hand, he endearingly proposed to the woman. Filled with love and tears flowing, she accepted with open arms. Strangers applauded and congratulated them as they passed. Their smiles would have brightened anyone's day. Sadly, that wasn't the case for me.

Witnessing the strong connection the two shared made me feel happy for them, but I highly doubted whether their love would ever survive the test of time. In the worst emotional state, reality hit me hard. I was heartbroken and needed to repair my heart, soul, and mind. That is when I decided to leave New York and get away for the month, as Mr. Gavin suggested.

But where could I disappear for a while and heal? I thought. Does a place like that even exist somewhere in the world?

"I don't care how much it costs. I'm going to find the most beautiful place on earth, and I am going there."

Walking into my apartment an hour later, frustrated beyond words, I noticed my voicemail alerting me of twelve messages waiting. A closer examination of my call display revealed they were all from friends and family who undoubtedly found out through the grapevine what I did hours before. Ignoring all of them, swiftly opening my laptop, I searched for the most secluded places on the planet and finally came across the Whitsunday Islands off the coast of Australia. The pictures made it seem like a touch of heaven on earth - the most tranquil, relaxing vacation sanctuary ever. I didn't even know it existed until now. One hotel caught my attention over the rest. The Qualia Resort was the most exclusive hotel on Hamilton Island. They had a world-renowned Spa, exciting excursions, tennis, golf, and a quiet, picturesque beach that would allow me to relax and listen to the waves - exactly what I needed. Figuring the cost of the trip would probably eat up most of my savings, I knew in the vast scheme of things, it didn't matter now since I didn't have to contribute to a wedding anytime soon. Within minutes, I spontaneously emailed Mr.

Gavin's travel agent, Barbara, and added a small request at the bottom.

"Please make all of these arrangements on a first available basis. I wish to leave as soon as possible," I said aloud as I typed the sentences.

When I pressed send, what I was doing became more real. The countdown was on. It made me focus on the next steps since there was a strong possibility I could be leaving in a couple of days. There was no time to waste. So, over the next hour, I created a list of things to pack and things to buy. All the preparation helped distract me from thinking negatively.

Heading out later that day, I hoped some relatively moderate retail therapy would make me feel better. Hopeful that I'd find a few new dresses for the trip, I scoured as many Manhattan shops as possible and was pleasantly surprised to find four pretty sundresses on clearance amongst all the fall and winter fashions on full display. Things were shaping up nicely, creating a hint of excitement and rekindling the bounce in my step that I seemed to have lost a while ago.

Later that evening, upon returning from my shopping escapade around dinnertime, I dug out my large suitcase amidst an abundance of unpacked boxes. Gathering and sorting through clothes suited for much warmer weather, I threw some in the washing machine before showering and getting ready for bed. Blindsided by apprehension, it made me question what I was doing.

"Are you actually going through with this?" I asked myself while looking in the mirror. Reliving my confrontation this morning with Scott solidified my answer of – "Yes! You bet I am!"

| 15 |

Let the Adventure Begin

Suffering through a restless, broken night's sleep, something that had, unfortunately, become the norm, I woke to the sounds of an email alert on my phone just after seven. Reading the message sent by Barbara, I was stunned to see the confirmation details for the flights and resort pavilion I'd requested. Not wasting any time, she'd promptly arranged for me to fly to Sydney out of LAX tonight.

"Well, I guess she did what I asked. That is certainly the first available," I said in disbelief.

Scheduled for departure on Delta's late afternoon flight, I realized it only gave me a few hours to finish packing and be on my way to JFK before two o'clock. In her email, she suggested I get to the airport earlier than usual since a significant storm was developing in the Carolinas. She warned that if I didn't get on this flight, there would be a pretty good chance I wouldn't be flying anywhere for the next week or so, given the impending weather.

With a million things floating about my mind, I jumped out of bed, partially coherent. Rushing around, feeling slightly panicked and out of control, I stopped in the middle of the room, took a deep breath, and tried to focus on getting myself organized. Usually thriving under pressure, this was new territory for me. Spontaneity was not one of my strong suits.

Having packed the rest of my clothes, neatly folding each dress and placing them on top, one by one, my suitcase, carry-on, and small crossbody bag soon found a spot near the front door. Worried about the trip, my soul desperately hoped it would help me heal and refocus my life for the better. Daydreaming of tranquil ocean waves, a lounge chair on the beach, and the warmth of the sun beating down helped to motivate my spirit.

Around noon, just as I was about to call Ellie, the building concierge alerted me of a messenger being escorted to my apartment with important documents to be signed for and received. Hearing a knock at the door, I greeted the young man with my tickets and itinerary in hand. After he left, the travel envelope and my passport got shoved in my bag. Figuring I'd look at the details later when I had a minute to think, I forwarded Barbara's email to my sister. Texting her shortly afterward, I hoped that she was free to talk.

Thankfully, Ellie called me. Diving straight into the conversation, omitting a gracious hello, she spouted, "Please don't be mad, but I sent your email to Mom and Dad," adding with a slight pause, "They were asking if they could be conferenced in on our phone call."

Surprised that they even cared, I agreed to speak to them despite it being months since we had communicated last. Ellie arranged the conference on her end, and soon, we were all there.

My father said, "Are you doing okay, Eva? We're concerned about you. Ellie has kept us updated on everything."

With some sincerity shining through his usual stoic facade, I tried to keep a stiff upper lip while it quivered. "Yes, I suppose I'm fine. As good as can be expected."

Confirming the contents of my email, Ellie made it quite clear she didn't want me to leave, but did realize why I felt compelled to escape New York. My parents couldn't comprehend the reasoning behind traveling so far away since this was very uncharacteristic of me. That's when Ellie asked where things currently stood emotionally.

Somewhat aware of my unhealthy physical and mental state, I told them I couldn't deal with any more hurt. The plan was to go away and relax before returning to tackle my dream job and, eventually, a solo existence in life once again. Sympathetically agreeing to help me through this challenging time, we soon reached an awkward moment that sparked the end of our conversation.

I checked the clock and interjected, "Umm, I have to go." Still met with silence on the other end, I added reassuringly, "I'll send you updates along my travels and let you know when I arrive at each destination. Alright?"

Happy with that, they thanked me for that courtesy and went silent again.

Hesitating, taking a chance, I desperately wanted to say something. "I love you all," I exclaimed, putting my feelings out there. A part of me wondered what response I would receive in return.

Hearing my mother and sister sobbing, I listened to each softly say, "Love you too, Eva."

My father stayed silent.

Ellie quickly added, "Safe travels."

"Thank you. Don't worry. I'll be back before you know it."

On that note, we ended the call. Saying our goodbyes, I couldn't believe that was the first time we had ever expressed those loving words to one another. After all these years, was that the silver lining hidden beneath my sorrows? Could my family be turning a page because of my heartache?

The phone rang amidst those thoughts. Answering it, I heard Eddie, the concierge, announce my car's arrival downstairs. Gathering my things, ready to depart, I wheeled my suitcase into the hallway, with carry-on in hand, and looked around my apartment for a split second. The space seemed quite bare, with the absence of every frame I'd packed away displaying photos that included Scott. Right then, I desperately wished that the pain in my heart would dissipate in a month and I'd return with a clear plan for my life. Locking the door, I went on my way.

Reaching the lobby, ducking into the waiting cab, and settling in while the driver stored my suitcases in the trunk, I quickly hid my tearful face behind sunglasses, regardless of the dense cloud cover blanketing the city.

In a blur, fighting traffic for almost an hour and a half, the taxi finally pulled up along the curb at JFK. Somewhat on time, I stepped onto the sidewalk and paid the fare. Tasked with now maneuvering the overly chaotic check-in desk at Delta, I slowly shuffled through the backlogged security check with the other passengers in a zombie-like state. Eventually, I made it with just enough time to purchase a bottle of water before proceeding to the gate. Eager to depart, sitting for only fifteen minutes, the boarding announcement came sooner than expected, which was fine with me since I was more than happy to get this show on the road. I thought the faster this plane leaves the ground, the faster I land in paradise.

In search of window seat 10 A, I stuffed my bag under the seat in front of me and peered out the window blankly after buckling my seatbelt. It seemed I was caught up in a whirlwind and was not in control of my actions - it was hard to fathom.

"I'm about to fly halfway around the world alone." Taking a deep breath, trying to muster courage, I quietly told myself, "Don't worry, you'll be okay," just as an elderly woman sat down to my right. Placing my earbuds in my ears, wanting to avoid small talk, continuing my antisocial behavior, I watched as we lifted off in New York, leaving the attractively lit city skyline to fade below the low-lying clouds. Closing the shade, feeling tired, I fell asleep once we got to cruising altitude.

| 16 |

The Journey Down Under

The coast-to-coast, six-hour and eleven-minute flight to California seemed to go by in a blink. Waking upon hearing the pilot announce that we would be landing shortly at LAX, I took out my phone and looked at the converted time, noticing it was now 9:35 p.m. Pacific.

Disembarking, making it through security, and claiming my bag at the carousel, I waited for the shuttle bus to take me to the Tom Bradley International Terminal. Along the way, opening Barbara's folder to locate the flight information for Australia, there, stuck to the front of the Qantas ticket, was a bright yellow Post-it note. Immediately, I recognized the handwriting. It read,

To Our Dearest Eva, We hope this trip to Australia renews your faith in life and love. The heart does mend; it just takes time. Wishing you to experience this life-renewing vacation in complete comfort, we booked you in First Class. Enjoy! You deserve all the happiness in the world. All our best, Mr. and Mrs. Gavin. (aka George and Sarah)

Eyes filled with tears, I had no choice but to stop in the middle of the hall. Clutching my heart, utterly speechless, I didn't care if people were watching my emotional outburst. What George and Sarah had done meant so much. It wasn't the first-class ticket that made me cry, but rather the tone of concern and optimism, offering encouraging support as any loving parents would for their child. No words could express my gratitude. Knowing they both understood my situation made me feel less alone in all of this.

Gingerly blotting the tears from my face, trying to pull myself together, I finally entered the doors of the Tom Bradley terminal. Not entirely sure where to go next, I asked an attendant for assistance. Spotting a woman standing beside the red Qantas First Class banner, I presented my travel information to her. She smiled pleasantly and escorted me to the designated check-in counter. There, the greeter introduced me to Lilly, a petite girl with blonde hair tied up in a perfectly smooth, sculpted bun. I learned she was the host assigned to maneuver me through to the First Class lounge.

Sliding my passport across the desk to the man behind the computer, I placed my suitcase on the scale while host Lilly looked on, trying not to invade my privacy too much.

"May I have your ETA Visa for Australia?" he asked firmly.

Taken off guard, I admitted, "Umm, I don't think I have one of those. I wasn't aware that a Visa was required."

Flashing a look of frustration while I frantically searched through the travel folder Barbara had prepared for me, coming up empty, I realized I didn't have anything matching what the man requested.

With very little emotion, he appeared somewhat annoyed.

Lilly calmly stepped forward without skipping a beat to advise, "Ma'am, my colleague, David, forgot to mention that you can electronically apply for one at the cost of seventy dollars, plus processing fees." Looking at the crusty face behind the monitor, she gave him the evil eye before signaling the Immigration Agent for assistance.

In an attempt to save face, David tried to smooth things over. "We must advise that there are no guarantees your application will be authorized after we submit the online form. In a case where an application is denied, the fee is nonrefundable."

Worried beyond words while agreeing to apply for the Visa, believing I would soon be returning to New York shortly if this didn't work, the agent with buzzed, dirty blonde hair and buggy eyes typed furiously on the keyboard as I crossed my fingers. Looking through Barbara's folder a second time, I found a checklist inside the front left pocket. At the top of the paper, there was an asterisk beside: You need to apply for an urgent ETA Visa upon arrival in LA. Pay the processing fee at the desk.

Whatever happens next, I thought, all I can do now is wait.

Almost ten minutes later, David looked up from his screen and said, "Alright. You can now enter the country. The Visa is electronically attached to your passport." Wrapping a baggage tag around the handle of my large suitcase, he issued my boarding pass.

Remembering what my Grandmother always used to say - *you get more with sugar than you do with salt*, I knew his mood would change if I departed with the words, "Thank you, Sir. Thank you so much for your help. I appreciate it. Have a good night."

With a nod of his head, seeing him display the pleasant expression that I had anticipated, he replied, "Have an enjoyable flight, Miss. Lilly will escort you through security." Looking to his next victim, he sharply shouted, "Next!!"

Feeling a bounce in my step, I followed Lilly.

"Okay, right this way. Off we go then." Walking along, she added, "So, where are you from, Miss...?"

"Thompson. Eva, actually," I explained. "I'm from New York."

"Nice to meet you, Eva Thompson, from New York. First time flying Qantas?"

"Yes, first time," I naively confirmed.

"Well, welcome. We are going to head through TSA Express Path shortly. It will help us avoid all the line-ups."

"Perfect. That sounds great."

"Are you flying to Sydney, Melbourne, or Brisbane on vacation or business?"

"Vacation. Work has been stressful, among other things, so my boss gave me some time off. I'm going to Sydney today en route to Hamilton Island."

"Wow, good choice. You will love it there. It's the best place to escape and relax. If you are looking for seclusion, that would be my first choice. Where are you staying?"

"Qualia," I replied.

"Lovely. That's a fabulous resort. Very high-end. It is so very peaceful."

"Well, that's what I am searching for - a quiet place to disappear for a while."

"Here we are. I will meet you on the other side," Lilly said, approaching the first-class priority lane. Showing her credentials while breezing through without issue, she greeted the security officers with a smile as I placed my carry-on and bag on top of the belt for scanning.

Once through, host Lilly waved me onward to our next stop.

"Right this way. We need to use the elevator," she instructed, pointing in the direction we needed to go.

After walking down the corridor, she pressed the lift button and waited for the doors to open.

"So, you've been to Australia before?" I asked.

"Yes, a few times. I usually stay in Sydney, but my husband and I went to Hamilton Island for three days on our honeymoon. I strongly suggest booking the Whitehaven Beach excursion and visiting the Great Barrier Reef. It is an experience like no other. You won't regret it. I promise."

Stepping into the elevator, contemplating what she said, and anticipating the fifteen-hour trip to Sydney, I felt a little more excited.

Lilly announced as the doors opened on the upper level, "Here we are. The Qantas First Class Lounge."

Double-checking the board while passing, she notified me that my flight was delayed and changed from 10:20 p.m. to 11:10 p.m. PDT.

Ten feet away, the honeycomb, frosted glass doors parted automatically to allow us access to the exclusive lounge. I stayed in Lilly's shadow while she approached the main counter and started speaking to a lady with a short, blonde, pixie haircut.

"Hello, Lilly. Who do we have here?" the energetic woman asked with an Aussie accent, trying to peek around her counterpart to see me.

Stepping aside, Lilly put me in full view. "Hey, Britt, this is our Qantas guest, Eva. She will be flying to Sydney tonight."

"Welcome to the First Class Lounge. May I see your ticket and boarding pass, please?" Britt formally requested.

Presenting my information to her, she said, "Thank you, Ms. Thompson."

Ready to depart, Lilly said, "You are in good hands now. This is where I leave you. It was a pleasure, Eva. Safe and happy travels. Enjoy your well-earned break."

"Thank you for your help, Lilly. Appreciate it."

When Britt said goodbye to my First Host, she described the services at my disposal inside the lounge. Listening respectfully, trying to look interested, I didn't want to interrupt and say that I was merely happy to find a seat in a quiet space.

Allowed to pass, I went around the corner to the left and quickly found an empty section to occupy. The area felt so light and airy as I sat in one of the ivory leather chairs positioned along a bank of floor-to-ceiling windows overlooking the airport's interior atrium. Grabbing my phone to send my parents and Ellie a text on my travel progress thus far, I composed a short note to say I had arrived at LAX safely. Surprised when each responded within minutes, I figured they were all worried about me and couldn't sleep a wink. Sharing the details of Mr. Gavin's travel upgrade gift, they were so happy and thankful that I had such a wonderful boss. Before ending our communications, each reminded me to alert them when I arrived in Australia. Promising I would, I wished them goodnight and signed off with a heart.

Wanting to freshen up before the next leg of the journey, I figured I'd use one of the shower suites to change into something more comfortable for the overnight flight.

Exiting twenty minutes later, now clean and in new clothes, I felt rejuvenated.

On route back to the main lounge area, noticing only a handful of people waiting around, I walked towards the long, modernly designed bar to grab a table. Intrigued by the autumn tasting menu, I read the seasonal shredded chicken salad description and decided to order that, thinking it would be a light dish.

In the end, I was right. It was substantial without being too heavy and boasted a combination of Latin and Asian flavors that blended well together.

Sitting there alone, with an idle mind, I ended my late-night dinner with an Americano to help battle fatigue. Remembering why I was sitting here, knowing I was trying to evade my broken life, a memory of our engagement party flashed before me.

Recalling Scott's mother's extravagant event the night of Christmas Eve, it seemed the party was more about her than celebrating Scott and me. That night, I learned what his mother truly thought of Yolanda. Avoiding a few annoying guests, I hid inside the butler's pantry attached to the dining room. While standing behind the pocket door, I overheard his mom talking to a group of gossiping women drooling for the scoop.

"I thank God every day that Scott met Eva. Last year at this time, I was certain he'd end up marrying Yolanda. He was with her forever. Remember that horrible girl?" she said viciously as the ladies giggled.

Grateful that Mrs. Egan approved of our relationship, I quickly wondered what her opinion of me would be as time passed - if she would talk behind my back eventually, too.

Regardless of everyone being happy for us that night, I still had reservations about whether our relationship was strong enough to start a marriage. There were issues, but I only started accepting that there were holes after we broke up. Being together five months at the time of the engagement party, I found myself caught up in the newness of our commitment and the allure of a wedding. Of course, with his mother planning most of the event, it also seemed I couldn't stop the momentum from swiftly moving forward anyway. Both sides expected us to marry within the year. I battled with the thought of disappointing everyone and embarrassing myself, too. Fortunately, my contract on the West Coast helped slow all of that down.

Hearing the boarding announcement for all passengers on Qantas Flight #12 to Sydney, I broke away from my thoughts and joined the other passengers moving along to the assigned gate.

While waiting patiently in the First-Class line, I gave the agent my boarding pass and passport when it was my turn. The lady assigned another stewardess to escort me and three others to our seats. Entering the long tunnel to the jumbo jet, the flight staff was pleasant and welcoming. Their upbeat smiles made me want to return the favor, which I hadn't done often enough over the last few months.

Near the front of the plane, turning right immediately after stepping aboard, the stewardess showed me to my First Suite. It was like a luxurious, tiny room where you could sit and watch TV in a recliner with a footrest or even flatten the chair into a six-and-a-half-foot single bed.

Excited to explore my cubicle, the petite, blonde-haired Aussie woman said before leaving me, "My name is Tricia. Please let me know if I can assist you during the flight. Here is our menu. We offer a wide array of options. The drink list is inside the folder. Should you have a request, please press the hostess button here, and I will be along shortly after."

"Thank you," I said with a smile while settling into the most comfortable armchair on the planet.

Soon, she returned with a glass of champagne and handed me a Qantas swag of packaged pajamas, slippers, an amenity kit, a pillow, and a blanket.

Despite all the luxury, I found it difficult to stop thinking about Scott - everything he'd done and the feelings I still had for him. It annoyed me beyond words, but your heart loves who it loves. Desperate to change that, I encouraged myself to stay on task over the next month. My job was to forget about him, move on, and close that chapter of my life for good. Taking a deep breath, I forced a smile, which prompted a subtle sense of nervousness for the trip to begin.

Finally, while speeding down the runway for take-off, I said quietly, "Okay, here we go. You're venturing into the unknown now, Eva. Let this be the start of your new and improved life."

Back in familiar territory, flying high above the clouds, the flight attendants gave the passengers in First Class permission to swivel and recline their chairs into a more comfortable position, along with the ability to move freely about the cabin. Quickly searching through several movie options, I wanted to find something that would distract me. That's when I detected a subtle lightness in the air. The suffocating feeling I was experiencing every minute of the day began to subside while the first few movie trailers rolled along. Wondering if it was just the relaxing environment surrounding me or the fact that Scott was so far away, I felt relieved and happy. In that moment of clarity, I had faith that this trip would heal my strength and confidence, something I realized he had gradually destroyed during our time together.

Upon finishing the famous Jason Bourne, my favorite movie of all time, needing to rest my mind, I switched the seat into a bed with Tricia's help. Somehow, acquiring an abundance of hope in such a short amount of time, I trusted my body would calm down enough to get a couple of hours of sleep before embarking on the final flight of this exciting adventure.

| 17 |

Halfway Around the World

Landing in Sydney, Australia, at 8:35 a.m. AEST, spending a little over twenty hours on two planes, I went through immigration and grabbed my suitcase at the baggage claim. Eagerly anticipating the flight to Hamilton Island, a short but scenic, two-and-a-half-hour trip, I got anxious for my vacation to begin.

Adhering to instructions from airport attendants directing passengers to the Qantas Seamless Transfer Desk to check in on my connection status, I realized there was no way I would make that flight on time. Departing over an hour late from LA had set everything back.

Standing in line for fifteen minutes, awaiting my turn, the attendant soon confirmed my fears and said the flight had already finished boarding. She suggested I book the next available, only fifty-five minutes away from departure. Exchanging my ticket for the 10:00 a.m. flight and rechecking my bag, I continued along and found a seat on the transfer shuttle bus heading to the domestic terminal a couple of minutes away.

More energized now, awake and alert, the shuttle pulled under the canopy outside Gate #15 Terminal 3. With an extra twenty minutes to spare, I walked through the doors to locate a washroom so I could freshen up and change into more summery clothes for the final leg of the journey.

Once dressed in a casual navy cotton tank dress with a cute ivory cardi over my shoulders, I sat at my designated gate. Ready to enjoy the soft-baked salted pretzel I'd picked up in terminal one, I took a bite before sipping the freshly brewed coffee I'd purchased just minutes before.

Boarding the Qantas connection mid-morning, locating my window seat in the relatively small, mid-sized plane compared to the past fourteen hours on the jumbo jet, it was surprising nobody was assigned the seat beside me. Scanning the tarmac out the window, knowing it wouldn't be long since the baggage handlers were moving away from the plane, with hands shaking and heels bouncing off the floor rhythmically, my body suddenly seemed stress-free. Antsy but happy, I watched the other passengers filing down the aisle. Amidst a few young families and senior vacationers, I spotted a handsome man with a backpack on one shoulder. Inconspicuously following him out of the corner of my eye, I noted how casually dressed he was. Sporting navy cargo shorts and a white t-shirt, with his hat facing forward and designer sunglasses resting on the brim, I felt a subtle flutter in my chest. Not at all surprised that I found the brown-haired, preppy type with dark eyes rather attractive, he passed me by, extending a bright, sexy smile, making me do the same before nervously looking away. Discreetly glancing at him, taking a seat a few rows back on the opposite side, I played it cool and tried to focus on the in-flight magazine I grabbed from the pocket in front of me. Flipping through the pages, not registering an ounce of its content, my eyebrows elevated. It was a positive reaction that made me feel a flood of warmth as it replaced some of the lingering loneliness. Without warning, a glimmer of hope made me think - just maybe I'd be okay. Perhaps my spirit hadn't died after all.

Taking off to embark on the final flight, I wondered what the islands would look like from the air. Some of the pictures I'd seen online were beautiful, but to see a photo and to experience it first-hand are usually two entirely different things. As the plane ascended into the clouds, the view from my window was erased. Showing only a blank canvas while moving upwards, the light slowly returned, illuminating a sea of fluffy cotton below and the bluest sky above. Mesmerized by the scenery, my subtle daydream got interrupted by a sudden series of sneezes that exploded a couple of seats back, instantly disturbing the peace. Catching a glimpse of the cute guy while looking over my shoulder, I decided to spy a little and see what he was doing. With head lowered and body slouched towards the window, I assumed he was sleeping. His sunglasses remained hidden under the brim of his hat, slanted down over his forehead. Filled with curiosity, I wondered why he was traveling alone. Perhaps he was meeting his family on Hamilton Island or had plans to dive the Great Barrier Reef. Unfortunately, I would never know what his story was.

Guess that forever leaves him a man of mystery, I thought, returning my attention out the window as we began our descent again.

Each passenger had the most incredible bird's-eye view of the islands on the plane's final approach. The sun cast an almost blinding glow across the Coral Sea. While circling above Hamilton Island, preparing to land, the turquoise waters and white-capped waves vividly shimmered.

Successfully touching down, the plane eventually stopped in front of the open-air terminal. Collecting my things from under the seat, I stood up and waited for my turn to disembark. While scanning the faces of the other passengers, in that split second, the cute guy just happened to look my way. He seemed happy to offer a subtle wave, adding a slight tilt of his head. Flashing a sexy smirk before grabbing his things from the upper compartment, sadly, the gesture immediately reminded me of Scott.

Exiting the plane on cue in an organized manner, I strolled up the aisle with everyone else and continued down the steps and onto the tarmac. Friendly attendants welcomed every passenger and guided us toward the small baggage claim area, where I located my suitcase when it arrived on the trolley. Escaping the crowd, heading toward the main doors, I saw a middle-aged, gray-haired man dressed in crisp, white linen clothing waiting outside the barriers. Holding a sign with my initial and last name written on it, the gentleman intently made eye contact with every woman departing the security area. Acknowledging him while inching closer, his face immediately lit up.

Pleasantly greeting me, he confirmed, "Ms. Thompson?" Nodding my head, he continued to explain, "Very nice to meet you. My name is Harry, the concierge. I will be escorting you to Qualia. This way, please."

Commandeering my large suitcase and passing him my small carry-on, Harry led me to the courtesy shuttle parked outside. After checking in at the Resort's Welcome Desk, I peered up at the sky, enjoying the sunshine and warmth, while he secured my bags on the back of the commercial golf cart. About to have a seat, my wandering eye caught the handsome guy from the plane walking past with his single-strap backpack positioned across his chest, two extra-large roller bags in tow, and another bashful smile that made me melt. With a flutter in my chest, recognizing those long-awaited butterflies from countless lonely Friday movie nights, reigning in my thoughts, I reminded myself of the purpose of being here. With a list of consequences revealing themselves not long after, knowing without a doubt that deviating from my original plan could cause irreversible damage, I quickly got my head out of the clouds.

Standing beside the cart marked with the Qualia logo, the beautiful feeling inside me faded.

I heard Harry's distant voice repeat, "Umm, Miss? Hello?" Turning my attention away from the cute guy, Harry requested, "Please have a seat. Qualia is not far away. We will be there shortly."

Sitting down, I noticed there were no cars here. They mostly had golf carts, which everyone called buggies, and the odd silver Volkswagen Minivan transporting family vacationers to their accommodations along narrow, paved pathways. Oddly driving on the opposite side of the road, we climbed a shadow-laden incline toward the top of a hill.

Harry broke the ice and said with a strong Aussie accent, "So where ya from?"

"New York," I responded, suddenly feeling pretty exhausted.

"You're very far from home."

Deciding to keep it simple, I replied, "Yes, I'm here to rest and clear my head."

"This is the place to do that then," he laughed before explaining the various activities the island had to offer, along with the excursions of the surrounding Great Barrier Reef area and Whitsunday Islands.

It was almost 1:35 p.m. when we reached the peak - a lookout area boasting unrestricted panoramic views of the neighboring islands and the Coral Sea.

Harry stopped the buggy. "This place is called One Tree Hill. Everyone gathers here at sunset for the complimentary cocktails and to experience the day-ending colors presented each evening between 5:30 and 7:30 p.m. It's very romantic."

"Well, I guess I won't be taking part in that at any point," I sighed, reminded of my current status in life.

"Oh, Miss, keep an open mind. You never know what the islands have in store for you."

Carefully driving down the other side of the hill, we soon arrived at the extravagant gates of the resort. Waving his fob over the lit security panel, Harry waited for the large wood and chrome doors to slowly open, granting us access to the exclusive enclave. With my key card in hand, there was an unbridled sense of excitement to see the Leeward Pavilion Barbara had booked for me, which had a view of the ocean through the trees.

Directed to my villa, taking a labyrinth of pathways, we eventually parked outside my temporary home. Harry slipped the stopper under the door after swinging it open, allowing me to enter the space on my own to have that moment to myself. Once inside the charming cottage, with vaulted ceilings and gleaming natural hardwood floors, I stood in the center of the room between the king-sized bed and the ample sitting area. The entire bank of glass windows included a double-sliding door that was partially open, allowing a warm, gentle sea breeze to cascade through the screen. As the drapes gracefully swayed with each subtle gust of wind, I turned to find Harry bringing in my bags.

Gently setting them just inside the entrance, handing him his tip, he said before departing, "Thank you so much. Remember what I said earlier? You never know what the islands have in store for you. Enjoy your stay here at Qualia, Miss."

Once again, thanking him for all his help, I closed the door, locked it, and found myself feeling hungry, sleepy, and surprisingly joyful. With my stomach growling, thoughts of the room service menu quickly crossed my mind. Locating its hiding spot, I ordered a fruit plate and a hot seafood appetizer that fit my mood.

Beginning to unpack, in desperate need of a shower, sadly, I heard the service bell chime sooner than expected. Enveloped in a plush white robe, I swung open the front door to allow the lady concierge into my suite. I stood in the middle of the room, watching her set everything up on the balcony. It looked so lovely.

After I'd signed the bill, she politely said, "Thank you, Miss. Enjoy your stay."

Sitting down at the table, topped with white linen, I positioned my chair to peer through the trees and see the turquoise water in the distance while texting my family to let them know I arrived safe and sound. Calculating the time difference, knowing they were fifteen hours behind, I realized it was 11:40 p.m. the night before in New York. While struggling to savor the delightful flavors before me, my body began hitting the proverbial wall as I finished the last few bites. Finding it hard to keep my eyes open while reading the texts from my parents and Ellie, minutes later, knowing I was fading fast, I responded as each wished me a spirit-renewing vacation, requesting that I check in from time to time during my stay. Agreeing to do just that while clearing the table, I brought everything inside before closing the sliding doors and pulling the blackout drapes to darken the room. Slowly opening the covers on the bed and slipping into the soft Egyptian cotton sheets, my eyes gravitated to the ceiling, unexpectedly feeling so far from home. While pondering everything I'd gone through to get here, proud of myself for successfully flying around the world, a more negative aura soon cloaked that positivity as I started analyzing again. Disappointed that I had somehow let Scott do this to me, I wondered if I had run away from my troubles versus facing them head-on. Had I taken this vacation to avoid things because I hated the thought of further confrontation? Or did I come here freely to invoke a fresh start with a clean conscience? Overall, did it really matter? I was here now.

To boost morale, I sat up in bed and promised myself aloud, "You are going to enjoy this experience. Think of it as turning a page and starting a new life. You need time to heal, so begin this journey with a level head and a forgiving heart."

Falling into the fluffy pillow, I drifted off to sleep that night and didn't wake up once.

| 18 |

Day One: Hamilton Island

Sixteen hours later, awakened by the loud rumbling sound of a seaplane flying overhead, the early morning light dimly spread across the room through an opening in the drapes. Sitting up, I fluffed my pillows and piled each against the wood plank headboard wall. Comfortably leaning back, reaching for my phone, the screen illuminated to show the time of 5:40 a.m. Shocked that I'd slept so long, feeling like it was too early to get up, it seemed my only option was to bury myself under the down duvet cover to rest a bit longer.

Tossing and turning for the next two hours, unable to fall asleep, I decided to get moving around eight. My stomach began to growl shortly after that. Anxious to get out of bed to start the day, I pulled back the drapes and sheers. Immediately, my eyes settled upon the gorgeous view of the channel and neighboring islands. The turquoise water mesmerized me as the choppy waves inundated the shore. Leaving the screen door open, allowing some fresh air to waft through while getting ready, I turned on the TV to the resort channel, hoping to become familiar with the many amenities and excursions available here. While watching the various segments, I got a little overwhelmed at the thought of tackling these activities alone.

Being a woman traveling solo did instill some fear. It almost made me revisit my sole purpose for being here. Intent on experiencing this Coral Sea adventure to the fullest, wanting so desperately to explore this beautiful place, a part of me felt reluctant despite being nestled amongst several vacationers and tour guides. All in all, I figured

I would be safe, and if I was lucky enough, there was even a possibility of meeting some new friends along the way. Determined to regain some independence, I compiled a list of attainable goals over the next few weeks - kind of like a Whitsunday's Bucket List. Looking at what I'd included thus far, every ounce of my being hoped it would give me the strength and courage to overcome these fears. I wanted to enjoy this once-in-a-lifetime vacation. Adding small steps like spa services, yoga classes, snorkeling, and exploring the island's shops and attractions seemed to help. Each would make me brave enough to book the Whitehaven Beach and Great Barrier Reef tours.

Proud of the list now neatly organized and recorded on the resort notepad, a spark of energy fueled my soul while I selected a pair of sandals to complement the casual white beach dress I had just put on. Well-rested but somewhat jittery now, taking the resort map to get my bearings, I nervously closed my cottage door to rejoin the land of the living. Heading in the direction of the Long Pavilion, located not far from my cabin, I followed the signs directing guests to the restaurant as the heavenly smell of breakfast guided me to the roof-covered entrance.

While passing through the lush jungle-like open-air breezeway, I approached the podium and noticed the incredible view displayed behind a gentleman who promptly asked, "Table for one, Miss?"

Acknowledging him with a nod, the question reminded me of what my life had been reduced to - a single person, by herself, table for one.

Escorted to the edge of the alfresco dining area, taking in every angle of the striking vista, looking left to right, I was in awe of the ocean's sights and sounds. Birds sang in the trees as the leaves wistfully blew in the updrafts while various shades of blue shimmered in the morning light. Immersed in the freshest air imaginable, sitting down near the balcony, my waiter stopped by the table, offering French press coffee and a warm morning greeting.

Able to offer him a smile, I happily thought, Maybe this wasn't such a bad idea after all.

Outwardly content, having had my favorite breakfast of eggs Benedict and a relaxing dining experience, I left the restaurant. While passing by the resort shop along the way to the Concierge Desk, I spotted an Australia-worthy hat from designer Helen Kaminski. Wholeheartedly prepared to make the sound investment, I held off to see what I could find in town later. Again, my true colors shining through, I knew spontaneity was not one of them.

Timidly approaching the front desk to speak with the Concierge Hostess, I inquired about the many spa services available and requested a map of the island, which I had every intention of exploring. Our conversation finalized a few appointment bookings over the next couple of weeks. While happily checking numbers five and six off my Bucket List in hand, that being reflexology and a massage, I noticed item number ten, a couple of lines below - the Whitehaven Beach excursion Lilly had mentioned. Hesitating a moment, cringing in the process, before taking the plunge, per se, I asked about the tour's availability.

The woman focused on her computer screen and said, "Yes, we have a spot for one person on a group excursion eight days from now, but we are fully booked until then. I suggest you reserve your trip because of this tour's strong popularity."

I reluctantly nodded while she took down my name and pavilion number. Fearful, I knew this excursion was way outside my comfort zone.

With that settled, she casually asked, "Enjoy your day. What is on your agenda?"

"I might go into town and explore a little."

Quickly offering one last piece of advice, she explained, "I strongly recommend, if you venture out, that you use the golf cart assigned to your pavilion. The walk back from the harbor is a rather long, exhausting trip."

I had never driven a golf cart, so I didn't know how to respond.

She read my facial expression like a book and added, "Should you require instructions on how to operate it, please call the Concierge, and they will offer a demonstration for you."

"I will keep that in mind. Thank you," I said. "Have a nice day."

"You as well, Miss."

Before walking away, I smiled and waved goodbye to her. Returning to my cottage minutes later, I arrived back where the day had first begun. Changing clothes into a skort and tank, I slipped on my running shoes and tied them tightly. Grabbing a water bottle from the mini bar, my phone, and a small backpack almost in one swoop, I left my pavilion, ready to scout the plantation on foot. Task number one was to find the pool and beach area.

Upon leaving the Long Pavilion behind me, strolling down the hillside slope, the signs efficiently pointed toward Pebble Beach. Discovering another building, I passed through the covered breezeway and found the pool just past the main entrance doors. In awe of the tranquil infinity edge that seemed to blend into the Coral Sea behind it, I stood and marveled at the view, almost looking like a piece of heaven. The perfect white sand and grey pebble beach was one level below the pool deck. Lined with black umbrellas and teak chaise lounge chairs, the black and white striped cushions looked invitingly comfortable. Scanning the beach from right to left, I caught sight of the artistic patterns engraved in the sand, welcoming guests to the shore.

"Wow," I whispered, disappointed not to have anyone to share it with. "That is so beautiful."

Reminded of my broken life, determined to carry on, I tried my best to keep my mind off Scott and his pregnant girlfriend. Thankful to be in this gorgeous place versus wallowing back in New York, I straightened my posture. Desperate for a distraction, while walking along the island's northern edge, I knelt to feel the temperature of the water as the tiny ripples hit my fingertips. That is when I saw my reflection and watched a tear leave my face and become part of the sea below. Standing up, deciding to rest for a second, I found a seat at the foot of an open lounge chair. Unable to sharpen my gaze through weepy eyes, I focused on the horizon. Lonely, sad, and unexpectedly homesick, the turquoise water mixed with the various blue hues helped send my thoughts elsewhere, alleviating some pain.

"Shades like this, you never see back home," I whispered.

Eyeing the fluffy clouds drifting by, my spirit followed suit, hopeful that, just maybe, there was a man somewhere in the world looking up at the same sky, wondering when he, too, would find the love of his life. That one person to call his soul mate. A woman he finds complete harmony with and a need to devote himself to. Knowing this may never be, I immediately shook off those sentiments since they seemed more detrimental than supportive and promised, "Starting now, you are going to live in the moment—nothing else."

Venturing up another path away from the water, I reached the main road to find guests driving through the resort in their golf carts with shopping bags dangling. Drawn to the downtown area, I continued my walk for another fifteen minutes, exploring the many little treasured nooks about the property before returning to my pavilion to pick up my buggy.

I was excited about driving up and over the steep hill, but did not know how this whole golf cart thing would work. Now, with the key in hand, locking my pavilion again, embarrassed to call the Concierge for a lesson on operating the machine, I assumed I was intelligent enough to figure it out on my own.

"Really, how hard could it be?" I questioned, looking at the cart sitting in front of me.

Behind the wheel, reading the laminated instructions, I inserted the key into the ignition and turned to the ON position. Double-checking the direction switch as indicated, I made sure the cart was ready to go forward. Gingerly stepping on the pedal, the parking brake released, making a clicking sound. Pressing my foot on the accelerator again, I slowly inched along. Maneuvering through the shrubbery-lined paths made me feel proud that I accomplished this feat. Surprised that it didn't take long to get the hang of it, I constantly reminded myself to drive on the left.

Cautiously navigating the narrow roadways, I threaded through the resort's main gates. Approaching One Tree Hill, where we stopped briefly yesterday, I remembered what Harry said about everyone meeting to take in the sunset over cocktails. Contemplating doing that as I passed by, I reached a divider where the name of the street changed. Referring to my map, I realized the road branched off into a small traffic circle.

"Right...hmmm. Which way?" I pondered. "Acacia Drive or the Great Northern Freeway? Funny how they used the name, freeway, to describe these small, two-lane, mini roads."

The allure of the marina made me turn right and meander down Acacia Drive. Traversing the hillside, other guests waved in passing, making me happily return their friendly gestures. Reaching the shoreline, I discovered the manta ray-shaped Hamilton Yacht Club Pavilion I'd spotted from the air. The street name changed to Front Street, which consisted of stores, restaurants, and a bakery. The downtown area was quaint, even though it was heavily tourist-laden at this time of day. Parking across the street from a string of stores, I found myself a spot facing the marina. Once again, reading the cart instructions, I checked to see if the parking brake was on. Removing the key from the ignition, I slipped it into the front pocket of my backpack before throwing it on my shoulder.

Slowly walking amongst the other tourists, I veered into a shop called The Hut. Stepping inside, hit by a wall of cool air, I took off my sunglasses and started looking around. In need of suntan lotion, not having brought any with me, I found a few brands that weren't familiar. Reading the labels, I eventually chose two types before perusing their vast selection of clothing and accessories, hoping to find a new sun hat. Quickly finding an entire wall of hats amongst many island guests flooding the store, a person standing to the far right suddenly caught my eye. Focused in, I froze. Could it be? Trying to act casual, I covertly pretended not to notice his presence.

Nervous, unsure of what to do or say, my hands shook at the thought of speaking to the guy from the plane. It sparked a flutter in my chest, making me gasp and unknowingly hold my breath for a second. That's when he turned around and recognized me. Smiling, with eyebrows raised, giving up a subtle wave in the process, he hesitated a moment before making his way over.

Unshaven, his short, free-spirited brown hair caught a burst of air as he walked past the main door and down the center aisle. He looked comfortable but super handsome, dressed in all-black athletic wear from head to toe. Casually resting his thumb behind the single strap of his backpack positioned across his chest, he approached and soon stood a mere five feet from me within seconds. My heart rapidly beat, and my cheeks felt flushed out of nowhere.

What do I say? I thought in a panic.

"Hi. Doing a little shopping?" he questioned in a low, curious tone.

Out of practice, I got up the courage and said, "Yes, I decided to explore a bit since I'm feeling less jet-lagged today. How about you?"

"Me? Umm, yeah, much of the same. I wanted to check out the local establishments and see what there is to do. I saw this little shop and figured I'd pick up a few things." Raising his hand to reveal a Whitsunday map and suntan lotion, he asked, "I guess you're looking for a hat?"

Turning toward the styles displayed behind me, I was disappointed not to see the Kaminski I liked. Selecting something similar, I said, "Yes, I think so." Boldly facing the mirror, not thinking through what I was about to say, I spouted, "So, what about this one? Does it look good? Do you think I'll blend in here?" Embarrassed, wondering if what I said was outwardly lame, I had no choice but to await his reaction.

Inspecting the first hat I'd chosen to try on, I felt somewhat insecure while the guy formulated his opinion with arms crossed in front of his chest. Unknowingly flexing the muscles in his arms in the process, deep in thought, he released an approving grin and said, "Think it looks great. You should buy that."

Acknowledging him with a subtle laugh and an uncertain smile, we encountered an embarrassing pause. It was almost as if we both had forgotten how to interact socially.

"Ah, I'm Ryan Davis, by the way," he said in a self-assured voice, offering his hand to introduce himself politely.

Following suit, I replied, "Eva Thompson. Pleased to meet you, Ryan."

"Likewise…" Faced with another uncomfortable moment, Ryan nervously revealed, "Well, I found what I needed, so I guess I'll get going. Might see you around then, Eva? Happy shopping."

"Yes. Have a good rest of the day," I said, trying to play it cool, almost offended that he chose to end the conversation. Cringing, replaying everything I just said, I felt so stupid.

How does a girl go about talking to a guy who looks like that anyway? I thought, No wonder he left.

Shifting my attention to the mirror, deciding whether or not I would buy the hat, I watched Ryan's reflection as he paid for his things and went out the door. Before leaving the storefront, I caught him peering in the window back in my direction. Bashfully lowering his head, unable to contain a smile, he seemed outwardly interested before continuing on his way. Funny how that tiny bit of attention made me feel good about myself for a split second. With my stomach still fluttering, it was hard to recover from the encounter. Feeling happy, a part of me hoped I'd see him again. It had been an eternity since I'd felt a spark fill my body like that.

Finally, deciding to wait and buy the Kaminski bucket-style hat I preferred at Qualia, I headed to the cashier to pay for a few other items. About to leave, putting on my sunglasses, a bit of loneliness returned. Thinking I would enjoy this whole experience more, I reminded myself that I'd spent the past seven months partially alone, so technically speaking, this was no different.

As my feet were about to hit the sun-drenched sidewalk, a vehicle suddenly pulled up tight to my right. Startled, trying to regain my footing, I saw Ryan sitting in a rather swanky custom cart, displaying a mischievous grin. Uneasy, with instincts going into overdrive, I immediately wondered what he truly wanted. Acutely aware of his striking good looks and sudden playful approach, my gut feeling assumed he was probably in the market for a vaca-girlfriend. Familiar with how summer relationships spawned in the Hamptons, I knew many guys who'd latch onto a girl for their vacation only to abandon her before Labor Day weekend.

Keeping that in mind, I heard him say, "So, where are you venturing...?"

With hands outstretched in front of me, I abruptly interrupted. "Umm, Ryan. Look, I am not interested in a short-term fling or anything along those lines, so thank you. I'm flattered, but I'm just going to walk away. I wish you all the best. Have a nice vacation, okay."

Shaken by my straightforward yet thoughtful reply, he sat back in his cart, wondering what my impression of him must have been to garner that reaction.

Turning around, feeling empowered, I walked to the next store, believing he had gone. About to open the door to a small art gallery, a masculine hand opened it for me. Instantly peeking over my shoulder to thank the person for their kindness, I saw Ryan standing there.

Right away, feeling defensive, I shouted, "Look!"

Before I could rip his head off, he raised one hand to stop my outburst. "Eva. Can we start over? I'm not some guy searching for a quote-unquote "good time" like you might think," he gestured. "I honestly thought you seemed kinda nice and, you know, wouldn't mind having a conversation or two."

Hesitating a second, I walked into the gallery, trying to ignore him while analyzing what he had just said.

"I'm on vacation alone—first time in years. Since arriving yesterday, I've only talked to one waiter and a store clerk. So yeah, it hasn't been fun."

Following me, he continued explaining his situation in a rather odd way.

"Guess I'm just looking for someone to talk to, like a friend. No strings. Just a person to hang out with and hopefully add a bit of camaraderie to an otherwise lonely vacation."

Part of me contemplated whether he was unstable. Giving him a chance, lending a sharp ear, I perused the beautiful works of art displayed on the walls. Strategically pretending to be uninterested, I cautiously questioned, "So, what do you think of this one?"

Put on the spot, he paused and silently pointed to the piece he figured I was referring to before he genuinely replied, "Truthfully, I know nothing about art, but I like the colors and the abstract way the artist made the setting sun evolve across the ocean."

Impressed by his description, happy to hear the word, truthfully, I relaxed a bit and said, "I like it too." Noticing the expression on his face, he seemed harmless enough, almost like the boy next door. Knowing I kind of felt the same way he did and would certainly feel safer not exploring the island alone, I hesitated before affirming my thoughts. "Friends? Fine, but nothing more. You keep your distance and no funny business."

Content with that response, his facial expression resembled a kid meeting his first buddy in kindergarten. "I promise. Ten-foot rule. Got it - no funny business. Right," he nodded. "So, how about it? Want to explore this side of the island together?"

In awe of how attractive he was, it seemed my head nodded up and down almost on its own. Thinking about it, I answered, "Sure. I'd like that."

Mutually settling on the terms I outlined, he walked the art gallery with me as the dry hardwood boards creaked beneath our feet. Discussing the many works on display created by local artists, I knew Ryan was right. It was far more enjoyable talking to someone experiencing the sights simultaneously, versus having an internal conversation with oneself.

Seeing the entire upper level of the building, we made our way back down the stairs toward the front door. Leaving the gallery, we stood outside under the covered boardwalk, sheltered by the heat of the sun, ready to decide on our next venture.

"So, where are you parked?" he said, looking up and down the street lined with golf carts. "Do you want to drive separately, or do you trust me to chauffeur us around for the day and pick up your cart later?"

"I'll drive my cart, and you can follow. How's that?" Needing to showcase my independence, I harshly reminded him, "Keep your distance rule, remember?"

"Right. Sorry."

With my guard up, I inquired, "So, where do you want to go next?"

Scanning the map, he suggested, "How about the Hamilton Island Yacht Club?" while pointing to the manta ray-shaped building adorning the harbor.

"Okay, sure. Let's head over there."

"I'm parked this way," Ryan said.

Easily spotting his custom cart wrapped in black and charcoal with matching rims and hand-stitched piping on the leather seats, blatantly standing out among the rest, I walked past his pimped-out ride.

Watching him place his backpack in the attached lockbox, he got in and turned his cart around before stopping close to me.

"Ready?" he asked.

"Ready."

Driving roughly a car length apart along Front Street, passing the marina full of yachts, and feeling considerable uncertainty, I found space along the fence line adjacent to our chosen destination. My heart unexpectedly raced while watching Ryan get out of his cart and look my way. As he approached with such confidence, it was hard not to stare. His dark eyes drew me in, and his bright smile was warm and friendly. Meeting up, anxiously walking side by side with a four-foot buffer between us, I said, "Wow... Why does your cart look like that, and mine seems so ordinary?"

Ryan thought for a second. "Ah, I'm staying at my friends' place just down from Qualia. He always likes his toys one of a kind."

"Well, that one certainly stands out. It's quite nice."

"Thanks," he said, not elaborating further.

Heading toward the lighthouse perched at the end of the peninsula, we marveled at the architecture of the creature-shaped building. Along the way, passing below the breezy upper deck, with white table linens dancing in the breeze, the fragrant smell of coffee and fresh-baked goods in the air was hard to ignore.

Surrounded by water, I started taking some pictures with my phone. The ocean sparkled like diamonds while the sunshine caressed the waves rolling into the harbor. The hillside, speckled with an array of glass vacation homes, had views of the marina teeming with watercraft of all shapes and sizes. As gulls screeched overhead in search of food, wind gusts created a subtle hum. Sitting on a bench just past the iconic beacon, I closed my eyes to take in the serenity of the awe-inspiring moment. Without warning, the smell of the air and the sun's warmth sent me back to standing on the balcony in St. Lucia, waiting for Scott to return and have breakfast with me. Remembering the salty breeze and some more unwanted details, I quickly stopped thinking about it further.

"It's been months," I whispered, "Get over it. Enough already."

Not wanting to relive the lowest point in my life to date, my eyes squinted tightly, hoping it would make the destructive thoughts leave. About to cry, lowering my head, I had almost forgotten where I was. Swiveling in Ryan's direction, I found him standing under a palm tree, not far away, watching me react how I did.

Embarrassed, I blurted out, "Sorry, I sort of left you for a minute there." Trying to save face, I added, "This place is magical. Don't you think?"

"Umm, yes... Yes, it is. The scenery is amazing," Ryan said, making his way over to the bench, silently motioning with his hand, requesting permission to sit.

About to break our distance rule, I acknowledged his request.

Sitting down, he said, "It is very peaceful here."

Immersed in the serenity surrounding us, I couldn't help but feel overly distracted by the pleasant aroma of coffee wafting from the Yacht Club Café, drawing my attention away. This gave me an idea. "So, can I treat my new friend to coffee? Maybe a mid-morning snack?"

Surprised by my invitation, a pleasant expression emerged upon his face. "I would like that, thank you. But as for you treating me, I am not sure that works. It's not how I do things."

"What do you mean, it's not how you do things?"

"I consider myself a gentleman, and they always pay for the lady. That may be old-fashioned, but I don't care. I consider it respectful," he explained.

"So, you were born in the '50s, then?"

With a chuckle, he said, "Laugh if you will. I can't change how my parents raised me."

"No, I think that's rather refreshing to hear," I complimented, staring at him, wondering where he came from out of the blue.

"Shall we?" he asked.

Leaving the bench, we walked to the Café steps at the end of the stingray building's tail. A young woman greeted us while ascending the stairs to the hostess podium.

"Table for two?"

Happy to answer yes to that question, Ryan held his hand out ahead of me, silently requesting that I lead the way. "Ladies first," he said.

Leisurely following the hostess along the upper deck, my mind started compiling a list of subjects to aid us in conversation during our coffee break. Feeling as though this guy might be playing a game, my guard remained alert, keeping me on my toes.

Following the woman, we admired the view from the elevated platform. Presented with a table along the ocean-side railing, the hostess set our menus down and placed a shiny, stainless steel, stone-shaped paperweight on top of them. About to sit, Ryan quickly grabbed my chair and pulled it back for me. Not used to that kind of treatment, I hesitated before having a seat, reminded of my loving Grandfather doing this for my Grandmother on many occasions.

He shyly joined me.

The hostess asked, "Would you fancy a brolly?"

Confused by what she asked, he caught me signaling the answer to him. Turning to another table sheltered by one, Ryan surveyed my facial expression and said to the woman, "An umbrella? Sure, that would be great."

"Very good. Someone will be by to take your orders, and another will arrive momentarily to shade you then."

Excited to flip open the menu, it didn't take me long to locate the decadent dessert options.

"So, what looks good to you?" I asked.

"How about the Lamington?"

Reading the description aloud, I said, "This traditional Australian dessert is a cube-shaped sweet slice of sponge cake, covered with chocolate frosting and desiccated coconut with a Hamilton Island twist of whipped cream and berry jam filling. That sounds rather interesting. Okay, want to go with that and coffee then?"

"Sure. I think that's a great idea."

Once we placed our order, we watched the sailboats effortlessly maneuver into the harbor. Glancing at one another intermittently, we lost our connection as the conversation went dormant.

So much for my list of questions, I thought, unable to remember a single thing. You look into the guy's eyes, and now your mind is all a muddle. Really?

To help reignite things, Ryan quickly posed, "So Eva... Where are you from?"

"New York. Manhattan, to be precise. How about you?"

"Me? California."

Knowing that his answer was quite vague compared to mine, I asked him to elaborate. "What part of California?"

"Malibu." Reluctant to share more, a sad expression hit his face. Taking a deep breath, clearing his throat, he added, "So what brings you to the Whitsundays? What are you trying to escape from?"

Uncertain how he knew the roundabout reason I was here, my attention redirected toward the water. Prepared to divulge the Cole Notes version of the truth, knowing I would probably never see the guy again after returning to New York, I said, "Well, let's just say... The truth of the matter is. Everything in my life was going great. I mean, I had my dream job and a dream guy. He asked me to marry him. I said yes. We were planning our wedding until my firm offered me a once-in-a-lifetime opportunity to further my career. The only problem with it all was that this dream job was out in California," I shared, motioning my hand in his direction to acknowledge his home state.

"Right. Okay," he acknowledged with a pause.

Once again, with another deep breath, I continued, "Since my fiancé agreed with me going, I took the job, but found out he was cheating on me when I came home for a surprise visit after being away for two months."

With a look of shock, Ryan could not say a word.

"Of course, I broke it off and returned to finish up the contract on the West Coast. Months later, when complications arose with my project, which is a long story, the team was ordered back to New York again. I tried to establish a new normal when I got there. But it wasn't easy. That first Saturday morning, I found my fiancé standing outside my apartment building, waiting for me to emerge for my routine walk through Central Park. Ambushing me, he said he was sorry about what had happened but confessed to always caring for his ex-girlfriend, dropping yet another bomb. To add insult to injury, he told me she was five months pregnant and recently asked her to marry him." Smirking and shedding a small tear, I felt emotional for a split second when I noticed the evident sympathy on his face. Pulling myself together, I said, "Long story short, my company gave me a month off in light of the construction delay, knowing I had worked night and day for the past seven months. They also recognized that I needed a break because of what happened in my personal life - little did they know how much. Immediately, I searched for the farthest destination I could travel to, other than the moon or Mars, and came up with this place."

Caught off guard, Ryan leaned back in his chair and said, "Wow, I am so sorry. That's horrible. If it's any consolation, it's his loss, you know. It'll be something he'll end up regretting for the rest of his life."

"Well, on the way here, I wondered if I would have stayed in New York and not taken the job; maybe this wouldn't have happened. Maybe I might have been able to keep him faithful." Playing with my napkin, I admitted, "Then again, maybe not... Guess it was better to find out that he is a cheater now than ten years down the road, right?"

Ryan sat up straight and placed his elbows on the table. "Hey, you came here for a reason, so let's enjoy this beautiful place. Forget about that guy. He's not worth it. You deserve so much more than that. Look, I realize we don't know each other, but no woman should deal with that. From this moment on, only happiness and fun, nothing less, deal?"

In agreement with his upbeat suggestion, trying to muster a smile, I said, "Deal," calmly feeling as though I was updating a long-lost friend on my current status in life versus spilling the details of my broken relationship to a total stranger.

A uniformed gentleman made his way toward us with our brolly and soon placed it overhead. Skillfully opening it, he suggested we change seating positions to both enjoy the shade.

Knowing the rules, Ryan asked, "Are you okay with temporarily breaking the distance pact?"

I nodded, realizing it made sense. "Sure. Wouldn't want you to have to sit in the sun," I humorously replied, knowing it could have come across as abrasive.

Subtly laughing at my dry response, he moved his chair tight beside mine, allowing him to shelter from the heat. Our waitress arrived seconds later with our aroma-filled coffees and the delicious-looking

Lamingtons. Sitting mere inches apart, we struggled to have a conversation. The warm winds caressed our shoulders. Overwhelmed by the view, I started snapping some pictures with my phone.

"Have you taken a lot of pictures today?"

Seemingly thrown off, he said, "Umm, no. No, I haven't."

Noticing he had nothing in hand, I asked, "Don't you have a phone or camera?"

"No, no camera," he replied.

"Are you an Android or Apple user?"

"Umm, neither," he bluntly answered, turning toward the harbor.

"Wait? What do you mean?"

"I don't have a cell phone. Don't believe in them," Ryan stated firmly.

"You're kidding, right?"

"Nope."

"Wow," I replied, stunned by this revelation. "I think my life would end without mine."

"I find life is less complicated without one," he said as that conversation died off.

About halfway through our dessert, needing to stir up some more banter, I got the courage to ask, "So, I told you my story... How about you? Why did you run away and come here?"

Noticeably uneasy, fidgeting with his coffee cup in one hand and a fork in the other, he shifted his weight forward in the chair, not knowing how to answer that. "Yeah, ahh... that's kinda complicated. Let's say, my long story short, as you put it, is that I needed a fresh start because of circumstances beyond my control."

Second-guessing his answer, with a level of hesitation, I noticed him tensing up from the statement he offered, so I quickly responded, "You know, I'm sorry. It's none of my business. Please, don't feel obligated to share just because I did. It's a girl thing, I guess. We can't keep secrets. Most of the time, we blurt stuff out to release what's bottled up. But, just putting this out there, if, at some point, you want to talk about it, I will sit and listen. No judging." Waiting for a second,

I quietly leaned over and comically whispered, "Just to be clear, you haven't murdered anyone, have you?"

Ryan turned to me with a look of shock. "No!" as his face scowled. "How could you even think that?"

Trying to defuse his astonished reaction, I calmly said, "I'm kidding. Thought we needed some comic relief - and - I kinda just wanted to make sure."

Laughing a little while listening to that voice inside my head - was he playing the sympathy card to gain my trust, or was he genuinely harboring a secret? Trying to stop my trail of social sabotage, I said silently to myself, just relax and keep an open mind.

Shortly after, our conversation dwindled. Reaching the bottom of our coffee cups, I could feel that Ryan had drifted deep in thought.

Out of the blue, he suddenly got up from the table and politely said, "Excuse me for a moment. I'll be right back."

Sitting there alone, our waitress returned to remove the dishes. When I requested the bill, she informed me that a gentleman had taken care of it moments ago. Knowing Ryan covered the check, I waited to see if he would return. Gazing out over the water, analyzing all the little coincidences that had to come together for us to be there right now, I smiled. What were the chances of being on the same plane and running into each other today?

"Ready to go, then?" I heard him say.

Startled, I looked up. "Yes. Sure."

Based on his facial expression, it seemed there was something wrong. His tone had changed, too.

"Thank you for treating me to coffee and dessert."

While this handsome, athletic guy walked along shyly, he said, "You're very welcome. As I mentioned, a gentleman always pays. I could never let you do that."

Captivated by his kind nature, never having experienced this in my twenty-eight years, we quietly went to the parking lot, not saying a whole lot. I noticed that the lightness of the day had somehow turned somber and assumed he was probably having second thoughts about spending time together.

"You seem to have a lot on your mind. You know, if you don't want to spend the day with me, it's fine. I mean, if you want to leave, I totally understand. Don't worry. I won't be offended."

Calmly snapping the single backpack strap across his chest, putting up a strong front, he said, "No. All good." With hands buried inside his pockets, Ryan looked down and then up at me with a tilt of his head. "Umm, so, you know that whole sharing thing you did?"

"Yes," I verified, assuming he might reveal more.

"Well, let's just say, the past few months have been kinda challenging for me too. I've been in this sort of transition. My trip here was supposed to be the first step towards moving through all that."

"Okay. Maybe you should take your advice. You know, happiness and fun?"

"Yes, I suppose you're right." Taking a second, he asked, "So, where to next?"

Somehow producing a half-smile, he turned and looked up at me, almost with a new sense of hope in his eyes, like today was the start of a new beginning. Strange how we were both in the same vote - each of us needing a fresh start and a new direction in life.

Referring to my island tourist map as we stood beside his cart, I pointed to an attraction listed and asked, "How about go-karting? That might be fun. Maybe I'll even beat you in a race."

Playfully irking him on, unsure what to make of my challenge, lowering his head again, he partially looked my way. "Really? Think I might have to prove you wrong there."

We scanned the map and our present location before sitting in our machines.

Confirming the direction we needed to go, he pointed towards the airport. "Guess we are heading that way?"

Slowly departing the Yacht Club, closely following Ryan, I felt a great deal of hesitation. Believing I should return to my resort and stick to the original plan of rest and isolation, he glanced back to check and see if I was still behind him. Waving to me, a few butterflies took flight and washed all the negativity away.

I thought one afternoon wouldn't hurt as we drove through town towards the airport before veering left on Palm Valley Way. Crossing a causeway with water on either side, we found the go-kart track coming up on the left. Ryan pulled in and parked. I stopped alongside him in front of the main building.

Approaching the ticket booth, taking out my wallet from my backpack, I strongly suggested, "This is on me. My turn now."

"Eva, please, I respectfully ask that you put your money away," Ryan said, grabbing his wallet from his back pocket.

"No, I can't let you do that. I owe you."

Quickly responding, Ryan said, "Honestly, you owe me nothing. I'm happy to do it."

"Dutch treat?" I insisted.

Not wanting this battle of wills to continue, he countered, "Fine, if that makes you happy."

Speaking to the person behind the counter and paying separate admittance fees, the woman instructed us where to go next.

"Down the hall to the right, you will be fitted for helmets first, and after that, there's a short safety reminder. Once finished, the attendant will escort you to your karts."

Basically, following the woman's instructions to a tee, we did as she asked. Once suited up, briefly learning how dangerous this could be, we buckled into our machines and started the engines.

As the roar of the motors echoed through the track, I heard Ryan say something along the lines of – "I'm gonna warn you. I can be pretty competitive!"

Noticing the traffic light had turned green, I floored it before he even had a chance to figure it out. Instantly seeing the astonished look on his face, I took off and immediately found myself about twenty feet ahead of him. While experiencing an adrenaline rush, my legs suddenly tingled and went weak.

The first section included a straight stretch, followed by a long curve, then a few sharp corners. Neck and neck through the middle track, he, unfortunately, caught up. Scheming to cut him off at the next corner, I swerved, recalling what my dear Grandfather had taught me years ago. Taking the corner a little wider, I caused him to veer straight into the tire barrier while trying to avoid a collision. Successfully achieving what I set out to do, I felt guilty. "Are you alright?" I shouted, stopping not far from his impact spot.

"Yep! I'm good! Have to say, though, I can certainly tell you are from New York!" he laughed in disbelief.

Unsure if he meant that as a compliment or an insult, I intended to keep things light and laughed with him. The employee overseeing the patrons came to Ryan's aid and got him back in the race.

Thinking I had somehow managed to hurt his ego, I figured I'd let him win that first lap and play the less competitive girl. But, starting the second whip around, Ryan caught on to what I was doing.

"You're not letting me win, are you?" he shouted playfully, noticing a difference in my level of aggression.

"What? No! Why would I do that?" I yelled across to him. Speeding up, cutting him off at the following three corners, and winning the second lap, I confirmed, "Now we're even!"

Intrigued by my competitiveness, he sat up straight in his cart and said, "Alright! Last one!"

The white flag waved. Accelerating towards the first corner and securing the inside, I made it hard for Ryan to manage the turn. The next few curves were mine. Knowing I could beat him easily, my foot edged off the gas. Waiting for him to catch up, we soon found ourselves approaching the finish line neck and neck. At the last minute, I took my foot off the pedal completely, allowing him to win by a hair. With hands raised in the air victoriously, I knew that the mood had changed to child-like fun. Expecting a lot of boasting, I prepared myself for what he would say.

Removing our helmets and handing them back to the employee at the exit gate, he walked beside me on the way out.

"So, where did you learn to drive like that? I mean, in the future, if things don't work out with your day job, you could definitely make a living driving a New York City cab," he humorously taunted with a smitten smile.

I smirked.

"I'm not kidding. It takes a lot of skill to drive in New York," he added.

Knowing what I had done, Ryan stopped in front of me. His finger pointed in my direction accusingly. "Why did you take your foot off the gas? You let me win."

Giggling, I said, "I didn't want to hurt your feelings - you know, getting beat by a girl and all."

"Right," he replied, standing tall with the wind removed from his sails. Arms crossed in front of his chest, he said, "Huh. Why do I feel like I just got played?"

"Truth be told, my sister and I would spend the summers with my Grandparents in Southampton. My Grandpa taught me to drive when I was sixteen, but taught me to drive a go-kart at age six."

"Ahh, now it all makes sense," he laughed. "Wow, those summers must have been great."

"Yeah, they were...." I said, with an element of sadness, missing them very much.

Needing to lighten the mood, he said, "Guess we'll have to say the whole thing ended in a tie then? Maybe we'll get an opportunity for a rematch. What do you say?"

"Sure, I'd be up for that. Absolutely. No holds barred next time? Deal?" I firmly stated, offering my hand to shake on it.

"Deal."

Hands tightly linked in agreement, surprised to feel a spark ignite, made for an awkward moment. It seemed Ryan felt it, too, since he quickly let go after spotting my eyes glued to our hands. "Oh, sorry," he said, "I forgot. Rule number one - keep my distance."

"No, umm, it's okay," I responded with a hint of uncertainty.

Concerned about the unexpected connection developing, we continued walking back to the parking lot, each focusing on the pathway before us. Approaching the vehicles, I looked at my watch and noticed it was around a quarter after three. The sun was hot, almost scorching, and the tropical breeze had died down, causing the humidity to rise.

About to start up our machines, he suggested, "It's boiling. Think it's time for a swim? What do you think?"

"Sure? Where do you want to go?" Immediately, I began rethinking what I had just said as he gave me this definite 'I like you' look.

"Umm, how about you follow me to my place? I have a pool overlooking the channel. There are trees overhead for shade, and being cliffside usually offers a nice breeze. What do you say?"

"Sure..." I replied hesitantly with an abundance of disappointment. There it is, I thought - the invitation he hoped I would accept because he thinks my guard is down. Without warning, this rather fun, relaxing day began to feel a bit stressful the second we pulled away and headed toward town.

In an instant, I wondered what Ryan's story was and whether he had an ulterior motive. I couldn't stop doubting his every word, which made me think, was I really that broken, or was my instinct setting off warning bells? To save myself the discomfort of spending time alone with a stranger in my swimsuit, I swiftly formulated a lame excuse while driving side by side along the deserted stretch of roadway.

"Ah, you know what, Ryan... I hope you don't mind, but I am kind of tired. Think I'm still jet-lagged. Raincheck on the swim? I'm going to head back to my resort for a short nap."

Disheartened, Ryan slowed his speed. "Umm, okay, sure. Will you still follow me to my place so you'll know where to find me?"

Cautiously agreeing to do that, I nodded.

While driving up the long hill towards the lookout, following him, he suddenly deviated right onto Melaleuca Drive. Passing all the secluded homes along the way, we finally reached the end of the street and arrived at his friend's place.

The house was an architectural masterpiece, graced with modern stone, wood, and steel elements, beautifully harmonized to blend into the surrounding landscape. The roof consisted of various angles, which, I'm sure, created dramatic ceilings within the structure. There were many artful aspects to the front of the property, including beautiful gardens, trees, and a pathway leading to the backyard. No doubt, there was an infinity pool, probably strategically positioned to take in the most scenic portion of the channel between the islands. I loved the seamless balance between design and nature. It was a mansion built with a million-dollar price tag attached.

"Well, this is where I'm staying. Sure, you can't join me?"

With my attention drawn in Ryan's direction, questioning everything, I knew as much as I wanted to cool off, it was better to be on my way to avoid anything more. I sensed a connection and was pretty sure he felt the same, but really, who was I kidding? It wasn't hard to see where this would lead eventually, so why would I allow myself to get my heart broken again, making it a hundred times harder to recover? Thoughts to stay or go started to parade through my head. "Umm, you know what...thank you, but I don't have my swimsuit with me anyway, so I think I'll head back. Maybe see you tomorrow at some point?"

Amidst the uneasiness, I could tell he felt rejected when he replied in a monotone voice, "Yeah...sure. Tomorrow then..."

Pulling out of his driveway, about thirty feet away, feeling guilty, I paused before shouting, "Can you join me for dinner tomorrow night around five o'clock? I just remembered, I booked spa services most of the day, but I have time after that!"

Happy to hear my suggestion, he confirmed, "Dinner sounds great!"

"Meet me outside Qualia's Long Pavilion! "

"Yeah, I'll be there!" he said, standing with his hands buried in his pockets, trying to keep up the manly façade.

"Good. See you then." Waving goodbye as he did the same, I drove down the road to return to Qualia and take my fictitious nap. It only took a few minutes for me to change, drive to Pebble Beach, and find a spot at the resort's infinity pool, ready to soak up some sun. While looking out over the water, that little voice kept reminding me that men can't be trusted. Flip-flopping, wondering how I should handle this whole thing, a part of me was angry at myself for even getting mixed up in such a mess in the first place. The lack of information he was willing to share worried me. Why was he so secretive about his life? That got me thinking maybe he was a criminal or a fugitive. But he didn't look like one.

Laughing, I thought, What does a fugitive even look like, Eva? Really?

To recap the day, I analyzed our conversations and whispered, "So, if things are above board, who is his 'friend' that allowed him to stay at his house on Millionaire's Row? Mafia, maybe?" My mind wouldn't stop reeling. Weighing in on the positive, I figured maybe he just had wealthy friends. Who's to say?

That night, I ordered room service and listened to the tranquil sounds of relaxing music playing on my phone. Pulling the blackout drapes, I cuddled up in bed after having a warm shower as visions of Ryan's memorable smile randomly played through my mind, knowing in my heart he wasn't a bad person. Not showcasing even a bit of arrogance, my gut feeling slowly changed as my opinion of him softened. There was something there when we shook hands at the go-kart track. I felt like I knew him from somewhere, but only his eyes gave me that impression. I couldn't put my finger on it. Thankful for the experience, I was relaxed and almost happy. It was nice to have something cheerful to think about for a change. Unsure if it was the excitement of this afternoon's events or just the fact of sharing time with someone, at that point, I didn't care. It was such a refreshing break versus the stress I'd been under for the past seven months. After everything that had happened, I hoped this was the start of my luck changing for the better.

| 19 |

Day Two: Anticipating Dinner

In the morning, faintly hearing the gardeners cutting the grass around the plantation, I shifted in bed and rolled from my left side to the right. A bit disoriented, I peered out the window while the sunshine spilled into the room. Not feeling as rested as I'd hoped, I knew I needed to get up, grab breakfast, and quickly make my way to the Spa Pavilion. Forcing myself to walk to the bathroom, I secured my hair in a bun. With a hint of makeup to brighten my face, slipping on a casual navy dress, I wondered how dinner would go tonight.

What would we talk about? Would he reveal anything more about his life? The thought then crossed my mind. I hope he doesn't get the wrong idea.

Out the door, locking it behind me, I sat in the buggy and enjoyed the short drive to the Long Pavilion. Parking to the right of the main entrance, listening to the birds chirping in the trees above, the warm breeze sweeping past made my soul joyful. Smiling, I figured it was going to be a good day.

Breakfast was beyond my expectations. There is nothing like eggs benny with a seafood twist.

Ready to move on with the day, I stopped by the concierge desk to inquire about the policy for friends dining with resort guests within the exclusive enclave before making the reservation for two in the dining room at five o'clock. Promptly receiving permission for Ryan to join me, the woman assigned us a table and entered his name in the guest registry for security purposes. Jumping in my cart shortly after, I swiftly drove the winding pathways to the Spa, arriving on schedule.

Throughout the reflexology session, I tried to immerse my mind in the calming sounds of tranquil music and flowing water. The entire time, I kept anticipating our dinner this evening. Convinced it wasn't a big deal – that we were just two people on vacation alone, looking for friendship - a small part of me liked the romantic flutter he caused, and I didn't want it to fade. What if things developed into something more? I mean, he is very handsome, gentlemanly, kind-hearted, and thoughtful despite his rugged, guarded exterior. Closing my eyes tightly, realizing what I just said, I stopped myself since that is what I thought of Scott initially, too.

"Look at how that turned out," I whispered under my breath so the lady couldn't hear me. Not wanting to venture down the same path, I outwardly said, "No. No. No. What are you doing? Haven't you learned your lesson? Get your head out of the clouds, Eva…."

The reflexologist must have thought I was crazy, talking to myself like that.

When my spa services ended mid-afternoon, feeling somewhat refreshed while leaving the soothing oasis, I got anxious thinking about my plans for the evening.

Arriving at my pavilion minutes later and walking inside, I took a deep breath and tried to calm my nerves.

"Just go out tonight and have fun. It's better than eating alone," I whispered, resting my back against the closed door with eyes glued to the ceiling before starting the shower.

After washing away the day, now wrapped in my plush robe, I applied some barely-there makeup and rolled my blonde locks up in a casual clip. Filing through my temporary closet, selecting a pretty floral dress didn't take long. Out of everything I had purchased, this one was my favorite. Boasting turquoise, black, and white colors, I matched it with a pair of gold wedge sandals. Dressed, taking one last look in the mirror, and grabbing my room card from the table, I went out the door, ready to drive to the Long Pavilion.

The building was beautifully up-lit, with dusk falling upon the island. Parking my cart in the shadows, it wasn't hard to pinpoint Ryan's custom ride standing out amongst the rest. For whatever reason, an intense uneasiness erupted, knowing he was already there waiting. Pausing a moment to gather my thoughts, I took another deep breath before slowly moving toward the covered entrance, raising the hem of my dress slightly as I walked. In search of him, peering down the hallway, it wasn't hard to spot Ryan. He was sitting on a sofa in the sunken seating area of the great hall. Flowers in hand, bouncing one leg, he soon found me gracefully approaching. Standing up with eyes locked onto mine, showcasing a confident grin, he inched closer, lowering his head from time to time, trying to disguise his nervousness while meeting me halfway.

Once face-to-face, he said, "Wow. You look beautiful," before handing me the colorful bouquet wrapped in tissue paper and cellophane, finished with a pink ribbon and bow. "These are for you."

"Oh, that is so sweet. Thank you."

Unsure if the *keep-your-distance rule* still applied, Ryan took a chance and offered his arm in a gentlemanly way. "Shall we?" he said.

Again, taken off guard by the traditional gesture, I placed my hand inside his bent elbow and walked alongside him toward the restaurant podium, reminding me of how my Grandparents used to stroll. Without warning, my body started trembling. Unable to calm down, with my jaws chattering, I stealthily kept taking deep breaths now and again, hoping to rid myself of the crazy nerves. It was hard to believe I was having dinner with such a handsome man.

The maître d' promptly welcomed us. "Good evening. Are we ready to be seated?"

Ryan acknowledged him proudly, with me on his arm. "Yes, Sir. Thank you."

Following the host to the table, our eyes were drawn to the view from the terrace. It was spectacular. The sky was painted with hues of pink and orange on the horizon. Enticed by the setting sun, the moon attempted to share its romantic light. Moving past the infinity pool at the edge of the dining room, only one star faintly sparkled in the distance.

Ryan pulled back my chair, ready for me to have a seat, as the maître d' let us know, "Your waitress will be along momentarily to assist you. Enjoy your evening."

Fidgeting, wanting to offer a compliment, noticing his perfectly pressed dress shirt and linen pants, I got up the courage to say, "You look very nice."

He peered down at his attire and cracked a subtle smile. "Dressing up is not exactly something I do a lot of lately. Since I didn't have any dinner-worthy clothes, I went shopping today. This is all new. Just bought it this morning. I figured I'd need to look presentable."

"What did you do for the rest of the day?"

"I hung out at the house after returning from town, watched some TV, worked out a bit, and swam some laps. Not much, really. Kind of wanted to save some more exploring for tomorrow if you're still up for it. Care to join me?"

"Sure. What did you have in mind?"

"Well, we haven't fully seen the other side of the island yet. Thought we could check it out?" he suggested.

"Sounds like fun."

"So, how was the spa?"

"It was good. I tried to relax, but that plan failed. Can't figure out why?"

"I know what you mean. It's like the island wants you to slow down and go with the flow, but we aren't ready yet. Guess it takes a few days to decompress."

Looking out over the ocean, we lost ourselves in the silence, unsure of what else to do or say. Luckily, our waitress arrived to introduce herself soon after.

Dressed in a black pencil skirt, a white blouse, and heels, she presented us with the wine menu. "Good evening. My name is Sandi. I will be your server tonight. Would you like to start with a glass of wine or a cocktail before dinner?"

While Ryan perused the wine list, he looked my way and asked confidently, "Red or white, Eva?"

"I prefer white, but if you like red, we can simply get a glass of each."

"How about an Australian Chardonnay to start? Sound good?"

Nodding my head, I watched him point to what he selected.

"The Penfolds Yattarna Vintage. Oh, very good, Sir," Sandi stated, sounding rather impressed, before leaving us.

Based on her reaction, I assumed he'd chosen something special. It made me curious to know if he was somewhat of a connoisseur.

Excited to open the formal dinner menu folders to survey our options, I hoped it would aid us in conversation. Discussing the many tantalizing entrees on the evening's tasting list, we decided on the six-course preset option. Confirming our orders with Sandi, a gentleman brought the chilled bottle of wine to the table in a silver bucket.

Ryan willingly participated in the customary bottle opening - a process he seemed fairly familiar with. When Sandi poured our glasses, he raised his between us and said, "A toast." Meeting mine in the middle, he offered, "Here's to a wonderful vacation and my new-found friend."

Eyes locked, clinking my glass gently, I was glad he kept it short and uncomplicated.

"Cheers," I said before taking a sip. Still unsure of who I was having dinner with, needing to know more, I decided to put Ryan on the spot and asked, "So… Does your family still live in California?"

Instantly, he started fiddling with the stem and base of his glass. "Umm…they used to…" he replied, leaning back in his chair and clearing his throat. "My parents…umm…died along with my older brother a few months ago."

Incapable of formulating a response, that piece of information was entirely unexpected. Knowing he was alone, without the presence of family, helped me make sense of his actions the other day. That's why he was having difficulty. "I'm so sorry… I didn't mean to, ah…"

Intent on diffusing the situation, hoping to sway from the sorrowful discussion, he said, "You know what... It's fine. I miss them a lot. Sadly, life must continue, and we need to keep living regardless. How about you? Do you have family back home?"

"Yes, my parents are still together - seemingly out of convenience, I believe. They live in New York and part-time in Scottsdale, Arizona, during the winter months. My sister, Ellie, is in Franklin Lakes, New Jersey. She's married to Ben, who is an Investment Banker. They have two children - both boys. I see and talk to them as often as time allows, but everyone leads busy lives." Pausing to think of another question, I asked, "So, what do you do for a living? Where do you work?"

"Before coming here, I hadn't taken a vacation in years. Needing a break, I opted for an extended sabbatical." Not elaborating, Ryan flipped it back to me and immediately inquired, "You said you worked, but didn't clarify what you do?"

Analyzing his statement, I caught on to what was happening. He was attempting to avoid topics relating to him.

Not wanting to be rude, I answered the question. "I'm an architect. My job in California was to oversee the construction of a modern art museum I designed. I love working for my firm. I'm just having trouble with the whole New York City vibe right now."

"Ah, yes... The ex-fiancé, right?"

"I'm still unsure what I will do about that situation. The thought of moving permanently to LA has crossed my mind."

"Do you want to leave New York? Why should you move elsewhere if you like where you live? Maybe he should be the one who leaves?"

"Well, not that I care, but his job is primarily in the city. With mine, I have the option of working in other office locations, so that means I'm the one who will probably have to make that dreaded decision. As for when? I don't know. I need to think about it some more. Being in California means I'd never have to bump into him ever again." Smiling, raising my eyebrows, I clarified, "That would be a bonus for me."

"Anywhere along the West Coast is a great place to settle." Stopping there, he quickly looked away. "I think that is our food coming," he said, trying to divert my attention again.

The food did arrive and helped change the flow of the conversation. Delivered the first course, we listened to the description of the meal artistically displayed on our plates. Marveling at the presentation, I kept wondering what Ryan wasn't telling me. Careful not to force the issue, I hoped things wouldn't get weird.

"So, do you know what there is to see on the other side of the island? Anything exciting?"

Raising his napkin from his lap to cover his mouth while finishing his last bite, he replied, "While shopping this morning, I came across a large hotel complex there, more shops, and some beautiful white sandy shoreline. Think the sign said Catseye Beach. It looks like we can snorkel, maybe kayak, or paddleboard. I saw some people doing that."

"Okay, we'll explore that side tomorrow then," I solidified to his surprise. "What time do you want to start? Maybe I can meet you at your place and go from there."

"Does ten o'clock work, or is that too early?" he added, excited about the plans we had just made.

Disappointed that I couldn't sleep in tomorrow, I happily conceded. "No, ten works for me."

When our waitress, Sandi, returned to remove the last of our plates, we received the bill shortly afterward. It included the cost of his meal and the wine we selected since I was part of the prepaid dining plan. Promptly insisting I pay since he was my guest, he outright refused. Being the person I am, I stood firm on at least paying my share for the wine. He had no choice but to surrender to my stubborn persistence this one time.

Leaving the table, we slowly strolled down the covered entrance toward the parking lot, exiting the Long Pavilion with a small gap between us.

For whatever reason, I didn't want the evening to end just yet. It was still early, so I suggested an extension. "Want to take a walk to the beach and pool area? We may be able to catch the last of the sunset and maybe see some stars. The view is stunning there."

His eyes brightened when I said that. A smile emerged seconds later. Burying his hands in his pockets, he extended his elbow. "Absolutely. I'd like that. Lead the way."

Grasping hold, now arm in arm, stopping by my cart, I placed the floral bouquet on the seat before we continued down the path toward the water. We didn't say much the whole way, but I noted how tall and straight he walked. He had a presence about him. Strong and confident. Self-assured but somehow shy. All evening, he had been a gentleman from start to finish and seemed the epitome of perfection. But aside from this immaculate façade, I still didn't know who he truly was. A mysteriousness surrounded him, making me nervous, and not in a good way. Because he'd shared his current situation and was obviously dealing with a lot, I decided to give him the benefit of the doubt for now and not judge him too harshly.

When rounding the corner, approaching Pebble Beach, the pool area was still draped in a subtle hint of burnt orange and red in the west. In contrast, the darkening sky presented the first signs of evening. One by one, the stars began to dot the sky. It looked so serene. Descending the stairs onto the beach below the pool deck, we found a seat across from each other on a set of lounge chairs.

With a need to take off my sandals and glide my toes through the granular sand, I revealed, "This resort is like a slice of heaven. It feels as though I'm in another world. I love this spot. It is just so peaceful." That is when I caught him staring.

"Yes, this view is something you don't see every day." With slight hesitation, he said, "Eva?"

I casually answered, "Yes," wondering what he was about to ask.

"Just wanted to say... I've enjoyed spending time with you. You know, I thought I'd come here on vacation and end up being alone day after day. It was a pleasant surprise meeting you."

My heart sank upon hearing that statement. Those were Scott's exact words. Again, I couldn't help but wonder, was I being played? Eyes glued to the sand below, I shuffled my feet from left to right as it began to stick. Unable to look at him, I said, "On the plane ride here, I felt the same. The thought of it wasn't enticing, but when we met yesterday, it was nice to know I had found a friend. You made me smile for the first time in a while, too, so thank you for that. But, in a little over three weeks, I'm returning to New York, possibly LA, and you will be - well, somewhere else..."

Immediately catching on to the point I was trying to make in a roundabout way, he replied, "Yes, this is true."

Despite the spark developing, I assumed things would inevitably be short-lived. Turning to the water's edge, feeling a need to guard my heart, I said, "Maybe it would be best to call it a night? Tomorrow morning will be here before we know it. Not sure about you, but I've been sleeping in until around nine-thirty." Bluntly expressing my thoughts out of fear, needing to make a stand, the last thing I wanted was a meaningless fling.

Surprised to hear I was ending the evening, nodding reluctantly, he agreed and stood up, ready to make our way back up the hill towards the main pavilion.

For some reason, guilt riddled me the whole way there. My insecurities had ruined everything. What if he was a nice guy with good intentions, and I pegged him wrong? What if he was harmless, and I was too blind to see it?

Beside my cart, moments later, we stayed awkwardly silent for a second before I said, "Thank you for joining me tonight."

Presenting my hand to bid him a handshake goodnight, he slowly placed his in mine and stepped forward, gently guiding me in close. Resting his left hand on the back of my shoulder, staying to my right side, he gave me a subtle, kind-hearted side hug of sorts. Calmly lingering a moment before backing away, our eyes met - a twinkling that took my breath away. It was as if he could see into my soul. My legs weakened. Feeling an overwhelming flutter, it made me gasp for a sip of air.

With senses heightened, he whispered, "I'll see you in the morning. Goodnight then."

On the way over to his cart, about to take a seat, he turned and glanced at me, then raised a steady hand to say goodbye.

Doing the same, watching him drive out of the parking lot slowly and disappear around the corner, I picked up my flowers and smelt their heavenly aroma. The remnants of warmth he left behind caused my heart to beat rapidly. Had I made a mistake? Oddly enough, I realized I hadn't enforced the *keep your distance rule* tonight, which made me wonder why.

The short journey to my pavilion had me second-guessing myself. Utterly convinced our lives weren't compatible, unable to ignore the red flags that had cropped up in conversation this evening, against all previous thought, the bottom line was - I just liked him. Even though Ryan's life was in limbo, to be fair, so was mine. We were two souls in the same place, hoping and praying this paradise would heal us.

Stopping my cart in front of my pavilion, I sat back in the seat. Out of left field, the more optimistic side of me contemplated everything that had to transpire for us to meet, making me realize - what if it wasn't a coincidence? Had fate stepped in?

Still analyzing every angle, being a romantic at heart, I started creating a list of pros and cons. I was here to recover from heartache. The last thing I wanted to do was create more. The purpose of this trip was to renew my soul, not go from the frying pan into the fire. But what if I made the first flight to Hamilton Island without getting delayed? Would we have met? If we hadn't seen each other on the plane, would we have spoken the following day? Had the universe strangely intervened? I didn't know.

"What do I do?" I questioned as I opened the door to my pavilion.

That night, as the rain shower cascaded over my shoulders, thoughts of Ryan were not far away. We both felt this subtle attraction – but I was the only one trying to ignore it.

Slipping into bed, I knew tomorrow had to be different. I hoped I wouldn't regret this decision somewhere down the line. Even if I did, would it even matter? Carpe diem came to mind. I encouraged myself to enjoy this vacation and everything that comes my way because one never knows what life has in store. My wise Grandmother once said, *If fate intervenes, you must give love a chance.* How very accurate this advice was right now.

Before falling asleep, I set my alarm for eight in the morning so I'd be on time. Thinking of him brought about the biggest smile, which caused me to roll over and bury my face in the pillow bashfully. Anticipating a restful night's sleep, I wondered if he was thinking of me, too.

| 20 |

Sleepless

Hardly sleeping a wink throughout the night, my brain kept spinning with many unanswered questions. Strangely, though, a sense of calm accompanied that doubt. Somehow, it seemed I'd known Ryan for years. It felt like we were old friends. Not strangers. But after spending only two days together, the fact of the matter was - I knew absolutely nothing about him. All the secrecy cultivated variations of stories that might fit his situation. Often waking with any new thought that came to mind, I started getting frustrated, knowing I'd have to get up soon.

| 21 |

Day Three: Beach Day

My alarm caressed the room with calming, tranquil sounds hours later. Tired beyond words, I mustered enough energy to leave my cozy bed. While getting ready for the day, a bit of excitement crept in. It was my first official beach day in Australia, and instead of experiencing it alone, I was lucky enough to spend it with Ryan Davis.

Eating breakfast at the Long Pavilion by 8:45, I sat on the oceanside balcony and appreciated the breeze while sipping my French press coffee. Remembering our short goodbye last night gave me a few butterflies. Funny how something so innocent could create such a stir of emotions.

After signing the bill, I swung by the resort shop to purchase the Helen Kaminski bucket hat I liked. With temperatures rising, I needed something to cover my head and offer shade.

Proud of my purchase, I headed back to my cottage with a shopping bag in hand, ready to change and be on my way. Thinking we would spend most of our time by the pool, I selected a sporty navy two-piece bathing suit with a wispy white cover-up and added my new hat. Packing a bag with a few essentials, I double-checked everything before going out the door and jumping in my buggy to head towards Ryan's house.

Driving through the main gates of my resort, I questioned how his friend could afford that beautiful place. What did the guy do for a living? These properties were going for at least $2 million or more. Hoping to lean toward something positive versus the criminal-infused thoughts creeping into my head, I made a mental note to gather what information I could throughout the day.

About to round the corner at the bottom of his street, I stopped and took a deep breath. "Try and have fun," I whispered before stepping on the peddle to continue up the hill.

Parking in front of the wrought iron gates not long after, Ryan must have heard me pull in. Before leaving my cart, I saw him exiting the front door to greet me.

"Good morning!" he said cheerfully, placing his hands in his pockets. "Excited to spend the day at the beach?"

"Yes, absolutely," I replied. His smile made me melt.

"Give me a second," he said, "I'm just going to lock up, and we can go."

It took him five minutes to secure the large house before joining me outside once again. Acting humble, with his head angled down and his eyes peering up in my direction, he opened the garage door and placed his backpack inside the lockbox attached to the cart. Backing it out, he drove over to where I was standing.

"So, do you have enough confidence in me to chauffeur you around yet, or are we driving separately?"

Trying to contain a partially smitten smile, still leery to a degree, I replied, "Oh, I think I might trust you a smidge more today." Grabbing my bag, I mumbled, "So much for being cautious."

Nervously sitting in his buggy beside him, he asked, "Ready?"

Before I could answer, he stepped on the peddle. Speedily pulling away from the house, we drove around the many corners on Melaleuca Drive. At that moment, I caught myself laughing. It had been so long since I felt happy and carefree.

Inspecting the fancy vehicle, I asked, "These seats are super comfortable. It's like a car. Mine isn't like this at all."

"Yes, my friend likes nothing but the best."

"Speaking of your friend. What does he do for a living?" Hoping to fish for more info, I wondered if he would answer the question.

"Oh, him... Yeah, umm, he's in the residential and commercial security business."

"Impressive. He must do very well."

Focused on driving, he added, "He does okay, believe it or not."

"Judging from the house, okay, is an understatement," I said as the conversation dropped off.

While passing the little white chapel, we continued towards the tall buildings along the beach and veered to the left. Turning onto Resort Drive, whisking by the Wildlife Center, we stopped under the covered breezeway of the large Hamilton Island Resort Center. The trees blew from side to side with the tropical winds as the salty ocean gusts tunneled through the open-air lobby, gently caressing our faces while ascending the steps of the beautiful facility.

The main reception hall was an architect's dream, boasting a horizontal wood plank cathedral ceiling supported by tall, decorative posts in the room's four corners. On top of each wall, creating a border of sorts, I marveled at several wood-carved plaques paying homage to the spectacular marine life inhabiting the waters around the Whitsunday Islands and Great Barrier Reef. Exploring the lobby's craftsmanship and soaking up the captivating pieces of art, Ryan and I headed outside and located the Beach Hut to the left of the picturesque waterfront, where the Concierge promptly welcomed us.

"Would you like beach chairs and a brolly, mate?" a blonde, curly-haired young man asked with a relatively thick Aussie accent.

"Yes, thanks. That would be great," Ryan said.

"Right this way." Nodding in agreement, the guy escorted us out onto the sand.

Captivated by the view, the tiny wave ripples hit the shoreline. This bay seemed more sheltered as the tide slowly rolled in. It was very different from the choppier marina side. Here, the water showed its genuine turquoise and dark blue shades in the mid-morning light, offering a bit of sparkle to the small waves. There was not a cloud in sight against the clear sky. In the distance, the other Whitsunday Islands seemed much closer.

Assigned two chairs in a quieter part of the beach away from the pool, we settled in and spread out our towels.

"So... What do you want to do first?" Ryan asked, clapping his hands together enthusiastically. "Kayak, swim, or paddleboard? Maybe go for a walk up the beach?"

"How about we take a couple of kayaks out since the water is so calm right now? Maybe we will be able to see the fish beneath us."

"Sure, that's a good idea."

Eagerly accepting my recommendation, he jogged toward the watersports hut to arrange things.

By the time I caught up to him, the young attendant was already pulling the kayaks to the water's edge. In the process, he suggested renting a locker to hold our belongings. Doing that, finding the ones assigned to each of us, I took off my cover-up and shoved it inside, as Ryan removed his shirt and did the same. With our backpacks secured, we walked back to the shore six feet apart, where the boats rocked gently in the waves. Struggling not to stare at his muscular arms and washboard abs, I kept my head down while we got seated. Shoved off by the attendant, we soon floated out over the water.

Pointing his paddle to our left, Ryan remembered, "The guy told me we should head to that dark blue spot over there. Supposedly, the reef is full of fish. Sound good?"

"Sure. Lead the way."

The location in question was about a hundred yards straight out from our departure point. Ryan paddled with precision and brute strength ahead of me. Surprisingly, I was able to keep pace with him pretty well. Glancing over, he seemed amazed and threw out a subtle jab.

"Didn't think you'd be able to keep up, you know - being a girl and all."

Smirking at his humorous comment, I cleverly taunted, "Need I remind you, this girl drove you into a pile of tires the other day?"

Impressed by the speed of my cunning reply, he laughed. Tilting his head, he knew I'd made an extremely valid point.

While drifting over the top of the shallow reef, we noticed fish everywhere. Dangling his fingers in the water, Ryan gently moved them back and forth while a school began swirling just below the surface. Curiously gathering under our boats, the tiny creatures darted from time to time to avoid us.

"This is incredible," I said in amazement.

With a nod, he scanned the water on either side of him.

Keeping my eyes peeled, I spotted a sizeable shadow about twenty feet away. It was moving.

Not wanting to panic, I whispered, "Ah, Ryan... What's that?" pointing in the object's direction.

Looking over his shoulder, he turned his kayak and paddled cautiously to determine what was lurking nearby. Given its size, I was scared. What if it were a shark? Immediately, our proximity to shore worried me as escape plans began to cultivate. Watching Ryan approach the ominous creature, moving dangerously close to him, I felt sick with visions of being brutally attacked. My hands uncontrollably shook when he peered over the side to see what was below.

"It's a turtle," he whispered, twisting his body around to me. "It's okay. Come and see?"

Relieved, I joined him, hoping to get a glimpse, too. Holding my breath, I saw the large creature glide through the water directly below us, appearing incredibly angelic as it diverted and moved on.

Five feet apart, resting his paddle across his legs, peacefully taking in the view, he said, "When I was a kid, I loved to visit the beach whenever I could. Some days, the waves were higher than normal, so my friends and I would go surfing, and on calmer days, we snorkeled or went free-diving in the bay. No matter how bad things might have been, the ocean would always wash away all the negativity. Given the makings of this year, there was no doubt I needed to visit the Coral Sea. It seemed to be the only logical place."

Not responding, letting his words sink in, I realized Ryan was slowly trying to open up and share small pieces of his life. I could only offer a reassuring smile before he turned the kayak and paddled further into the bay.

Exploring the reefs for the next hour, we eventually hit the shore and stepped out of the kayaks. Not skipping a beat, Ryan grabbed each rope attached to the bow and easily dragged them in line with the others. After handing in the paddles at the watersports hut, we retrieved our bags from the locker and walked over to our chairs. The whole time, I listened as he shared his love for the ocean along the way. It made me take note of his boyish charm, which occasionally seemed to crop up during our kayaking journey. Somehow, his reactions, comments, and stories made the experience even more fun, mainly because it allowed him to let his guard down.

Feet shuffling through the sand, we made it back to our spot on the beach, ready to bask in the warmth of the midday sun. Sitting comfortably under the partial shade of our umbrella, another blonde, wavy-haired waiter approached, dressed in khaki shorts and a white-crested polo shirt.

"Ga day, Mates. Would you fancy somethin' from the bar?"

Ryan asked, "So, Eva? What'll it be?"

Not sure what to choose, I replied, "Surprise me. Nothing too strong, though."

"You heard the lady," Ryan chuckled. "Can you surprise us with your most popular beach drink?"

"Gotcha, Mate. No problem. Back in a jiff," the young man noted with an enthusiastic smile.

Ryan turned to me and casually said, "Man, I hope he comes back with something good." Nudging my arm playfully, he left his hand resting against it.

With my eyes glued to it, he saw my reaction. It took him a second to realize what he had done. Moving it back to the armrest on his chair, I'm sure he wondered if he'd crossed the line and made me uneasy.

"It's a beach bar. Nothing they bring to us could ever be bad," I explained, nudging him back, successfully lightening the mood again.

Lying on the chaise, relaxing, with my eyes closed a majority of the time, I did open one eye for a moment to sneak a peek at him beside me, wondering why such a good-looking guy would ever care to spend any time with me. Not wanting to obsess over it, I told myself just to be thankful. Focusing on my suntan, I figured, if nothing else comes of this, at least being around him reassured me that my sense of attraction for handsome men hadn't died or been negatively impacted by my break-up with Scott.

Moments later, feeling the ocean breeze caressing our faces, the guy returned with a tray bursting with light blue decadence.

"Oy, Mate. As promised, I've brought you our most popular Australian specialty. It is called – Bondi Blue. We blend Blue Curacao and Malibu Rum with ice cream, pineapple juice, lemon, and crushed ice. On a hot day like this, it's quite refreshing."

Carefully taking the drinks from his tray, we thanked him for looking after us so well. When Ryan passed him the money, the guy's eyebrows raised at the sight of the generous tip.

"Thanks, Mate. Appreciate it," he said before departing.

Sitting up in our chairs, Ryan steadily raised his logoed cup. "A toast to our adventures here in Australia. I am so happy to have met you and even happier that you wanted to spend time with me. Cheers."

"Cheers."

Not taking his eyes off mine, we sipped the tasty cocktail before returning to sun-worshipping as his toast replayed through my mind. It was such a genuine sentiment. Little did he know I, too, was happy we had met.

Upon reaching the bottom of our glasses, the conversation dwindled. Overheated, I felt the need to cool off.

"I'm going to go for a swim. How about you?"

Opening one eye, he asked, "Sure. Ocean or pool?"

"Pool, of course. There is nothing to worry about in there."

"Eva, you're in Australia. You gotta swim in the ocean. Come on. Let's go snorkeling and see if there are any fish offshore. We won't go out far."

Still scared of what could be lurking in the water, I hesitated, wondering if I should venture in, especially with our earlier experience.

Confident, he urged, "Please?"

"Fine, but if we see a shark, he's eating you first," I conceded.

"Deal," he replied speedily, pointing his finger at me, reacting to my comment. Catching my look of concern, he added with great sincerity, "Don't worry; I'll protect you. I promise."

In an instant, somehow, I believed he would.

With the cove now at high tide, we walked to the watersports hut and signed out the snorkel gear. They also insisted we wear stinger suits as a precaution, just in case we had an unfortunate run-in with a bluebottle or jellyfish. Taking everything to the locker area, I was scared. Not wanting Ryan to pick up on it, I put on the suit and tried to walk towards the water bravely. Quiet while wading in a bit, submerged to our knees, I scanned the water around me while slipping on the fins and these unusual full-face masks. Never having used anything such as this, I tested out the breathing apparatus before leaving the shallows.

As I got comfortable with how it worked, Ryan asked, "You okay? Got the hang of it?"

"Yes," I replied, giving a thumbs up. "Think I'm good now."

Immersing ourselves in the water, floating above the surface, we perused the ocean floor. With anticipation, I hoped to see the colorful marine life that lures tourists here from around the globe. Swimming along in a muffled state, it wasn't long before we found a small reef filled with abundant movement. The tiny fish were almost translucent with bright yellow tails. Swimming around the perimeter of the ridge, it was full of brilliant, multi-colored fish frolicking about, completely unaware of our presence.

Ryan suddenly pointed at something along the sandy bottom. Wondering what he'd noticed, he moved closer so I could hear what he was about to say.

"It's a small stingray hiding under the sand."

Slowly hovering above it, we got too close since the ray gracefully flapped and rose out of the white granules, trying to evade us. Safely following it, we came across a jagged section of the reef, where I caught sight of something emerging from a stone cropping not far away. The creature was stoic and stayed close to the rocks until it exposed its big, open mouth and fierce stare. Heart pounding, terrified, I raised my head above the surface and frantically swam in the opposite direction, having visions of it biting at my fins.

Ryan saw my reaction and immediately came after me. Following a short distance behind, he tried to get me to stop. Amidst it all, he removed his mask and shouted, "Eva, it's just an eel. He won't hurt you!"

With my heart beating so rapidly, barely able to breathe, I could not hear his muffled words.

Finally, catching up to where I had stopped on a small sandbar far from the reef, standing a few feet away, Ryan witnessed the terror in my eyes. Unable to regulate my breathing - almost claustrophobic, I flipped the mask off. Head on a swivel, my sights glued to the 360-degree space around me, hands out of the water, pressing them tight to my chest, I scanned every angle. My first thought was that the creature had followed us. Paralyzed by fear, I could not move another inch.

Cautiously approaching, knowing he should keep his distance, Ryan boldly inched closer. Reaching out, he presented his hands and took hold of mine. Feeling them trembling, he slowly brought them below the waterline.

Hesitating, I abruptly pulled them out and tucked them under my chin.

"Eva. You're okay," he said reassuringly.

Intent on helping me face my fears, he took hold of them again and submerged each under the water. His gaze did not waver from mine.

"See. It's alright. Just focus on me. The eel is more afraid of us than we are of it. Trust me. They only attack if provoked, and we did not do that." With every encouraging word, his thumbs caressed the tops of my hands, giving a sense of calm. "Do you want to keep going or head back to shore?" he asked.

Embarrassed, I stayed silent for a minute, trying to muster the courage to continue. With slight hesitation, I replied, "No. Umm, I'll... I'll keep going."

"Okay. I'm glad."

He moved a few rogue strands of hair away with one finger before helping me with my mask.

I tried to be brave from that point on. Looking into his eyes, emitting a sincere look of concern, I inhaled deeply, hoping to expel some nervousness and anxiety.

He stayed tight to my right side and extended his hand to me. About to return beneath the sea, without question, he said, "Take my hand. Swim with me."

Very self-assured, he seemingly wasn't afraid of anything.

In that split second, there was a shift. This increased connection between us - a feeling I could not describe. Holding his hand, I felt utterly safe. Against every previous careful thought, I suddenly found myself trusting him with my life. That sense of security, somehow knowing that he would protect me from whatever came our way, allowed me to relax. Able to leave the paranoia behind, we floated above the reefs teeming with tiny fish, colorful coral, and patterned white sand, as the whole situation surprisingly brought us to an entirely different emotional level.

Over the next hour, while exploring the world beneath the sea, it felt like we were the only two people left on this earth. Enjoying the incredible experience with ease, he finally turned to me and pointed toward the beach, suggesting we head back.

Waterlogged and shriveled, wading in the shallows along the shore, we reluctantly disconnected and walked a couple of feet apart while taking off our masks, returning to reality.

"So, what did you think of that?" he asked, grinning from ear to ear.

Remembering my horrible freak out earlier, I confessed, "That eel was massive. Sorry about that. I'm kinda embarrassed."

"Don't be silly. You continued regardless. Did you enjoy the rest?"

"Absolutely. It was unbelievable," I sincerely added.

"Doesn't it feel like you just returned from a different planet or something? On days when I haven't sat by the water, I miss it. It's like part of my soul exists out there," he genuinely confessed, looking toward the waves. "Oh, and for the record, that eel was a good size, but it wasn't massive," he laughed.

"Yes, it was! What? Are you kidding me?" I argued humorously as he chuckled.

Now, on dry land, talking about our adventure, we stopped by the hut to hand in the gear and pick up our things. In need of water, grabbing some from the bar before returning to our chairs, I could hardly wait to crack it open and take a sip.

That afternoon passed by in a blink. The tide started to recede more and more around four o'clock while the sun descended on the other side of the island. Casting shadows of palm trees along the shoreline, I loved the orangey-colored glow it painted over the Whitsunday Islands in view.

Having recapped our snorkeling excursion, Ryan asked, "So, do you want to walk up the beach now? It looks as though there are benches at that end. With the tide out, maybe we will find something interesting along the way."

"Sure. Let's do that."

About to begin our stroll, snapping our backpacks on with flip-flops dangling in hand, we walked barefoot to the pebbly shoreline. Ryan casually glanced over once we reached the water. Sending a smile my way, receiving one in return, taking a chance, he boldly outstretched his arm and offered his hand again. With eyes affixed to mine, he hoped I would not decline. Feeling like I was starring in the makings of my very own romantic movie, I slowly grabbed hold as he affectionately gave it a couple of gentle squeezes. Convinced, my face was glowing, we continued our walk side by side. Noticeably content, he showed a hint of shyness but tried not to break away from his tough exterior. His hand was much bigger than mine, quite strong, and seemed rough to the touch. It was surreal to be connected like this to another man.

With the cool sand squishing between my toes, we stopped here and there to pick up a few seashells and unique pebbles. I tried not to get caught up in my thoughts too much and just appreciate the moment. Surprisingly, I felt at ease with it all.

The setting sun was emitting bright, angular rays over One Tree Hill. Reaching the end of the beach, we found a seat on the weathered bench and simultaneously looked upward to bask in the final minutes of sunlight.

Alternating his breathing, subtly clearing his throat, Ryan nervously followed the motion of his feet while each slid back and forth through the sand. Thinking he was working himself up to say something, I remained quiet.

"Eva?" he asked, breaking the silence between us.

"Yes?"

"Have to say, everything we've done together so far has been effortless. I've enjoyed our day today." Not sure what to add, he looked out at the ocean, then over to me, hoping to find a positive reaction to what he had thrown out there.

Almost whispering, I said, "I've enjoyed our time together, too. It's like I have known you for years - not days. I can't explain it."

Bumping his shoulder prompted him to put his arm around me as I naturally leaned in.

"Thank you for a wonderful afternoon," I softly noted.

Glimpsing down at the waves breaking on the shore, he genuinely replied, "I should be the one thanking you. Haven't had this much fun in a very long time."

I purposely didn't peer into his eyes after that, fearing it would open the door to another step forward. I felt we were on the cusp of something more, but weren't quite there yet.

The sun descended further in the west, disappearing far from sight.

Ryan asked, "Guess we should head back then? I'm getting hungry. How about you?"

"I could definitely eat something."

Not giving it a second thought, we wandered hand in hand down the quiet beachfront. It seemed many tourists had already retired for the day.

Gathering our towels, we placed them in the bin outside the hut and washed off our feet at the outdoor shower. After slipping on our flip-flops, we bypassed the main building and walked down the path to the parking lot.

Seated in his buggy, Ryan's hand rested conveniently in the space between us. Mine softly covered his before he grasped hold to intertwine our fingers.

The drive to his house on Melaleuca was surreal for me. It was humid outside, so the gentle breeze cooled us off while moving up the hill. When rounding the corner at the bottom of his street, feeling like I was dreaming, we pulled up in front of his friend's house. Sadly, disconnecting, I fumbled through my backpack to find my golf buggy key and jumped out to switch to my machine a few feet away.

Close behind, illuminated by the setting sun, he said, "So, for dinner, do you want to try one of the Marina restaurants or eat at Qualia?"

Thinking a moment, I figured it would take me an hour to shower and get dressed.

"Umm, how about, since it's already late, we just eat at Qualia and try another place tomorrow?"

Happy to hear I was contemplating plans for the following day, he said, "Sounds good. What is your cottage number? I'll swing by and pick you up."

"I'd like that," I said with a smile. "Drive to the Long Pavilion and turn left instead of right into the parking lot. Make the first left again and follow that to the very end of the road. I am cottage number 33."

"Okay, that sounds easy enough. Got it. Does an hour give you enough time?" he asked, leaning against my cart while I found a seat on the driver's side.

Nodding my head, I faintly replied, "Yes. I'll be ready."

"Great," he confirmed in a low tone of voice. "See you shortly."

Turning the cart around, I drove down the road with butterflies soaring, bringing a joyful feeling when thinking of what we'd found. Tightly holding the steering, about to explode, I waved while turning the last corner. Ryan watched from the deck perched high above me on the hill.

Deep in thought on my way to Qualia, I knew things with him were escalating. No longer did I feel a sense of dread. Contemplating it all, I didn't care anymore if I eventually got hurt. This newfound feeling made it worthwhile since my many emotional scars showed signs of healing. It had been so long since I'd felt cared for and wanted. But what surprised me the most was that these feelings were mutual.

| 22 |

A Night to Remember

Maneuvered the cart into the spot beside my cottage, I quickly swung open the door and turned on the shower faucet. While the water warmed up, I called the Concierge to confirm Ryan's arrival with security. Requesting permission once again for him to join me for dinner, they quickly approved the arrangements.

With only forty-five minutes left to get ready, I had little time to rid myself of the sticky sand and salty film. Moving quickly, wrapping myself in a towel, I cleared the steam from the mirror.

It took longer to put on my makeup, with my hands shaking nervously. Beautifying my face with natural tones, I swept my hair in an updo and secured it with bobby pins.

Happy with how I looked, it was time to select a dress. I chose the cranberry one with a halter top and high-low hem tonight. Stepping into neutral woven wedges, I added some delicate jewelry to finish it off. Taking one last glance in the mirror, I clenched my hands together, content with the overly excited person before me. She immediately seemed very different from the one I saw the week before. Showing more life in my eyes, I noticed the darkness of my spirit slowly fading away and my face brightening as the days passed. It wasn't hard to figure out who was responsible for this transformation.

A few gentle knocks on the door unexpectedly interrupted these jubilant thoughts. Checking to confirm who was there, I saw Ryan standing outside. Flexing straight arms out in front of him, quickly positioning each behind his back militarily, he patiently waited for me to answer. When I opened the barrier between us, his eyes lit up to match his smile.

"Wow. You look beautiful," he confessed.

I was not used to hearing compliments, so I simply replied, "Thank you."

Ryan stood there smartly in navy linen pants and a white long-sleeved shirt rolled up to his elbows. Reaching out to me, taking hold of my one hand, he twirled me around, making the lower hem of the dress elevate slightly, along with my spirits.

"Shall we go?" he asked.

Acknowledging him with a nod, I took the room key off the table and placed it in a small clutch. Escorted out to his buggy, Ryan helped me take a seat, mindful of my dress, making sure it did not get dirty. Walking around the machine to the driver's side, he, too, jumped in, and off we went.

Unwelcome thoughts of Scott reminded me of his lack of gentle-manly qualities in contrast to Ryan's. It was so refreshing to be treated like a lady, finally.

When we parked in front of the Long Pavilion, Ryan said, "Wait one second."

Gallantly swinging around to my side, he reached for my hand so I could step out. Offering his arm, I took hold.

While passing through the covered walkway lined with candles nestled in beach sand, the flames glistened romantically inside the tall glass cylinders. Arriving at the front podium inside the entrance to the restaurant, Ryan's opposite hand caressed mine lightly as I clung to him. Greeted by the maître d', we noticed he was the same gentle-man from the night before.

Immediately recognizing us, he said, "Oh! The happy couple is din-ing with us again. Table for two. Right, this way."

"Thank you, Sir," Ryan replied.

The man grabbed our menus and instructed, "Follow me. We have a special spot for you."

Escorted to the far end of the restaurant, taking in the 180-degree view of the Coral Sea, the man presented us with a table bordering the infinity pool. About to have a seat, the soothing waterfall sounds complemented the breeze circulating amongst the trees.

"Is this to your liking?" the older gentleman asked while the space sparkled with candlelight.

Delighted with the location, we both said simultaneously, "Yes, thank you."

The place was lit by an array of lanterns and votives, each creating a flickering reflection on the varnished wood-paneled ceiling. The music was tranquil and light. Ryan pulled out my chair - something I now had expected from him. Joining me, he casually rested his hand on top of the table between us. Mine naturally covered his. It was strange how at ease I was around him. It was like we'd always been together. Was that even possible?

While perusing the wine list, feeling his fingers gently moving over the top of mine, negative thoughts began to seep in and wreak havoc. Doubt emerged destructively, forming a hole in the pit of my stomach. What if the allure of this man and the hope of finding love is blinding me? That is when reality hit, and the damaged part of me surfaced. If it's too good to be true, I thought, then it probably is. I have to make sure I don't lose sight of that fact. Not be naïve and stupid like before. Had I played into what Ryan had planned all along? Had I become the vaca-girlfriend he wanted initially? Was my gut feeling the first day correct? Throughout our dinner, I vowed to stay sharp and not be so vulnerable and awe-struck. I wanted to see if I could get him to divulge his reason for being here. Looking into his eyes, I couldn't help but notice they still seemed oddly familiar, but from where? His face did not give me the same impression, though - just his eyes.

Ordering our drinks and making our menu selections, Ryan asked, "So, when do you want to explore Whitehaven Beach with me? There is also the Great Barrier Reef excursion, too. I think that one is a full-day thing, but it would be an adventure, don't you think?"

"Actually, after watching the guest attractions video in my room on the first day, I reserved a spot for Whitehaven Beach through Qualia next week. Maybe you can register for the same one?"

"Okay, I'll look into that. I'd love to join you. How about the Great Barrier Reef, then?"

"Honestly, that one scares me. I mean, being in the middle of the ocean surrounded by nothing but water?" Glancing across the table at him, I knew what he was thinking. "I know... I know. I'm in Australia – I have to see it."

He showed a hint of happiness through his tough exterior. Had I inadvertently given him the answer he wanted?

Squeezing my hand, he said, "You'll love it. Trust me."

In a split second, his facial expression and eye movement gave off another sense of familiarity, but I still couldn't pinpoint the reason why or who it resembled.

Unable to stop staring at him, he questioned, "What is it?"

"Umm, it's your eyes. They looked vaguely familiar for a second. Don't know why? Sorry. I didn't mean to stare."

Directing his gaze away from me, feeling uncomfortable, I noticed a scar. "What happened to your head?" I asked while pointing to the mark, needing to know more.

Chuckling, he said, "Ahh, nothing major. I cut it open, hitting the side of a boat. I was trying to climb out of the rough water a while back and hit it pretty hard."

Disappointed that there wasn't a better story to go along with it, I confirmed, "That's it?"

"It's boring, I know. My life is not overly exciting."

Veering away from anything personal, we mostly discussed world news, politics, and travel to fill the time. Sadly, I didn't discover any new information about him or his past, which concerned me even more. What was he hiding?

Our waitress arrived to remove our plates. Ryan politely requested the bill. Upon her return, he pulled a money clip from his pocket, bursting with cash, and slipped some inside the folder casually.

"Ready?" Standing up, he pulled my chair back.

"Yes," I replied. "Thank you for the wine."

"You know you don't have to thank me every time," he smiled.

"Yes, I do. I appreciate it."

With a pleasant expression, he added without hesitation, "I know you do."

Passing by our maître d', he said, "Have a pleasant evening."

Both of us graciously bid him good night.

While wandering down the long corridor again, arm in arm, dusk had fallen upon the island. Small pathway lights automatically illuminated when we reached the parking lot. The warm breeze was welcoming, and the salty air seemed to be calling us to Pebble Beach.

"So, do you want to extend the evening?" I asked. "Maybe head down to the water?"

Turning to me with contentment on his face, he replied, "Definitely."

It didn't take us long to reach the pool pavilion. Rounding the corner, we noticed the bar was open. Stopping to order another one of the island's Bondi Blue cocktails for dessert, we found space on two lounge chairs conveniently placed tight together amidst a handful of other guests. Only able to see the makings of pitch-black emptiness before us, hearing the waves hitting the shore, it was hard to distinguish any ocean, land, or sky; it was so dark. Enjoying our cocktails, we stretched out on the chairs. Blanketed by a ceiling of stars, Ryan reached his arm over and placed it along my shoulders, allowing my head to rest comfortably.

"Guess the distance rule no longer applies?" he humorously pointed out.

Based on our current position, I had no choice but to say, "Yes, it looks that way." Instantly, half of me wondered if he was proud of that fact, while the other half knew my reaction was a solid reminder that I was still broken. Despite everything that had happened today, I found myself having doubts. My guard went up again, and that constant internal struggle returned. Listening to the music playing, blending seamlessly with the conversations surrounding us, I counted two falling stars passing through the night sky. Trying to work up the courage to ask him some personal questions, he said, "So, what's with the fear you have of the ocean?"

Knowing the answer, I sighed. "Well, that all stems back to a childhood memory I'd rather forget."

"Oh?"

He prompted me to elaborate. So I did.

"Let's just say, one summer, I had a run-in with a jellyfish."

"Yeah? Well, that explains it. Enough said." Laughing a little, he sincerely added, "You know, the ocean isn't all bad. You have to look past the scary parts to find the beauty in it."

His comment made me think it had more meaning, like, just because you got hurt by Scott doesn't mean all men will do the same thing to you.

With the door open per se, I asked, "So, man of mystery? Why are you here?"

Initially, not saying a word, he knew he had no choice but to expose his more vulnerable side. Something he wasn't used to doing, I'm sure.

Sitting up and grabbing hold of his drink, he stayed seated on the chaise facing me. "Truth is...umm... Death is a heavy subject. I needed time to grieve. Had the option of coming here, and I took it."

Upon hearing this, I replied, "Can I offer some advice?"

"Sure."

"Sometimes it helps to talk things through – then it doesn't seem so bad."

Appreciating my concern, he said, "Thank you. I'll keep that in mind."

Our conversation dropped off there. Only recalling our beach adventures today, sharing a little more detail about my museum project in LA and my life in New York, covering my yawns, we called it a night as the pool bar closed.

"I guess we should turn in. I'm pretty tired. Aren't you? We did a lot today," I said while sitting on the end of the chair beside him.

"Yes, we did." Moving his feet through the sand, not saying much, he reached over and took hold of my hand in his. Almost inspecting every finger, not wanting to let go, he asked, "What should we do tomorrow?"

"I'm not sure. Have any ideas? By now, I thought you'd be sick of spending time with me." Remembering Scott would have lost interest by now.

"First of all, one – I will never get sick of spending time with you, ever, and two – maybe we can hang out at my place for the day, sit beside the pool, and grab some lunch at the marina? I thought we could also have a special dinner tomorrow night. My friend has a Chef arranged to cook for me. How does that sound?"

Intrigued by his suggestions, I accepted. "That sounds – nice."

"So, it's a date?"

"Yes. It's a date."

Ready to leave, we wandered arm in arm up the path back to the parking lot. Sitting in his cart with some assistance, Ryan drove from the restaurant to my pavilion.

I was anxious en route, not knowing how the night would end. Thinking about it further, I thought it had been so long since...

Pulling in front of my cottage, arriving sooner than expected, interrupting my last thought, Ryan came around to my side and offered his hand. Upon leaving the cart, we walked to the door, hands tightly connected. The tension between us was difficult to ignore. Apprehensive, knowing I was still unsuccessful in getting him to open up about his life, I decided not to invite him in since that would inevitably lead to something more.

"Well, here we are," he said, quietly standing in the shadows.

Facing me, he grasped hold of my other hand and lifted both in front of him to fill the gap between us while contemplating his words. Comfortably wrapping my arms around his waist, happy with their position, he let go. Doing the same, he pulled me in close as I timidly caressed his back.

Swaying from side to side, Ryan leaned forward to rest his forehead against mine as those dark brown eyes gazed deep into my soul. "Thank you for an exciting day and a memorable evening. Tomorrow night, you will be my guest." Pausing, he stood tall and confessed, "Eva, I know our lives are complicated. That is what brought us to Australia. Perhaps we are both here for a reason. What I am about to say is probably the last thing you want to hear, but it needs to be said. I'm not sure if you've noticed, but we seem to have this unusually strong connection." Hugging tighter, I could feel his heart pumping in his chest while he awaited my response.

Nervous beyond words, I whispered, "Yes. It seems we do."

With eyes locked on mine, his expression brightened. "I find myself feeling overly protective of you. Since we met, you haven't been far from my thoughts. Suppose that is what happens when you start to fall for someone."

Hearing that made me gasp.

Not wasting another minute, Ryan reached up and gently traced my hairline with his finger before tucking a few strands behind my ear. Resting his hand along my cheek, I pressed against it as his thumb drifted across my cheekbone from right to left. The light touch caused me to shiver. Breathless, legs weakening, arms tingling, he took a step toward me. Then another. Inching me backward, my body soon leaned against the pavilion door. My eyes fluttered intensely without leaving his sights for a second. Dangerously close, they soon fell shut just as Ryan's lips washed passionately over mine. Taking his time, his touch caused an incredible warmth to spread from head to toe.

Oh, I thought in the heat of the moment, how could I not invite him in?

Parting from the soft, gentle kisses, he nestled his cheek alongside mine and quietly said, "Until tomorrow. Goodnight. Sweet dreams, Eva."

At that point, I realized he'd decided for me, continuing that gentlemanly respect displayed since day one. Trying to recover and formulate a sentence, I looked into his eyes. Towering above me, he kissed my forehead, leaving his lips pressed firmly before stealing one last embrace.

Backing away with hands still connected, our arms outstretched, still floating, I asked, "So, what time do you want to meet in the morning?"

"How's eleven? That way, you can sleep in. Think we will have a lot to talk about tomorrow."

Elated, I responded, "Eleven it is. I'll see you in the morning."

Ryan held on until the very last second before letting go. Waving to me with a steady hand, bidding him goodnight in the same manner, I watched him drive around the corner and disappear. Part of me wished the evening could have ended differently, but rationalizing it while standing in the doorway, I knew this was the right decision to make for now.

Moments later, I slid open the large glass doors to my balcony before getting ready for bed. The ocean breeze cascaded in, making the draperies gracefully sway from side to side. Walking over to the railing, I grabbed hold of it. The moon was now lofting high in the night sky, creating sparkling diamonds on the ocean's surface. Without warning, the reality of Ryan streamed through my mind. Had I misjudged him? Were my first instincts wrong? My gut feeling said he was different – not the guy searching for a fling. He seemed too kind. Too sweet. Our first kiss replayed, prompting me to close my eyes and run my fingertips over my lips while envisioning the tender moment. Tonight made me question if I was ready for another relationship. Because it seemed that was the direction we were heading. What would happen when I return to New York? Where would he be? Would he come with me? What if he didn't? Once again, I would be utterly heartbroken and, sadly, still alone. Could I withstand any more pain? I couldn't get past wondering what his entire story was. Why the secrecy? Was the reason that bad he couldn't share it?

Slipping under the covers, I recalled our less innocent goodbye. How is it that just the touch of his hand made me feel loved and safe? Something I had not felt in my lifetime. The words "falling for you" fully embraced my heart, giving way to a radiant brightness and this enamored glow. Thoughts of kissing him made me adoringly content while snuggling with my fluffy pillow. Remembering what Harry, the wise Concierge, said when I arrived made me laugh. He was entirely right. You never know what the islands have in store for you. Emotionally confident, I knew we couldn't have met by accident. I felt in my heart that our paths had crossed for a reason.

| 23 |

Day Four: Something Amiss

Tossing and turning for the third night in a row, I got up feeling overly tired. Surrounded by peaceful silence, desperate for an additional fifteen minutes, I wholeheartedly knew if I slept in, there would be a good chance I'd be late to meet up with Ryan.

Famished, I ordered room service to start the day and save some time. While waiting for the food to arrive, stepping out onto the balcony, I rested my arms along the railing and drifted deep in thought, thinking about my life and wondering what would happen when this dream vacation ended. A part of me loved my career immensely. Still, the other half began contemplating the possibility of marriage and starting a family, since I couldn't imagine my life without either one intertwined in it. All of that seemed possible months ago, but got violently ripped from my future by the absence of faithfulness and the presence of deceit. Frankly, my heart wasn't sure if it believed in everlasting love anymore. Analyzing what was developing between Ryan and me, I tried to figure out whether we were experiencing lust for each other or, perhaps, feelings of love were genuinely beginning to grow. Due to my relationship inexperience, I didn't fully know for sure.

While getting dressed, I gathered a few things I figured I'd need to survive the day. About to place them in my backpack, I heard a knock. Breakfast had arrived.

Swinging open the door, I met the concierge with a smile. I'm sure the woman was a morning person based on how she hummed while she worked. Within minutes, she had set the table beautifully with crisp white linens and silverware. On her way out, she wished me a pleasant day. I did the same.

Closing the door behind her, I found myself alone once again. For some reason, after I sat down, my stomach felt unsettled. Eating what I could, I figured it was a burst of nervousness brought about by the thought of spending the day in seclusion at Ryan's place.

Eating what I could, I gathered a few things and finished my coffee before leaving. Upon locking up, I started my cart and maneuvered the winding pathways of the resort before ascending the long hill to the lookout.

The sun was shining brightly. Despite it being a beautiful day, my anxiety kept running at an all-time high while making the tight turn onto Melaleuca Drive.

Slowly rounding the last corner below his place at the end of the street, I inhaled deeply. Expelling the apprehension, allowing my chin to almost hit my chest in the process, I prepared to refrain from getting overwhelmed and doing something I would regret. I felt I could trust him, but now, could I trust myself? He was drawing me in, and I feared there would be no turning back once my damaged heart was fully vested.

About five minutes late, I parked in Ryan's driveway and strolled down the path to the back of the house, where I found him in the kitchen, making toast and sipping a coffee.

"Morning," I said, subtly trying not to scare him.

"Hey! Good morning. How are you?"

"I'm fine. Did you sleep well?"

"Oh, you know, it was hard for me to drift off last night with thoughts of you," he said charismatically, moving in my direction, cautiously wrapping his arms around my waist. Finding the need to lift me off my feet and swing me around playfully, he added, "But I'm glad you're here now."

Apparently, picking up a little further from where we left things last night, my guard went up. Heart pulling in his direction, I almost could not defy its power. Placing my feet on the ground, he took hold of my hand and turned to guide me into the kitchen casually.

My leeriness returned.

"Can I offer you something to drink? Did you have breakfast already?"

"A bottle of water would be great. I had something to eat before I left, so I'm good for now, thank you."

Taking a seat on a chair along the kitchen counter, part of me contemplated again whether he was a player – someone who always had a girl wherever he traveled, figuring I was the flavor of this trip. Unable to control my negative thoughts, I stopped analyzing our situation but kept my mind in a rationally coherent place. Desperate to break away from the apprehensiveness, I put on a happy face, wishing I could just let things happen naturally if this was meant to be, not sabotage it beforehand.

"So, swimming and lunch at the marina? Can we pencil in a little shopping, too? There were a few stores I didn't get to see the other day since my plans were interrupted," I pointed out in jest.

Setting a bottle of water in front of me, he said, "Hey? I'm glad I interrupted your day."

With a snicker, I said, "Yeah, me too," wondering if I truly believed that.

"We can do whatever your heart desires. I am up for anything. Sure, you wouldn't like something to eat?" Ryan asked, spreading a little butter on his severely darkened toast.

Raising my hand, I declined. "Umm…no, it's okay. Besides, it might end up like yours. You know, slightly crisp and, well, burnt."

"I'll be honest, I'm not much of a cook." He opened the fridge and said, "I ordered a fruit platter early this morning from the store. They delivered it about half an hour ago. Maybe you'd like some? I promise, my hands never touched it." Professing his truth, he awaited my answer before taking another bite of his breakfast.

"Sure, that would be nice," I conceded in amusement.

Carefully taking the platter from the fridge, Ryan carried it to the outdoor dining table beside the pool. He returned to the kitchen seconds later to grab two small plates, forks, and pieces of paper towel to use as napkins. While I sat overlooking the ocean, he brought a pair of binoculars.

"Here, look at the view through these. You'll see people on the sailboats below and the waves crashing against the rocks on the other islands."

Moving his chair right tight beside mine, sitting down, he leaned in to point out the different things he'd already observed days prior. With his arm resting on the top edge of my chair, passing the binoculars between us, we discussed our newest findings while eating the fruit from the tropical display.

With little left to discover, Ryan asked in a low tone, "Hey, would you like a tour of the house?"

Excited to see the interior of this beautifully designed home, I replied, "Yes, I'd love to see it. Thought you'd never ask."

Passing through Fleetwood doors to take our dishes and the platter back inside, making sure the birds wouldn't take advantage of it unattended, we left everything on the counter. That is when he said, "Follow me."

Offering his hand, I took hold.

First, Ryan led me to the middle of the open-concept central living space.

"Of course, this is the interior living room, dining room, and kitchen, which can be open-air or closed off when needed. It mirrors the covered outdoor living spaces. I love the up-lit cathedral wood-paneled ceiling that spans the length of the room, especially the exposed beams. Something you would appreciate, I'm sure."

Mesmerized by the craftsmanship of the ceiling, sparkling with pool ripples reflecting upon it, I wondered what I might find touring through the beautiful house. Making sure to pay close attention, I figured something might stand out and shed some light on who the real Ryan Davis was.

In awe of the home's grandeur, with walls painted ivory and natural tone, wide-planked hardwood floors beneath our feet, many little accents made it unique.

The front door was four feet wide. It had a full pane of glass showcasing a series of arched wood branches, creating the likeness of an abstract tree inserted in the middle. On the wall opposite the foyer hung an exquisite eight-by-six-foot, three-panel, hand-carved bamboo art. LED lights inset into the floorboards accented the decorative piece to give the room a gallery look. The entire space was painstakingly created with great care, detail, and thought.

After peeking into the many bedrooms and bathrooms, we ended up in the media room before returning to the kitchen. That is where Ryan showed me an advanced monitor inset in the wall.

"This security system operates everything within the house. Multiple cameras with motion sensors display every ounce of the grounds. I can control all of the automated blinds from here. Even the lights can turn on and off this way," he explained expertly before focusing on the importance of hurricane-proof windows and doors in case of a severe storm.

About to head back outside to the pool, Ryan opened the linen cupboard and grabbed a selection of beach towels. By this time, it was almost 12:50.

Feeling uneasy, I suddenly blurted out, "Instead of swimming right now, how about we head to the marina to shop a little and grab lunch before coming back?"

"Sure, we can do that." Placing the stack of towels on the interior living room couch for later, he added, "It'll take me a minute or two to lock up, though."

At the press of a button, the Fleetwood doors rolled automatically along their tracks. Ryan seemed to have a process for closing the house. Before leaving, he entered a code in the unit inset in the wall. Hearing the loud beeping as it counted down, we stepped outside the front door so that he could lock it.

Moving toward the garage, he looked over. "Want me to drive?"

"Sure, if you'd like," I said before he got in the cart to back it onto the driveway.

Jumping into the seat beside him, we were soon on our way.

Drifting along Melaleuca Drive, we commented on the weather and what I hoped to find today. In search of gifts for my family, I explained that I always liked finishing this task early instead of leaving it to the last minute. Ryan offered a few suggestions, which I took into consideration. Our light-hearted conversation made me feel like the day was off to a good start.

The sun went in and out from behind the clouds, giving us a break from the heat. Met by strong, gusty winds, we both were wary of debris floating through the air as we arrived downtown. Ryan luckily found a parking spot not far from where we'd met four days ago. Amidst the many yachts parked in the marina, we looked at the stores, trying to decide where to go first.

Drawn in by the thought of having Fish and chips for lunch, I asked, pointing at the restaurant, "So, do you want to go there and grab something later? What do you think? Eat-in or take-out?" Not receiving an answer, I turned to find Ryan's eyes affixed to something further up the road. Wanting to see what had caught his attention, I followed his line of sight but saw nothing unusual. "Ryan? Hello?" I said, waving my hands in front of his stoic face.

He broke from the trance. "Yeah? Sorry. What was that?"

Repeating my question, I asked, "Fish and chips? Eat-in or take-out?"

"Either is fine," Ryan replied.

Before crossing the street, he tightly held my hand and intertwined our fingers.

Dipping in and out of the first two stores, strangely, I happened to catch him looking about often. Entering one building, he glanced behind us. Once inside, he stayed overly alert and faced the windows the entire time, never turning his back to the street. His sights moved from left to right when exiting, scanning a full one hundred and eighty degrees. Passing the Fish and Chips restaurant and the Pharmacy, we visited a store called Breeze. Consisting of beautiful women's swimwear, I could tell Ryan wasn't interested. Saving him the grief of standing idly by while I browsed, we left and moved onto the souvenir shop hand in hand. By this time, I had deemed this behavior rather odd. It was like he had become paranoid.

Finishing that thought, he turned to me and said, "Hey, Eva? I'll be right back. I just remembered. I need to pick something up. You go ahead. I'll join you in a moment."

Caught off guard, I didn't know what to say. "Umm, sure, no problem," was the only thing that came to mind.

Never elaborating on what he intended to buy, I watched him move down the boardwalk to the Pharmacy, kind of in a hurry, as a big man dressed all in black followed behind him.

When he was out of sight, I went inside the tourist shop and began roaming the aisles, searching for trinkets with the Hamilton Island logo branded on them. Not sure what to bring home for my parents and sister, brother-in-law, and nephews, I was happy not to purchase anything for Scott. It felt surreal to know that I was spending time with someone other than him, making me question whether my relationship with Ryan would be long-lasting or short-term.

That's when an eerie feeling hit me. Curiously peeking out the store's front window, I kept a close eye for any signs of him returning and examined a few theories of what may have caused him to bolt so quickly. Focused, I suddenly saw him exit a few doors down. Scanning the streets with his head on a swivel, his hands were buried in his pockets. There was no shopping bag to be seen. Seconds later, the man dressed in black also left the store and made eye contact with him before venturing the opposite way.

Who was he? What was their connection? Or was that just a coincidence?

About to walk into the store and find me, I instantly hid amongst the shelves, making it look like I was trying to decide what to buy my family.

"So, did you find what you were looking for?"

Hesitant, he removed his hand from his left pocket and said, "Yes, just needed to grab some lip balm. Forgot to get it the other day." Opening his hand, he revealed the brand he preferred.

Suspicious, I analyzed his actions as he paced the store aimlessly. With eyes peeled, I hoped he'd tell me more about himself in the coming days - the absolute truth. Desperate to make sense of our situation and why he hadn't confided in me yet, I figured he probably didn't feel I was trustworthy enough. Realistically, being together only a few days would certainly not warrant divulging that level of information anyway, especially knowing our escape to this island would inevitably end.

Thoroughly needing to shake off my current frame of mind, I picked out things for my Mom, Dad, nephews, brother-in-law, and sister, and met up with Ryan to explain who each item was for on our way over to the cashier. As I paid for my trinkets, it wasn't hard to see that he was a little quieter all of a sudden. Not wanting to make a scene, figuring something was wrong, I decided to wait until we left the shop to ask what was bothering him.

On the way out the door, I watched him wander to an open picnic table alongside the marina. I followed close behind.

"Is everything alright?" I asked in a concerned tone.

Uncertain if he would respond, we sat on the bench and gazed at the boats.

Ryan periodically scanned the area around us. "It's nothing," he said, "Everything's fine."

That's when I felt the need to push him a little further. "No, really... Is it me? Did I do something?"

Hastily turning to me, he said pleasantly, "No, it's not you at all."

"I noticed you scanning our surroundings as we walked in and out of the shops. Why are you doing that?"

"I'm sorry, Eva, you won't understand..." Ryan stated firmly, lowering his voice, filled with frustration. "Yeah, I can't do this right now." Getting up from the picnic table, he walked down the street, leaving me behind.

With no choice but to allow him to depart undisturbed, I thought I'd give him some space if that's what he needed. This confirmed that something had happened when we arrived at the marina, but what? He was fine before we got here. Things got weird when that man showed up, and Ryan ducked into the store with him.

Stressed, losing track of his whereabouts, I went to wait at the golf cart, hoping he would surface shortly.

Thirty minutes passed. I locked my sights on every person that came into view, but there was no sign of him. Part of me figured he was not coming back or, perhaps, he was patiently waiting for me to leave so he could return home alone.

Not given a choice, I went to the Qualia Shuttle Service hut to arrange a drive to my resort, assuming I would grab my buggy from his place later. Turning in the direction of Ryan's cart one last time, I spotted him standing nearby, watching me move farther away from him. He was now wearing a baseball cap. Facing each other, not losing eye contact, I stood in the middle of the street, unsure what he would do. With each step I took, he, too, moved closer, bridging the gap.

About four feet apart, barely able to look me in the eye, with sights focused on the marina more so, I could feel something was amiss.

"Eva… I'm sorry."

Sensitively surveying this tall, muscular, emotionally damaged man standing before me, I peered upward into his eyes, now filled with uncertainty. Inching toward him, reaching out, I placed my hands on either side of his expressionless face. "You'll have to let me in eventually. You can't keep these walls up forever."

Sliding my hands over his shoulders, I pulled him in close. His arms encircled my waist acceptingly. Desperate to comfort him, I could feel his pain as he hugged me tightly. It was almost as if his life depended on it. Motionless, while buggies whizzed by, he stood tall.

"Can we go? I can't stay here any longer," he quietly whispered.

"Sure. We can leave."

Taking a seat in his cart, tilting the brim of his hat down over his forehead, Ryan gazed out at the marina. "Can I ask you something?"

"Sure, anything," I immediately responded, scared of what he might say.

Leaning forward, resting his arms on the steering wheel, he took a deep breath, still avoiding eye contact.

"Look, I've been thinking a lot about the two of us, and I understand that we agreed early on to be nothing but friends, mostly because we think our lives are incompatible. But I believe we've drifted well beyond all of that now. When I told you how I felt last night, you said you felt the same way. When I returned home, I sat down and thought about our situation. I know we literally just met, but as crazy as it is, I think when you know – you just – know."

Unexpectedly hearing my grandmother's depiction of true love, he caught my attention, and the conversation took on a more serious tone. Feeling an unusual flutter in my heart, I thought, Is this what it feels like?

His eyes overwhelmed me with emotion as tears developed in mine.

He added, "I've never felt anything for anyone like I do for you. I can't explain it. Look, I didn't come here searching for anything but an escape from my problems. Never in a million years did I think I'd fall…" Stopping, he hesitated, then bravely said, "…in love with someone on this trip. Finally, after all this time, the thought of spending the rest of my life alone seems to be fading the more we are together. Are you drifting in this direction with me?"

Caught off guard by the rawness of his words, watching this confident man wear his heart on his sleeve, allowing me to see a more vulnerable side, I paused and replied, "Ryan, I honestly do feel this strong connection with you, too. But is it love? I'm not entirely sure. As you said, we only met a few days back. I can't deny that being around you makes me happy. You've helped me smile and laugh again. Something I thought I'd forgotten how to do, given what's happened in my life recently. When we were snorkeling yesterday, and I bolted in fear, you swam after me, willing to protect me from harm. You calmed those fears. That is when our relationship changed in my eyes. I believe I can trust you with my life, but I need to be honest. The secrecy surrounding yours is holding me back. I confided in you and shared why I'm here - the good, the bad, and the ugly - but you won't share your full story with me. Those questions run through my head daily, keeping me cautiously at arm's length. I hope you understand what I am trying to say." I paused. "Why can't you let me in? I won't judge. I'll just listen."

"I'm sorry, Eva. I can't." Looking away from me, he seemed frustrated beyond words. "I get what you're saying. Just wanted to know where you stood."

"You don't trust me? Is that it?" I asked, lowering my head in desperation.

"No, that's not it at all. This is far more complicated than you could ever imagine," he said, placing the key in the ignition before starting the cart and pulling away.

Driving through town, back to Melaleuca, we stayed silent. Arriving at his place, parking in front of the garage door, we found ourselves lost for words. I contemplated what to do or say next. It was so awkward.

Unsure where we go from here, I bravely whispered, "So, do you still want to have dinner tonight?"

His mind noticeably reeling, he tried to break from his weary thoughts. "I would love for you to join me if you still want to."

My hand immediately grasped hold of his. Not skipping a beat, he silently turned, reached out with the opposite arm, and clung to me. This time, it felt like he was the one who required my unrelenting support.

About to let go, he asked, "Can you meet me at One Tree Hill around six o'clock? Maybe we can have a cocktail and watch the sunset before coming here for dinner? That should give me enough time to do a few things first."

I didn't have to think twice. "Yes, I'll meet you there," I answered, concerned by what the evening could bring.

Reluctantly separating, happy to hear me accept his invitation, I got out of his cart and moved to mine before waving goodbye and returning to Qualia with nothing more said.

Descending the long hill, the strange events from our afternoon together haunted me. Somewhat numb, I was shell-shocked by his unusual behavior. What was so wrong with his life that he needed to keep it a secret? I speculated whether this was an act or a sympathy ploy to make me feel sorry for him. That would be something most girls would fall for, and then he'd have them right where he wanted them.

Conversely, I thought he was carrying an enormous weight on his shoulders. The latter made me wonder how tonight would go after hitting this symbolic bump in the road. Analyzing everything, I remembered he said his situation was far more complicated than I could ever imagine. Despite that subtle warning, I knew I needed to move forward regardless, especially since my heart suddenly seemed more vested after what had transpired. Knowing he was falling in love with me gave me a sense of hope. While mentally replaying the moment, I realized I hadn't said it back. Did that mean something? Flipping back and forth between the red flags, I didn't know what to do. Was this a wise idea? Was I being naïve - trusting a total stranger and feeling love for him so soon? Was the desperation on my part fueled by not wanting to be alone anymore? Doubt rained over me as I drove through the Qualia gates.

Arriving at my cottage, I turned off the ignition and stayed seated. I couldn't stop thinking about him. Shaking my head, needing to calm my nerves, I decided to go for a swim. About to go inside, I gave myself an ultimatum.

"Give him one more night - one chance to come clean and confide in me. If he doesn't, I'll have no choice but to move on."

Not fully believing I'd do that, I changed into my swimsuit, convinced a line needed to be drawn and abided by without question.

Immersed in the tranquility of Pebble Beach not long after, I wished my mind could find a little peace and stop analyzing our situation. Consuming every ounce of me, I prayed that he'd reveal something. Anything to say – yes, I trust in you, Eva. This is my story. I'm ready to share it.

| 24 |

Romance in the Air

Time passed by ever so slowly. About an hour before I needed to meet Ryan at One Tree Hill, I selected another pretty dress to wear. This one was my favorite – a long, flowy, navy blue dress, elegantly casual with a draped cut-out in the back. Adding a teal pashmina for a hint of color in case the evening got chilly, it soon came time to walk out the door.

Slightly before six, driving up the long hill, I could see the street was lined with buggies parked everywhere near the top. A crowd had already gathered to take in the sunset and complimentary cocktails. Close to the popular tourist destination, I could see Ryan there waiting. Dressed in dark linen pants, with the sleeves of his white shirt rolled up to his elbows, the setting sun illuminated him with the most incredible ocean, land, and sky backdrop beyond that. In his hand was a single red rose.

I smiled while parking beside him. Unable to leave his eyes for a moment, I walked over.

"This is for you. You look so beautiful. But then again, you always do," he said, presenting me with the flower.

Lost for words, I whispered, "Thank you. You're looking very handsome yourself," as other tourists joyfully looked on.

With so many people staring, Ryan got uneasy. Turning away from the crowd to hide his face, he said, "Let's leave your cart here. I'll drive us to my place. We can see the last of the sunset from there. I have a surprise for you."

Mindful of my dress, he helped me get seated in his gentlemanly way before slipping behind the wheel. Nervous, my body shivered while descending the hill towards Millionaire's Row.

When we arrived at his place, he pulled into the driveway and parked the buggy in the garage.

Escorting me to the left of the house, I marveled at the sky, brilliantly glowing a bright orange, red, and yellow amongst the clouds. About halfway to the back, lanterns lined the walkway, with flaming candles nestled inside. Turning to Ryan in amazement, I noticed he had stopped. Silently prompting me to continue down the path, I found the pool magically accented by white spheres of light floating in the water. The lit, tethered beach balls swayed gently in the breeze as the sunset blazed over the horizon, reflecting a soft sea of liquid fire at the far end. Filled with calming music, the atmosphere around the patio created the most romantic setting I have ever experienced. Surprised by what he had done, part of me felt scared as to why.

Finding him lagging a few feet behind, I assumed he wanted to survey my reaction to everything from a distance, quietly anticipating what I might say next.

Filled with excitement, I was almost speechless. "You did all of this for me?"

He confidently nodded.

"No one has ever done anything remotely..." Emotionally overwhelmed, tears developed, stopping me from speaking.

Visibly happy, he inched closer. "I'm so glad you like it." Pointing at the Chef cooking in the outdoor kitchen, he humorously reminded, "Remember I said I don't cook much. Well, lucky for us, he does."

Guided to the table, decorated with white linens and fresh flowers, he pulled out my chair and poured us a glass of white wine before sitting beside me while the Chef served our appetizers.

Impressed by the abundance of flavors on white rectangular platters presented, I timidly asked, unsure if he would answer. "How are you doing?"

"I'm fine," he replied. "Sorry about today. I'm not usually like that. I'm working through a few…things. I knew this would come up eventually. I just wasn't prepared for it to be so soon."

Seemingly speaking in riddles, Ryan looked away. An awkward silence fell upon us.

Deciding to change the course of the conversation, I suggested, "How about we enjoy this lovely evening? No talk of baggage and such? Deal?"

He nodded, relieved to hear my suggestion, while the Chef presented the main course.

While eating, we enjoyed the unobstructed vista of Whitsunday Island, accented by an orangey hue of day-ending light flooding over its darkened silhouette. Watching the ball of fire disappear in the western sky, leaving small, colorful remnants behind, and saying goodbye to another day in paradise, I felt Ryan's hand reach for mine. Fingers intertwined, sitting silently, he raised my hand to his lips and kissed it.

"Thank you for joining me," he said before sipping his wine.

"There is no place I would rather be."

Taken by my words and intense stare, assuming he was thankful I had not been scared off, he affectionately slipped one arm around my shoulders while the other cupped my cheek. Sweeping his thumb below my sight line, eyes not veering away, he gently moved his fingertips through my hair before slowly bridging the gap between us. With the scent of red wine still upon our lips, he brushed his gently across mine once, then twice, before passionately breathing each other in. Reaching out, I felt my hand instinctively clench and knot in his linen shirt as I pulled him closer. Magically connecting body, mind, and soul, the warmth of it radiated. Never had a man stirred such a sense of longing.

Shyly biting my lip as we parted, now cheek to cheek, I found his eyes fixated on the house behind us. He looked disheartened and weighed down, somehow burdened.

In an uplifting way, I wrapped my arms around his neck, hoping our embrace would distract him, if only for a minute. Nothing needed to be said as the moon greeted the world with its muted light. The feelings we shared spoke volumes. And just like that, all the negativity disappeared when he smiled.

To offer a cozier spot, Ryan asked, "Want to move to the sofa?"

I nodded happily.

Extending his hand, getting up from the table, he led the way, where we sat in the corner of the plush outdoor sectional. Almost completely enveloped by him, he lifted both my legs across the top of his. Fixing my dress to cover them respectfully, I rested my head on his shoulder. A sense of calm blanketed us.

As the flames inside the cylinders danced about, he whispered, "I love you, Eva Thompson."

Hearing those endearing words, unafraid, I said softly, "I love you too."

Sensing movement along my forehead, I assumed he reacted positively to my sentiment. When I peered upward, his eyes lovingly found mine, and that gentlemanly sweetness appeared out from under his unwavering, masculine exterior.

"I've never met anyone like you before," he said, gently kissing my forehead.

Fully immersed, my hopeful heart wanted to believe him and embrace every ounce of what was happening. Realistically, though, I knew I was not yet part of his real world - this void concealed behind a black curtain to which I was denied access.

The two of us sat listening to the wind gusting through the trees. Faintly, I could hear my grandmother's words. She used to say that when *you love someone, you must love and accept their past as much as you exist in their present.* Part of that for us remained absent, but my heart needed Ryan now. Regardless of the complications, I could never fully describe or explain the emotions developing. There was this bond - a burning desire to be with him. Whatever he was experiencing, I somehow felt it, too. It was like he'd always been there, except now, a physical body was attached to the person I'd seen in my dreams.

Not taking notice of the Chef standing beside us, he interrupted civilly. "Excuse me, Sir. Are we ready for dessert and coffee now?"

Ryan replied, "Yes, thank you. That would be great."

The Chef departed to prepare our final course with coffee freshly brewed while we took those last few moments to enjoy the peaceful twilight. When he returned, we broke our embrace to appreciatively listen to the culinary description of what he had created.

Picking up the delicate bowls to enjoy the berry and custard treat, sipping our coffees, Ryan asked, "So... What shall we talk about that doesn't involve home, family, and our past lives? Guess that only leaves the future."

"The future, huh?" Deep in thought, I looked to the sky, needing one answer above all others. "Can I ask you something?"

"Sure."

"Where do you think you will go after leaving Hamilton Island?"

"That's a tough one." Taking a second, Ryan said, "Because I know the weather is about to become blistering hot here in the coming months, I think I might change it up and say Iceland will be next on the list."

Confused, my face scrunched unexpectedly. "Iceland? Why?"

"Figured by the time I leave Australia, I'll have had enough of the hot weather for a while and might like something a bit cooler."

"That is certainly cooler."

"You know, Iceland is incredible. The mountain ranges and glaciers are amazing. Ideal for hiking. They have the Blue Lagoon there, which I've always wanted to experience. It's a geothermal lake. They also have countless waterfalls and natural wonders." Disappointed that he wanted to venture farther away from me after our trip ended, he asked, "How about you?"

Understanding wholeheartedly that another vacation would be miles away after this, I said, "Sadly, nowhere, I'm afraid. When I return to New York, I'll need to continue my job in LA, and depending on how things develop with the museum project, I probably won't experience another vacation for quite a while. If I do, it will have to be a short getaway, maybe four days if I'm lucky."

Troubled by my reply, I noticed his mind beginning to reel again, selfishly taking him away. While the flames swirled about and flickered, we hit another lull in the conversation. Amidst the silence, I saw the Chef close the kitchen's glass walls along their tracks before leaving for the night. Giving us privacy, I thought about what had happened between us the past few days. That's when I decided just to come out with it.

"Ryan, what happened beyond your family's passing that brought you to Hamilton Island? I know whatever you are running from is never far from your mind. It's a part of your every thought, and you can't help but be distracted by it. I know you want to tell me more. I can feel it. What you are hiding can't be that bad, whatever it is…."

He looked straight ahead. In a rather solemn tone, he confessed, "I don't want to go to Iceland. The life I chose dictates that I keep moving."

About to share more of his troubling past and the secret he has been harboring, I sat up and turned to him, prompting, "But why? Why do you need to do that?"

"Because it's not safe," he solidified sternly before leaning forward and resting both elbows on his knees. Hands tightly bound together in a white knuckle grip, he seemed incredibly torn. "I'm sorry, Eva. I can't elaborate…"

Witnessing his heightened affliction, not wanting him to hate me for bringing up the subject, I stood and asked for his hand as the song, *Hands to Heaven, by Breathe,* played in the background. Knowing it would lighten the mood, I asked, "Will you dance with me?"

Hesitant, his eyes moved upward, almost mournful. Standing to oblige, he got up and slowly approached. Holding my hand flat against his chest, his other arm around my waist, I could feel his heart beating rapidly. Little did he know, mine was, too. Clinging to him, our bodies dangerously close, we rhythmically swayed to the music, cheek to cheek. Now, all alone, seemingly leaving the world behind, he leaned back slightly and kissed my forehead. Cloaked by a ceiling of stars twinkling above, he kissed me softly. Immersed in each other, everything changed. I knew I loved this man despite knowing him for only a short time. And just like that, I was his.

Parting from his affections, his forehead pressed against mine, he quietly asked, "Can you stay?"

Afraid our relationship wouldn't go beyond the Whitsundays, I said, "I will stay, but only so that you're not alone."

Ryan interrupted. "Eva, I would never pressure you to do anything you don't want to. I'm not that guy. I hope you believe that. Our connection, above all, has been a gift. I would never do anything to jeopardize what we found."

His words resonated as we walked around, hand in hand, extinguishing flames before securing the remaining glass walls of the house.

Dimming the lights, he set the security alarm before we went to the media room to stretch out on the deep sectional sofa. With his head on the pillow near the one end, I decided to sit and cuddle up alongside him.

He lifted his arm to welcome me. A bit surprised, he asked, "Are you sure?"

"Yes. It's fine," I whispered, trying not to second-guess myself.

"As long as you are comfortable," he said genuinely.

I nodded.

"Goodnight, Eva."

"Goodnight. Sweet dreams," I answered whimsically.

With a subtle chuckle, he replied, "Yes. You too."

Not saying another word, I felt his arm get heavy. It wasn't long before Ryan drifted off. Trying to do the same, I realized he wasn't the guy I painted him out to be when we first met. He was different, and it was hard to overlook the intense feelings that had developed in just a few short days. Closing my eyes that night, for the first time in a while, I could finally say, without a doubt, that I was where I needed to be.

| 25 |

A Break in Time

Nervous to wake with the dimness of dawn spreading across the room, careful not to move a muscle, I wondered if he was still sleeping. Not wanting to disturb him, I stayed in the same position a while longer. Listening to him breathing, our conversation from the night before came to mind. Inevitably, drifting back to my relationship with Scott and striking up a comparison, I knew my feelings for Ryan were much stronger. There was this comfort he seemed to exude - this familiarity. A simple look from him would melt my heart and give me this irresistible flutter, something that had almost become addictive. His protective instinct was a rare trait not found in men these days. Often, with most being too relaxed, self-involved, and oblivious to danger, a woman would be hard-pressed to find one willing to risk everything, including his own life, to save the woman he loves. Captivated by the knight in shining armor featured in my grandmother's treasured fairy tale stories told to me long ago, I always dreamed of finding a man like that. As I got older, the whole theory seemed foolish and unrealistic. I believed he didn't exist - until now. This valiant human being - courageous yet kind and loving. A balance that made up the perfect man. The one meant for me.

How on earth will I ever be able to let him go? I thought. That's when I felt a sinking feeling, making me lightly shake my head, trying to force the negativity out.

Abruptly lifting his arm, assuming I'd startled him, I peered over my shoulder and quietly said, "Good morning."

"Morning," he replied, slowly finding my eyes. "Did you sleep well? Probably not the best sleep, I'm sure."

"No, it was good. Are you doing okay?"

"Suppose so. Thank you for staying," he said, kissing my cheek before resting his head on the pillow again.

"What time is it?" I asked, seeing the sun now shining brightly outside.

He looked at his watch. "It's almost ten o'clock."

That jogged my memory. "No, really?"

"Yeah, why?"

"I'm pretty sure I have a massage appointment at the spa in an hour."

Eyebrows raised, he glanced at me, waiting for direction.

I hoped he'd understand and not take offense when I asked, "Can you drive me to Tree Hill? I can go to the appointment and see you right afterward. I'm so sorry. It's too late to cancel."

Reluctant to give up my company for a few hours, Ryan agreed. "Sure, no problem. But promise you'll come back here right afterward."

"Absolutely," I smiled, rolling over. "Promise."

Cuddling, not wanting to let go, he reluctantly said, "Okay."

Running out the front door and locking up, we jumped into his cart and sped quickly around the corners and up the steep roadway toward One Tree Hill.

With my buggy now one of five parked there, Ryan stopped and said with a hint of seriousness, "Please hurry back."

"I will." Mesmerized by the look in his eyes, he kissed me goodbye.

While descending the long hill to the gates of my resort, I looked in the rearview mirror and noticed his sights on me as I drove away. Disappearing around the corner, I assumed he would then venture home.

Close to my cottage, maneuvering the winding paths, I couldn't believe the appointment had almost slipped my mind. Parking beside my pavilion, I plugged in the cart to allow it to recharge. Upon opening the door, there sitting on the nightstand was a beautiful floral bouquet with a note attached that read,

Dearest Eva,

Despite spending the entire day together, I still miss you the second you leave.

Thank you for a memorable evening.

Love Ryan

Tickled pink, having no choice but to smile brightly, I realized he'd arranged the flower delivery before our dinner. I felt so appreciated. He meant for me to find the gift last night when I returned home from his place, and the fact that I stayed was indeed unplanned based on the card. It took every ounce of my being to try and decipher where things would end up after our Australian vacation ended. Having changed into comfortable workout wear, I stopped for a second and stood silent, believing everything happens for a reason. People just don't cross our paths by accident, I thought. With everything that had taken place, I desperately hoped at this point that fate had brought Ryan to me. Maybe that was a romantic notion, resembling my grandparents' relationship, but still, a part of me wanted to see if this would grow into something long-lasting, given our feelings. It made my heart hopeful for the future, whether it was reckless or not. There was something about him. It was like he'd always been in my life.

Confident with all of that finalized, I closed my cottage door and jogged over to the Spa Pavilion, arriving seconds before my scheduled appointment. Dreadfully failing to relax during the session, finding it hard to turn off my thoughts, guilt soon took over.

"What if he was hurt by my abrupt departure this morning?" I muttered.

| 26 |

The Note

When I returned to my pavilion, two hours had passed. Anxious to get back to Melaleuca Drive, I opened the door and stumbled upon an envelope lying on the floor. Picking it up and noticing my name on the front, I slid the card out and read what it had to say.

Eva,

I apologize, but I will not be able to spend the rest of the day with you.

I've had some business come up that needs my full attention.

I'll see you soon.

Ryan

Confused, slowly setting the note on the side table beside his flowers, I questioned, "How can he tell me to hurry back, then suddenly change everything? Wouldn't he have known this beforehand? It's only been a couple of hours." Thinking about it a bit further, I said outwardly, "Wait. He went on a sabbatical from his job before arriving here. What business is he referring to? Was this his way of blowing me off?"

I took a second to sit down and analyze what was happening. The final few minutes of our time together came to mind.

"Why did he watch me drive away?" Bombarded by countless theories, our conversation from the night before stood front and center as I recalled a comment he made. "…because it's not safe," I said. "Because it's not safe?" I repeated a second time.

In a moment of clarity, trying to decipher the vague note a bit more, I thought maybe his past was catching up to him, and he needed to distance me from whatever 'business' he needed to handle. He'd also signed it with just his name, omitting the Dearest and Love part like the previous card had, which got me thinking it wasn't from him.

Sure of what I needed to do, I left my pavilion and drove toward his house with a sense of urgency, hoping to find him there. Cautiously rounding the corner at the bottom of his street, I counted a few more people hanging around the other estate homes along Melaleuca Drive. It looked as though something had happened since people were standing around in groups, talking and pointing. While moving closer, it wasn't hard to see that Ryan's house had oddly changed in appearance. Every door and window was encased in some sort of retractable metal shielding. Uneasy with the people watching me drive by, not stopping, I quickly turned around in the cul-de-sac, trying to act casual, like a tourist taking a leisurely drive.

"What's going on?" I asked myself on the way back to Qualia. "Is he gone? Were the flowers meant as a goodbye gift? Is that why he had that look on his face when I left him this morning? That would explain his behavior in town yesterday and his sadness last night."

Safe inside the confines of the resort, I walked into my cottage, hoping to find a message from him, but sadly, there was nothing. Crawling onto my bed, desperately grabbing hold of a pillow, my eyes filled with tears, fearing something had happened. Would I ever see him again? Was he in danger? Who sent the second note?

| 27 |

Leaving My Life

Time passed by ever so slowly. I tried to stay positive and held out hope that he might show up. In need of something to calm my nerves, I ordered a pot of herbal tea and toast and opened the patio door to let the breeze waft through.

Strangely, the doorbell rang within five minutes, which immediately made me think he had returned. After peeking through the hole in the door, I was disappointed to see the concierge waiting for me and not Ryan standing there. While unlocking the door, I wondered how they could deliver my order so fast. Graciously greeting the woman as she smiled, suddenly, out of nowhere, two male figures barged in on either side of her. Forcefully grabbing my arms, they pulled me into the middle of the room, slamming the door behind them.

Scared beyond belief, I bravely shouted, "What are you doing? Get out of here!!"

The men let go and started scouring my closet.

About to scream, the woman launched at me. Roughly swinging my body around, holding one of my arms tightly behind my back, she stood there and covered my mouth with the other hand to stop me.

Sternly, she said, "Miss! I need you to listen very carefully."

Given no choice but to adhere to their demands, seeing the men with guns, I knew they were robbing me.

The woman unexpectedly released her hand from my mouth. Angered that they were gathering my things from the closet, stuffing clothes into a carry-on bag, the woman revealed, "We are getting you out of here. Your safety has been compromised."

Stunned by what she said, it seemed my mind froze, making me unable to move a muscle. Did I hear her correctly?

Aware that I was in shock, the woman said urgently, "Miss, you need to listen to me. We must leave now."

"Who are you? What do you want?" I questioned with a hint of courage.

Lightly taking hold of one arm, she ignored everything I said and stayed on task. "Leave your passport in the safe. Power off your cell phone and gather a few personal items to make it look like you went on an excursion."

Not even thinking, I robotically did what she said, not fully knowing why. Within seconds, we were walking out the door. That is when I took note of everything I was leaving behind.

"Wait... I can't abandon the rest of my things."

"Miss, I am sorry, but you don't have a choice."

Panic-stricken, skimming the room with my wallet and phone in hand, the woman did a final sweep and grabbed a baseball cap and the Kaminski from the table.

Tucking my backpack under her arm at the last minute, she instructed, "Eva, follow me."

Eerily hearing my name made me realize this was real. Confirming the coast was clear, the two men led the way and took my small carry-on bag with them. Guided through the trees, still holding on, she ran alongside me through the densely wooded path to the resort's seaplane docks at the shore, two tiers down from my cottage. Tethered below was a boat waiting. With its engine running, the two men ahead of us quickly boarded before scanning the hillside and tossing my bag on the floor of the vessel in the process.

Dread engulfed my body when one of the men untied the boat and stayed to hold it steady.

The second my feet hit the edge of the platform, I stopped in my tracks. What am I doing? I thought. "No! Wait? I'm not... No!" Refusing, raising my hands, and resting them atop my head, I felt the urge to run.

The woman looked my way in desperation. "Eva, we are taking you to Ryan," she revealed. "He asked us to extract you, but we must go now. There's no time."

Mechanically responding to her words, my apprehension softened upon hearing his name. Naïvely trusting what she said, I stumbled across the dock, inching toward the forty-foot boat as my legs weakened. Helped aboard by the driver, kindly offering me a hand, the woman sat by my side to provide support, knowing the transition I was about to make.

Was this a glimpse of the world that usually remained hidden from sight?

Seeing the man forcefully shift the throttle forward, the engine roared as the boat sped across the water while the two men surveyed the coastline.

Suddenly, one reported in a low tone, "Targets in view."

Witnessing their defensive actions aimed at a few figures invading the shore, the woman in charge shouted, "Eva, get down!"

Shoved to the floor, she shielded me while pulling her gun and covering my head. The other men followed suit in the blink of an eye.

Shaking beyond words, I found it hard to breathe. Amidst it all, the boat accelerated to lightning speed.

In minutes, leaning close to my ear, she affirmed, "We're okay. You can get up now. We are far enough away." Hesitating before I did so, my eyes still closed tightly, her face brightened before she said, "My name is Kayla."

Incapable of offering a gracious hello, still trembling, the boat maneuvered into open water. I watched the island that I unknowingly attached so much security to move farther and farther away in the distance. Frightened beyond belief, there was no turning back now.

Fearful of where they were taking me, I saw Kayla grab a white object under her collar. Placing it in her ear, she said, "We have her."

Hoping and praying I'd be safe, absolute fear instantly muddled my thoughts while trying to decipher what had happened. Speeding through the channels around the other islands, I could see we were not far from the Queensland coast.

My head soon got heavy, and my stomach queasy. Feeling somewhat seasick, I rested my head along the side of the boat. Kayla covered me with a blanket while her eyes systematically scanned the horizon.

Oblivious to how much time had passed, I saw the driver turn around and point over the bow. Looking ahead to see what he was referring to, I noticed a rather large boat positioned off a long peninsula, with the sun descending behind it.

We are going west, I thought, trying to remain coherent.

Reducing our speed to adhere to the roughness of the waves, we carefully pulled alongside the stern of a massive yacht named the De Lisle II. Kayla threw a rope to the guys, seemingly awaiting us, just as the driver cut the engine. Maneuvering closer to secure the vessel, I saw some people move down the stairs from the main deck. One of them was wearing a baseball cap and sunglasses. Terror set in. What would happen to me now?

Docked, the man standing on the lower platform had three other men flanking either side. Overwhelmed with emotion, I stared at him. Flashing a reassuring smile, he removed his sunglasses.

"Ryan?" I mumbled as the engine shut down.

Immediately, his hands reached out for me. With assistance, I grabbed hold and jumped straight into his waiting arms. Clinging tightly, I still couldn't believe it was him.

"Don't worry, I got you," he whispered. "Sorry, it took me so long." Cradling my face in his hands, checking to see if I was hurt, he hugged me again. "Are you alright?"

Thoroughly shaken, I whispered, "Yes, I'm fine," before he guided us to the upper deck.

Safe and sound, I recognized the overly muscular man standing guard in the corner. It was the guy who followed Ryan into the shop the other day. I assumed he was security personnel since he had a gun holstered in a shoulder strap.

Kayla tossed one of the men my baseball hat, then spoke to another blonde woman on deck, who seemed similar to my height and build. Dressed in black yoga pants and a tank top resembling mine, she had pulled her hair back into the same ponytail style. Slipping the hat on her head, she threaded her hair through the hole before jumping into the boat with the three men who brought me here. Before leaving, they removed my bags from the vessel. The big, burly guy got them on board and set each on the deck chair.

Securely wrapped in Ryan's arms, he glanced at me and said, "It's alright. They know what they're doing. Trust me…"

With my stomach in knots, his words angered me. Wait? Trust you, I thought. Strangers just forcefully kidnapped me, and he says – *trust me?* On the verge of a panic attack, my heart began racing, and my breathing labored. What do I do now? I'm in the middle of the ocean. There's nowhere to go.

Hearing the engine roar, I watched the craft take off across the water, returning in the same direction we had just traveled. Amidst all this, the big, muscular security guy gave something to Ryan a small box in passing.

Taking hold of my hand, he said, "Come with me. You're safe now."

Lead down a spiral staircase, with a blur of emotions, I followed him below deck. At the bottom, he opened the door to a beautifully decorated room. Timidly walking in, I sat at the end of the bed, positive I'd made a horrible mistake. The trembling returned. Buckling forward, I placed my hands over my face.

Ryan tried to comfort me, knowing full well what I had just experienced was extremely traumatic.

A torrent of feelings then erupted.

Holding me tightly, he said, "It's okay, Eva."

In a fit of rage, I said, "No! It's not! I thought something had happened to you. What the hell is going on? Why did you leave? More so, why did you bring me here? I think I deserve an explanation, don't you?"

Taken off guard, he stood and turned his back to me. "I had to leave as a precaution. They received Intel that was a cause for concern."

"Who's they?" I questioned meanly.

"I can't tell you that. I'm sorry. You have to trust me. I promise, when this blows over, I'll tell you everything."

"What about those men along the shore? They were obviously after us when these people kidnapped me. Why?" I questioned, hoping he would divulge that much.

"Yes, they've been watching us for a few days. That's why I needed to get you out of there. They've seen us together. Eva, I promise I'll do anything to protect you and keep you safe. I hope you know that." He walked over and rubbed my arms.

Abruptly pushing him away, I wasn't sure what to think.

He seemed shocked by my adverse reaction but knew I didn't fully understand.

At that point, a knock came on the door. Ryan opened it to find his security guard with my bags. Bringing them into the room and placing each in the walk-in closet, the man departed without saying a word.

Ryan moved toward the windows with his arms crossed in front of him, deep in thought.

"I'm sorry, I want to be alone for a while," I demanded.

Disappointed, he turned and silently nodded, understanding that I needed time to process everything. Before leaving without reservation, he placed a small box on the bed. The door closed behind him seconds later.

Now, by myself, I examined the room before my eyes focused on the tiny box he had placed beside me. Pulling the ribbon and lifting off the lid, I found a pair of diamond earrings sparkling inside. A note then fell to the floor. Bending down to pick it up, I unfolded it.

Dearest Eva,

I got you a little gift.

It's the first time I've bought something for someone in quite a while.

I hope you like them.

Love Ryan

Closing the box, I got up and placed the earrings on the side table. My mind began examining the events that got me to this point. Stomach feeling queasy, emotionally exhausted, and scared, I didn't know where we were going and what I'd gotten involved in. Curling up in bed, I gave in to all the stress. This brought me back to my greatest fears. I started reexamining all the things that initially came to mind when I first met Ryan, namely, him running drugs, having mafia connections, or something negative along those lines. I knew I'd made the worst mistake of my life. Disappointed by my naivety, a part of me questioned what I was to him now. An accomplice? A prisoner? A hostage? I felt tapped lying there, trying to gather my thoughts.

| 28 |

The Truth Surfaces

A short while later, with my eyes closed, the sound of the door opening and softly closing startled me. Alarmed, I quickly lifted my head off the pillow to find Ryan standing with a tray of tea and snacks.

After placing it on the round table, he asked, "How are you? I thought you might like something to eat."

Shaking my head, I did not know how to answer.

Walking over, he sat on the bed and leaned against the headboard before crossing his arms and stretching his legs out casually. "Please don't be angry with me," he pleaded. "I did what I had to do to keep us both safe. I know you don't understand why I can't explain things more, but please tell me you still have a little faith in me."

Not moving from my spot in bed, lying with my back to him, I offered absolutely nothing.

Ryan paused, understanding the only way to gain my trust was to divulge information about his past. That prompted him to blurt out nervously, "Okay, I know how stressful today's events were for you. How you were forced from your reality and thrown into this world - the rawness of it all. I know the feeling because I had to do this at one time myself."

Stunned by what he just said, believing he would convey more, I rolled over halfway, ready to pay closer attention.

"I had to leave my family and friends behind five months ago. Eva, my family is not dead, but they think I am...." Pausing a second, he took a deep breath before confiding in me. "I had to lie to them, and you, for that matter, because it's the story assigned to me. I've technically had to end my life to save it. That's the reason for all the secrecy. These people on the boat are here to keep me alive. When I arrived on Hamilton Island, I never intended to meet someone, wrap them up in this mess, and subject them to this existence. I also never really rehearsed or thought much about what I would tell someone if they asked about the details of my life. During our conversations, I opted to stay quiet or run around the subject, knowing whatever I said wouldn't be true. I was struggling with having to lie to you about my past. For that, I apologize, but I'm not sorry we met. You are the very first woman who genuinely accepted me for me, someone who lovingly cared. I tried to let you go and carry on with your life uninterrupted, but when my contacts said you were in danger, I had to bring you here. Eva, I still can't tell you everything, and I am running a huge risk even sharing this much, but I trust you. Now, I need you to trust me, too."

Vaguely understanding how complicated his life was, thankful to hear a small part of his real-life story, I put my arms out to him.

Without hesitation, he quickly wrapped me securely in his. "I promise I will never let anyone hurt you."

As I cried with a mix of emotions, he kissed my forehead. While lying there in silence, intent on providing as much comfort as he could, we eventually fell asleep without saying another word.

| 29 |

Off The Grid

20°15'00" S / 148°44'44" E
20°05'23" S / 148°51'25" E

Rolling over in bed, I found myself alone. It took me a minute to get my bearings. In great detail, I remembered what transpired yesterday. All of it felt like the makings of a nightmare, but sadly, I knew otherwise. Unsure where Ryan had gone, I was too scared to search for him.

Somewhat awake, I timidly walked into the ensuite and found everything I needed. Uncertain what the day would hold, surveying the limited wardrobe available to me, I hung up a few things, strangely trying to create normalcy, hoping he would return at some point.

A subtle knock came to the door just after I'd secured my hair in a ponytail. Opening it an inch, I peeked into the hallway. Thankfully, it was Ryan. With his back to me at first, he turned around and offered a familiar tilt of the head and a warm half-smile, wondering whether I was in better spirits.

"Good morning. Can I come in?" he asked as I opened the door. "How are you doing today?"

"I'm fine - think so anyway." The shock still hadn't worn off.

"Thought you might like some breakfast?" Nodding my head, knowing I hadn't eaten much the past twenty-four hours, Ryan added, "Great, follow me."

Carefully climbing the stairs to the main deck, we approached a table set with white linens waving in the breeze. Waiting for us was a platter of fruit and freshly brewed coffee. On one side was a woman dressed in a casual uniform. Opposite her was the same big, burly security guy sporting black cargo shorts and a tight, athletic, short-sleeved t-shirt, accentuating his intimidating physique.

Holding onto Ryan's hand, he introduced them both.

"Eva, this is Jenn. She will help you with anything you need. The big guy there is Rob. You may or may not have seen him lurking about on Hamilton Island. He is part of my security detail."

The main salon doors slid open. The woman from yesterday exited.

"And, of course, you have already met Kayla."

Behind her was an older woman with stylish white hair, armed with a small platter of scrambled eggs, Belgian waffles, and slices of bacon and sausage.

"This is Diana, our onboard Chef."

The Chef's face lit up. "So nice to meet you," she said jovially. "We've heard nothing but good things since we left the docks. Mr. Davis hasn't stopped talking about his Eva."

He quickly lowered his head bashfully.

Gathering a smile, somewhat confused by their casualness, I sat in the chair Ryan had pulled out for me. Staring over the horizon while the ship moved slowly along, I tried to determine our current direction. About to place my napkin on my lap, a young gentleman walked by in a hurry.

"That's John. He is our Bosun. He helps the Captain run the ship and keeps it in order," Ryan introduced.

The guy acknowledged us with a raise of his hand.

"By the way, you may have seen more people when you arrived. The others on board can not be named, nor will they interact with us, so don't take offense."

"Okay," I acknowledged, not having noticed yesterday. "Where are we going? Can you share that with me?"

"Of course. We were anchored in Woodwark Bay overnight and are now en route to Hayman Island. It is situated three islands north of Hamilton, in the Whitsundays chain. We'll be making a quick stop there first before carrying on to Blue Pearl Bay, on the west side of Hayman."

A middle-aged, white-haired man with a full beard dressed in a sharp uniform introduced himself without skipping a beat. "Good morning, everyone. How is our special guest doing? From what I hear, you've already met the crew. My name is Captain White. I will be your guide on this Great Barrier Reef excursion."

"We are going there?" I questioned.

Ryan smiled. "The plan is to sleep in the middle of the Reef under the stars tomorrow night. If that's okay with you?"

Hearing this made me feel less anxious. Thankfully, it brought my alert level down a notch.

"We can snorkel the reefs or go on a submarine tour. Whatever you'd like?" he added.

Just then, another unfamiliar gentleman rounded the corner and stretched his hand across the table. "Hi, my name is Brad Fergus. I'm the deckhand."

I shook his hand. "Nice to meet you, Brad. I'm Eva."

"Yeah, heard a lot about ya. Welcome," he warmly replied in a strong Aussie accent.

Skeptical but feeling somewhat safe, I realized these strangers were the good guys.

About to eat breakfast, Ryan suddenly rested his hand on my leg under the table. Lightly placing mine on top, I did not grab hold fully. I could sense that it bothered him.

Having poured me a coffee and one for himself, he stared at his cup while blending the cream with the spoon. "This was the only way I could keep moving. I couldn't stay on the island any longer. There wasn't another option."

I assumed that was all the information he could divulge, so I nodded to confirm I understood.

We dished out some breakfast onto our plates.

In the process, Jenn approached and asked, "Would ya like to have a tour of the ship after your brekkie?"

"Yes, we should show you around. It would be best to familiarize yourself with the layout," Ryan stated quite concretely, taking a bite of bacon.

Tension mounted between us as the minutes passed. I noticed him glancing over from time to time. The air felt heavy.

Out of the blue, he unexpectedly questioned, "Eva, are we good? I mean, you seem quiet. Is everything alright?"

"I'm just disoriented and confused. I mean, who I thought you were isn't who you truly are, but I never entirely knew who you were, to begin with…." Agitated, silently repeating what I'd just said in my head, desperate to keep the facts straight, I asked, "So, your name isn't Ryan Davis?"

Careful about answering the question, Ryan looked down at his food before responding. "Umm, no… No, it's not. But it has to be now since that is who I've needed to become."

Not fully comprehending why I agreed to let this all slide, he soon placed his left arm behind me. Feeling his hand rubbing my back, trying to give reassurance, it seemed his touch always made me less fearful, but now, it had an adverse effect.

Almost finished our breakfast, Jenn brought up the tour once again. I figured it was important to know where I would be living for the next few days.

Ryan and I followed her as she took the lead. Stepping indoors, leaving the main deck, my attention drifted toward the beautiful design of the grand room. Adorned with richly colored mahogany paneled walls, beige tiled ceilings, and neutral plush area rugs, all of it created a luxe custom look. I loved the contrast between the upholstered ivory furniture sitting atop the dark hardwood floors in places.

Upon reaching the bottom floor, Jenn explained our sleeping arrangements. I found out Ryan's room was directly across the hall from mine.

"I hope your room is to your liking. If there is anything else you need from me, please do not hesitate to ask," she added.

Before following her up the small staircase, Ryan requested, "Eva? Can I talk to you alone for a minute?"

"Sure," I replied reluctantly.

Jenn disappeared upstairs.

Now alone, Ryan bridged the gap between us while standing in the middle of the hall. "So, are you sure you're okay? I feel as though you're scared of me now. Something's changed."

Breathing unevenly, very nervous, I answered, almost unable to look him in the eye. "Yes, I mean…You kidnapped me from Hamilton Island because it wasn't safe - because I was in danger. Now, we are on an excursion to the Great Barrier Reef?" Throwing my hands in the air, I added, "On top of that, everybody on board is acting so casual about all this. I don't know what to think."

"I realize, and I'm sorry. As long as we keep moving, we're good. They can't track us as easily."

"Who's they? Who can't track us?" I asked, staring at him with conviction.

Ryan turned away. "Eva, look, the more you know, the further you will get pulled in."

"Pulled into what?" I pried, hoping to get more information. "I'm already deep in - whatever this is!"

"Please, Eva…"

Losing my patience, I lashed out. "You know, you asked a moment ago if I was afraid of you. I am! I'm sorry. I can't help it. Part of me knows you're the same person, but this. I'm already recovering from a relationship filled with lies and deception. Honestly, I can't…"

Stopping mid-sentence, lost for words, resting my hand on my forehead in desperation, he sincerely looked into my eyes, now welling with tears. Upset to see me like this, he moved closer.

Standing mere inches away, wrapping me in his arms, he said, "I'm sorry."

Gently kissing my forehead, I could sense his endearing aura while his heart pumped anxiously.

Not sure if our closeness convinced me otherwise, he declared, placing my hand over his heart, "I'm still in here. It's still me, Ev. I haven't changed."

"Sadly, a kiss or embrace can't solve this problem…I wish it could."

Solemnly walking into my room, he followed and closed the door.

"What do I need to do? How can I fix this? I've told you all I can."

"No. You're keeping me in the dark, and I hate it. I have to be in New York in a little over two and a half weeks. What do I do now?"

"I can't answer that. We just need to keep moving."

"Then what?" I asked frantically. "You said you left your life behind. Tell me the truth! Am I still able to return to mine?"

Utterly silent, he looked down at the floor. "I don't know," he replied with great uncertainty.

Approaching me again, I put out my hands to create a buffer. My mind reeled while his last comment resonated. Immediately, I thought of my sister, my friends, my career, and the life I worked so hard to achieve. What if I couldn't go back?

About to explode, feeling enormously frustrated, Ryan kept his distance and waited for me to make a move.

Not knowing what more to say, looking up at him, finding his arms crossed in front of his chest, he noted strongly, "Eva, the day we met, I'll admit, I should have walked away, but I couldn't. I just…." he paused. Shaking his head, running his hand through his hair, he tried to gather his thoughts. "Please believe me when I say I never intended to bring you into this. Based on what's happened, I did what I had to, and I'm sorry. Right now, we can only take one day at a time. That is what I can offer. Ultimately, I hope you know I'm still the guy who couldn't help but smile at you on the plane and talk to you in the store that day. The guy who lovingly sat across from you at dinner and tried to deny his feelings." Shifting to face me, he added, "And I am still the man who told you, without an ounce of doubt in his mind, that I love you. No matter what happens, I vow to protect you at all costs."

"I know. I know you're that person. I do." Trembling like a leaf, utterly distraught, I fearfully confessed, "Should I be scared? Because I am."

Inching closer, with arms outstretched, I conceded and found comfort in them.

"As long as you are here with me, you should never be afraid. Don't worry. I will keep you safe. I swear."

Taking a deep breath, aware that this situation was now out of our control, I had no choice but to accept it.

"We still have time to figure this out before I fly home, right?" I asked, not wanting to fight.

Hesitant, he nodded, trying to conceal his uncertainty. Still wrapped in his arms, he kissed my forehead and silently held me.

Eyes affixed to mine, needing to lighten the air, he suggested, "So, shall we continue the tour?"

Unable to find humor in that, I disagreed. "No, I don't think that will be necessary."

Leaving the room, we established a temporary truce. Holding his hand, moving up the spiral staircase, now on the middle deck, the southern tip of Hook Island came into view.

Politely offering me a seat on the upholstered bench facing the shoreline, he and I watched the panoramic views slip by, boasting turquoise waters and lush green island foliage all wrapped amidst the bluest, cloudless sky. It was mesmerizing despite the level of panic creeping in as I analyzed everything.

Jenn came through the sliding salon doors and asked, "Is there anything I can get you?"

"What would you like, Eva?" Ryan asked.

"Just sparkling water would be great. Thank you."

"Make that two, then. Thanks, Jenn."

"Good. Two fizzy waters coming right up."

Soon to arrive at our destination, she returned with glasses of sparkling Badoit and lemon on the side.

Kayla walked up behind her and asked in a business-like manner, "So, Ryan. How are things going?"

Ryan turned to her and said, "Fine. How is it on your end?"

Optimistic, she responded, "So far, so good..."

| 30 |

Hayman Island

20°03'37" S / 148°52'53" E
20°02'49" S / 148°52'41" E

Shining brightly, the sun's rays cast a shimmer across the water. Its warmth was invigorating. While cruising northeast through open water, less than an hour from our planned destination, John, the deckhand, walked by on his way to the bow and pointed out a few dolphins trying to keep up with us. Carefully peering over the side to see our marine friends frolicking in the waves below, I saw the Whitsunday Islands move further in the distance. At the same time, Captain White stopped to check in on us.

"I suggest you both move to the top deck. We will be passing Langford-Bird Reef shortly. It is a popular place for tourists to anchor."

Taking his advice, we headed up the staircase to the top of the vessel. Amidst the intense gusts of wind, the polka-dotted backdrop of sailing yachts gracefully taking advantage of the crosswinds within the channel created such beautiful scenery. Opting to sit on the wraparound sofa to enjoy the one-hundred-and-eight-degree unobstructed view, Ryan kept his distance, uncertain where he stood in my eyes. Lifting his arm invitingly, boldly taking a chance, I could not deny him and carefully nuzzled beside him.

A multitude of vessels passed us along the journey. Met by warm greetings each time, a loud-sounding horn, a high-pitched ring of a bell, a wave of the hand, or a tip of the hat made me feel that everyone on the water was now a friend. Noticing the wind picking up and the sun beating down, John brought us a light blanket to continue embracing each other in total comfort.

Gliding toward the northern tip of Hook Island, we discussed the very different landscape of this island compared to the others. The coastline seemed noticeably riddled with massive boulders and towering evergreen trees growing there, somehow surviving in the more mountainous terrain with little soil. Just before that was an Inlet full of anchored sailboats enjoying the calm waters sheltered between both islands. It was reassuring to see so many vessels surrounding us - each with plans to sleep under the stars tonight. Guess we were included in that, too. Thinking about it further, I was a tad nervous about being on a boat in the middle of the ocean.

Curious to know whether he felt this way, I asked, "So, how often have you slept on a boat?"

"Lots of times," he smiled. "A few of my friends' families had boats. My parents couldn't afford one, so I'd always tag along with them when they'd cruise south to Baja."

Starting to open up more, I was happy to receive any information he would share.

About to pass Langford-Bird Reef, the sandy shoal had started breaching the surface with the receding tides. Nearing our destination, the resort windows reflected the sunshine on our approach to Hayman Island. The Captain slowed the yacht and listened to the deck crew relaying information on the visible jetties installed on either side of the dredged harbor entrance.

"We will be anchoring for the night on the west side of Hayman Island, but I have a surprise for you first. I've arranged some shopping at The One & Only Resort Boutique this afternoon. You'll need some clothes to wear. I assume your wardrobe is pretty limited right now. Jenn told me they have stylish brand names. Upon returning to the boat, we will continue to Blue Pearl."

Not knowing what to say, I was sure the resort shop would be expensive. How could I pay for such luxury items, especially when I never splurged on clothes like that, even when living in New York or Beverly Hills?

"We don't have to go shopping, you know. My wardrobe is sparse, but I have enough to get by until I go back to Qualia. As nice as it would be to have that experience, this trip is already costing me a lot of money, so I must be mindful of my spending, or I'll be working for years to pay for it."

Despite presenting my case in an overly honest way, Ryan leaned in and whispered, "We can't use anything other than cash. No credit or debit cards. Nothing traceable, so consider this my treat."

Maneuvering to read the expression on his face, I paused. "Oh...." I felt uneasy. "I can't let you buy me clothes. You need to save your money too, although this yacht, I must say, was probably not a sensible way to do that."

Amused, he stopped and flashed an overly assured smile, something quite uncharacteristic of him thus far. "Please do not worry about me. I'm well taken care of."

Wondering what he meant by that, I figured it was another clue to his puzzling past. Did it imply he's wealthy? Where was he getting all this money? Should I ask or leave it alone? After having a silent mental debate, I decided to let it rest.

As the yacht approached the small resort marina, I questioned whether the channel was too narrow for such a large vessel. As the crew carefully navigated the ship through the small opening, we could see two other yachts about our size in the dredged harbor.

Deckhand, Brad began running this way and that way, as Bosun John assisted with their walkie radios, communicating from either side of the ship. Both men helped Captain White easily maneuver the yacht into the cove. Once inside, the loud sound of reverse engines roared so the Captain could sway us to the left. We marveled at how he and the crew could skillfully park the massive boat beside the berth at the end of the docks.

Like clockwork, the vessel got tied off with assistance from the marina attendants on the island, each working to ensure our arrival was safe and secure. The Captain emerged from the bridge to announce our arrival.

"Mr. Davis. Ms. Thompson. This is your first destination. We have exactly ninety minutes before the tides begin to change significantly. Also, protocol dictates that we do not stay long. Please be mindful of our scheduled departure in an hour. Enjoy your short visit to Hayman Island."

Ryan got up from the sofa. "Guess we should get going then," he said.

Descending the staircase to our cabins, I quickly selected one of the two dresses the men had stuffed in my bag before departing Qualia. Unable to take an iron to it first, I was happy to have the comfy navy maxi dress with the draped cut-out. But sadly, I found only one pair of suitable flats. Dangling the sandals from my fingers, I hoped they would suffice. About to leave, I spotted the small earring box resting on my side table. Wearing them, I wasn't sure if he would notice.

Ryan was already waiting in the hallway when I emerged from the room. He looked picture-perfect, wearing a white polo shirt and black shorts with designer slides in hand.

Immediately spotting the earrings, he commented, "They look great on you. Do you like them?"

Given the circumstances, I realized I hadn't thanked him. Turning around, I said apologetically, "I am so sorry. With all the confusion, I didn't even thank you. But yes, they are lovely." Needing to explain myself, I added, "I hope you know you don't need to buy me expensive gifts for me to love you."

Holding my hand, he smiled, "Yes, I realize. I wanted to."

I thought about how much they cost and where he got the money to pay for them. All of it gave me a bad feeling.

Walking up the stairs, he was close behind. I questioned whether or not I should leave. This would be my last chance. After that, we were heading to the Great Barrier Reef, and there would be no escape. I thought about catching a shuttle boat back to Hamilton Island. Once there, I'd pack the rest of my things and take the next flight home. Faced with a decision, contemplating what to do, seeing him glance at me with those loving eyes, somehow, my heart couldn't do it. I couldn't leave.

"Ready? Shall we go?" he asked excitedly, taking me by surprise while I was deep in thought.

Agreeing, I let him lead the way.

While departing to explore the resort, we met the concierge at the end of the dock with security guard Rob and the two unnamed agents shadowing us. The driver swiftly chauffeured our group to The One & Only in a tandem golf buggy. The crystal blue waters in the bay on the way to the main lobby were mesmerizing.

Greeted by a hostess with a welcoming smile, the woman offered directions to the resort shop close to the fitness center. Both agents stealthily went about their duties while Ryan, Rob, and I moved under the covered pathway, surveying our surroundings and watching a few people breeze by.

Together, we walked into the airy, bright space designed in neutral tones. With my eyes drawn toward a wall of custom-built-ins showcasing skincare, bags, totes, and hats, I hung a right past a selection of designer dresses boasting brilliant colors and intricate beading along each neckline. Able to find a few casual pieces on the other side of the store, I noticed Ryan had pulled two dresses from that upscale display. Moving in my direction with them in hand, the store attendant asked if she could open a change room for us. I recognized that one was quite possibly a brilliantly colored Camilla Babylon and the other a silk coral-colored kaftan with tassels hanging along its edges. Both were hand-embroidered along their seams, making them more like art pieces than clothing.

Immediately agreeing with the attendant's offer, he requested, "Do you like these? Want to try them on?"

"Although they are beautiful, I don't think they fall in the category of casual resort wear. Shouldn't I focus on something simpler to get me through the next few days?"

"Yes, perhaps. But I know how much you like dresses," he presented quite observantly.

Knowing he was right, I followed the lady to the changing room assigned to me. Each opened up to an area with mirrors and three designer chairs in front.

Seated under a seashell chandelier, tasked to wait patiently, Ryan anticipated what each dress would look like on me.

About to walk into the cubicle, looking back at him, I subtly said, "I'll try them on, but it does not mean we are buying them."

Closing the linen drape, I quickly found the price tags on the dresses. My heart sank seeing the cost of the long one. Being a Camilla designer maxi, I expected it to be expensive. A little out of my element, I tried it on first, mainly because Ryan favored it. Painted in bold shades of royal blue, red, orange, and yellow with hints of white and black, it boasted a V-shaped beaded neckline to complement the intense colors. I thought it resembled flames and sky – maybe even lava and storm clouds. Sliding open the curtain, his head quickly popped up when he saw me standing there.

"Wow! Beautiful. Do you like it?" he said expressively.

"Yes...but...." Grabbing the price tag, I shook my head and bluntly mouthed the word, NO, with my eyebrows shockingly raised to make my point. "We need to focus on less formal choices."

With his index finger moving back and forth in retaliation, he said, "Ah, yes. You have to have this dress." Walking over to me, he whispered, "Remember...my treat," before adding, "How about the other one, then?"

Returning to the room and closing the curtain, I changed into the kaftan. Before showing it to him, I looked at myself in the mirror. It fit perfectly. Showing him moments later, I got the same positive reaction.

Even though I loved the long dress, the kaftan didn't cost as much and was more practical right now, so I compromised and told him, "This one, yes – the other one – sadly, no."

"How are we doing here?" the attendant asked us on the way by.

Ryan spoke up and said, "We'll take everything."

Completely blindsided, I looked at him in disbelief.

Seeing my reaction, he chuckled slightly. "Why are you so worried? It's fine."

Concerned by his actions, opting just to get changed, I tried to decide how I would stop this purchase from happening.

Meeting up in the middle of the store, the woman took both dresses from me. He was already paying for them and the casual wear I'd placed on the second chair. It was too late. The attendant was neatly packing each dress into a garment bag. Hanging them up, she folded the rest of the clothing in tissue paper and placed the piles in a complimentary logoed tote.

Before leaving, I also grabbed a swimsuit, flip-flops, and a cover-up at the last minute, and both of us found a pair of water shoes just in case we needed them on our travels.

Joyfully handing us our purchases, she noted, "You are one lucky lady. Your husband has great taste."

Not having time to respond to her, Ryan whisked me out toward the front of the store. On the way out, he turned and spotted a Hindmarch Iman straw bag with black piping and a side tassel prominently displayed on one of the upper shelves. Examining the quality of its leather trim and braided handles, he insisted I have one to remember our visit here, since it came with a logoed Hayman Island silk scarf attached.

Sternly shaking my head, not wanting to create a scene, I looked at Ryan and quietly said, "No, definitely not." Despite him still eyeing up the bag, I calmly repeated, "I am technically compromising with these dresses. I don't need anything more."

While perusing the jewelry displayed in the brightly lit cases nearby, believing he'd gotten the point, I turned and noticed he'd disappeared. Nervously walking around the store, I found him speaking to the same woman at the cash, reaching for another large shopping bag with a large gift box inside.

"What did he do?" I mumbled.

Coming up behind him, he felt my hand on his back. "What did you buy?"

"Oh, nothing… I'll show you later. We need to keep going."

Rob stuck very close to us on the way back to the lobby while the two agents appeared out of nowhere and followed. At the last minute, we took a short detour around the pool and beachfront area. The view was spectacular - turquoise water, the bluest of skies, and cliffs bursting with lush shades of green.

Reminded of our time constraint, we returned to find our driver waiting in the breezeway. Once seated in the cart, he quickly whisked us back to the marina with shopping bags in hand.

Climbing the ramp beside the yacht, Captain White met us, happy to see we were on time.

Taking our packages to our rooms below, I wanted to freshen up and change into something casual. About to slip into the new swimsuit I'd bought, I heard a knock at the door.

"Come in," I said on the way out of the bathroom, still in my navy dress.

"Is it okay?" he asked while peeking inside.

"Sure. It's fine."

Ready to thank him for the shopping experience, I noticed he had something in hand. Presented with the luxe package, I sat at the end of the bed.

"As I said earlier, I wanted you to have this as a memento of our trip."

Of course, having a pretty good idea of what was inside the black box with white trim, I untied the ebony ribbon and lifted the lid. Enclosed in a striped, logoed, drawstring fabric bag was the Hindmarch tote. Captivated by how beautiful it was, I still couldn't believe he had bought it for me.

"Oh, Ryan... I love it, but this was so expensive," I expressed guiltily. "Thank you."

"I know what you are going to say."

"Like I said earlier about the earrings, I don't need expensive gifts to have feelings for you. I had those feelings without all of this."

"I know. All the more reason to spoil you - it's appreciated."

"More than you know."

Reaching out to hug him tightly, he soaked up every minute.

"You go ahead and get changed. I'll wait in the hall. Hopefully, we won't miss our departure from the marina."

"Don't worry. I'll be fast," I said.

"Take your time."

Minutes later, we ambled up the spiral staircase to experience the last few moments before hitting the open water. Captain White precisely guided the yacht through the channel like threading a needle. Happily returning to the depths of the Coral Sea, the engines roared while making a wide right turn, veering northwest toward Blue Pearl Bay.

By this time, the sun was beginning its descent in the clear blue sky, providing much-welcomed warmth. It wasn't long before we reached our anchorage destination close to a few boats with the same idea - all perfectly spaced, allowing each to swing freely in the currents. The ship maneuvered above the edge of an ominous drop-off. Hearing the clanking of chains when the anchor plunged into the water, the crew communicated call signals back and forth to secure the boat safely in place.

Rob stayed alert and scanned our surroundings, closely monitoring the other vessels nearby.

"Well, we are here, Blue Pearl Bay - this is where we will be staying tonight," Ryan divulged, sitting beside me on the sofa near the stern.

Moving to the upper deck, with a bird's eye view of Hayman Island's steep western shore and a rocky cliff separating two secluded beaches, the water around us was so clear. We spent the next half hour crisscrossing the ship's perimeter, peering over the railing to scan the reefs below, spotting fish of varied sizes against the sandy floor. The drop-off was a mass of black water. Nothing could be seen swimming in its depths.

Brad suggested we take the paddleboards and explore the rocky, coral-laden Blue Pearl Beach. Doing just that, the time spent with Ryan was like he had described - effortless - a feeling I never wanted to be deprived of.

The time passed quickly. Returning to the yacht, desperate for a shower after enduring the high humidity, we descended to the lower deck and parted ways outside our rooms to prepare for an early dinner.

Honoring the plan to meet in the hall within an hour, Ryan soon knocked on my door to escort me back to the main level. Wearing the coral kaftan, he smiled when he saw me.

"Beautiful."

That was all he needed to say.

That night, after soaking up our surroundings, having had a casual meal filled with general conversation, happily recounting our day together, he asked with a hint of excitement, "So, are you ready for our first unbelievable nighttime ocean experience?"

"What type of experience would that be? I hope we're not swimming," I inquired, staring at him, terrified to swim in black water.

"No swimming involved, but I promise it'll be something you'll never forget."

Pulling my chair out, he offered his hand and led me to the railing at the back of the boat. All the deck lights suddenly went out, leaving us in the dark. Only small lights were left on at the stern, the bow, and one on the mast. The eeriness made me a bit edgy. Without warning, about forty feet in diameter, a section of water was illuminated by exceptionally bright lights floating over the trench beside our anchorage point.

Brad and John moved around the water-level deck at the rear of the boat as Ryan suggested, "Let's go up to the top. We can probably see better from there.

Climbing the stairs to the highest point, we arrived at the stern and leaned on the railing to watch what was happening.

"Brad said it would take a few minutes, so we might have to be patient."

"Patient for what?" I questioned as he inched closer behind me.

Arms wrapped tightly around my waist, he attempted to shelter me from the gusts of wind swirling at our backs.

With eyes glued to the beams of light, I didn't know what to expect. Suddenly, out of the dark abyss, we spotted a huge shadow moving swiftly in line with the farthest light.

"What was that?" I whispered.

Shifting his body to see the reaction on my face, he replied, "Watch."

Instantly, I started counting the number of giant sea creatures gliding erratically through the depths. Putting on a choreographed performance for us, each curiously investigating the lights floating above the surface.

"Are they stingrays?" I questioned.

"Close. These are manta rays. Their average wingspan can be upwards of twenty-two feet. The light entices plankton, which happens to be one of their main food sources, so in the process, they put on an unbelievable show for us as they feast. Isn't it amazing?"

"This is incredible..." I added, fascinated by the graceful movements of about six rays of varied sizes. It was almost ghostly, tracking their movements in and out of the illuminated area. The odd shark inquisitively joined in on the action occasionally, dodging the rays as they frantically sped in every direction, gathering food. I had never experienced anything like this. It was just unforgettable.

Entertained for almost an hour, our underwater friends soon went on their way, leaving us in the dark when the spotlights shut off.

"The evening is not over yet," Ryan said, nuzzling his cheek against mine. "I have another surprise for you. Follow me."

Gently taking hold of my hand, with a small flashlight in the other, he led me to the front of the top deck, where a high-powered telescope stood. Just then, the mast light turned off, also leaving us immersed in the blackness of night. It made the stars in the sky pop and seem closer. Each brightly sparkling, we gazed upward at the beauty presented before us.

Spotting the first cluster of stars, he sent positioning coordinates wirelessly to the advanced-looking apparatus using an iPad application.

Peering through the eyepiece, he explained, "From what they tell me, most of these southern constellations can only be seen here in Australia. Also, a star in this region is closest to the sun. It's called Gacrux, a Red Giant." Focusing briefly, he said, "Ah, there it is. Take a look."

Ryan moved back to let me see what Gacrux looked like. That's when I saw the bright reddish ball glowing, clearly visible against the darkness of space.

"Gacrux is the northern tip of the Southern Cross. If you look from left to right, you will see two more bright stars on either side and another below, which is Acrux. If you draw a horizontal and vertical line to each, they make a perfect cross in the sky," he added while expanding my view to include each star, making it easy to see what he meant.

Skillfully repositioning the telescope, he said, "The middle of the Milky Way goes straight through here," offering me another look, he revealed the mass collection of stars shimmering in the night.

Appreciating the brilliance of Mars, Saturn, Antares, and Hadar, among many others, I heard footsteps around us. Turning to see who was there, I was surprised by the romantic scene I encountered after the crew disappeared. Lantern candlelight now surrounded the entire deck as music filled the air.

Captivating me with his smile, tilting his head, Ryan put down the iPad on the table and reached out his hands. "Will you dance with me?"

Wholeheartedly joining him, the slow opening tempo of the melody revealed a *Lady A* song that was so very fitting. It seemed we always ended our evenings innocently with a kiss goodnight.

In perfect unison, we swayed from side to side, with the moon lofting high in the sky and the winds swirling around us. Noticeably allowing his guard down, the music carried us away. Not sure who selected the song; I assumed it was Jenn since we saw her sneak a peek from the lower level. Clutching her heart, she seemed to melt at the scene unfolding before her. Leaving us alone, entirely taken by the stars above and the ocean below, immersed in the breeze and each other, I cherished every minute.

Overwhelmed by many thoughts and feelings, forgetting our current circumstances, I wrapped my arms around Ryan's neck as he pulled me in tight. With bodies tight together, I peered upward into his dark brown eyes. Kissing me below a billion galaxies, it felt as though I was floating. It was an unforgettable moment that surpassed all others. I could never fully describe this unparalleled affection we shared. Where did this seemingly perfect man come from? No matter how hard I tried to ignore it, this strong connection could never be lost or broken.

When the song ended, we felt a few drops of rain.

"Maybe we should go inside now," he said softly.

I agreed as my hair tossed about with the wind.

Packing the stargazing equipment in its molded foam casing and securing it safely inside the waterproof bin, he turned to me and offered his hand.

About to walk down to our cabins, I pulled him back. Turning to look my way, concerned that something was wrong, I nervously asked, "Would you please stay with me tonight? Just in case something happens. I don't want to be alone."

With eyes glued to mine, he replied, "If you'd like," adding reassuringly, "Don't worry. Nothing is going to happen. I promise."

Carefully descending to the lower decks in the dark, following the faint staircase lights, step by step, John passed us by to pack away the equipment box we had left behind.

Reaching the lower level, standing outside our doors, exhaustion set in. Not saying much, he confidently hugged me.

"I'll see you shortly."

"Okay," I acknowledged with a nod before opening the door to my room and closing it behind me. Leaning my back against it, anxiety surfaced, making me stand there for a second. What was I doing? Again, forcing myself to block out the negative, I walked into the bathroom to get ready for bed. Slipping on a silky nightgown and brushing my hair, I secured it in a messy bun.

Within a few minutes, I heard a knock at the door. Slowly opening it an inch, Ryan quietly asked, "Is it okay to come in?"

"Yes," I replied from my spot, already under the covers.

Walking to the other side of the bed, joining me in the middle, he lay on his back with one hand placed behind his head and the other securely around me under the fluffy duvet. Respectfully kissing my cheek, we fell asleep in silence, like we had two evenings before at his house.

That night, encircled in his arms, my heart hoped and prayed our lives could resemble some semblance of normal. But was that just a fantasy? The makings of a childish fairy tale – a fictitious happily ever after? Over the next hour, I found myself recapping all the things he had told me so far.

His family believed he had died.

He needed to end his life to save it.

Continuously moving, so he'd be harder to track.

His life is in danger.

Unable to tell the truth about his past because his past no longer existed.

Putting all the pieces together, I knew he was part of a witness protection scenario, and the people aboard the boat were there to keep him alive at all costs. But who was he running from? If the crew had gone to these great lengths to keep him safe, the person hunting him down must be a monster – a killer. Hugging Ryan tighter, I was terrified as the truth sank in.

| 31 |

The Great Barrier Reef

20°02'39" S / 148°52'41" E
19°44'15" S / 149°08'23" E
19°44'44" S / 149°10'57" E

I woke to find Ryan fast asleep with his legs entangled in mine. Not hearing a sound from the upper decks, I focused on a beam of light marking the opposite wall. Hypnotized by its rhythm, I watched it brighten and dim while the sun peeked in and out from behind the clouds. Counting how many days I'd been in Australia, each seemingly attached to an unparalleled experience shared with a man I barely knew, I realized we'd only been together a week. That is when this irresponsible feeling taunted me.

It is not in your nature to be so spontaneous and reckless, I thought, squinting my eyes, trying to rid myself of the relentless self-doubt.

Possibly sensing my internal debate, Ryan's head lifted off the pillow to bid me good morning. When I looked back at him, for whatever reason, all the worry magically melted away.

"How did you sleep?" he asked, pulling his pillow up a little more to support his head.

"Pretty well. You?"

"Best sleep ever," he replied, stretching a bit.

"So, what's on the agenda for today?" I quietly questioned.

"Ah, yes, let me see if I can remember… After our quote-unquote brekkie, we will travel to the island's northern peak before heading to the Great Barrier Reef. We will probably arrive there sometime late this morning and will anchor. The guys will have the Brig ready for us to use. It's a smaller tender boat stored onboard. We'll be situated close to an enormous tourist barge alongside Hardy Reef. They have a lot of activities, from what I understand. How do you feel about snorkeling in the middle of the ocean? You know, the odd eel might be hiding in the rocks."

Frowning at his comment, expecting my adverse reaction, I nudged him playfully, making him defend himself against my incoming pillow.

"Hey! Hey!" he shouted comically. "No need for violence."

"You've spent your whole life around the ocean, while I've been the city kid, spending most of my time at the water's edge, not necessarily in it. I'm just afraid." Pausing, I repeated my confession. "I'm just afraid. There, I said it. When I got stung by that jellyfish, it was excruciating. I've never forgotten the pain of it. My grandparents panicked while driving thirty minutes to the hospital, where I got stabbed with needles to manage it all."

Chuckling at my dramatic performance, he gazed into my eyes. Motionless, he genuinely replied, "Eva, as long as you are with me, you never have to worry. I swear nothing will ever hurt you. I promise."

Inches apart, sending him mixed signals, he raised himself off the pillow and hovered over me, sights locked to mine. Desperate to read my thoughts, he pulled me close, hoping his instincts were right. Smothered with gentle kisses, taking his time, caught up in the moment, I placed my hand against his chest and subtly pushed against him. His eyes immediately opened, and he flashed a confused look.

Realizing I was the problem, I built the courage to share another piece of my past.

"I'm sorry. Please don't think this has anything to do with you," I whispered. "I can't stop these feelings of…" Pausing, I divulged, "Umm….there is something I need to explain."

Ryan leaned back to give me his full attention.

"The only man I've ever been with was Scott. I promised myself a long time ago to wait for that special person. Focusing on school and my career made that whole subject easily avoidable. I've often asked myself why he cheated on me. Contemplating many theories, especially on the way to Australia, I figured it was because I was inexperienced, unlike his old girlfriend, I'm sure."

Ryan's face changed to a more weighted look. "Eva, what Scott did was not a reflection on you. None of that was your fault. The bottom line is he wasn't faithful. That was his biggest mistake. Don't ever think that you were to blame. And in regards to, well, that…I'll be honest. I'm just happy to hold you whenever you'll allow me. Our relationship is so new. There's no need to rush things, and I'm okay with it."

His answer surprised me. Unable to look him in the eye, I said, "Thank you." Fidgeting with the edge of the duvet, feeling uncomfortable, I added, "It's been worrying me. You know, I also promised I wouldn't be that girl. Everyone sees the blonde hair and assumes I'm an easy target."

"I have never thought of you in that way. Beautiful, yes, but not an easy target. The second I spotted you on the plane, your eyes drew me in. There was just something special about you. When we saw each other at the store the next day, I felt compelled to make introductions. It's not something I make a habit of, especially now, given my situation. Still, I would never have forgiven myself if I didn't say hello." Ryan kissed my forehead and tried to rebuild my confidence, understanding my position now.

"Well, I'm glad you did," I whispered.

"Me too."

Moving back to give me space, conscious that I wanted to wait, he respected my wishes as we talked, merely holding hands under the covers.

An hour went by. Before long, the heavenly smells of breakfast seeped into our room, prompting us to start the day.

Ryan helped me make the bed. Across from him, on the opposite side, I noticed the light reflecting off his eyes. Something was wrong.

"Your eyes are so red."

"Umm, yeah… It's, ahh, probably the salt in the air. I have eye drops in my room. They help a little." Trying to change the subject, he said, "So, you get ready. I'll go change and see you in a minute."

Watching him walk out the door, he closed it quietly behind him, leaving me too much time to think. While getting dressed and freshening up, reminded of my problems, I said frustratingly, "Live in the moment, no matter what happens. Live in the moment for once in your overly predictable and calculated life, for goodness sake!" Angry at myself, lashing out, that verbal declaration seemed to create a paradigm shift - a new start - one less cautious and more open. It helped me prepare for our adventure at the Great Barrier Reef.

Meeting again in the hallway, Ryan hinted, "Today will be amazing. Are you excited?"

I nodded, fearfully contemplating the scope of what we were about to do, and hoped he was right. As for being ready? The truth is, I was still scared out of my mind.

Lured by the aroma of food, having a seat, the crew tried to contain their smiles. They could see the closeness developing between the two of us. It made me wonder if the rumor of our dancing last night had already made its way around the ship.

Ryan parked his chair closer to mine. Given a kiss on the cheek and pouring me a coffee, his arm found that comfortable place along the back of my chair. Without warning, the sounds of the anchor rising from the depths of the ocean below broke the silence on deck. We could hear loud chants from John, Brad, and Captain White as they prepared the yacht to move to our next anchorage.

Turning to me, Ryan said, "Here we go."

Simultaneously excited and nervous, I knew, beyond a doubt, that today would be the most memorable adventure either of us had ever experienced.

The roar of the engine slowly directed the boat away from the island shore, pointing us toward the open sea. For me, there was no turning back now. Mesmerized by the mighty swirls created in the water, the yacht increased to a higher speed while we said goodbye to Hayman Island. Just then, the sun came out from behind a few clouds to cascade its warmth upon us.

When rounding the northern tip of Hayman Island, heading Northeast, we marveled at the flat rocks appearing to have risen vertically from the ocean floor. I still couldn't fathom how the trees could grow lacking soil. Even the roots were exposed.

On our way, nothing ahead of us but the open waters of the Coral Sea, the Whitsunday Islands soon faded in the distance. I felt as though we were heading into uncharted territory, which I suppose, in reality, we were.

Opting to take in the view from the upper deck, we ascended the stairs to our favorite spot. The vast waterscape was unnerving. It was scary to see only one other vessel in sight. Resembling that of a pirate ship, it gracefully floated a mile away, heading in the same direction. Ryan then pointed out another large boat veering around Hayman Island, not too far behind the sailing ship, probably with the same daily itinerary in mind.

Seated on the sectional sofa, Ryan spread the thin blanket over our legs to protect them from the sun.

Enjoying the peaceful serenity, I hesitated and asked, "So, can you tell me anything about your family?"

His pain still fresh, outwardly reluctant to share that information, he bowed his head and fidgeted with a corner of the blanket.

Not sure where to start, trying to think of what he was going to say, he solemnly revealed, "My Mom and Dad are married forty years this year - exactly six weeks from now, I believe. We were supposed to have a party for them - my brothers and me. I have two brothers - Curtis and Corbin. They are older by four years; twins, actually. They always ganged up on me as a kid - forever wrestling me to the ground, pinning me there." Ryan shook his head, adding a chuckle. "They weren't all bad, though. Both of 'em protected my friends and me - even taught me how to defend myself because our community wasn't safe. That made me tough." Pausing a moment, he barely kept his composure. Determined to maintain a strong façade, he refocused and continued the story. Clearing his throat, he said, "I remember the last day I saw them like it was yesterday. I'd stopped by my parents' house unexpectedly hours before I was supposed to disappear. It was a normal day for them. Not for me. While having dinner, I studied their faces, hoping never to forget what each looked like. Having to do this, you leave everything from your old life behind. Nothing can come with you in case it ties you to the person who no longer exists. Even now, I still recall hugging my mother, desperate for her love to rub off somehow and stay with me always." Stopping, trying to control things, he cleared his throat several times. "Umm, when shaking my Dad's hand, he pulled me in for a manly hug, as he normally did with us boys. Bidding my brothers goodbye the same way, I offered each a firm pat on the back and stood in the doorway, painting a mental picture of them laughing and joking around the kitchen table. About to walk away, I knew I was leaving them forever. It was the hardest thing I've ever had to do." Tears streamed down his cheeks as he silently kept a straight face and looked forward, not saying another word.

Holding him tightly, offering every bit of comfort I could give, the story made me understand part of the secrecy and emotional torment I've seen thus far, all stemming from a state of grief. He, too, lost his family as if they'd died.

"So, there it is…umm, the moment I departed my old life to save it technically. Sometimes, it doesn't make sense to me, you know, since there isn't much left without family and friends. But I did this for the greater good. At least that is what I keep telling myself."

Ryan knew he had said way too much and tried to shake off the personal sentiments. "You are the only person I've told this to. No one else knows. Nobody would anyway because I haven't had a real conversation with a single person outside of protective services all this time. By now, you probably know I'm being protected for a reason."

Knowing he couldn't say anything more, I said, "Yes. I figured as much. Don't worry. You're not alone now." Smiling, I squeezed him tightly to provide the same reassurance he'd given me.

"Thank you," he whispered.

Both of us sat in silence for the next half hour. It allowed him to think of his family and the memories they shared peacefully.

Given a minute to reflect on our time together, our talk validated most of his comments and actions.

Ryan spotted the barge far in the distance. Pointing, he said, "There's the Marine Base. We're close."

Hearing footsteps from the side staircase, Jenn appeared and asked, "Sorry to disturb you both. Would you like some lunch?"

He nodded to her, conveying a silent - yes.

Leaving us, we folded our blanket and placed it in the deck box for the next visit. Steps away from the staircase leading to the main level, my arms found a home around Ryan, hoping to reassure him that everything would be okay. Kissing my forehead, he held on tightly before letting go and presenting his hand to escort me to lunch.

Ready to eat, we arrived at the table.

Rob pulled out a map of the Great Barrier Reef and explained our plan for the day. All business, he said, "We are approaching the canal between Bait and Barb Reefs, here and here. The Captain will guide the yacht to our assigned anchorage at Hardy Reef. From this location, it will be easy to maneuver the Brig to that Marine Base. The guys will drop you at the platform and will stay close by. Any questions?"

"Nope. Sounds good, man. Thanks."

"I believe Jenn has reserved your ReefWorld e-tickets. Confirm that with her."

Nodding, Ryan said, "Thanks. Will do."

Finished giving his update, the burly bodyguard resumed his duties while Jenn and Diana came through the sliding doors holding a selection of steaming seafood on a white platter. Setting it in front of our seats, already conveniently placed tight together, they also brought a small salad and sparkling water.

Jenn informed us of the arrangements she'd made for our excursion. Having personally spoken to a representative there, she assured us our experience would be seamless.

Slowing our speed to a crawl, we could hear Brad and John communicating back and forth with the Captain while maneuvering the yacht into position. With the engines turned off, the boat drifted into position. Entirely stopped, we could hear the clanking of chains as the anchor dropped deep below the blue sea.

While finishing our lunch, we watched Brad and John prep the small Brig tender for us.

Thanking Jenn and Diana for our lovely meal, we stepped onto the lower water-level deck along the stern. With the hatch raised, displaying a multitude of fishing, diving, snorkeling, and water sports equipment, all nicely organized in the compact space, the tender was now secured to the back deck and was floating freely.

Brad handed us our wetsuits. "Put these on. It's a safety precaution in case blue bottles or jellies are in the area."

With a heightened fear emerging upon my face, knowing my history, Ryan reassured me, "You've done this at Catseye Beach. Don't worry, I promise you'll be fine."

We took the wetsuits below to our rooms and quickly changed into our swimwear, layering the full-body suit on top. Prepared for our afternoon of snorkeling with the most beautiful marine life in the world, we soon returned to the water-level deck, ready for this once-in-a-lifetime adventure.

The small boat bounced around in the waves. Rob looked on while John and Brad held it steady for us. Stepping one foot in the boat, then the other, I noticed the two nameless agents on standby and the jet skis tethered to the back.

Rob passed Ryan a black bracelet, which he quickly secured around his wrist and tucked inside the wetsuit sleeve. I'd seen it on occasion but thought it was an activity tracker or a new modern-style watch. Wanting to learn more, I thought I'd wait until we were alone.

Ready to go, the two of us jumped into the boat. Pushed back from the deck, we floated away with the current. Starting the engine, Ryan turned the vessel around and slowly accelerated our speed. The two agents on jet skis followed.

Somewhat concerned about the depth of the water below us, I held on tightly to the side of the small craft while he maneuvered skillfully through the channel.

Now, a short distance from the yacht, I asked, "What did Rob give you to wear on your wrist?"

Exposing the band under his sleeve, he said, "This? It's a security device. It has red, yellow, and green button lights on it. We can't use verbal communication because someone is always listening, so they gave me this to send signals back and forth. Yellow is for caution or heads-up. Stay alert. Red for danger - follow protocol and escape. Green is for – the coast is clear, A-OK."

"Has the red button ever lit up?"

Knowing what his answer was, looking away, he answered, "Yeah, a few times."

Now understanding its function, we headed toward the Marine Base barge with our snorkeling equipment on board.

Skillfully docking along the front of the platform, Ryan cut the engine and jumped on the deck, surprised to see me climb out on my own to join him. Handing off the line to one agent, the guy towed it from the barge to their designated surveillance location.

We walked hand in hand toward the main desk, carrying our snorkeling gear. In seconds, a woman with a clipboard promptly welcomed us with a smile. Assuming we were VIPs, she gave a brief presentation before letting us move freely. It was apparent she had been instructed to do so by the crew.

Drawn to the view of the reef, I noticed many tourists enjoying the sights above and below the waterline. Unfamiliar with our surroundings, we found the steps leading to the partially submerged steel grate floor below. Slipping our wetsuits on and zipping them up, I was somewhat scared. But seeing the ocean floor through the crystal clear water made it not seem as ominous. Having a seat, Ryan dangled his legs off the edge. Comfortably sitting beside him, securing the unique full-face masks didn't take long. They resembled the ones we used at Catseye Beach. Slipping on our fins, we tested the breathing mechanisms one last time. Hesitating, I was concerned whether I could do this again.

Ryan pushed himself off the platform into the water and began treading, waiting for me to join him.

"Okay, Eva, ready on three?"

Quite nervous, I reached out my hand.

"Three!" he said in a muffled tone from behind his mask.

Not giving me time to think, I used my opposite hand to push off into the open space beside him. Still holding on, he tended to me, skillfully keeping himself afloat.

"Are you okay?"

Swiftly checking my status, I confirmed, "Yes, I'm fine."

"Remember, you've done this before. Put your face below the surface and breathe normally. Double-check that the mask doesn't leak. If it does, I'll adjust it."

I submerged and looked around. Able to breathe and talk simultaneously, I confirmed everything was okay by giving a thumbs-up.

"Ready to go?" he asked.

Nodding, I reached out and took hold of his hand to weightlessly float along the edge of the towering boulder coral walls of Hardy Reef. Amazed at the brilliant variations of fish surrounding us, it seemed we were in a different world as the fear and uncertainty washed away.

Immersed in the turquoise waters, Ryan scanned our field of view and checked the location of the agents. Both had their sights on us.

Finding a green sea turtle swimming below with schools of tiny silverfish circled in unison, we hovered above, watching them quickly divert if anyone got too close.

Slowly rounding the corner, the reef came alive with fish moving everywhere, of every color imaginable. The majestic beauty was captivating, making me wish this vacation would never end. Thoughts of my old life back in New York occasionally flashed through my mind. That reality reminded me I would eventually have to say goodbye to this man. Trying to stay in the present, I told myself to focus and enjoy every minute of this place in time because the chances of visiting this natural wonder would never happen again.

Distracted by a group of snorkelers along a populated, active part of the reef, we admired the area filled with hundreds of bright royal-blue fish that changed to a silvery color depending on their direction. Weeding through everyone and breaking free of the crowd, to our surprise, we encountered three tourists taunting the fish, making the school frantically avoid their strange visitors.

Angry, Ryan suddenly said, "I'm diving down to stop this. Wait here."

I watched him confidently descend toward the bottom, instinctively willing to protect the marine life. From my location high above, floating almost motionless, without warning, the group of grey-colored fish began swirling in my direction as snorkelers waved their arms frantically before Ryan signaled for them to stop. On a collision course with me, I braced for impact and put out my hands to try and create a barrier. At the last second, a few made a sharp left-hand turn in front of my face, encouraging the rest to follow in unison. Thankfully, the school went on its merry way. Witnessing what happened, Ryan ascended and rushed over.

Lifting our heads above the surface, he laughed. "Are you alright? Sorry about that. They scared them in your direction."

"Figures," I said, trying to put on a brave face. "Out of all the open space, they had to come this way."

With little sympathy to convey, Ryan urged me along. "You're okay," he chuckled. "Come on. Let's keep going."

Laughing, realizing I was acting overly dramatic, my face returned below the waterline.

For the next hour, we discovered many unforgettable sights along the reefs. We even met the very friendly and enormous local Māori Wrasse named Angus. Gray in color, painted with hues of green, Angus was three and a half feet long, maybe a bit more. This permanent resident seemed happy to greet and follow you around, almost like he was the tour guide for his neighborhood.

Comfortable with the experience, my confidence grew by the minute. Swimming along, feeling happy, I noticed movement alongside a section of boulder coral to my right. Silver in color, the speckled creature moved within the shadows. Not knowing what it was, believing it might be a strangely shaped eel, I brought my head above the surface to nervously check our proximity to the Marine Base. Finding us countless yards away, I had no choice but to tread terrifyingly.

Ryan immediately noticed what I'd seen. Recognizing the fear on my face, he quickly grabbed my hand and said from behind his mask, "Eva, it's a squid. I promise you. They're harmless. He's just a little curious, that's all."

Unable to speak, slightly panicked, I nodded and tried to calm down. Placing my mask beneath the water to see where the creature was situated, I knew it had gone.

"Okay. Okay, I'm good now," I muttered.

Lovingly reassured by Ryan, I took a deep breath and continued swimming beside the red sea fans, elegantly waving in the currents. Checking our location, discovering that we were all alone, having arrived at the edge of the roped-off area, about fifty yards from the pontoon base, he removed his mask while latching to the floating barrier. Not sure what was wrong, I took mine off, assuming he wanted to take a break. Slowly bridging the gap between us with a smitten smile, he wrapped his arm around my waist and pulled me in tightly. I clung to both him and the barrier rope. With love in his eyes, he kissed me in a heartfelt surge. There, in the middle of the most beautiful place on earth, I figured if this wasn't the perfect environment to fall in love fully, then I didn't know where that could be.

Leaning back, he locked his sights on mine before turning away briefly. Seemingly deep in thought, he lowered his head and stated, "I don't believe in coincidences. I know we met for a reason."

"It's as if fate intervened," I whispered.

"That's quite possible," he paused. "Being in my situation, you gain perspective on what is truly important in life. Over the past few months, I told myself never to take anything for granted." A sincere smile appeared on his face. "I see my future with no one else but you. I promise I'll never betray you and will always protect you."

Beaming, only able to say one word through my tears, I nodded, "Yes," understanding what he was trying to say. Somehow, my heart trusted every word.

"And, if anything should happen, remember, I love you, Eva Thompson. Never doubt that, okay?"

Emotionally unable to speak, our conversation brought back the harsh reality he faced. Even in the middle of the ocean, danger lurked despite the protective measures in place. Attached to the man that now held my heart, I adoringly said, "I love you too."

If someone were to ask me to describe these feelings, I wasn't sure if I could do it justice. This connection just ran so deep; it was like our souls were intertwined. Maybe we existed previously in another life or a different dimension and found each other here? I didn't know.

Granted one more kiss, I wished we could stay there in that place forever. The serenity of it was awe-inspiring and safe - the type of environment he probably hadn't had in a long while.

Feeling waterlogged, we started swimming in the direction of the barge. Hand in hand, we floated below the docks of the pontoon vessel and slipped off our fins one by one. Ryan set them on the platform before pulling himself out of the water to help me do the same.

Climbing the steel grate steps to the upper deck, equipment dangling from our fingers, we casually discussed our reef experience. He raised a hand to signal the agents and let them know we were ready to leave. At the same time, people were staring, assuming we were celebrities.

Regardless of the unwanted attention, Ryan took my hand and gently pulled me into his arms.

"Today was incredible," he said. "Thank you for sharing it with me."

"Thank you for taking me out of my comfort zone. I don't know if I would've been brave enough to do this alone."

With absolute certainty, he replied, "Sure, you could. You're strong. I believe you can do anything you set your mind to."

Staring confidently into my eyes, I ran my hands along his cheeks and guided his lips to mine as we temporarily left the real world behind - if only for a minute.

As the agents brought the Brig closer, Ryan tossed our gear into the boat and jumped in. Arms outstretched, he carefully helped me. When we were about to leave, he peeled his wetsuit down to his waist, as did I.

The men on the jet skis backed off and continued scanning our surroundings systematically. Ready to escort us, we could hear them communicating with the yacht. Getting clearance, they gave a thumbs up.

Ryan double-checked his bracelet. The glowing green light gave a sense of calm. Departing, he slowly turned the boat toward Line Reef.

"All good. We're clear. Ready?" he asked, slowly accelerating with the agents flanking either side.

The wind whistled while we cautiously sped across the water. I noticed the tide had changed. Some reefs were now surfacing, making the water seem more aqua-colored than deep blue.

On approach, we saw John waiting for us to pull up. Tossing him the line, he kept the Brig steady so we could climb onto the water-level deck. Securing the craft, he increased the line, allowing it to trail behind us before lifting the jet skis onboard.

Removing our wetsuits and handing them over to the guys to be rinsed and dried, Ryan grabbed a couple of towels and wrapped me in one.

Reaching the main level, Jenn offered us water as we sat at the dining table. Rob soon emerged from inside and took watch. There weren't too many boats in sight. Just the sailboat that resembled a pirate ship anchored farther away, opposite the barge, and another smaller yacht that looked similar in shape to ours in the distance. The tourist boat remained docked, waiting for the guests to finish their excursion at the Marine base. At the same time, the last seaplane took off from the aviation platform with some VIPs escorting them to their next destination.

Tired from swimming, Ryan asked, "Do you want to go to the upper level to enjoy the sun and regain some energy? Maybe take a short nap?"

"Sure, that sounds nice," I said, getting up from my chair.

Ascending the stairs, we found a spot on the sun-drenched deck bed where Ryan easily fell asleep.

Still feeling the floating sensation of being on the water for more than three hours, it took longer for me to drift off. Seeing him peacefully lying there, his head supported by a pillow, my heart ached. Despite how perfect things seemingly were today, in reality, I knew that was far from the truth.

| 32 |

Below the Sea

19°44'15" S / 149°08'23" E
19°44'44" S / 149°10'57" E

Waking a while later, startling myself, I opened my eyes and looked around, quite disoriented. Hearing only happy banter from the lower decks, I realized where I was and knew everything was okay. Ryan suddenly kissed me on the cheek casually.

"So, what do you want to experience next? Maybe go back to the Marine base and take a submarine ride?"

Drenched in the sun's brightness, shielding my eyes, I squinted one side and replied, "I've never been in a submarine before."

"Well, lucky for you, I've been in a couple in Hawaii. It would be amazing to see what's living outside the barriers in the deeper water. Want to try it then?"

"Sure."

"Submarine, it is. I'll be right back. Just need to put some more drops in my eyes."

"Yes, you definitely should. They are very red," I agreed, noticing their distinct color.

We left the upper deck and continued downstairs to our rooms, parting momentarily.

"I'll meet you up on the main level, alright?" he said before entering his room. "I'll get Jenn to make the arrangements for us."

"Okay. I'll be there in a minute."

Closing my room door, I walked into the closet to slip on my cover-up. Washing my face and brushing my hair, I grabbed a pair of flip-flops and climbed the stairs again to find Ryan in a rather intense conversation with Rob, the security guard, and Kayla, the person in charge. Turning his back on me, Ryan quietly continued their discussion with arms crossed in front of him.

It made me uncomfortable. Instantly, the air seemed a bit thicker.

Ending things, he said, "Thanks, guys." Eyes locked on mine, with a clap of his hands, he said, "Alright. Ready to go?"

"What's wrong? Is everything okay?" I asked, needing to be informed of any issues.

"Yes, all good," he quickly responded, flashing an uneasy expression.

Not wanting to cast doubt, I cracked a slight smile, suspicious of what had just happened.

As we ascended the steps, the agents stood by while John and Brad kept the Brig steady. We got in with ease and took our positions.

Guiding it away from the stern, John tossed the line to me. I pulled it in while Ryan started the engine. Moving away from the yacht, he gradually accelerated and maneuvered us toward the barge. Once again, the agents were flanking both sides.

The tides were low when we docked at the platform this time. I reached up and jumped out of the boat to climb the ladder. Impressed by that, Ryan waited and tossed the bow line to one of the agents on approach. With it secured, he climbed up and joined me. At the top, we watched the men drift away and take their positions. Ryan then put on a hat and sunglasses to hide his face - something he hadn't done recently. It made me wonder.

In an instant, the same woman welcomed us back. Giving instructions on what to do, she said, "Better hurry, you two. The sub is leaving shortly."

Escorted to the submarine at the far end, she introduced us as unnamed VIPs to the vessel's Captain. The older gentleman smiled, shook our hands, and invited us to descend into the capsule. Doing just that, finding open seats near the exit, we sat together as the hatch closed above our heads.

Sitting there, I recalled what had happened before leaving the boat. Because it bothered me, I asked, "So, umm, if something was wrong, would you tell me? Because I got a bad feeling when you were speaking to the crew. So, would you? Would you fill me in if anything was wrong?"

Taking hold of my hand, he said, "Yes, absolutely. Please don't worry."

With my mind reeling, I tried to focus on the underwater trip but told myself to stay alert just in case.

Thankfully, spotting marine life on the other side of the sub, our guide quickly pointed out a group of slender silver Remora fish swimming in search of a shark to cling to. All around us were brilliant blue and yellow Surgeons, one round-faced Batfish, and another green sea turtle floating a few feet above the seafloor. Peering upward toward the surface, I could see the bottom of our boat and the jet skis floating in the distance. It gave me comfort knowing they weren't far.

Alerted to a school of beautiful, tiny black and white striped zebra-like fish, we listened intently to our guide's observations. Numerous creatures were hiding amongst a large patch of spaghetti coral, gracefully waving in the current. His presentation reinforced the need to protect the marine park, pointing out that it takes years for the boulder coral to heal and repair itself if damaged, citing the surprising fact that it only grows about two mm per year. Enjoying the tranquil views, Ryan wrapped his arms around me while looking out the window for most of the trip. It was one of the most amazing experiences of my life.

Returning to the pontoon base an hour later, we were the first to disembark when the hatch opened. The afternoon sun blinded us slightly. Pressing the green button on his bracelet to alert Rob that we were preparing to head back, we waited for the signal to come through, signifying that things were secure on their end.

The agents approached with the Brig and kept it steady. Ryan descended the ladder and jumped in. Extending his arms upward, he then helped me. Safely lowered, I sat beside him while he started the engine. About to turn us around, I heard a strange tone emanating from his bracelet. Quickly checking it, he confirmed it was flashing yellow and not green.

The men shouted at him, "Go! Go! Go!"

"Eva, hang on," he said urgently, shoving the throttle forward.

Immediately accelerating, his eyes affixed to the yacht, still a thousand yards away, Ryan skillfully maneuvered the channel, scanning the horizon from left to right, keeping watch for any rogue boats. The agents stayed close. Both pulled weapons from inside their wetsuits.

Closing in, we realized the Captain had already raised the anchor and swung the vessel in the opposite direction.

Trembling, my heart pumped fearfully.

With his head on a swivel, we coasted toward the stern.

Ryan shut down the engine. "What's going on?" he shouted to John as we got closer.

The Bosun tried to defuse the worry on my face. "We are just tracking a storm developing off the northeastern coast. Gotta roll!"

Stepping onto the platform, Ryan turned and offered his hands for me to board while John kept it steady. At the same time, Brad signaled the agents to bring the jet skis around to the port side so he could lift them out of the water.

Escorted up the stairs, Rob and Kayla met us on the main deck. Before speaking a word, Rob motioned for Jenn to take me below.

"Ev, please go with Jenn. I'll be there in a minute," Ryan requested in a monotone voice.

Agreeing to do as he asked, locking eyes before leaving the group, I saw the two unnamed agents join Rob and Kayla. They were already conversing with Captain White, John, and Brad. Placing a map on the table, each hovered over top of it.

Jenn and I descended below deck and walked into my cabin. Sitting on the bed, she stayed with me and waited. About to ask her a question, Kayla entered the room.

"Jenn, can you give us a moment?" Leaving us, closing the door behind her, Kayla stated firmly, "Eva, you should gather up your things in a bag just in case...."

"In case of what?" I questioned with a feeling of dread.

"Just in case, at some point, you and Ryan have to leave everything and go. You know what his situation is now. I'm sure he's filled you in somewhat. I realize this is scary, but believe me, he will do everything he can to keep you safe. We will, too, I promise. It's our job. We know what we're doing."

Switching my mindset, I was sure everyone on the yacht was involved in some way, shape, or form. Standing, grabbing hold of the backpack they provided, I threw a couple of water bottles in, light clothing, and my hoodie, hoping it wouldn't take up too much space. Changing clothes, putting on cropped yoga pants and a tank, I got out the water shoes we bought the day before. Sitting on the end of the bed, slipping them on, my feet began to bounce rhythmically off the floor. While waiting for an update, Kayla left the room, and Jenn returned. She had gotten Ryan's pre-packed exit bag to place with mine. Looking at it, I remembered he had taken that bag with him whenever we went anywhere on Hamilton Island.

Casually walking over to the window to see how fast we were going, Jenn turned and said, "Don't worry, we are not running at high speed. It's probably just a precautionary redirect due to the storm."

Ryan appeared the second she said that.

"Jenn, thank you for staying with Eva."

Giving the nod, leaving us, she quietly closed the door behind her.

Now wrapped tightly in his arms, his chin resting upon my head, he whispered, "Captain White is tracking a cyclone developing off the northeastern coast of Australia. That is why we had to leave the reef. I'm sorry our trip is about to be cut short, but I hope we can stop by Whitehaven Beach for an hour or two while traveling south."

Running his fingers through my hair, not making eye contact, I knew something was wrong. "When my caution signal went off, I immediately thought of how I would keep you safe. One of these days, they will find me - that is a reality I face every day." Hesitating, he took a deep breath. "It might be best to part ways until this is all over. The team can send you to another safe house, and I will join you later."

Holding me even tighter, outwardly feeling my objection, I didn't say a word.

"Originally, the plan was to move on to Airlie Beach and leave together from there. But with the storm, we have to divert to avoid the weather, and Brisbane may not be the optimal departure point for us. With everything going on, I will have to continue moving and stay one step ahead. That said, we've arranged for a seaplane to pick you up at Whitehaven and transport you out. Kayla will go with and protect you."

Backing away from him, still holding on, I said with a wavering voice, "No... No, I am not leaving you."

"Ev, I'm sorry. You have no other choice." Breaking our embrace, he sat at the end of the bed. Resting his elbows on his knees, hands clenched together, he firmly stated, "If you stay with me, I guarantee your life will be in danger. Please understand. I never want you to suffer because of me. I didn't tell you this earlier, but these people are old school. They abide by this ancient rhetoric - this code of an eye for an eye. If they capture you, Eva, they will rape, torture, and murder you because of your connection to me. It's a gruesome, barbaric, and revengeful mindset. They will have no remorse. I'm sorry for being blunt. But it's the truth."

Speechless, I didn't know how to respond. My hands moved into a praying position and uncontrollably shook while trying to process what he'd just described. Thinking of leaving and doing what he asked, believing it to be the only way, I realized he might inevitably suffer an even worse fate. Lip quivering, trying to contain my emotions, the thought of never seeing him again was excruciating. In a panic, the air left my lungs. I gasped and started to cry. Refusing to abandon him, needing to be as strong and gain the courage, I wiped the tears away and stood my ground before him. With my head held high, I bit my lip and tried to spit out the words. "Please, I can't...umm. I can't leave you. Not now. I won't...."

Seeing such desperation on my face, Ryan quickly got up to comfort me, unable to fathom the thought of having to let me go. Hugging tightly, he could never ask me to make such an enormous sacrifice, either.

Frustrated, he let go and rubbed his hand across his forehead. "Please, don't cry. Listen, you can stay for now, but if there is any escalation, I am sending you to safety - no questions asked. Honestly, you will have no choice at that point. I will make the call, and you will have to go, agreed?" Not acknowledging him, he added, "You have to promise you will do this for me, Ev. If I know you're safe, I can focus on surviving too. Do you understand?"

I reluctantly nodded.

"I'm sorry for bringing you into this..." he whispered. "I'm truly sorry. I should have walked away."

"I'm thankful you didn't."

Clinging to him, I knew our time together was ending. Nothing more needed to be said as fear set in.

That night, trying to continue some sort of normalcy, we had a quiet dinner. Captain White emerged from the bridge to inform us that we were approaching the eastern coastline of Border Island, situated en route to Whitehaven Beach. Selecting the yacht-designated anchorage point for tonight, he assured us that we would be safe in the hidden cove.

While sitting in the main salon on the sofa, trying to pass the time, we didn't converse much as reality hit hard.

Around the north peninsula of Border Island, the setting sun dipped below the horizon. As the yacht slowed to a drift, gentle raindrops hit the windows.

Worried about me, Ryan asked, "Are you doing okay?"

"It's been a rough day," I answered, emotionally drained.

"Listen - about those things I said earlier. At the time, I wanted you to understand the severity of what we are facing. Behind all this luxury, I'm fighting for my life. It was not my intention to come across in such a cruel way. I shouldn't have shared those details. I apologize."

Focused straight ahead, I replied in a solemn tone, "Don't be sorry. I needed to know. Whatever happens, we are in this together now. You and me."

"Ev..."

Ryan tilted his head to the side upon reading the frightened expression on my face. Putting up my hand to interrupt him, he stopped.

"Don't...," I said. "I meant what I said. Nothing you can say will change my mind." Reaching out, I rested my hand on top of his. Ryan intertwined his fingers with mine. Rubbing his burning eyes, I said, "They are very red. Are you sure they aren't infected?"

"No, it's just the saltwater. I need to get my drops, and they'll be fine. Don't worry. Come on, let's go downstairs."

He offered his hand to help me up off the sofa. Quietly moving along, we descended to our rooms below deck.

Parting ways in the hall, Ryan divulged, "I will see you in a few minutes, okay?"

"Alright." I watched him enter his cabin while I went into mine. Now alone, I opted for a quick shower to freshen up and remove the salty residue before Ryan returned. During that time, I kept circling back to the same decision made hours earlier. No matter the outcome, I would see this through to the end with him.

Ready for bed, I was surprised he wasn't waiting for me when I exited my bathroom. Concerned, I decided to peek in on him. After knocking gently and not receiving an answer, I opened it an inch. Peering inside, I found him fast asleep. Utterly exhausted, unsure what to do, I softly closed his door and retired to my room to get some rest.

In bed, snuggled under my covers, I got thinking. What was ultimately waiting for me back in New York? Even though I was excited about my promotion and the museum project finally finishing two to three years down the line, I knew work would never love me, have dinner with me, marry me, or have a family with me. The crossroads where I found myself seemed very unfamiliar. Usually, I choose the safe, more predictable path, not the one with bumps along the way. But what if this bumpy road led to everything I desired out of life? What then? Do I take the chance or keep the status quo?

Going to sleep that night, I felt like my life had a new direction. A new host of possibilities, regardless of the uncertainty. Not entirely sure what the makings of this future entailed, I decided to move forward with blind faith, knowing sometimes that's all it takes to find a little happiness.

| 33 |

Targeted

20°09'58" S / 148°02'20" E
20°14'47" S / 149°02'08" E

Disturbed by an unknown commotion upstairs in the early morning hours, I quickly sat up in bed and listened. Focused on the sounds and voices, I soon recognized regular staff activity from the upper decks, remembering it was now day eight of the vacation. Somehow, it seemed much longer than that.

Hearing a soft knock on my door, Ryan quietly entered the room, unsure if I was awake. While sending a smile his way, he came over to the bed and cuddled up beside me. It didn't take long to notice his eyes had improved drastically. Only a slight redness remained.

"Good morning. Your eyes look much better."

"Yeah, umm. They are. Sorry about last night. I came back to your room, but you were in the shower. I didn't want to disturb you, so I thought I'd lie on my bed for a few minutes before returning, but I must have fallen asleep."

"It's okay. Think you needed it."

Getting more comfortable, he said, "I'm sorry we won't get to spend more time at Whitehaven Beach today, but at least we'll get to see it."

"That's alright. I'm just happy to share the experience with you. It doesn't matter for how long." Knowing it might sadly be our last day together, I wanted to make the most of it. "Come on! Let's get up and get ready. The pictures I've seen of this place are so beautiful. I can hardly wait to go for a swim there."

"This, coming from the person who was scared of going on this excursion last week."

Proud of myself, having gained a surprising amount of courage and strength, I honestly said without a doubt in my mind, "When I am with you, I feel like I can do anything."

Elated, he replied, "Yes, I know what you mean."

"So, are you going to hurry and change so we can go?"

Attracted by my sudden bossy but endearing demeanor, in a low tone, Ryan joked, "Yes, Ma'am," before walking out the door.

Freshening up in my bathroom, I got organized, tied my hair back, put on my swimsuit and cover-up, and even added a bit of makeup to my face.

Opening my room door, I found Ryan sitting on the steps, waiting for me.

"Ready?" he asked.

"Oh, have you been here long?"

"No, not long. I guess all men wait for their girlfriends at one point or another. That doesn't bother me. I would wait for you all day if I had to."

"Aww… that's so sweet, but it's not how you truly feel. I bet you were thinking – I wish she'd hurry up," I smirked humorously.

"Well…maybe the last 5 minutes," he chuckled, making me tap his shoulder, before running up the stairs to breakfast waiting.

The smell of food was easy to follow. The ladies had set the table beautifully. Ryan requested that the crew join us to share this time together. The air lightened as the group gathered around, bonding to the level of a family. Amidst all the banter, Ryan seemed a little quiet. Given the circumstances, I knew he was concerned for my safety now, so it was understandable. But I didn't want to think negatively.

On our final approach to Whitehaven Beach, passing the north side of Esk Island, everyone watched the white sands around Hill Inlet come into view and divert our attention away from each other. The magnificence of it was indescribable. Exposed sandbars above the waterline created a series of patterned swirls in the turquoise sea. Boats plotted their path through the canals, carefully staying within the deeper sections, while a handful of tourists stood high up on the Hill's lookout to soak up the view. The picturesque scene was as perfect as a postcard.

Anchoring the yacht, Captain White announced, "We have arrived at our Whitehaven Beach location. The middle section is quite crowded right now and is not suitable for a vessel of our size. We will anchor here. Feel free to take the Brig out to explore the inlet. Keep in mind - we only have a one-hour window."

Brad quickly got us ready to board the small craft. Slipping on our water shoes, prepared to depart on the next adventure, Jenn and Kayla brought our exit bags up from downstairs and placed them inside the Yeti waterproof container on board.

As Kayla secured the lock, she turned to me, noticing my sights on her. "It's just a precaution," she said. "Don't worry."

Carefully stepping into the rocking boat, unstable with the high winds today, we soon drifted away from the yacht. Looking to the upper level, I found the agents standing with binoculars in hand. I assumed they stayed behind based on our proximity, but would be watching us with eagle eyes nonetheless.

Jenn happily waved. "Have fun, you two!"

Raising my hand and waving back to her, I wondered what this day had in store for us. Fixated on our destination, I was excited to experience the beauty of this place firsthand since pictures did not do it justice. I had never seen such clear, blue water, and the white sand resembled that of baby powder.

Accelerating across the sparkling ocean, we headed toward the natural wonder. The crew had packed us a picnic basket with snacks, a small cooler with chilled drinks, beach towels, a brolly, and two folding chairs. While bouncing over the waves, the wind sprayed a salty mist upward, helping to cool us off from the sun's heat.

Ryan slowed our speed to move into the swirl of canals cautiously.

Reaching overboard, I placed my hand in the water to feel the refreshing temperature change the closer we got to the shallows. The water was so warm.

About a third of the way inside the channel, the beach was empty, so he brought the boat ashore. Feeling he was on edge and not as relaxed as earlier this morning, I sensed a bit of paranoia. His head continuously scanned the horizon from left to right when we jumped out of the boat.

Content to help unpack the things we needed, I touched Ryan's arm and said, "What's wrong?"

With an unsettled tone, he responded, "Nothing, I'm good," just before securing the umbrella in the sand.

I placed the chairs underneath, along with the cooler bag and picnic basket, within arm's reach - creating our perfect spot.

Pulling out two bottles of water, we each took a sip before Ryan asked, "Care for a swim?"

"Would love to."

Calmly moving hand in hand along the soft, powder-like sand to the shoreline, wading into the crystal-clear water, it didn't take long to submerge and cool off fully. Clinging to each other, we looked about, trying to enjoy the peacefulness. The tranquility seemed to wash away my worries while floating on our backs, with our ears in a silent state.

Aware of the time, we walked down the beach barefoot, surprised that the sand didn't retain any heat. Along the way, we spotted a school of tiny silverfish swimming past a mere six feet from shore.

Back at our chairs, minutes later, opting to have a little snack, I pulled the sandwiches from the picnic basket before we'd have to pack up and return to the boat, adhering to Captain White's instructions. Finishing our last few bites, Ryan stopped and stood up. His attention was affixed on the open water. Concerned, I followed his line of sight and spotted two boats approaching the yacht at high speed, causing a dire look to flash across his face.

In disbelief, he pressed the red button on the security bracelet and immediately received a solid red in return.

"Eva! Get in the boat! Hurry!" he said alarmingly.

I grabbed our water shoes and threw them into the craft before Ryan shoved us away from the shore. Tossing his tracking bracelet on the chair and abandoning our belongings on the beach, he started the engine.

"What's wrong?" I said, trembling fearfully.

He didn't answer.

Moving us away from shore, he instructed, "Ev, sit at the bow and help me navigate the channel. Use arm signals to direct me if I get too close to the sand bars."

I did what he asked and took point as he stood tall behind the wheel and carefully steered us out of the inlet at medium speed to open water. Leaving the shallows, pushing the throttle, Ryan headed towards a few other tourist vessels along the six-mile stretch of shoreline so as not to bring attention to us. In horror, I watched the rogue boats circling the yacht, fearing for the lives of our friends on board. Praying that God would keep them safe until we got there to help them, I felt the boat unexpectedly divert, making me realize Ryan was turning in the opposite direction and heading away from the yacht.

"Where are you going? We have to help them!" I shouted.

"They will be alright. We can't go back," Ryan blatantly declared, displaying a change in body language. Standing militarily, he distanced us further and further from the confrontation taking place.

Guiding the vessel southwest toward Hamilton Island, we quickly passed by half of the expansive section of Whitehaven Beach.

Looking back at the yacht, I noticed smoke billowing from the main deck. "Ryan!" I pointed. "The yacht is on fire!"

Afraid to confirm my observation, he focused on the task of getting us to safety. Unable to stop, thinking the worst, he saw several Coast Guard vessels tending to a tourist boat seemingly hung up on a shallow reef while rounding the southern tip of Whitsunday Island. All the commotion helped cloak us on the way by.

Following protocol, staying in check, he said firmly, "We have to get to the safe house."

"Where's that?" I asked, utterly confused.

"My house on Melaleuca."

"Wait? Your house? What do you mean?"

"It's a long story, Eva. We'll discuss it later," he said coldly.

Blasting past the island's southern shore, we could see the tall white hotel towers in the distance.

Not far from our destination, hoping we wouldn't run out of gas before reaching our landing point, Ryan asked, "Are any boats following us?"

I leaned to the left and then right of him. "No, I see nothing there!"

With a slight nod, he acknowledged my report, knowing they probably didn't see us depart the beach. "Keep watch until we get to shore. We can't let anyone see us go to the house."

Keeping a close eye behind him, I saw no activity other than the dark, ominous clouds rolling in from the east. Secure in the fact that nobody was following, a sense of calm began to creep across Ryan's face when nearing the coastline below the house.

"Can you climb the rocky cliff to get to my place?" he questioned with little expression.

Confident I could, I said, "Yes," willing to do whatever he asked.

Ryan scoured the shore for a softer incline versus the steep bluffs right below the steel Melaleuca structure on the hillside. We both put on our water shoes as we got closer, knowing the climb ahead would not be easy. About to hit the rocky edge, some boulder-sized, all jutting out of the water, he stepped out of the boat onto one very carefully to hold it steady for me.

With my exit bag on my shoulders, I handed Ryan his and held onto the boat tightly before stepping onto a submerged boulder, careful not to slip. Facing the boat toward Catseye Beach, he pushed the throttle and let it float away, knowing it would be out of gas shortly and drift the rest of the way.

"Let's go..." he said, holding my hand.

Leery about climbing over the sharp boulders, with the risk of coming in contact with something poisonous hiding in each crack and crevasse, we could now hear the rumbling sounds of thunder in the distance. Black clouds started encompassing the northern part of the Whitsunday Island chain sooner than expected. Noticeably paranoid, Ryan scanned our surroundings systematically, focusing on the water, not seeing anything suspicious. Creeping toward the first row of houses on Melaleuca, he seemed distant. With our heads down, I followed his lead, afraid to say anything. Sneaking along the cliffside, we stopped at a wall of shrubbery growing tight against the rock, just down from his place. Carefully shoving some branches aside with his hand, he uncovered a black door and an access pad hidden behind the leaves and debris. Calmly entering the code, showing little emotion, it opened with a click. The tiny panel light turned from red to green. Shoving the heavy door, he pushed it forward and escorted me inside. Slowly closing it behind us, I heard the two, three-inch steel pegs slide back into place, securing the entrance again. With a snap of a light stick he'd grabbed from the ledge, Ryan cracked a second one to offer us more light. Feeling somewhat safe, we inched through the dark tunnel.

"This corridor leads to the house. We will be safe there." Arriving at the end, Ryan said very quietly, "Wait here. I'll come back to you when everything's secure."

Agreeing, still shaking with fear, I said, "Please, hurry back."

"I will. Stay quiet."

Opening the next door, thoroughly searching the space on the other side, Ryan slipped into the void, leaving me behind. Frightened beyond belief, the silence surrounding me became deafening. I couldn't stop my body from shaking and gasping for small bits of air. It was hard to stay completely quiet.

Intently listening for the faintest of noises, hearing nothing, the door finally opened minutes later.

Ryan peeked in and said, "The coast is clear. You can come out now."

Thankful that he'd returned, I sighed. Leaving the dark tunnel and entering a windowless room, he locked the door before guiding me up a ladder, where we climbed out from under the bedroom closet floor. Standing at the end of the bed after leaving the hidden exit, my legs felt prickly and weak. Flipping the trap door closed, Ryan hastily brought his attention back to me, realizing I was wavering and had become quite pale.

One arm around my waist and the other holding my head tightly against his chest, he glanced down. "You're okay. You're okay. We're safe here."

Nodding, unable to speak, Ryan led me to the living room. With legs giving out sporadically, he picked me up and brought me to the sofa. Elevating my feet, he went to grab a bottle of water and a blanket. Back within seconds, supplies in hand, he tucked the blanket around me and rubbed my arms briskly.

"We're safe now. I promise."

Barely able to respond, I said, "I'm good," even though I knew I wasn't. It took a few minutes, but eventually, I felt better.

Confident, I was over the worst of it, he said, "Give me one second. I'll be right back."

Not wasting time, he ran to the security panel and quickly punched in a numeric code, explaining, "This is a distress signal. It goes directly to my extraction team. They'll see our location and get us out." Analyzing the monitor's security camera footage, he added, "The seas are rough. I don't see any boats approaching the island, just the Coast Guard still tending to that tourist vessel. There's no movement along the perimeter, so we're fine."

Relieved the coast was clear, Ryan returned to the living room and pushed the coffee table off the rug in front of me. Rolling back the carpet, he revealed another trap door in the floor. Effortlessly pulling the flush handle, I watched him lift the hatch upwards to swing it open, exposing a secret room below. I curiously followed when he entered the hidden space. Gingerly, sitting on the upper part of the stairs, I watched him open a cabinet encased in the wall. Shock swept over me when he shifted to one side to reveal a selection of weapons. Expertly grabbing hold of a handgun and a high-powered rifle, he loaded the clips with ease. Scared of what I was witnessing, I promptly got up and returned to the main floor.

Joining me moments later, with guns in hand, he strategically placed the weapons about the room. He soon realized this was frightening me, even though it seemed a reasonable course of action for him.

"How do you know where all these things are?" I asked with a multitude of questions going through my mind.

Guns placed safely on the tables within arm's reach, he faced, knowing his secret was about to be exposed. Prepared to tell the truth, Ryan approached and sat tight to my left, ready to share specific details about his life.

"I know where everything is because I designed it that way. It's not my friend's house. It is one of the many safe houses I have at my disposal."

Stunned, knowing what I thought to be true, once again, wasn't, my mind fell into a state of confusion, making me ask with slight desperation, "So, that was all a lie?"

"Please don't think of it that way. It's complicated, Ev. You have to understand that I never wanted to lie to you, and from a security standpoint, I couldn't take the risk and tell you the truth either, so...."

Annoyed by his blunt statement, I stood and left the room with my exit bag. Needing a moment to think, I did not say another word.

"No, Ev, wait. Please..."

| 34 |

The Past

20°14'47" S / 149°02'08" E

Not looking back, I found a bedroom at the end of the hall and locked myself inside the ensuite bathroom. Able to wash the excess dirt from my arms, hands, and face, staring at myself in the mirror, part of me was disappointed in my naivety. Deciding to shower off the salty residue, I changed into dry clothes from my bag and repositioned my wet hair in a ponytail. Knowing he had no choice given the situation, I couldn't blame him. He did what he had to.

Again, a fight-or-flight response grabbed hold of me. Do I stay or go? I couldn't help but feel I was in over my head. I knew Ryan had technically told me the truth about ending his life to save it. Inevitably, given a new identity, he was denied access to any form of ordinary life. All that said, my heart was still deeply connected to his, no matter how I tried to deny it. The thought of parting ways was unfathomable.

Leaving the bedroom, I found him sitting on the sectional with his eyes glued to the flat-screen TV, simultaneously watching a montage of security monitors.

Sheepishly moving in his direction, he turned and stood up. "Is everything alright? I mean…"

"Yeah, I just needed to process this whole thing."

In that somewhat awkward moment, I felt the need to run and the pull to stay. Staring into his eyes, seeing the beautiful soul I found days earlier, I sat at the far end of the sofa. He returned to the same place where he had been sitting and focused on the security footage silently.

Concerned about who would rescue us and when, I asked, "Who did you say is coming to get us?"

"There is a group they refer to as the Stealth team. They're alerted in emergencies to extract people to safer locations."

"How many times has this Stealth team rescued you?"

"Twice so far. As a precaution, though. Never in the case of an imminent threat," he mentioned casually. "I'm constantly on the move, so it hasn't been a huge problem. When arriving on Hamilton Island, I hoped to hide for a few months and stay in one place. Venturing out one too many times may have given away my location, although I still can't figure out how that could've happened."

Minute by minute, the impending storm engulfed the house in darkness. Seeing anything clearly through the cameras with a standard view was difficult. Grabbing an iPad, Ryan switched the footage over to night vision. Not moving from my chair, keeping my distance, I caught him glancing my way and then back to the screens a few times. There was only one way to fix things between us.

Running his hand through his hair nervously, he knew I deserved answers. Exhaling, probably wishing the world would stop for a moment so he could take a breath, his eyes moved to a spot on the floor in front of him.

"You know, I never wanted this to happen… I mean, all of this to turn out as badly as it did. I'm sorry, Eva. You have every right to be angry with me."

Getting up, I walked over and sat down beside him, ready to listen. Like offering an olive branch, I reached for his hand.

He took hold and rested it on top of his knee. Lowering his head, he said, "I want to tell you everything. You need to know why this is happening, but first, I need to show you something."

Oddly rolling his eyes back, he carefully removed a pair of dark contact lenses, seemingly tinted black. Turning in my direction with his eyes closed, he slowly opened them and revealed their actual color - barely-there baby blue.

While focusing in, tilting my head, staring intently, I suddenly realized who was hiding behind them. Astounded, I whispered, "Wait? Are you Anthony Morgan?"

Afraid to look me in the eye, he turned away. "Now you know… This is the reason why my eyes have been so red. I've been wearing these contacts steady. They are a part of the disguise. That's the reason they've been so irritated. Last night on the boat, I purposefully fell asleep in my room to remove the lenses and take a break from them."

Leaning back on the sofa, with both his hands resting on his legs, still perusing the camera images on the screen, he clarified things further.

"My brothers and I grew up in the rough neighborhood of National City in San Diego. Every day, we witnessed a crime and were exposed to the violence between gangs feuding over drug territories. When I was seven, my brother's friend overdosed on drugs and died right at his feet. He took his friend's death pretty hard. Sadly, there was nothing he could have done to save him. My brothers were into sports, so it kept them out of all that. They hoped to play football in college one day and get away from our neighborhood, determined to take my parents and me with them. When I was about eight, the plastics factory where my Dad worked let go of about half of their employees. After looking for a job for almost two months, my Mom decided to call back this showbiz agent who had approached us a while before, giving Mom her card when we were picking up a few groceries one Saturday afternoon. Since I was a pretty good-looking kid, and we were out of options, my Mom thought I could help make the family some money if I got discovered. Using the stage name Anthony Morgan instead of my real name, Anthony Morgani, I luckily started modeling for a few kids' clothing ads and eventually got cast in some commercials. Within a few months, I landed small roles on after-school TV shows since I always liked putting on a show. Over the years, things went pretty well. Not only did I earn money to help my family, but I made enough for us to move out of the projects. My family and I left our friends behind to relocate to Los Angeles, hoping to be closer to the casting calls. Eventually, I saved to pay for college after my brothers went years before me. As I got older, I often thought of the old neighborhood, feeling the need to help protect the people there, believing nobody would if I didn't care about them. This led me to want to become a cop, which I ultimately did, despite my mother's constant pleas to consider other professions. After leaving the Academy, I worked the streets as a patrolman for four years. Moving up the ladder, I completed a series of competitive detective exams and a formal interview before finally getting assigned by request to the undercover Narcotics Unit. Weeks after securing that position, I realized defying death was about to become a daily occurrence. I spent most of my off-hours alone. Usually, I went to the gym or stopped by the gun range. Working long shifts for over three months on this one case, I began rethinking my career choice, especially when tragedy suddenly struck our unit. Late one night, I received a call from the Chief. He informed me that my partner had been brutally murdered outside his assigned secret housing location about an hour before by this young, crazy assassin named Tomás, a newly known Cartel hitman. Sadly, it didn't stop there. Afterward, this guy went to my partner's home and killed his wife, two young children, and his parents, who lived with them. Telling me my partner had died wasn't the only reason for his call. Supposedly, word on the street was I was next."

Fearfully captivated by his story, sounding more like a movie script than real life, I thought about how much fear these people must endure daily. Not only for themselves but for their families too. All in the name of trying to protect innocent people from such horrible circumstances.

Not finished with what he needed to share, Ryan continued. "They took me off the case immediately. It wasn't entirely clear how our identities became compromised, especially how they located my partner's family. We were always following protocol, never deviating from it. The experience shook me, though. I feared for my family's safety above anything else, never wanting any harm to ever come to them. So, in the days that followed, I moved my parents to a new home in Santa Monica, registered them under assumed names, and decided to request a transfer back to being a patrol officer, expecting to return to the streets to keep the local neighborhoods safe. Denied my request, the only option they offered was to sit behind a desk for the next year in another district. Fully knowing I couldn't do that day in and day out, regardless of whether I was still part of the Narcotics Unit, I opted to take a leave of absence for a month to figure things out and never did go back. Upon finding a small apartment in a quiet suburb in Santa Barbara, I took on the odd construction job before landing a position as an installer for a hi-tech residential security company. Reluctantly leaving my old life behind, needing to make some extra money, and wanting to open my own security business, I signed with an acting agent in hopes of continuing that temporarily so I could fund my start-up. It was the only other thing I knew how to do well. Reinstating my stage name from when I was a kid, I superficially altered my appearance as much as possible to keep my troubled past a secret, not wanting to dredge up anything. Not long after, I started to get attention from a few people in the business, many remembering me from different shows I had done a while back. That opened the door for the opportunity to be cast in the series of films you've seen me in. Once the first installment was under my belt and nobody had connected me to my past life, I figured I was in the clear after that. Now having the money to move closer to the beach off the coast of Malibu, I found a small three-bedroom house along the coast badly in need of renovation and established roots there once the construction had finished. Arriving on set, the first few weeks of the third movie, we weren't entirely aware of who the major investor in the production was this time, and didn't care as long as our contracts got paid out. Very late one night, I returned home from a shoot to find a van parked across the street from me. Obviously, knowing the drill, I was certain it was more than just a serviceman working at one in the morning. Getting out of my truck, I stayed alert in case there was a problem. Suddenly, the lights went on, and the van came barreling towards my house. As the doors swung open, I was forcefully grabbed by four guys and tossed in before they sped away. Blindfolded and gagged, I thought the worst. That's when I figured my life was about to end. I sat there, preparing to die, and hoped it would be a fast." Pausing momentarily, he cleared his throat and said, "Long story short, the Cartel didn't take me. It was a group of DEA agents under the threshold of SOD, a Special Operations Division. Driven to an undisclosed location, releasing me from my restraints, they requested information on a wanted man named Constantine Consuelos. He was heavily involved in many arms of the Colombian Cartel and was on their high-priority list. When they revealed the guy was responsible for the increase in drug activity along the Tijuana border into the Chula Vista area, my interest piqued immediately, realizing that this place bordered my old neighborhood. They believed he was in California and asked me if I recognized him. Looking at the picture, I knew with little doubt it was one of the investors I'd noticed around the movie set from time to time, always checking in with the crew to see if we were running on schedule. Confirming his identity, the detective asked me to go undercover for them, completely aware of my law enforcement training and the fact I was a former narcotics investigator. Understanding what I was about to be roped into, having evaded this for years prior, I initially declined full involvement. Immediately thinking of my family's safety, knowing what these guys were capable of, the cop buried deep inside me emerged, making me change my mind. After agreeing to help, I got released hours later. They said they'd be in touch. Over the next week, I kept an eye on Consuelos when he made his unscheduled appearances on set. Noticing my focus on him one day, looking straight at me, I knew something was up. That night, on my way home from another late shoot, I realized I'd forgotten my cell phone. Remembering I left it on the charger in my trailer, I turned around and returned to the lot to get it. Reaching the front gates, I was surprised to see the guards were gone and everything was locked. Deciding to slip through the fence, I walked to my trailer to retrieve the phone. On the way back to the truck, I got distracted by the sounds of loud, violent yelling. Curious, I investigated and came across a group of men, the on-site security guards, and Consuelos. Peering through the windows of a few vehicles, entirely out of sight, I saw the men had guns pointed at three other guys on their knees, gagged, with their hands tied behind their backs. My first instinct was to record what was happening, so I pulled out my phone. Within seconds of doing this, Consuelos shot the three men in the head one by one. After witnessing the murders, I left the lot and tried to remain undetected. Driving around for about five hours, needing to think up a plan, I understood all too well that Consuelos probably had contacts everywhere, including the police department. Upon returning home, I wasn't surprised to see the same mysterious van parked outside my house again. Unafraid, I walked straight up to it. They opened the door and let me in. Already aware of what had happened, the agents inquired whether I had any information for them. I presented what was recorded on my phone, explaining that I returned to the set because I had forgotten it in the first place, adding that I'd stumbled upon the scene while going back to my truck. Analyzing the faces of the murdered men, they confirmed that one was an undercover DEA agent, and the other two were FBI. Updated further, they said they discovered Consuelos also had contacts working within many levels of the government and had ties to illegal weapons dealers and terrorist organizations overseas. Claiming their unit to be one of the precious few still untainted by Consuelos and his payoffs, the man in charge told me not to trust anyone else. Once my evidence was validated and copied, they said not to draw attention and to continue the production. I was to watch for Consuelos since they had lost track of his whereabouts hours before. They knew he had gone underground for a reason. So, that week, I returned to the set. Consuelos only showed up once, for less than ten minutes. While shooting this one scene, he watched over us like a hawk, giving me a bad feeling. As quickly as he showed up, he disappeared. Early the following morning, must have been around three a.m., a bunch of men converged on my house, breaking in from the back. Thankful, it was the SOD agents and nobody else; the guys informed me of an authenticated Intel alert they'd received. Consuelos had just put out *a hit* with my name on it. Supposedly, the informants said his men reviewed the security footage from the night of the murders, found out I was there, and witnessed everything. That's when the United States Marshals Service intervened and told me my life as Anthony Morgan was about to end since they had just located Consuelos. A sting operation was underway to arrest him for killing the three agents, and I was their prime witness." Ryan continued, somewhat unsettled, "They said they wanted me to testify against Consuelos by creating a video interview to describe the footage from my phone. The only catch was, by submitting the evidence that would indict one of the DEA/FBI's most wanted, along with his men on site that night, I would need to disappear right afterward if I wanted to live."

Changing positions on the sofa, he leaned back, locked his hands behind his head, and waited a second to pay attention to the cameras as each made one complete loop.

"So, that night, I agreed to do as they asked, thinking about the families of those men who died. I finished their requested interview and stayed in an unknown safe house location that night. They gave me instructions for the following day – first, not to divulge to anyone what was about to happen, and two, take my boat out fishing later that afternoon to the coordinates given to me and wait. Issued a different vehicle, I covertly passed by my house, knowing I had to leave everything behind. With nothing but the clothes on my back, cell phone, and wallet, I nervously drove to my parents' house, unsure if that was a good idea. I knew I needed to see them one last time. Paranoid that someone had followed me or, worse, was already waiting on their street, I told you what happened when I was there. Rather not relive that again."

Remembering where he left off, he explained, "Umm, so when I was about to leave their house, I told my family I was taking the boat out fishing for a bit, which wasn't unusual. Arriving at Marina Del Ray Harbor, I started the boat and texted a buddy of mine to meet up later at the pub down the street from his place, knowing full well I wasn't ever going to follow through on those plans. It needed to look real – whatever was going to happen. Receiving the confirmation text from my friend, he said he'd see me around 8:30 p.m. While leaving the harbor, knowing the direction my life was about to go now, alone, kinda feeling scared and guilty for leaving my family behind, inevitably about to also put them through the pain of losing a child and sibling, I did as instructed and set the GPS for the coordinates given to me. When I reached the location miles offshore, I could see rough weather developing in the distance. Inside the boat to stay warm, I waited for almost two hours, continuously repositioning myself as I drifted off course while the storm started to make its presence known. The waters began to surge through the rain and fog. Amidst it all, I suddenly noticed a large ship approaching. Almost in total darkness, a smaller craft rushed towards me with a group of men dressed in black. Boarding my boat, providing further instructions, they said to leave my phone and wallet behind, asking me to enclose them in the waterproof bag handed to me, knowing someone could easily salvage them. Transferring onto the military inflatable, turning on a dime, the officer skillfully drove us back to the larger vessel. When climbing the ladder, the heavy winds bounced us around. That caused me to hit my head on a piece of steel while pressing upward toward the main deck. That is how I got this scar," he explained, pointing to what I had asked about earlier. "Once aboard, they took me to another undisclosed location. There, I watched the news coverage of my death and witnessed footage of my family and friends in mourning. Left with tremendous guilt for what I had put them through, I wished life could return to normal. Days later, I read a news report by the California Coast Guard, and from what I could gather, technically, the storm hit my boat pretty hard since they showed reporters pictures of it capsized with pieces missing. They salvaged both my wallet and phone as planned. That caused an immediate media frenzy. All of it, I believe, was orchestrated to get maximum exposure. By the end of that week, they again transferred me to another government facility, somewhere overseas, I assumed, since I was placed on a plane for over ten hours before landing on an abandoned runway in the middle of nowhere. There, I met an unnamed agent who informed me that I had three choices. Due to my status in life, being well-known and photographed often, they said I could leave at will and live anonymously in another country - but I would run a risk of eventually being recognized, hunted down, and killed. The second option was to spend the rest of my existence hiding within the walls of that facility under armed guard, technically living in captivity, to continue a restricted life. Lastly, the third option was more drastic. Listening to the specifics, the agent presented a process that entailed altering my appearance, which meant I could hopefully continue a sense of normalcy after everything was said and done. Given what you see, it's obvious I chose door number three," he said, putting on a fake smile in a humorous attempt to lighten the mood. "Within a week, I had met with surgeons to discuss the procedure and spent two and a half months recovering. Taking off the wrapped bandages, the only thing that looked familiar to me was my eyes. They at least had stayed the same, but I had to wear the contacts in public to hide them even more. Case in point, you recognized them immediately. Upon being released from that place a few weeks after making a full recovery, they compensated me by granting access to significant funds, multiple safe houses around the globe, and 24/7 stealth security until they could prove that my life was no longer in danger. Afterward, we agreed that my lifestyle would remain at the standard I was used to, rewarding my cooperation and sacrifice. Remember that home security business I had built? While making the movies, I hired someone to run it and invested what I could to expand. When all this happened, the agency orchestrated its sale after my death. That has provided me with additional funds to live off of at some point down the line. All of that was magically executed without anyone knowing. The general public is not remotely aware of what they can do. It is mindblowing, actually."

Taking a break, scouring the screen images, he continued, "Anyway, umm, moving on, I decided to integrate back into society and opted to try and settle here off the coast of Australia. Always wanting to visit the Great Barrier Reef over the years, I felt a need to be reacquainted with the sea. When I saw this house for sale, I had it renovated and altered to how you see it, hoping I could stay here for a while and start a new life. After spending so much time alone in other safe houses around the globe, finally en route to Hamilton Island when this house was ready, I noticed you on the plane. When walking down the center aisle, your eyes and smile caught my attention and gave me this warm feeling - something I had not felt in a very long time. Unexpectedly meeting you at the store that morning, I was initially searching for a friend. As I said, I never intended to bring anyone into all this, but as time passed, I could no longer ignore the feelings I was developing for you." Reaching over to take hold of my hand and kissing it, he moved closer, hugging me, all the while keeping watch on the monitors. "The day the two of us went shopping in town, a newly assigned officer to my case passed updated intel to Rob lurking nearby. They informed him that Consuelos' crew had somehow infiltrated my USMS file, breaching my current status and compromising my whereabouts. That is why I left you so abruptly outside the shop, citing that I forgot to buy something. Rob had signaled me minutes before to meet up so he could pass along the warning and share the plan in place. Making you stay overnight was not only a personal request of mine but also a safety measure. They had the house surrounded by security personnel staying in an adjacent home, and everyone agreed that you needed to be protected as a precaution. I also selfishly wanted to spend those final hours together because, in the morning, the plan was to leave the island. Your spa appointment helped me do this seamlessly. I etched into memory every second you drove away from me that morning, knowing that would be the last time I would ever see you. Like I said before, I wanted you to continue living your life, so I had to let you go. Kayla was assigned to keep an eye on you, at least until you got back to New York. I vowed to find you again one day when this whole thing ended, but when they told me that I was not the only person on Consuelos' radar and that he had his sights set on you as a way to get to me, placing you in grave danger, I had no choice but to bring you here. I'm sorry. There was no other option."

Staring at the ground, unable to respond to what he had just explained, I watched Ryan take a deep breath.

"They've validated the two precautionary redirects I experienced a few weeks earlier and are now investigating a third Intel breach. It's believed the Cartel knows Anthony Morgan was placed in protective custody and did not die at sea as originally reported. Footage showing me living within the government facility where I underwent surgery has now been listed as accessed and distributed. The USMS and SOD agents discovered that photos of my new face were passed along to the Cartel using this footage. It accompanied 'the hit' personally ordered by Consuelos, who is currently behind bars. From the FBI and DEA to USMS, every organization immediately began scanning my files to try and discover who the embedded mole was and how they were successfully evading security systems protocol to supply info to the Cartel. This was not easy since the DEA and SOD had about 800 Intel analysts to scour through. Given the situation, my security team went on high alert and had to extract me to the yacht to keep moving. Long story short, over seventeen of Consuelos' men are now in custody since this all took place. My testimony and video of Consuelos killing those three agents prove beyond a doubt that he is guilty of three accounts of first-degree murder. His trial will begin around three months from now, and he'll probably receive life in prison, if not the death penalty, because he was the one who pulled the trigger. Until then, I must continue relocating, trying to stay one step ahead. I am Ryan Davis now. Anthony Morgan is dead, and he needs to stay that way."

Seeing the astonishment on my face, almost unable to comprehend it all, he turned to me and said, "I've completely terrified you now, I'm sure. This is a prime example of what happens when you see the criminal world hidden behind the curtain. Much of the population is oblivious to the truth. The government does an excellent job of keeping it that way. This is not a movie – sadly, this is my life. It's complicated, and I'm sorry, but now you understand why."

Still shocked by the story he shared, I was lost for words. "I don't even know what to say."

"It's fine. I know it's a lot to take in."

Processing what he revealed, Ryan watched the monitors as the storm made landfall. The trees started to sway violently in the surging winds, and the rains fiercely pelted the steel shields, creating a lot of noise. Turning on the radio to listen to the island news report, we learned they'd upgraded the storm to a category four cyclone as anticipated. Most of the island's guests had been evacuated to the mainland. Anyone remaining had been instructed to go to the nearest storm shelter over the past few hours. They kept rhyming off a handful of locations in rotation.

Frightened, I sat beside Ryan on the sofa. He tried to keep me calm.

"Don't worry. This house is a fortress. I had it reinforced to withstand hurricane winds of over two hundred miles per hour. We'll be okay. I have lots of supplies in the bunker, solar backup power when the electricity goes off, so yeah, we're good."

Knowing the truth now of what happened to him and where his life stood, I couldn't help but wonder where this left us.

"Can I ask you something?"

He turned his focus my way, ready to answer any question.

"Umm, with everything that's happened - where do we go from here? What happens to us now?"

Slowly taking hold of my left hand, needing to think positively, he focused on one of my fingers. "You know, while snorkeling the reef the other day, I was thinking how perfect things were. There was no violence, no killing, and no fear. For once, I was immersed in the moment, not once thinking about this entire situation. My world was peaceful, and you were the reason for that. In the water, far away from everyone else, I felt compelled to ask you something but didn't, figuring I'd scare you off..."

Having an inkling as to what he was about to say, I turned to him, peering into his strangely bluish eyes.

"Eva, in the middle of the ocean, I wanted to ask you to marry me, right then and there, in that pristine place, where I knew I loved you and wanted to spend the rest of my life with you, no matter how long or short that might end up being. Living apart wouldn't be living anymore. As bad as my life has turned out, I can confidently say I'd do it over again if I knew it led to a future together. Fate might decide who comes into your life, but your heart decides who stays. Ev, I need you to remain in mine."

With tears streaming down my cheeks, unable to speak, I nodded. Oddly staring into the eyes of a stranger, I closed mine as he lovingly leaned in. His precious kisses were unchanged despite his appearance, tenderly offering this unparalleled affection like no other. Falling back onto the sofa, taken away as the rains fell above, I knew I needed him. Longing for that pure, soul-melding closeness, without any reservations, my hand slid under his shirt and along his chest, making him freeze. Backing away, caught off guard, not moving a muscle, our eyes met again. Stoically hovering above me, he tried to analyze the expression on my face.

About to speak, I softly pressed my finger against his lips to stop him. All I whispered was, "I love you."

Not hesitating, his eyes sparkled. "I will always love you more," he said lovingly.

Bodies pressed tightly together, he gently lifted me off the sofa, effortlessly supporting my weight as my legs wrapped around his waist. Clinging to him, he carried me through the darkness to his room at the top of the stairs. Gently set on the fluffy, light-colored duvet, I innocently inched backward and fell into an abundance of pillows stacked along the headboard. Crawling across the bed, the gravitational force between us brought him closer. Eyes locked to mine, he hovered a moment and hesitated. Affectionately caressing my cheek and showering me with dreamy kisses, I knew the timing was right. Reaching to slide his shirt over his head, he did the same for me, not speaking a word. Legs intertwined, bodies snugly bound together, we found a spot under the covers. Feeling fully alive for the first time, the flood of euphoria emerged as it naturally should. Not awkward. Never nervous, unsure, or afraid. He was my protector, my safety, my strength. It was our secret moment of sheer ecstasy while hiding from the world.

Nestled beside him, watching him calmly drift off, I, too, tried to fall asleep but felt compelled to study his face. Not seeing his eyes, I knew I had fallen in love with Ryan Davis - not Anthony Morgan.

Lying there, the sounds of the rain hitting the roof created nature's music while gusting winds joined in from time to time. Thinking back to what he said, I thought meeting him was fate. Deciding to become his friend was a choice I thankfully made, but falling in love, without a doubt, was beyond my control. That made me realize why it never worked out with anyone else. I just wasn't meant for anyone but him. Resting my hand against the side of his face, running my thumb along his cheekbone, he slowly opened his eyes and granted me that sexy grin that would warm me from head to toe.

Startled by the steel shields rattling violently with the high wind gusts, sounding alarmingly unstable, I looked at him fearfully. Amidst the questionable weather beating down on the island, bringing us back to reality, three loud bangs hit the roof out of nowhere. Feeling my heart pounding, Ryan immediately threw on a pair of shorts. Swiftly sliding open the side table drawer, he took a handgun from a concealed box. Cracks of thunder shook the whole house.

Loading the clip, he stood unafraid and racked the slide on the gun. "Stay here."

When he left the room, I gathered my clothes, attempting to get somewhat dressed. At the top of the stairs, I crouched down, trying to see what was happening using only the dimness of the TV screen. To ensure the lower level was secure, Ryan enlarged each camera image on the monitor and reviewed it individually.

Turning to where I was, he said, "It is okay. The coast is clear. A tall tree fell on the slope behind the house. I see a few large branches have broken off and hit the roof. They are lying on the same side. The storm is increasing. We need to stay on this level just to be safe. When the worst comes through, we might be safer in the bunker below. Unfortunately, this storm is going to slow down the stealth team."

Making my way down the stairs, I went to the great room and switched on two battery-operated lanterns to help create a faint, inconspicuous light while Ryan watched the screen.

Sitting down, cuddled on the sofa, his arms tightly around me, our fingers intertwined, he said, "So… I seem to recall a question I asked you a little while ago. Technically, I never actually heard an answer from you."

With eyes glued to his, in the sincerest of tones, I confirmed, "Yes, Ryan Davis, I will marry you," feeling slightly shy given what just happened.

Waiting for a second, he said, "When this is all over, I want to start my life with you."

"I want that too," I replied, clinging even closer, hoping to discuss more of what awaited us in the future. Curling up with my legs draped over his, feeling utterly content, I immediately thought about how we would make this work if I lived in New York or worked in California. Deciding not to ruin our moment, I figured I'd leave that discussion for another time.

While reveling in the peacefulness of the house, a beeping signal from the security console rang out.

Getting up quickly to see what communication had been sent through, Ryan read the message aloud. "Pickup time: undetermined?" Setting off the emergency beacon a second time, we waited for another response, hoping the next one would be more concrete. Once again, the monitor went off, listing the exact details: "Pickup time:

undetermined." Knowing the weather was to blame, he concluded, "Well, we're going to have to sit tight and make it through this storm."

Walking back over to me, placing the guns on the floor close to the sofa, he fluffed up the pillows at one end. Lying down on his side, he said, "Care to join me?"

Tight beside him, he took the blanket draped over the back and covered us both. Holding me, we continued monitoring the pictures presented on the screen. Falling asleep for a couple of hours as the rain and winds prevailed, opening my eyes for a split second, I watched the cameras to make sure all was clear. Drifting off again, I knew whatever happened, I didn't care as long as I was in the arms of the man who truly loved me.

| 35 |

The World Behind the Curtain

20°20'21" S / 148°57'15" E

Hours passed as the hurricane-force winds continued to surge, causing the shields to rattle nonstop. Both of us began to stir as a result of the noise. Seeing the battery-operated lanterns had faded, immersed in darkness, it was not easy to distinguish the time of day. Half-awake, I noticed Ryan's eyes open. Immediately drawn to the monitor that had gone black, he lifted himself off the sofa, flinging the blanket in the process. Grabbing a gun off the floor, his actions frightened me. Hastily descending the steps into the bunker, he hoped the power had just gone off and nothing else. Within seconds, the screen flickered. Each camera soon returned to its sequence in line.

Guess he switched over to solar power now, I quietly assumed.

Back upstairs, Ryan analyzed the footage in great detail. Thoroughly accounting for every angle of the house, he seemed confident that the perimeter was clear. We found the storm still ripping the island to shreds when changing the feed from night vision to standard view. Convinced everything was now secure, I went to get cleaned up a little.

On the way back from the main floor bedroom, I felt hungry. It didn't take long to scout out the food storage lockers for something that would constitute a healthy breakfast. While searching the shelves and opening each cabinet door one by one, I selected a few items and placed them on a nearby table. With peanut butter, sealed crackers, and some canned fruit in hand, along with two more water bottles, I climbed the stairs to return to the kitchen.

Seeing me emerge, carrying everything awkwardly in my arms, Ryan came to my aid. He placed the food on the counter and grabbed some dishes for me to prepare two plates. Content with the rationed meal I'd brought into the media room, Ryan kept studying each full-screen image and stayed alert.

Aware of his intense expression, I sat to his right after placing the food on the side table. That's when I gave him a slight nudge.

His stressed appearance brightened when he looked my way. "Sorry for frightening you earlier. I needed to switch the power source to the solar supply. We should be okay for two to three days, but no more than that. If they don't pick us up by then, there is a chance we'll be trapped in here, completely blind. I don't mean to scare you. I just want to prepare you for what may happen. I'm being honest."

"Whatever comes our way, we will just face it together, deal?" Concerned, my head rested on his shoulder.

He placed his hand on top of mine and confirmed with a whisper, "Absolutely."

The day rolled by at a snail's pace. Ryan sent out another secure distress signal late that afternoon. Waiting patiently to see if the storm had subsided enough for the extraction team to rescue us, we watched the security console, hoping to receive a positive response.

In minutes, Ryan read the message aloud. "Pick-up time: undeter-mined."

Frustrated, he switched on the radio to try and gather a report on the storm's severity. We heard the news anchor state that the winds were averaging 175 km/hr with added gusts reaching a whopping 210 km/hr as the rains continued to fall heavily, with flooding and mudslides confirmed in many areas of the island, along with severe damage to coastal structures. A voluntary evacuation occurred a few hours before the storm made landfall. Unbeknownst to us, most island guests relocated to the mainland in case the airport and marina were damaged after the storm. Now relaying a shelter-in-place warning to a handful of permanent residents and guests who chose to remain, a list of instructions went on repeat.

With his arms around me, not having a choice but to sit tight, the two of us walked to the sofa. Monitoring the cameras for any sign of movement, he and I played card games to pass the time, desperate to keep our minds off things.

Over the next few hours, I made trips to the bunker for food to keep our stomachs from growling. Shifting our bodies into more comfortable positions from time to time, now with my legs elevated on the back of the sofa, we discussed some personal likes and dislikes, which somehow filtered into our thoughts and opinions on world issues. We even debated corporate and government corruption. That created an in-depth conversation on how to solve the skyrocketing food and water crisis in third-world countries.

"If the wealthy of the world got together, they could wipe out hunger in a matter of a week, even provide clean water and sanitation to the masses, who do not have access to these liberties. I've always funded projects that make a significant difference. High impact in a short amount of time. Especially the causes that benefit children. We've been so fortunate as kids to grow up in a country where basic needs were supplied. Many don't have these luxuries. Thirteen percent of children in the world grow up in poverty. My heart goes out to each one of them. In the past, I've funded school breakfast programs and food banks back home to support efforts locally. Then, I branched out to humanitarian missions, where I vowed to have a substantial impact every year. When I updated my Will a couple of years ago, I allotted some money to continue supporting those charities. I assigned the task to my beneficiaries under my lawyer's direction, hoping they would abide by my wishes. That crosses my mind often."

"I'm sure they are. If they knew it was important to you, they would continue your work, right?"

"Depends. Hopefully, my family feels the need to help as much as I did."

After such a heavy conversation, Ryan switched gears. "So, Eva Thompson, what would you consider a perfect wedding?"

Not needing to think at all, I replied, "An intimate beach wedding has always been a dream of mine. While visiting my grandparents in the summers, I always saw so many of those. Each one always gave me a warm feeling in my heart."

"I think that sounds perfect," he said in the sincerest of tones.

By nine o'clock that evening, having covered a lot of territory in conversation, Ryan got concerned when we were preparing to go to sleep.

"We should take turns watching the screens tonight while the other gets some rest. The longer we stay here, the more worried I am that they'll find us. If that's the case, we have to be diligent. We are safe inside the house as long as the walls remain intact. We can't risk falling asleep at the same time."

Understanding, I rose to the challenge and said, "Yes, I can do that."

"Okay, then. I'll take the first shift. You get some sleep. I'll wake you when we need to switch." Positioning the guns on the table to his left, he sat at the end of the sofa while I found a comfortable spot with my pillow placed at the opposite end. Ryan grabbed my feet, positioned each on his lap, and massaged them gently, helping me relax and drift off.

| 36 |

Abandoned

20°20'21" S / 148°57'15" E

Faintly hearing someone talking, feeling a little nudge to my shoulder, I woke to find Ryan sitting alongside me.

"Eva? I'm so sorry, but we need to switch. It's 5:30. I hate to wake you."

Rising from the pillow, unaware of where I was, quite disoriented, I focused and realized he had stayed up most of the night. He looked so tired.

"I am so sorry. Why didn't you wake me sooner?"

"You looked so peaceful. I couldn't. I just need to recharge. Can you take over so I can rest for an hour? I should be okay, then. The storm is dying down. Be sure to watch for any movement. Wake me if you see anything."

Agreeing with his instructions, I reassured him, "Yes, I will."

Lying in the same place I had slept, Ryan positioned the guns on the floor within arm's reach and closed his eyes once his head hit the pillow. Legs outstretched over the top of mine now, I gradually woke up while rubbing his calves and feet lightly, trying to repay the favor he so kindly bestowed upon me. With the dimness of dawn beginning to appear, shedding a hint of light on the damage around us, I flipped through the camera images. Trees were blown down or uprooted, and debris filled the pool. Even the deck chairs were flung off the platform or submerged under the water. The winds were still gusting, causing the trees to sway violently back and forth as fragments flew past the cameras. The channel pictures showed the waves still invading the coastline at around a height of eight to ten feet, maybe more.

The clock on the screen soon changed to 6:22 a.m. I was still wide awake while Ryan slept soundly. Three days had gone by since we arrived at his house. The worst of the storm had passed over, but the winds were still strong. As the rains hit the roof in a persistent vertical dousing versus violently tossed buckets, I felt better knowing the danger of the system had eased somewhat. In the grand scheme of things, though, the weather seemed to be the least of our worries. If anything, it was the one thing keeping us alive all this time.

By now, I assumed most of my family and friends back home were concerned for my safety and well-being since the cyclone hit the island. For the most part, Ellie came to mind. Remembering my last telephone call with her, wishing I hadn't planned a trip so far away, suddenly made my heart ache. Thoughts of Antonia surfaced, making me wonder how she would survive being in New York without me there. Who would help her not miss Carlo when he was in California? Moving on to poor Mr. Gavin and Sarah, knowing he had encouraged me to take this time off, I figured they would feel responsible if anything bad happened.

Contemplating how I could get in touch with each of them to let them know I was okay, I remembered Kayla instructed me to turn off my cell phone when we left the Qualia cottage the day I arrived at the yacht. Unable to recall where it went after that, I may have stashed it in the bedside table drawer on the boat for safekeeping because it was not in my bag. Understanding that my sister was probably trying to get a hold of me all this time, not getting an answer made me highly anxious. Mindful of how worried she must be and how helpless she'd feel, not knowing if I was alive or dead made me cry. I never wanted to hurt any of them. It was never my intention. This trip was supposed to be an escape from my damaged life - a break from the relentless pain and suffering - a month away to heal and clear my head before returning home with a new perspective on life - thoughts of how selfish that was worsened the guilt because it was unlike me. I always considered everyone when making decisions, regardless of my feelings. Desperate to ignore the negative thoughts and replace them with something more positive, realizing I could not change the past, I felt grateful to have found love.

"How could that be considered negative?" I muttered.

Looking over at Ryan while he slept, I knew I loved him despite our circumstances being far from ordinary. Thinking ahead to one day making it through this horrible nightmare, I thought about what it would be like to return home, but doubted whether that would even be possible now. My mind took me down a million different paths, trying to establish a way our lives could blend seamlessly. Sadly, there was only one answer to all of that. I would inevitably have to disappear with him.

Off task, very distracted, my attention returned to scanning the images on the screen again, looking for any movement. Making the rounds a few times, I was happy there was nothing to report. Determined to stay focused, switching the cameras over to standard view, I could see far more than with night vision. The damage surrounding the house suddenly appeared worse. A roof on the home, just one street below, was entirely blown off. Getting a closer look at the images on the screen, I was shocked to see what little was left untouched. The pool had gone from a tranquil blue oasis to a muddy mess as the pictures looped around and around, eventually causing my astonishment to wear off.

With my legs slightly numb, I needed to shift positions. That subtle movement caused Ryan to stir. The clock read 8:55. Turning to see if he was awake, I leaned forward, hoping to greet him. Seeing his one eye open, feeling my presence, he peered down toward his feet at me.

Offering a half-smile, he asked, "Is everything the same?"

"Yes, nothing to report other than severe damage, rain, wind, and waves."

"Well, that is good and bad," he pointed out, sitting up to analyze the images, stretching a bit. "The extraction team will have difficulty getting us by land since debris is blocking the road. That will force an extraction by air or water - if the winds ever die down."

The calm in his voice made me feel better about the thoughts I had earlier. But I couldn't help but think further about everyone back home, knowing they must be so worried.

"Ryan, I was thinking about my family and friends. Is there any way to get a message to them saying I'm alright? I know we can't use phones, so."

"I'm sorry, Eva. We can't contact anyone on an unsecured line." He hesitated a moment before adding, "I forgot. Your family still knows you're alive." As his eyes moved to the floor, he said, "Mine wouldn't be looking for me."

That comment made my heart go out to him.

Concretely responding, Ryan said, "Until we make it out and get further instructions, we can't do anything. I'm sorry."

Understanding what he was saying, I knew it could jeopardize our lives if we attempted to call anyone.

In agreement, he hugged me tightly. "Don't worry, they'll be here soon. I promise."

With that said, I got up from the sofa to stretch my legs, deciding to quickly freshen up and change before gathering up a few things from the bunker for breakfast. When I returned to the living room, Ryan asked me to watch the screens while he did the same. He submitted another distress signal along the way to see what would happen. While waiting for a response, ten minutes passed with no word, then an hour, then two as I paced the house up and down.

Desperate, inevitably losing hope that people would rescue us, I went into the main floor bedroom, closed the door slightly, and lay on the bed. Tightly hugging a pillow, I started to cry, wondering if this was it. If this was the way, our lives were going to end.

In search of where I had disappeared, Ryan came to the bedroom looking for me. Opening the door a crack to peek inside, he saw my tearful face on the pillow.

Empathetically inching closer, realizing I was distraught, he sat on the edge of the bed and said, "Eva, I know things seem hopeless right now, but we are going to get out of this. Please don't cry."

With tears streaming down my face, I sat up and tightly wrapped my arms around his neck, hoping he could offer solace.

"I know you're scared, but we're gonna be fine. I promise. The team will get us out of here and take us somewhere safe so we can be together."

Just as we were about to part ways, Ryan heard the message notification from the security system.

Hoping for good news, he said, "Come with me."

We ran to the screen, hand in hand.

Ryan read the message. "Pick-up: 23:00," he said with relief. "There! Finally! See, the team is coming to get us at 11:00 tonight."

Quite relieved to know that they hadn't abandoned us, I had mixed feelings of happiness and fear simultaneously.

On our way back to the sofa, after gathering our thoughts, he said, "Are you alright?"

"Yes… It will be better once we leave and go somewhere far away. Do you think these people will follow us?"

"No," he said. Pausing, he added, "Truthfully, yes, they will. But it will take them some time to figure it out. Hopefully, they've discovered who the person is giving out Intel at HQ. But let's not think of that right now. Let's focus on getting out of here."

With no choice but to smile at his handsome face, beaming with delight, I immediately replied, "I love you, Ryan Davis."

"I will always love you more, Eva Thompson." Mischievously leaning in, he kissed me with meaning and specific intention. Breaking intermittently to pay attention to the images flipping past the screen, he suddenly tackled me on the couch and said, "Come here."

Knowing this may be the last opportunity to love each other, we took advantage of the peaceful seclusion before leaving the house. How was this man so perfect for me? Sweeping me off my feet and giving me butterflies, just as I prayed for it to happen months earlier. I knew then we were just meant to be. This was the person I was destined to love - nobody else.

| 37 |

Into the Darkness

20°20'21" S / 148°57'15" E

Anxious, while preparing to depart the house that night, my stomach was in knots as the clock dwindled. It was hard to breathe with the persistent pressure on my chest while we covered the furniture with white sheets. Closing the bunker door, hiding it from sight under the area rug, we knew we wouldn't be back. I thought about how much I would miss this place. Even though our happiness here was short-lived, ruined by chaos, uncertainty, and fear, we weathered the storm and even found a moment of peaceful bliss amidst it all. Now, facing a journey through the unknown, I could hear my grandfather's words quoting Vivian Greene. *Life is not about waiting for the storm to pass. It's about learning to dance in the rain.* Glancing over at Ryan, I hoped and prayed I would have enough courage and strength to do that. Seeing him smile at me with such love in his eyes helped me believe I could.

By ten o'clock, we were sitting nervously on the covered sofa with our backpacks strapped on, ready to leave at a moment's notice. Ryan listened intently for any noise, surveying the cameras for signs of life. Suddenly, the security monitor alerted us to another message.

Casually walking over to read it, Ryan said, "Pick up time: 22:10?" Pausing, he questioned, "Wait? Ten minutes?"

Detecting a level of confusion and concern off him, Ryan removed his backpack and paused for a split second. Bolting over to the large

TV, knowing there was a reason for the drastic change, he flipped through the camera images one by one, then stopped and froze. Intensely magnifying a specific frame, he spotted various dark figures emerging from the trees along the perimeter to the north.

"There's movement outside. They're not Special Ops."

Unable to produce a single word, knowing the Stealth Team was extracting us now because we were dangerously surrounded, Ryan grabbed the iPad and scanned all the cameras at full screen to gather more detail. He counted the bodies hiding in the shadows. Inching closer, all armed with guns, they converged upon the house. Powerless, not moving a muscle, staying close to him, we listened and waited. The silence was deafening. Not knowing what they were planning, able to feel their evil presence, we knew they were lurking. Hunting. Hit by a percussive blast, the steel shields rattled violently.

"Oh my god, Ryan!" I screamed, reaching up to protect my head, feeling the instability beneath our feet. Terror flashed across my face.

Sheltered by him, the place shook amidst a second explosion immediately after.

Inspecting the shields, traces of smoke began to creep in through the small cracks on that side. Thankful, the barriers held up, sustaining minimal damage; he physically distanced me from that area and went into action.

"Run upstairs. Hide."

"No, I want to stay with you and fight," I yelled in a determined voice, not wanting him to confront this alone.

"No, I can't lose you. Go. Hurry. Run!" he said, flipping open the bunker trap door and darting inside to grab more ammunition and weapons.

Fearfully adhering to his words, skipping steps, my heart pounded with the impending doom. Once upstairs, I turned to look over the railing into the living space below. The popping fury of gunfire filled the air with countless rounds attempting to penetrate the barriers. The shields stayed solid but buckled slightly in two places, making it easy to see the shadow-like figures trying to force their way inside.

My heart raced, and my hands quivered while I lay motionless with my stomach flat on the floor. Emerging from the bunker, Ryan flipped over the kitchen table, exposing a silver panel underneath where he quickly released ammunition and additional weaponry mounted strategically with duct tape. Loading clips into multiple weapons, he glanced up at me in utter desperation.

"Ev, whatever happens…" he said firmly.

Crying, I replied, "I know…."

"Stay back! Hide!"

Covering my ears, I stood up to move further away. Hit by a blast from above, it threw my body backward, twisting me awkwardly against the wall. Knocking the wind from me, leaving my lungs gasping for air, the thunderous sound temporarily hampered my hearing, causing a high-pitched ringing and cognitive confusion. Pain in every extremity, needing time to recover, the situation escalated violently, making me realize this was it. They were going to kill us.

Rain poured through the hole in the roof and flooded the hallway. Black smoke and the smell of sulfur spread through the place, making me choke while struggling to breathe. Barely coherent, crawling to the edge, covering my mouth, I tried to locate Ryan's whereabouts but couldn't focus. Eyes brutally burning and watering severely, unable to find him, another series of explosions buckled the barriers, causing a large sheet of glass on the backside of the living room to shatter into a million pieces, spraying shards in all directions, chiming as they fell. With a barrage of bullets now firing alarmingly, I stayed down and covered my head, knowing the love of my life was dead, and I was about to be, too. That's when I saw them - an army of killers stepping through the wreckage into the fiery room below.

Panicking, rushing from the hall to the nearest bedroom, opening the closet, I found space to the far left of a stack of boxes. Smoke crept into the room. I closed the closet door, pressing my fingertips along the bottom edge to pull it completely shut. Instinctively, grabbing a robe hanging above me, I used it to block the bottom half-inch opening, hoping to stop the engulfing smoke from seeping in, knowing there was no escape. Accepting the inevitable, I knew this was it - this was how I would die.

The floor beneath me vibrated with every explosion. In seconds, the battle increased, sounding like an all-out war with an incredible number of rounds drowning out the men yelling in the combat zone. Then, as fast as it started, the gunfire stopped. Nothing. Not a sound. It went deathly quiet.

Petrified, my blood ran cold. Every part of me - numb. That silence broke with the sound of footsteps approaching. Rhythmically causing the hardwood to creak, the heavy boots lurked ominously. Shutting my eyes and bowing my head, I knew these were my final moments. With tears streaming down my face, I prepared for the worst. Attentively listening, someone entered the doorway of the bedroom. Careful not to make any noise, I leaned forward on my knees to peek through the narrow gap between the doors. There, a man holding a rifle with a red laser scanned the room systematically. Fearfully, witnessing the beam of light cut through the smoke, my throat burned. Huddled back in the corner, I spread the robe sleeve over my nose and mouth to act as a filter. Afraid to cough, tears spilled onto my fingers while I pressed the fabric tighter, desperate to absorb my weeping. Feeling the slight draft of the closet door swinging open, revealing the black barrel of a gun, I held my breath as the red light searched the space in front of me. Following the scarlet target marker, with hands now clenched together in a white knuckle grip, praying, I knew it wouldn't be long before the love of my life would greet me in heaven.

BANG! BANG!! BANG!!

My body jumped with every shot. A thud followed. It sounded like a body had hit the floor. Taking inventory of my vital signs, I knew I was okay. That is when I heard it - a voice cut through the darkness.

"This is Bravo Delta 3-3-6. I have her."

The closet doors flung open. In seconds, a man dressed all in black, face faintly glowing green, offered me his hand.

"Miss? You're safe. Come with me! We must leave now!"

In shock, still unable to fully comprehend what was happening, I spotted a man lying dead on the floor with blood seeping from his head. Grasping hold of the soldier's hand, I tried to stand up.

Through the tears, in a muted tone, he asked, "Are you hurt?"

Unable to speak, shaking my head, *No*, I coughed uncontrollably. My lungs stung with every breath, and my legs gave out while trying to stand.

The man picked me up and placed my arm across his shoulders, helping me move with his other arm supporting my waist. "Quickly, Miss..." he said in a deep voice.

In a blurred state, we descended the stairs amidst the fire, smoke, and destruction, dodging dead bodies on the way through the opening where the front door once stood. Behind the house, climbing the muddy slope, the rains fell sharply. Through the tall grass, fallen trees, and mangled shrubbery, stumbling almost every step, I heard an engine roaring on top of One Tree Hill. Finally, on level ground, the man ducked my head as we approached the noisy machine shrouded in the thickness of night. Taking a seat on the helicopter, I noticed no light visible anywhere. All I could see was the green glow around the eyes of multiple dark figures on either side of me.

While the craft lifted off unsteadily, it was hard to decipher which direction we were heading. Feeling something hit my leg, I soon realized it was a hand. Terrified, I pushed it away, not knowing who it belonged to. Fearful, shaking uncontrollably, I faintly heard my name. Straining to filter the voice through the noise, I heard it a second time. It was almost inaudible.

"Ev?"

"Ryan?" I questioned, hoping with every ounce of my being it was.

"Sorry, Miss. Mr. Davis can't talk now," the dark shadow interjected.

Feeling his hand hit my leg again, I tightly grabbed hold of it and said, "I'm here! I'm here!"

Facing the ghostly figure, I bravely asked, "Please tell me he's okay?"

"Mr. Davis was hit. We are doing everything we can."

Unable to see Ryan's face, I moved my hand up his arm until I felt his cheek. Blindly leaning down to kiss it, I whispered in his ear, "I'm here. I love you. I'm here. You're going to be okay."

Focusing on the cyber eyes surrounding us, I desperately tried to see the outline of Ryan's body while flying roughly through the violent crosswinds. Out the window, noticing lights in the distance, it seemed like we were approaching a small city with a landing strip.

Touching down, a uniformed man instructed, "Please stay seated, Miss."

When the helicopter door opened, the winds and rain flew inside. Not wasting time, the men carried Ryan on a stretcher to a small plane waiting a few feet away. Forced to release his hand, I waited my turn to disembark and join him. Suddenly, the door on my side of the chopper opened.

"This way!" the man shouted above the whirring sound of the rotors.

Knowing they were expecting me to get out on the opposite side made me realize - I wasn't going with him. They were splitting us up. Seemingly moving in slow motion, I immediately bolted out the other door, attempting to get to Ryan. Feeling arms holding me back forcefully, I tried to press forward regardless. Unable to break free, my efforts were in vain. Dragged to a second plane, I watched the craft Ryan was on as it turned and taxied down the runway before ascending into the air, leaving me behind.

"No! No!" I shouted, falling to my knees! "No!"

Escorted away in a frantic state, continuously screaming at the officers, I heard a familiar voice call out.

"Eva! Eva? I need you to focus, alright? Focus here for a second."

Falling into a heightened state, trying to decipher who the voice belonged to, a woman stated, "It's Kayla. Eva, it's Kayla! You're okay. You're safe now."

"Kayla? Kayla?" I repeated, beginning to crumble in tears. Taking hold of her so tightly I could break her, I pleaded, "Where are they taking him? Is he alright? I want to be with him! Please, please, help me! I want to go with him, please! I'm begging you! Help me!"

"Eva…we had to split you up, but he told me to say he will see you soon."

Numb, I conceded to their demands, having no choice but to comply. A familiar feeling of abandonment returned - a childhood mix of emotions I hadn't experienced in years, yet it still haunted me to this day.

Seated on the aircraft, Kayla buckled me in.

When we took off, I felt very cold…prickly…faint.

| 38 |

Where Am I?

33°00'00" S / 71°32'34" W

Unconscious, with eyes closed, in a dreamlike state, I noticed a brightness unexpectedly appear, along with a captivating view of the Hamilton Island Yacht Club. Hazy, somewhat confused, looking around at the beauty, somehow untouched by the cyclone, I realized I was all alone. Needing to find Ryan, strangely unable to remember the past few days fully, I desperately searched for him.

Physically and mentally exhausted, I found no signs of life anywhere in the outwardly deserted downtown area. Tears flowed with vague flashes of our ordeal emerging piece by piece. Legs buckling, my knees hit the pavement. I felt hollow - a shell of a person. It was a level of grief that was hard to comprehend. Unwilling to accept the truth, knowing he had left me behind, I started shouting his name, finding my voice strangely muffled. Frantically scanning my surroundings, not sure what to do, out of the corner of my eye, I saw a figure standing at the end of the peninsula beyond the marina. Unsteadily running in that direction, I followed the boardwalk to where the man stood. Slowly turning around, the love of my life greeted me with a bright smile and those endearing eyes. Relieved, inching closer with an abundance of tears streaming down my face, the first thing I wanted to do was hold him so tightly and never let him go. Steps away, with open arms, close enough to see the sparkle in his eyes, our attention moved to a faint beeping sound emanating from the sky above. Leery, with my sights drawn toward the clouds, a blinding light temporarily distorted my vision. The intensity of it gradually dimmed, allowing my eyes to adjust and reveal more. Soon, the clouds transformed into lines of fluorescent lighting across a sterile ceiling. Lying on my back, I tried to raise my head slightly. Mentally, taking account of multiple IV lines and tubes running from my arm and nose, it didn't take long to know that someone was holding my hand. Unsure who it belonged to, I slowly rolled my head in that direction to see the person sitting alongside me. Intensely trying to focus, blinking repeatedly, the fuzzy figure revealed a woman's face. Concentrating, I realized it was Kayla.

In shock, I faintly whispered, "You're not dead," still unclear if she was, in fact, real or not.

Offering a relieved grin, she said, "Hey, there."

Knowing it was her, recalling that Ryan and I abandoned the crew on the yacht, leaving them defenseless, a feeling of tremendous guilt overtook me.

Hoping to explain, I desperately said, "We didn't come back and help... He said we couldn't. I'm so sorry. Please don't hate me. I'm so sorry. I'm sorry...." Uncontrollably sobbing as the remorse inflicted pain, knowing he said we had no choice but to leave them behind, I hoped she wasn't angry.

Reassuring me, gently rubbing my arm, she solemnly said, "No, Eva, I am fine. Our training prepares us for situations like that. Ryan followed protocol. Coming back for us would have put both of you in danger. There was nothing you could have done."

"Where are the others? Is everyone okay?"

Kayla lowered her head and revealed, "John and Jenn didn't make it." Shedding a tear, remembering her fallen friends, she quickly wiped it away to show strength.

Becoming more aware and in tune, I tried to sit up. That news settled in deeply. "Wait... What? They died?" I asked, hoping I heard her wrong.

Not receiving a response, only witnessing her somber reaction, I knew I need not ask again and observed a moment of silence.

Memories began to rekindle and flash in waves, making me whisper, "Where am I?"

Kayla stood up and confirmed, "We are at one of our government facilities, far from your extraction point."

"Where is Ryan? Is he okay? Please tell me he made it through, please…." Not receiving a response, tears streaming down my face, and my voice quivering with desperation, I begged for an answer. "Please, tell me he is alright? Kayla?"

Watching her turn her back to me and walk across the room, my heart sank since that simple gesture confirmed my worst fears. With my heart aching and my body searing in pain, tears flowed in an unstoppable flood. My fists closed tightly. Punching the bed over and over, I realized he had died.

Kayla rushed over and hugged me, offering support while I mourned. She stayed silent as I released blood-curdling screams. There was nothing she could do or say to calm me down. My body went lifeless as my mind produced memories of him and me. All the special moments we had shared. Our first sight of each other on the plane. Coincidentally, meeting at the store. Beating him to the corner on the race track. Walking hand in hand up the beach, enjoying the sunset. His face, bashfully tilted to one side, smiling when he proposed - even the times spent alone loving him in that less-than-perfect moment in time. Clinging to these mental images was all I had left.

Unavoidably sinking into denial, this dreadful, relentless feeling of loss spread through me with such emotion. This surge of anger unexpectedly boiled over, making me scream as I frantically yanked the IV tubes from my arm.

"He's not dead! Where is he? Tell me! He's not dead!"

As I yelled irrationally, Kayla left the room to find help.

Getting out of bed in a weakened state, I could hardly stand.

A group of nurses entered with urgency. The mob picked me up and forcefully restrained my arms and legs as I screamed and fought. In an instant, I felt a pinch. Seconds later, my body went limp, and the lights above me faded into darkness.

| 39 |

Alone

33°00'00" S / 71°32'34" W

Groggy and confused, I emerged from sedation the following day as a female doctor woke me with a soft voice and a caring hand on my shoulder. Unable to open my eyes fully, feeling extremely weighted, I sluggishly nodded to provide the answers required, trying to return to the land of the living. Knowing Ryan was dead, I went in and out of consciousness and suddenly lost the will to live.

In the days that followed, I didn't show one ounce of anger or violent behavior since the feeling of loss was so intense. It stole every bit of energy I had. Opening my eyes from time to time, mostly staring straight ahead, I attempted to comprehend how I had loved and lost the most loving person in the world. Doubt overpowered me, realizing my life would never resemble that happily ever after ending I'd envisioned for so long. Trying to find the silver lining, I cherished our shared experiences and felt grateful for what I had been gifted.

Unaware of time passing, I was more awake than asleep most days. Disoriented by feelings of lifelessness that engulfed my soul, I knew my heart would always seem partially there now, making healing an almost impossible task with so many shards unaccounted for.

One morning, upon waking to the faint sound of my name, a dim light crept in, allowing my eyes to adjust slowly. I eerily found multiple blurred figures standing on both sides of the room and heard them request my undivided attention. Struggling to seem coherent, I saw a group of doctors, military personnel, and men dressed in suits.

With a nurse by my side, a man sporting a black suit, tie, and white dress shirt said, "Ms. Thompson. My name is Officer Raymond. I work with the United States Marshals Service Witness Security. Please listen to what we have to say without interruption. It is imperative."

In muted agreement, nodding my head, he presented the information from inside a file folder in hand. "Ms. Thompson, we rescued you from Hamilton Island almost three weeks ago. We have cautiously monitored your progress and allowed your body to recover from the post-traumatic shock of your ordeal. Over the past couple of days, we have been happy with your recovery. Currently, you are staying at an undisclosed location for security reasons. Early afternoon, the day the cyclone ravaged the Queensland coast, the Whitehaven Beach excursion vessel you registered with hit a shallow reef called Frith Rock while experiencing mechanical issues just off the most south-easterly coast of Whitsunday Island. As a result, it eventually sank. Your name was left falsified on that ship's manifest as one of two unaccounted for by the rescue teams. Since then, the Australian Coast Guard has notified your family of the tragic loss, which aligns with what we need to say. I am sorry to inform you, Ms. Thompson, but this means you are not at liberty to return to your life in New York City. And with just cause. During our investigation, we recovered Intel, suggesting that Constantine Consuelos' men had been tracking you and Ryan Davis for a few days before transferring to the yacht. Some of these men killed at the safe house during the extraction had very recent photos of you both. Ms. Thompson, these criminals know what you look like, and if they find you, they will kill you for having an association with Ryan Davis. We are here to explain your options. Do you understand the details presented?"

Agreeing with a nod, overwhelmed with emotion, I listened as he continued to outline my current situation with little empathy.

"When you have fully recovered, we advise you not to resume life outside the confines of this facility for the time being. We have placed shadow security on your sister, brother-in-law, nephews, and parents to guarantee their safety in light of your situation. Furthermore, we now need to discuss the following options, should you wish to integrate back into society at a much later date."

Holding up two fingers, with my wrists still resting on the bed, hoping to ask a question, I asked, "Can I speak, please?"

"Yes, Ms. Thompson." Officer Raymond responded in a formal, monotone voice.

With my eyes beginning to well with tears, gasping, trying not to break down uncontrollably, I questioned, "Is Ryan alive? Can you please, umm? I'm begging you. Can you answer me that?"

"I am sorry, Ms. Thompson, but Mr. Davis succumbed to his injuries the night of the extraction. My condolences." Coldly moving along with their agenda as his words hit me, I remained silent. "Upon choosing to integrate back into society, you will be assigned a new identity, along with access to multiple safe house locations around the globe and 24-hour stealth security, should you require extraction, for as long as a threat to your life exists. You can freely leave on your own accord at any time, but we firmly advise against that. Since the Cartel knows what you look like, they will likely hunt you down and dispose of you. That is their mandate. If you choose to remain under our protection in this facility, we must keep you safe. We can assign jobs on-site to occupy your time. There is one last option to consider, as well. Your appearance can be cosmetically altered by simply changing your eye and hair color or overall hairstyle. And, as you are aware, Mr. Davis had a more drastic procedure performed, given his level of recognizability and celebrity, which allowed him to start an entirely new existence after his death. This procedure would give you complete control over the severity of the changes to your facial features. Ultimately, it would offer the freedom to blend into a new, somewhat normal life undetected. How you wish to implement these changes and to what degree is at your discretion." Looking over the notes written inside the file folder in hand, he paused and said, "I suppose that is all for now. We will leave you to think over these decisions and answer any further questions you may have as needed. If there are any disgruntled or depressed feelings to discuss, a psychiatrist can be assigned. Submit a request, and we will arrange an appointment for you."

As the group exited the room, I knew my life in New York was now a piece of the past. I'd lost everything I'd worked so hard to accomplish. Leaving my grieving family behind, I knew I couldn't hide forever. Determined to remain in control of my life, I didn't have to think about my decision. Watching the last person walk out the door, I carelessly shouted, "I want the surgery!"

Stopping upon hearing my request, one of the men dressed in a military uniform instructed the doctors to speak to me further about the procedure the following day.

That night, with the sounds of thunder rolling overhead and sheets of rain hitting the window in my room, I spent almost nine hours thinking things through. It seemed I didn't have a choice in the matter. I had to do this. It was either that or living my entire life in fear or captivity, maybe both. For years to come, I couldn't see myself permanently staying in this facility or any other like it. Keeping my face wasn't even an option since, technically, on all accounts, I was dead. I no longer existed.

Contemplating the severity of having to start fresh somewhere else was terrifying, but the thought of doing it alone was far worse. Still numb and overcome by loss, the world around me was dark. After much consideration, there was only one conclusion. I needed to live out my days and *simply just exist*, no matter what capacity. I figured those three words would become my mantra, summarizing what I was emotionally capable of doing right now - nothing more, nothing less.

Late the following morning, I solidified my wishes a second time, reiterating with clarity that I opted for the more invasive procedure versus the superficial alteration. Meeting with the plastic surgeon shortly after to discuss the details, listening somewhat coherently, I still felt a piece of me was missing or had died. Waiting for the man to finish his speech while disclosing the dangers and complications one could experience when choosing this root, I signed the consent form with a scribble and asked him to leave the room.

Days later, while being prepped for surgery, lying on the gurney before the anesthetic took effect, I hoped I would possibly, by some fluke, not make it through. That way, I could be with Ryan, knowing he was watching me from above. Beginning to count backward from ten, temporarily leaving the world, I wondered how things…would…eventually……turn………out.

| 40 |

Awake

33°00'00" S / 71°32'34" W

Hearing faint beeping sounds, I partially woke in the recovery room as disappointment silently hit me. My fingertips were bound in gauze and throbbing. Immobilized, I could feel the bandages wrapped around my head to the bottom of my neck. In significant pain, I realized I had survived...

Barely able to see through the gauze slits, with my face extremely swollen, I raised my hands slightly as the nurse explained, "You must not speak or move your head around too much. They altered your fingerprints, too, Miss."

Giving me a shot of morphine in my IV, I felt sleepy and drifted away yet again...

| 41 |

No Longer Me

33°00'00" S / 71°32'34" W

Not knowing how much time had passed, startled by the sound of a closing door, I mumbled to the nurse who had entered the room. "How long? How long have I been here?"

Fixing my IV and changing the fluid bag, she caringly answered, "Almost five weeks, Miss. It's been eighteen days since your surgery."

Shocked, a rush of emotions flooded my soul. Five weeks? I thought, realizing the extent of this entire situation and how it has affected my life.

Thinking about my family enduring a month without me, knowing I had died, sparked immediate anxiety. Scott came to mind. I figured he was probably relieved since I was now out of the picture permanently - one less complication for him. Fully accepting that I was not returning to work at the firm or finishing my beautiful museum, knowing I had let Mr. Gavin down, I wondered who would take over the project in my place if and when construction resumed. Pausing, understanding that everything I'd worked so hard to achieve throughout my life was gone, every piece erased - for a moment, I didn't know who I was anymore. I was no longer me.

Gathering courage, restoring my focus on the present and the things I could control versus those presented beyond it, and not wanting more time to slip by, I believed I had to concentrate on getting stronger so I could find out what happened to Ryan. This need to know the truth was weighing heavily on my heart.

Just before noon that same day, a nurse announced, "Well, Miss, the doctors will arrive shortly to remove your bandages. Are you ready for the reveal?"

Scared and excited, I hoped I'd be happy with my slightly changed appearance and not be disappointed.

When the door opened, not long after, a plastic surgeon and two doctors entered my room with a young nurse.

The lady doctor in charge said, "Hello, Miss. Are we ready to remove your bandages then?"

Nervously nodding to agree with her, seeing another surgeon enter the room, standing nearby, I noticed nobody had called me Ms. Thompson.

"Can I ask a question?" I muttered through the gauze.

"Yes," she answered, washing her hands before placing the gloves on.

"Why are you not addressing me as...?"

Solidly interrupted, she raised her hand to stop me from speaking. "I am sorry, Miss, but that person doesn't exist. Shall we proceed?"

Realizing Eva Thompson was now a piece of my past, I waited as the unwrapping began, slowly exposing a new, unnamed person.

With scissors ready to cut through the gauze, she commented, "There may be some residual swelling, so don't be alarmed. For the most part, everything has healed up very nicely from what I can see."

Given a mirror, I peered at the reflection and focused on my eyes, which had stayed the same. Inch by inch, she revealed my new face. Watching the last piece of the white covering cut away, I surveyed my unique features, pleased to see how pretty I still was despite some inflammation along my jawline, nose, and forehead. My skin was flawless and firm, but slightly bruised in two places. A little overwhelmed, my smile seemed somewhat unchanged as it tried to welcome me back to life. Turning to the surgeon, I thanked him while he confidently observed my reaction to the masterpiece he had created. Everyone left the room shortly after to allow me time with my new self.

Within an hour, I was transferred from the medical wing and assigned a small apartment on the long-term resident floor. As I walked around the suite, I found it homey. With a spacious living area, small kitchen, private bath, and a bedroom off to the left, in a way, it resembled my apartment in New York. It seemed all that was missing was my artwork, a few decorative accents, and my treasured drafting table.

Finding the need to stare in the mirror regularly as that day went on, I desperately tried to get used to my new appearance, imagining what I'd look like after it fully healed. Knowing it was still me inside, even though a stranger had taken over, I kept focusing on my eyes to confirm my soul was in this body somewhere.

The doctors arranged mandatory counseling sessions over the next week to help me through. It was a strange transition, mentally. Seeing your reflection, expecting to find your old self, but meeting a different person staring back at you is disturbing. Remembering that Ryan had dealt with the same situation months prior made me understand why he always lowered his head and peered upward, versus looking straight at me most of the time. He, too, was not confident in his looks even then. It was oddly comforting to find myself making the same gesture once in a while.

Day after day, I was determined to show improvement. When finally allowed to begin light exercise, an additional six weeks had passed. Starting with short walks up and down the halls, I felt I had made it through the worst. Meandering through the facility's corridors, nameless, I realized many others were in the same vote. Some looked like mummies, all bandaged up, and others were in a daze, passing by like zombies, still shell-shocked by their ordeals. Most were antisocial, and some seemed depressed or afraid to speak as a result of their circumstances.

To keep my mind active, I regularly visited the library within the compound to sign out books to read in my free time. Trying to stay current on what was happening in the world, I read the daily newspaper and perused a selection of magazines, hoping that I hadn't missed too much. We did not have access to the internet, phones, or computers since contact with the outside was listed as strictly prohibited for security reasons.

Thankfully, reaching the seventh week post-op, the swelling in my face had almost entirely reduced. Not paying as much attention to my new appearance these days, it now felt like the novelty had worn off. The lack of mirrors and glass in the facility's common areas offered little opportunity to see your reflection, which helped, I suppose.

One morning, after breakfast, I went to my room to read. Halfway through the fifth page, a knock unexpectedly came to my door. Opening it, I was surprised to see US Marshals Service Officer Raymond standing there.

"Hello, Officer Raymond."

"Hello, Miss. May I come in?" he formally asked.

"Yes," I responded, stepping back and opening the door wider.

Having a seat in the living room chair, I followed him and sat on the adjacent sofa.

"I see you have recovered well from your surgery," he said, studying my new face. "Not a drastic change, which is good. For you, subtle was better."

"Yes, so far, everything is fine. The doctors are happy, and I am, too."

He didn't waste any time. Leaving the casualness behind, he got down to business and opened the file folder in his hand to read his notes.

"Before leaving the facility to embark on your first external posting, we provide survival training. Unfortunately, your doctors have advised against strenuous combat instruction for at least another three to four weeks. Usually, instructors prefer that the students in our care partake in the activities, but watching others train must suffice in your case. You will also be issued a handgun and receive instruction on its usage. In the meantime, we will introduce you to extraction protocol should Intel receive word that you need to relocate." Taking out a camera, he instructed, "I need to take a headshot of you to process your new documents."

"Alright. One second." Going into the bathroom to brush my hair and see if I was presentable, I wished I had a bit of makeup to brighten my face. Knowing I couldn't do that yet, given the healing process, I thought, Well, this will just have to do.

Returning to the living area, I stood along a blank wall as Officer Raymond got what he needed.

"Perfect. Thank you," he said, double-checking the parameters of the picture.

Wondering where I would go from here, I asked him, "What are the next steps? I mean, once I have the option to leave?"

"We will allow you to start your new life in any of our high-security government-monitored districts since a threat on your life remains evident. Here is a list of twenty secure safe houses you may consider. When you leave this facility, you will be assigned a security team on staff 24/7. Someone will know your whereabouts every minute of the day. We will ensure your safety at all times. Once settled in your chosen location, you will slowly become accustomed to your new identity. Should you wish to work in the community of your choice, we will assist you with those arrangements." Pausing, he looked over his paperwork and said, "I guess that's all for now. Someone will be by to escort you to these training sessions beginning tomorrow at 9:30 a.m. Do you have any questions?"

Shaking my head, unable to think of anything, I replied, "No."

"Good. I will be on my way. Goodbye, Miss."

Walking towards my front door, he swung it open, as a half-smile quickly came to my face while glancing at the locations listed on the piece of paper. Locking the door behind him, I knew where I wanted to be.

Ryan had said that his next stop would be Iceland. After spending so much time in the sun and warmth of Australia, I remembered he wanted to try a cooler environment for a while. Recalling him mentioning the Blue Lagoon, the waterfalls, and going hiking, I hoped starting my life there would help my heart stay emotionally connected to him.

That week, I spent most days learning self-defense in the morning and survival techniques and extraction protocol in the afternoons. I also visited the indoor gun range, where I received instructions on firing a handgun after having one issued to me. The gun box had a fingerprint scanner built into it, similar to what Ryan had in his side table drawer.

During the first lesson, they taught me how to aim and shoot at targets. With others firing all around me, the sound rehashed memories of the extraction from Hamilton Island. It echoed through my head repeatedly, creating devastating flashbacks. Given no choice but to walk out of a few classes, I hoped to rid myself of the emotional scars left behind and prayed I'd never have to use any of the training I'd received to date, knowing violence was not in my nature. I could never fathom having to pull the trigger, inevitably killing someone in my sights.

That week, everything revolving around my recovery and release preparations caused a lot of stress. My handlers said recovering from the trauma and loss would take time. Their experience reassured me that, eventually, things would evolve to a new semblance of normal - whatever that meant. Deep down, my heart hoped they were right.

| 42 |

Three Months

33°00'00" S / 71°32'34" W
32°56'55" S / 71°28'47" W

When the training ended, I realized I'd been at this facility for almost three months and couldn't believe how fast the time went by - everything considered. Disappointed that I missed Christmas and New Year's somewhere along the line, all of that seemed trivial compared to what I suffered through.

Walking the hallways one afternoon, I noticed Anthony Morgan's picture flanking the newscast on the small TV tucked inside the security office checkpoint along my route. Waiting for the guard to leave and make his rounds, I snuck in the second the guy turned the corner.

Eyes locked on the actor's face, I approached the screen to hear the update on what had happened.

The trial for Colombian Drug Cartel leader Constantine Consuelos ended today. Consuelos was captured nine months ago within the state of California and indicted on three counts of murder in the killing deaths of undercover government agents last May. It seems the principal witness in the case arose from the dead, as actor Anthony Morgan's taped interview was authenticated earlier this month and viewed within the courtroom as the jury looked on with an eerie sense of intrigue. According to court records, Mr. Morgan taped footage of Consuelos murdering the agents, brought the information to a reputable source, and completed the video testimony just days before his untimely death. The DA has called for an added investigation to determine if Consuelos or his counterparts were in any way responsible for the disappearance and suspected murder of Anthony Morgan just days after the dated interview. Currently, the judge has passed the death penalty sentence for Consuelos, which now means, within the State of California, life without parole, given the moratorium on capital punishment. We will update you on this breaking news story as further details arise.

Staring at Ryan's eyes in the photo to the right of the newscaster, I tried to remember his face while leaving the security cubicle in silence. Missing him terribly, I felt dreadfully alone - the same feeling I assumed he had months before.

In the days that followed, I started dreaming of Ryan, almost feeling his presence in the bed beside me at night. Believing his spirit was watching over me and protecting me, I began attaching hints of happiness to my thoughts of him.

After finishing every training requirement and passing all the tests, officials escorted me into an empty boardroom late one afternoon. Shortly afterward, US Marshals Service Officer Barry Raymond joined the meeting. With a thick brown manila envelope in one hand, greeting me with the other, not addressing me by name, he asked that I open the package. Doing what he requested, I found my new passport, driver's license, phone, bank card, GPS security bracelet, and sixteen bundles of cash wrapped in yellow, brown, and violet straps.

"We were able to salvage your baggage from the yacht," he disclosed discreetly. "They informed me of a few sentimental articles enclosed inside. Normally, protocol prohibits taking any personal effects, but we are willing to bend the rule in light of what has happened in your case."

Leaving the room after placing the bag on the table, I read into what he meant. Ryan was gone, and he wanted me to keep a few treasured items from our time together. Approaching the only piece of me still connected to my past, I slowly opened the small tote. Immediately finding the One & Only signature bag Ryan bought me, underneath it, nicely folded, was the colorful Camilla Babylon dress.

Boasting all the bright, beautiful colors he loved so much, I pulled it from the bag, along with the short coral kaftan with the tassels and intricate beading. Mustering a smile through my tears, I knew I'd always have a part of him with me, no matter where I ended up. Gathering most of the clothes from the bag, I opened the passport to reveal my new identity. Seeing AVA THOMAS presented boldly beside my changed appearance, a sense of familiarity overcame me since it seemed similar to my original name.

Officer Raymond re-entered the room. "So, where are you off to, Ms. Thomas?"

Hearing that for the first time, it was strange being referred to as someone else. Knowing there was only one place for me to be, I confidently said, "Iceland."

He confirmed my request with little emotion as a familiar face entered the room. It was Kayla.

Approaching with a smile, she hugged me and said, "Ava, my friend. You look fabulous." Shedding a tear, trying to remain professional, she stated, "So, I heard you want to relocate to a much colder part of the globe."

With feelings of uncertainty running at an all-time high, responding to her comment with only a nod, I took a deep breath, knowing my new life was about to begin.

Packed and ready, we left within hours. In the darkness of night, Kayla and I exited the building I'd been staying in for months. Getting into a shuttle van, we soon passed through a set of white-guarded gates and merged left onto a deserted highway. Within fifteen minutes, we entered a military airfield. The driver pulled up to a private hangar with a mid-sized private jet waiting inside. Boarding the empty plane, we quickly got settled.

"So, can you tell me where we are right now?" I asked, hoping Kayla could divulge that information while we taxied down the quiet runway.

"You have been hidden inside a Naval Hospital in Concón, Chile. This is their Naval Airport. Ready to start our long journey?"

Acknowledging her with fearful hesitation, she knew I would never be the same without Ryan. Swaying my attention to the darkened scenery out the window, I secretly hoped I would see him soaring among the heavenly clouds along the way.

About an hour into the flight, not having said much to each other, I finally broke the silence and asked Kayla, "Who do you work for technically?"

Kayla turned away from me and peered out the window. "That's a lengthy story," she replied.

"Well, we have a few hours, right?" I chuckled.

"Yes, I suppose…" pausing a minute to decide what pieces she was willing to share and those that needed to remain a secret, Kayla turned my way and answered, "Well, where should I start? Like most of us who take up this line of work, many don't have relatives, and most have endured a tragic past. I grew up an orphan. My father was killed in a car accident when I was three, and my mother died of cancer when I was seven. My father was an only child and had no known next of kin. My mother had a sister who declined to take on the responsibility of a kid since she wasn't exactly the motherly type. Being placed in an orphanage, I watched as the other children got adopted, and I didn't. By age ten, believing the world had tossed me aside and didn't care about me, I turned somewhat rebellious and became like every other troubled teen. Having been returned from nine different foster homes in three years, I knew I wasn't exactly daughter material anymore. One morning, a military officer came to meet with the headmaster at the orphanage when I was about to turn eighteen. That day, they offered me an opportunity to leave the facility, take what had happened to me, and change it for the better. This secret organization gave me a reason to live - a purpose in life. I have to say, out of all the missions I have been privy to, you and Ryan have felt the most like friends to me. You found a special place in my heart."

Beaming with delight, I was happy she thought of me like that, especially now since she was also my only friend in the world.

"So, that is the long and short of my sad story. Believe me. I would not change a single thing in my life to do over. My disastrous childhood taught me to be tough and to survive anything. Nothing I've dealt with has come close to the trials I've conquered as a child. Being alone in this world at that young age was terrifying. My past has prepared me to help people, and I have to say I love my job. I technically work for a government special operations group. The rest I can't tell you - it's classified," she said, smiling with one eye slightly closed, signifying a hint of secrecy. "Just know the main thing is I'm here to keep you safe. That is all you need to understand."

Landing once in a very secluded location to meet a fuel truck and a second time in a smaller city airport, we then continued on our journey. Kayla and I looked at magazines, watched movies, grabbed a bit of sleep, and talked some more throughout the twenty-two-hour flight. During this time, we became close friends, laughing, joking, and sharing our thoughts on life as we knew it, almost like she had now slipped into the role of the sister I missed so much.

"Do you think you'll ever get married?" I asked somewhere over Eastern Canada.

Kayla looked at the floor and thought to herself. "You know, I sadly don't know if marriage is in the cards for me. But that said, I have been seeing someone casually in the past couple of months. We share a common interest, but it's too soon to tell."

"Details?" I asked, knowing she probably wouldn't divulge much.

Giving off smitten vibes, she declined my request. "Sorry. Not ready to do that yet. It's still new."

Happy for her, I nodded and said, "Fair enough."

"You know, this line of work gives you little downtime, and technically, nobody is supposed to know who you work for, too. Those secrets alone would be hard to keep from a spouse. It's like the movie Mr. and Mrs. Smith, for example. Both had assassin jobs and fictitious careers, which created a façade of their somewhat perfect life. Some people actually do that, you know. They blend into society and covertly harbor their secret profession. I don't think it would be fair to my husband, not knowing where I might be for extended blocks of time. My conscience would not allow me to lie to him. How about you? Think you will ever get married?"

Shaking my head, knowing the answer, I said, "No. I have only truly loved one man and will never find another like him. So, no. I think it is not in the cards for me either."

| **43** |

Iceland

63°58'49" N / 22°35'06" W
64°00'28" N / 22°20'05" W

Finally, after spending so much time in the air, we began our descent in the early evening of the following day. Landing at the Keflavik International Airport, taxiing over to a private hangar away from the central terminal hub, we noticed a black Suburban awaiting our arrival.

Before the plane door opened, Kayla handed me a fur-trimmed, hooded parka and said, "Welcome to Iceland."

Enveloped in the warm jacket, it wasn't as cold as I expected. A military officer escorted us to the truck while another loaded our bags into the back of the vehicle. Settled in the middle seats, scanning my surroundings, I started having second thoughts about choosing a location as desolate as this. My initial impression made me think it was a dismal place to begin my new life.

Driving along the barren, moon-like surface of the island, we watched the sun descend in the west, creating an array of colors never seen before. Amidst the many hues of blue and black, radiant wisps of orange, burnt red, and yellow blended seamlessly. Taking that minute to offer gratitude for our safe arrival, I prayed that I would eventually appreciate this second chance at life despite everything that's happened.

Twenty minutes into the journey, we spotted a faint porch-lit building ahead, surrounded by brown grassy, rocky hills, slightly covered by a dusting of snow. I assumed it was my new home, the closer we got, since it was the only place we had seen for miles. Veering left towards the structure, driving up a long, uneven, gravel driveway, the quaint three-story home had white walls and a red tin roof. There was even a small, partially frozen pond out front. Situated yards from the shoreline, the view of the departing sun on the sea was utterly captivating.

Slowly advancing to the back of the house, waiting in front of the two-car garage situated in the basement of the raised building, the driver opened the one retractable door remotely before we drove into the empty bay. Safe inside, Kayla got out of the truck. I followed close behind. Being handed my duffel bag, she guided me to the steep, narrow staircase leading to the main floor. Once at the top of the stairs, we entered the main living area.

Kayla explained, "I will stay a while until you get settled. We'll arrange for food and supplies regularly after I've left. The town of Grindavik is about fifteen minutes away, and Reykjavik is about thirty minutes out. There is a compact car at your disposal should you wish to explore a bit. We also offer secured transportation if you're uncomfortable going anywhere by yourself. Plain-clothed agents can accompany you."

Timidly perusing the great room comprising a living, dining, and kitchen, the house included warm walnut hardwood floors, white walls, and sparkling ivory granite tiles. Examining the modern surroundings with a little more hope, cautiously moving about the open-concept space, I saw the all too familiar security monitor on the wall, similar to the one installed at Ryan's house. To the right of the steps leading down to the garage was a room harboring the computer systems that controlled all the equipment on-site. Inside, security personnel sat on shift around the clock.

Noticing that I found the staff office, Kayla added, "Someone is always stationed here 24/7, and a stealth team is at the airport base where we landed, with an extraction time of fewer than seven minutes if need be. Would you like me to show you to your room?"

I agreed while silently moving to the upper level. Exhausted, I could hardly wait to shower and go to sleep.

"Oh, there's one thing I forgot to mention. Another person is also here before being relocated shortly, so I should probably introduce you since he will be around us the next few days."

Not in the most positive mental state to meet anyone, tired and out of sorts, I reluctantly replied, "I'd rather not do that right now if it's okay. Can it just wait until tomorrow?"

"Well, that may come across as rude. It'll just take a second. I promise."

Unhappy about it, still self-conscious about my face, I wondered what this person would think of me.

Kayla knocked on another bedroom door before opening it slightly. "Excuse me, Bryan?"

"Yeah?" a deep voice said before welcoming her in.

"There is someone I'd like you to meet."

Following in Kayla's shadow, hiding behind her, I could see a person standing in the far corner.

"Sorry to bother you," she apologized.

Vaguely seeing a silhouette emerge from in front of the bright, sunset-drenched window, I noticed that the man was wearing a warm hat. He didn't seem welcoming or happy. Nor did he speak a word. Limping slowly with a cane in hand, it seemed he, too, was not in the mood for company.

Kayla pushed for the introductions regardless. "I'd like you to meet Ava Thomas. She will be staying here a while."

Stepping aside, putting me on the spot, I moved to the middle of the room. Believing the guy had become a recluse after suffering a horrible ordeal, probably shell-shocked based on his actions, I was a bit afraid. Yet, given the degree of injury he had noticeably sustained, I felt sorry for him and politely reached out my hand to introduce myself. Unable to see his face clearly since he kept his head lowered, seemingly not wanting to make eye contact, the lack of light did not help matters. Now six feet apart, I looked upward and leaned to the left to greet him. Deciphering a few facial features now dimly illuminated on one side, feeling a sense of utter confusion, it was as if I was hallucinating. In disbelief, incapable of taking a breath, tears quickly developed when those familiar baby blue eyes that captivated me with love turned to stare with a sense of bewilderment.

"Ryan?" I mumbled.

"Eva?" he answered with a perplexing element of hope upon hearing the sound of my voice. Perking up, he looked past me in search of someone else. Only seeing Kayla there, his sights returned to me.

In shock, I suddenly broke free and raised both hands to cover my mouth. Inching forward, the tears flowed. "They said you were dead. They said you were - gone."

Staring at me with intense emotion, somewhat apprehensive, I figured he was confused by this stranger trying to portray his long-lost love. Not knowing what else to say, he gave a fragmented response. "No, umm…No, I'm… I'm okay." With paralyzing uncertainty, he asked, "Eva…is it really you?" Surveying my face, Ryan broke down upon seeing tiny remnants of his Eva.

Awkwardly approaching, gently cupping my cheeks, he studied my new features.

Confused by the light brown hair, he blocked out my nose and mouth with his hand and looked deeply into the eyes that had stayed the same. Staring intensely, he ran his finger along my eyebrow, now slightly different.

I reached up and placed my hands along his face. He closed his eyes and focused on my touch while I gently wiped the tears away.

Opening them again, he saw Kayla give him a thumbs-up sign, verifying it was me.

Witnessing our reunion with a content smile, she hoped that throughout this painful experience, we would feel the same for each other despite the time apart and the changes made to my appearance.

Leaning back, I examined his scarred complexion, now more rugged and unshaven. His smile was unchanged, and his eyes remained the doorway to his beautiful soul. All I could whisper was, "You're alive."

Tilting his head the same way he always did, he said reassuringly, "No…I am here…so that you are not alone." He hugged me tightly and said, "I've missed you so much."

With her mission complete, Kayla closed the door behind her.

Wrapped in each other's arms, needing to get reacquainted, we had a seat on the sofa near the window.

"What happened to you after leaving the house?" he asked. "Were you hurt?"

"No, I was okay. Guess I suffered some kind of post-traumatic shock or stress. They wouldn't tell me what happened to you and led me to believe you had died. That took me a long time to accept."

"Protocol also kept me in the dark, not offering any information on your condition or whereabouts. I hoped you were alive but never thought I'd ever see you again," he stated bluntly, reaching out to grab my hand. Staring at my face, he tried to ignore his uneasiness, confessing, "Please bear with me. This is going to take some getting used to."

"Is it that bad?" I fretted.

"No. Not at all. You are as beautiful as ever." He smiled lovingly.

Knowing my appearance had altered things between us, I wondered how I could help him along. Realizing how strange this must be, I had an idea.

"Close your eyes," I said, wanting to try something.

Obliging, shutting them, Ryan asked, "Okay. Why?"

"Listen to the sound of my voice. Hearing it will help reinforce our connection despite the changes to my appearance. Do I sound like me?"

"Yes," he said without hesitation, cracking a smile, never thinking he would ever hear that sweet sound again.

"Anytime you are in doubt, close your eyes. Focus on my voice. I am still in here." Firmly holding his hand, I clutched it tightly under my chin while his eyes drifted open.

"Okay. I will."

"What happened when you left the helicopter?"

Ryan turned and looked out the window. "During the attack, I took a bullet while attempting to get to you upstairs. The hit shattered my hip bone on impact. The team grabbed me, and I don't remember much after that because the pain was so intense. I kept fading in and out. I remember hearing you say my name once or twice and holding my hand before everything went black. From what they tell me, we got separated after the extraction. I was taken to a rapid response center and underwent emergency surgery to repair the extensive damage." Running his fingers over his scars, he unnervingly pointed out, "Glass from the explosion sent splinters of debris, causing little nicks here and there. Most have healed up nicely, considering. Just a few remain noticeable."

"To me, you are as handsome as I remember." Changing the subject, I said, "So, you stuck with your original plan and came to Iceland."

Closing his eyes, noticeably trying to deal with my altered appearance, taking my advice, he replied, "When they asked me where I wanted to transfer to, the only place that came to mind was here. Honestly, I felt the need to fall off the face of the earth - never be seen or heard from again. All I had left was a bleak existence without you in my life. What made you choose this place?"

Recalling our conversation beside the pool that night in Australia, I replied, "You mentioned Iceland was going to be your next travel destination, remember? You wanted to go hiking and visit the Blue Lagoon. I came here hoping to feel close to you, thinking I could experience some of the things you had mentioned, figuring you'd be watching in spirit."

The bond our souls shared now seemed more intense. After everything we've been through, our love was very much there.

Pausing a moment, not wanting to think negatively anymore, Ryan opened his eyes and said out of the blue, "So, Ava Thomas, huh? It suits you."

"You kind of look like a Bryan, too," I chuckled.

While discussing our new names, we decided that even though the old ones no longer existed, we'd use them behind closed doors, making sure to refer to the assigned titles in public when needing to keep our situation believable.

In desperate need of a shower and a change of clothes, I said, "Umm, please don't take offense, but I want to freshen up a bit. It's been a long journey to get here. I'll be right back, okay?"

"Yes, for sure. I'm not going anywhere," he said with that smitten smile.

"Okay, make sure you don't," I stated while leaving the room.

Gone briefly, thankful to wash away the remnants of the trip, I returned to him shortly afterward. Walking around to the opposite side of the bed, we rested our heads on the pillows and stared at each other. Reaching over, he carefully caressed my forehead, eyes, nose, and lips, struggling to see Eva behind the face of Ava. Closing his eyes, moving closer, wrapping me in his arms, he knew from our embrace it was still me.

| 44 |

Beginning Again

64°00'28" N / 22°20'05" W

Our first few weeks together went by quickly as spring arrived on the rolling hills of Vogar. It was now almost April, and the days were becoming longer.

After staying with us an extra week, Kayla announced she needed to return to the mainland. Leaving three security guards on shift every eight hours at the house, they kept a close, constant eye, giving a sense of comfort.

Having established a routine, our days mainly consisted of Ryan's continued rehabilitation, reading together, talking, and taking short walks up the laneway when he could. The changes in my appearance became less and less apparent as the bond we shared got stronger as time passed. I began documenting our experience in a journal, thinking maybe in the future, we could look back on this and remember how the two of us came to be despite its dire complexity.

While becoming accustomed to our new Icelandic surroundings, we both decided to make a valid attempt to settle into ordinary life. Only supplied with a few clothing items upon arrival, we thought it wise to invest in a few additional layers if we stayed here for an extended period. Figuring a trip to Reykjavik was our best bet, being the most modernized, we were sure it would have most of the necessities. Asking the security guard for directions and advice on where to go, he devised a plan for us to visit the Main Street shops the following day and assigned a security escort as a precaution.

| 45 |

Reykjavik

64°08'47" N / 21°55'59" W
64°09'03" N / 21°56'37" W
64°08'31" N / 21°55'37" W

Waking up early the following day, excited to embark on our little adventure, a part of me expected that it might be short-lived, with Ryan still having difficulty getting around. Before departing, we both expressed concern for our first public outing, but he seemed far more bothered by it.

Nervous about leaving the safety of our four walls with his visible scars for all to see, Ryan put on a stylish beanie and grabbed a pair of sunglasses, hoping to hide behind them.

"Please don't be concerned about your face," I said supportively, walking over to place my hands along his cheeks. Looking into his eyes, I reassured him, "You are as handsome as ever."

Smiling and lowering his head as he usually did, I quickly raised it and said, "No, you don't need to hide. Everything will be fine."

"Okay," he answered, not entirely convinced.

Outside, a black Suburban arrived right on schedule. Meeting our security detail, we introduced ourselves to the man dressed in civilian clothing as he opened the back passenger door for us.

"Hello. Good morning. How are you?" I asked him, presenting my hand, remembering to refer to our new names. "My name is Ava, and this is Bryan."

Addressing us with the same friendly gesture, he responded, "Nice to meet you both. I'm Demus. I'll be escorting you to Reykjavik today. The trip will take thirty-five minutes or so. I hear you want to visit the shopping district?"

"Yes, that is the plan. We need to buy some clothes. Are there any shops you would recommend?"

"Well, there is Cintamani or 66◇ North if you want outerwear and warm base layers. They have a wide variety of regular spring clothing, too, if I recall, and both stores are on the same street. That whole section of the city is a shopping mecca for tourists."

Looking over at Ryan, I asked, "Want to try there then?"

Staying quiet, he calmly replied, "Sure. That sounds good."

Having a seat in the SUV, we departed and began driving north along the western shoreline, noticing how barren and flat the landscape was, consisting of only low-lying hills in the distance. Finally, linking up with what looked to be a central, four-lane highway, the beautiful views on either side captivated our attention. With the icy waters of the ocean to the left and mounds of volcanic rock on the right, it was odd not to see any greenery anywhere.

The highway then changed to a minor two-lane road with signs of corporate industry beginning to crop up along the coastline on the outskirts of Reykjavik.

When noticing our interest in the large factory we were passing, Demus commented, "This is Rio Tinto Limited. One of the biggest industrial companies in Iceland. It plays a big role in our economy and produces some of the world's highest quality, lowest carbon footprint aluminum."

Entering the city limits, we could see low-level apartment buildings and residential subdivisions becoming visible as the highway changed back to a people-moving freeway, which resembled any other city in the United States. Demus merged west off the main road and drove along a waterfront area close to downtown. He navigated onto a one-way street while heading back towards the city center, attempting to stay inconspicuous.

"Here we are. Cintamani is around the corner, and 66° North is a couple of stores down on the same side," Demus pointed. "I will wait for you here. Do you have your bracelets on?"

After exposing the black security bands from under our sleeves, we got out of the truck and walked hand in hand to the first store. Ryan opened the door for me and systematically scanned the perimeter on the way in. In search of a small wardrobe, we began scouting out our options. Finding a few pairs of comfy tights for myself, t-shirts, two long-sleeved base layers, a raincoat, waterproof hiking boots, a fleece, and a light, three-quarter-length down jacket, I felt that would get me through however long we remained here. Ryan did the same, and we met to settle the bill at the register.

Deciding to go to the 66◇ North store, even though we had most of what we needed, Ryan realized I did not have a hat, warm socks, or mitts - things they had supplied him upon arrival at the safe house. Purchasing additional pieces to add to our wardrobe, with packages in hand, we explored a little more. When walking past a place called Ísey, I stopped and went in. Ryan followed. There, I found stylishly warm accessories to protect my hands, feet, and head from the cooler temperatures later in the year.

About to pay for the things we wanted, speaking to the lady at the cash register, I asked, "Do you know where we could find a nice restaurant with a fairly relaxed atmosphere, preferably by the water?"

Not fluent in English, she did not really understand. Simplifying my question, I said, "Good food?" and provided hand gestures to provide clues. "Where? Eat?"

Understanding somewhat, she timidly answered in broken English, "You like Kopar. Seafood. Very good."

I turned to Ryan and said, "Want to try there? Maybe we'll drive over if it's too far to walk?"

He nodded in agreement.

Bringing my attention back to the woman, she said simply, "Walk. Ten minutes." Raising her right hand, she happily pointed in the direction we needed to go.

Thanking her for the advice before leaving the storefront, we opted to head back to the truck parked not far from where we were.

Meeting up with Demus, I asked, "We want to grab lunch. A lady suggested a place called Kopar. Do you know of it?"

"Sure do. I'll take you." He pulled away from the curb cautiously, minding the many pedestrians surrounding us.

Within five minutes, we arrived at the walking path leading to the restaurant.

"Do you want to join us?" I asked Demus, knowing he may be hungry too.

"No, Miss. I'm fine," he politely refused. "I'm on duty. Please don't take offense. Appreciate the invitation, though."

When we exited the vehicle, I noticed Ryan had difficulty moving. On our way to the restaurant, walking hand in hand, he opened the door for me to head inside first. Right away, I loved the rustic, eclectic atmosphere, with exposed brick, plank wood floors, and wrought iron railings. Being escorted upstairs into the loft, spying a beautiful starburst chandelier hanging to our left, the lounge boasted a long, unobstructed picture window overlooking the busy marina and snow-capped mountains. Offered a seat at the round dining table assigned, the waitress handed us our menus.

Happily submitting our orders not long after settling in, I could feel something was wrong.

"So, how are we doing? Are you okay? You've been fairly quiet since we arrived here. Please tell me what's bothering you."

Glancing over with an almost sorrowful gaze, I figured he would stay quiet.

"Do I have to pull it out of you? Remember? No secrets. All we have is each other now. You have to talk to me. Have I done something wrong?"

With eyebrows raised, he replied, "Why do you always think you are to blame for my moods?"

Shrugging my shoulders, not sure why I do that, I replied, "I don't know. Guess my parents always blamed my sister and me for things like that."

Knowing it was not the case, he conceded, lowering his head, knowing he had to clear the air. "Alright... Do you want the sugar-coated explanation or the straight-up, point-blank version?"

"Straight up version, I think... What's wrong?" I replied, squinting my eyes, reaching across the table as a part of me was scared to hear what he was about to share.

Holding my hand, squeezing it intermittently, he explained, "All my life, I've been tough, a survivor... I mean, I've seen some pretty horrific things throughout the years, but I've always been strong through it all, not once doubting myself or my abilities. I don't know. Maybe I'm having a bad day." Ryan paused, glancing out the window at the fishing boats arriving in the harbor, thinking about how he could describe the feelings he was experiencing on such a profound level. "This year has tested my limits beyond comprehension. It's been the most difficult thing I've ever had to endure, mentally, physically, and psychologically, but now, it's not just about me anymore. It's not about my safety, my awareness, my surroundings, my life. It's about you - us. Being out amongst the living, trying to lead a somewhat ordinary life today, is and may never be entirely possible. We don't have control over what happens to us anymore, Ev. Maybe, to a degree, we do, but continuously moving isn't having control. It's prolonging the inevitable. Every time we step outside the confines of a safe house, we will always be putting ourselves at risk. I'll be honest, that scares me - not much does, but this..." He hesitated, then added, "So, yeah. Umm, we've seen first-hand what these people are capable of doing. Every ounce of my being wants to save you from further harm and protect you from danger, and I'm not exactly in peak condition to follow through on that. I feel like it's my job to keep you safe, and right now, I highly doubt I can."

Looking into my eyes for a split second, having shared his concerns freely, he continued watching the boats in the harbor, frustrated to a degree, almost as if he was embarrassed by the statement he made.

So happy that he trusted me enough to share his feelings, I replied, "Ryan, what we've been through is something you wouldn't bless on your worst enemy, and I know it is far from over, but we can't let these criminals win. We will remain strong. We will remain in control of our lives. You've always made me feel safe, secure, and protected from day one. That's just one of your many talents." Mischievously smiling, squeezing his hand a few times, I hoped to get his attention and bring his eyes back to mine.

With a bashful smile and a tilt of his head, he looked my way as I continued to rebuild the confidence he had seemingly lost.

"You know, after a while, hopefully, we'll be able to settle into a quiet life, but until then, we'll take one day at a time and deal with whatever comes our way. You must focus on your healing and recovery stages. You've gone leaps and bounds thus far. I promise I'll be here for you every step of the way, without fail. We are a team now, you and I. I know we'll get through this. So, are you with me?"

He released my hand and gave me a silent clap. "Now that, ladies and gentlemen, was the greatest pep talk I have ever received. Thank you. Yes, of course, I'm with you. There is no place I would rather be than with you."

After such a heavy conversation, we opted to people-watch and enjoy the lobster and crab risotto dishes placed in front of us with a glass of white wine - something we had not had in a very, very long time.

Hours later, while departing the restaurant, we talked about stopping somewhere on the way home for fresh fruits, vegetables, bread, and maybe a few bakery items for the house. Demus didn't even hesitate when we asked his advice. He knew just the place. Along the scenic route past the majestic Hallgrimskirkja Cathedral, we arrived in front of a store called Frú Lauga, a tiny gourmet food market. There, we found organic peppers, carrots, tomatoes, homemade jams, freshly made pasta, cheeses, and homemade sauce. They even had gourmet popcorn, dried fruits, and nuts for snacking. With many new ingredients packed inside the cloth shopping bags, Demus insisted we visit his favorite fresh fish market also. Doing just that, purchasing white fish, crab, and shrimp, Ryan then asked that he drive us home.

Thirty-five minutes later, pulling into the long driveway, Ryan seemed antsy. Getting out of the truck, stiff and slightly unstable, we ascended the stairs together to the main level. A security guard passed Ryan a small package on his way past. Not saying a word regarding its contents, taking it, he quietly headed in the direction of his room. Realizing that our activities today took a lot out of him, I unpacked the groceries, knowing he was tapped out.

| 46 |

Aurora

64°00'28" N / 22°20'05" W

Later that night, I heard Ryan stirring at around three in the morning. Suffering from insomnia lately, he would often take a walk around the house before coming back to bed. Half asleep, I closed my eyes and drifted off, assuming he would return shortly.

When he returned, I heard him softly trying to wake me. "Ev? Ev, wake up."

Wondering what was so important that I needed to get out of our cozy, warm bed, I whispered, "What? What is it?"

"Come on, Ev. You should get up. You really need to see this," he insisted before disappearing downstairs again.

Groggy, slowly moving, I sat up in bed. Placing my feet on the chilly hardwood floor, I got dressed in a few layers, knowing how cold and damp it was outside. Greeted by the night watchman at the bottom of the stairs, I confirmed we were both fine while putting on a winter hat. Spotting Ryan standing outside on the back porch, I slipped into my parka and boots and opened the door as the darkness seemed strangely illuminated. Immediately upon stepping onto the patio, my eyes drew upward to a spectacular display of lights. Flowing like a river overhead, an array of green, yellow, and white colors danced above us - it was the most beautiful Aurora Borealis. Feeling as if we were on an alien planet, this was one spectacle a person had to see to believe. The lights were so low that it felt like we could reach up and touch the sky. Their movements were quite erratic and un-predictable, making it even more mesmerizing. Embracing me with warm arms, we stood and watched nature's show for almost an hour before sadly needing to surrender inside with cold cheeks, fingers, and feet.

Returning to bed, Ryan opened the drapes so we could continue watching the dancing lights through the window. Eventually, we both drifted off, ready to meet a new day within a few short hours.

| 47 |

The Blue Lagoon

64°00'28" N / 22°20'05" W
63°52'46" N / 22°26'53" W

Ryan got moving much earlier the following morning - a relatively rare occurrence. Sitting on the edge of the bed, I watched him stand and gingerly stretch before going for a shower. When he closed the bathroom door, I peered out the window and noticed it was a dismal day. Weather like this usually prompted me to sleep a few extra minutes. Hearing the water running, I enjoyed the quiet time alone and tried to relax. Thankful to see Ryan more energetic, I closed my eyes and remembered what he said at the restaurant yesterday. It made me realize I needed to be more involved in our day-to-day survival, so he didn't have to worry about us as much.

While resting peacefully, he soon returned, showcasing an unusual abundance of energy.

"Ev?" he said, gently rocking my shoulder.

Not sure what he was up to, I quickly hid my head under the covers. "Five more minutes," I whispered.

"Wake up. We should grab some breakfast. Daylight is burning." Not receiving a response, he added, "I've planned a surprise for you."

Rolling over and flipping the covers back, I said, "Really?"

"Yep," he replied with a smile before leaving the room.

Curious about this surprise, I quickly jumped out of bed to prepare for the day. By the time I got downstairs, he'd made us something to eat.

Sitting at the table, I took a bite of my toast and asked, "So, will you give me a hint?"

"Sorry. You will have to wait and see," he replied, refusing to elaborate, sporting a mischievous grin.

Once fueled for our afternoon excursion, Ryan and I placed the tracking bracelets on our wrists before leaving. Already checked in with security personnel, Ryan had gotten dressed in a warm hat, jacket, and sunglasses. I did the same and grabbed our exit gear – now a part of our regular routine when departing the house.

Receiving destination clearance, Ryan led me downstairs to the small car parked in the garage bay below.

Graciously opening the passenger door, he said, "Right this way, my lady."

"Why, thank you, kind sir," I replied to his dramatics while he closed it behind me.

Carefully going around to the driver's side, I watched him get in, clearly stiff from shopping in Reykjavik. Securing his seatbelt with a click, he turned to me and said, "Ready?"

"I guess so."

He grabbed hold of my hand and said, "Okay. Here we go."

Backing out into the dim sunlight, pressing our green lights, and receiving a confirmation green in return, we tucked the bracelets under the cuffs of our jackets. Slowly proceeding down the rough driveway, Ryan turned onto the highway and headed south.

"Where are we going?" I asked, noting the two additional overly stuffed backpacks he had tossed into the back seat with the exit gear.

"We, my dear, are going to the Blue Lagoon today. The geothermal lake I told you about. It's one of the twenty-five Wonders of the World. I've read that the water originates thousands of yards below the surface, where freshwater and seawater combine at extreme temperatures. The locals believe it has healing qualities, which, I believe, we both could benefit from right about now."

Amazed by his description, I was excited to finally go on a solo adventure, especially with him feeling confident and happy. Given the map to help navigate, I directed him where to turn. Driving through the very flat, desolate surroundings, searching for a collection of white Blue Lagoon flags as pictured in the guidebook, I spotted mounds of rock and steam billowing in the distance.

"There it is," I said, pointing to the entrance coming into view.

Arriving at the famous tourist landmark, Ryan parked steps from the welcome monolith. Locking up the vehicle, we followed the long path lined by walls of black lava rock to the main building.

"After you," he said, holding the door open for me.

"Thank you," I replied kindly on the way past before lining up to register.

When it was our turn, Ryan seemed uncomfortable speaking to the person behind the counter. He continuously lowered his head and tried not to make direct eye contact with anyone.

Grabbing hold of his hand, he turned to me and smiled while the woman gave instructions and passed a set of blue electronic wristbands across the counter. Explaining that each granted access to a locker in the changing rooms and allowed us to charge food and drinks during our stay, she added that the final bill would be available when we were ready to depart. Placing them on our wrists beside the GPS bracelets, we located the modern change rooms and had to sadly separate for a brief moment, with robes, flip flops, and towels in hand.

Entering the sleek, gray stone room with walls lined with rich wood, I found myself amongst a handful of women. It was quiet and peaceful while changing into the new one-piece white swimsuit Ryan must have bought yesterday and packed in my bag. A sign advised that the patrons shower and use the conditioner on their hair since the mineral-rich water caused it to dry out quickly. Doing just that, slicking my hair back and rolling it up in a tucked bun, I wrapped myself in the robe provided and slipped on the flip-flops.

Exiting onto the main deck, Ryan was already waiting for me by the railing, enjoying the view.

Gently running my hand along his back, he turned and said, "Isn't this amazing? Look at this place. It is even better than the pictures. Are you ready to go in?"

Super excited, walking hand in hand along the boardwalk slowly, I stayed by his side. Neatly hanging our robes on the hooks and stashing the flip-flops inside the pockets, we reached the water's edge. The zero-entry area made it easier for him to manage. Sliding our toes into the overly warm water, the first few steps were shocking. But eventually, as it passed our waists, we soon got used to the temperature. Fully submerged in the milky, aqua-colored, crystallized water, Ryan waded over to me and placed his arms around my waist, while mine quickly found a home around his neck. Floating weightlessly in the middle of the lagoon, hidden amidst the steam emanating from the surface, I felt so relaxed but, most of all, safe.

Ryan whispered in my ear. "This place is so peaceful. It reminds me of our time at the Great Barrier Reef." Leaning back, looking into my eyes, he added quietly, "I love you."

It meant everything to hear those words. Happy, with my heart leaping, I meaningfully replied, "I love you too."

Cloaked by a sea of clouds, he leaned in and gently kissed me. It felt like we were the only people left on earth. How I wished we could just stay in this place forever.

Spending three hours in the lagoon, immersed in the natural steam saunas and waterfalls, we ended the day trying the silica mud masks.

Hungry, with shriveled skin, feeling water-logged and parched, we returned to the changing rooms after watching the incredible colors of the setting sun. Ready for dinner, having slipped into a pair of skinny jeans and the white turtle neck he'd packed for me, I was surprised to find a few make-up products in a small bag, realizing he'd thought of everything. Finishing the outfit with a warm, colorful pashmina encircling my neck, I smiled at myself in the mirror. "He has good taste in clothes," I said softly.

When I walked into the front lobby, spotting him in the gift shop wasn't hard. Dressed in a grandpa-like bulky sweater with a full zip, he handed me a heavy, hand-knit poncho matching the tones in his.

"What do you think?" he asked, "Want to try it on?"

I slipped the poncho over my head and stylishly modeled it for him. It was a perfect fit. I thought we looked so cute in the mirror - like an old married couple. Taking hold of my hand, we paid the bill after taking off the blue wristbands and submitting each in the electronic slot.

Given directions to the Moss Restaurant, moving on, Ryan spoke with the maître d', who was strangely expecting our arrival. The kind gentleman escorted us to a special table draped in white linens overlooking the water. It looked so pretty with a fragrant floral arrangement placed in the center. The votive candlelight spread a romantic vibe throughout the room.

Ryan pulled back my chair the way he usually did. Taking a seat, he moved directly beside me, continuing the proximity we had become accustomed to months prior. Comfortably placing his left arm behind me, we peered out over the illuminated Blue Lagoon, mesmerized by the steam gracefully disappearing into the dimness above.

While admiring the scenery without saying a word, Ryan turned to me. Nervously taking both of my hands, allowing his eyes to survey them quietly, he broke his silence.

"Eva… Fate found us despite all our plans. On the plane to Hamilton Island, the beauty of your eyes and the warmth of your smile captivated me. Granted, the privilege to know you and spend time with your heart has made me realize I want to share my life with you. Months back, I asked this very question, and you said yes, but a gentleman should always propose to the woman he loves and create a moment they will cherish for a lifetime."

Presented with a small box he had pulled from his pocket, he slowly revealed a glimmering ring nestled inside with a pear-shaped aquamarine center stone, surrounded by a halo of diamonds that continued around its band. Enchanted by the unexpected moment, enveloped by the sincerity on his face, I couldn't believe what was happening as he held the beautiful ring between his fingers, watching it sparkle in the light.

Able to gingerly get down on one knee, he proudly asked, "Eva, from the moment we met, I knew you were the one for me. That feeling has never left. I need you in my life forever. Will you do me the greatest honor of marrying me? I love you and will do so until the day I die."

Unable to speak through the tears cascading down my face, feeling an undying sense of everlasting love so deeply rooted, it was etched on my soul - nodding my head, I peered into those all too familiar eyes. The eyes that made me fall in love with a man I hardly knew. Wrapping my arms around his neck joyfully, I couldn't have asked for anything more. The moment was perfect. Tightly holding him, I immediately thought, there it is, precisely how my loving Grandmother had described it. That feeling when you just know. It's the promise of faithfulness, paired with mutual respect, never wanting to be apart, incapable of imagining your life without him. The only thing I would add to her words of wisdom is this feeling of my heart overflowing with happiness and love.

Slipping the ring on my finger was a very proud moment for him. He couldn't stop smiling. It was the most romantic experience of my life. After all this time, our lives had come full circle. I believed fate had brought us together, and now, nothing could rip us apart.

Amidst our memorable moment, I spotted something rather odd. "Wait..." I whispered and pointed. "You're wearing your contact lenses?"

My heart melted when he tilted his head and lowered his sights, grinning at my observation.

"Being out in public tonight, unable to hide behind sunglasses, I thought I shouldn't take the chance."

"Well, it seems fitting since those eyes were present for so many milestones during our time in Australia. They, too, caught my attention on the plane, even calmed me down, and protected me from that eel."

"You didn't need protection from the eel," he laughed, recalling the drama.

"Yes, I did." Giggling with embarrassment, I knew full well I had panicked. "And I will never forget the shy look you gave me when you offered your hand to take our walk up the beach."

He nodded, then glanced up and said, "Ah, yes. That is when things changed between us. I decided to take a chance. Little did you know - I fell for you on that walk."

Unable to hold back, I kissed him and whispered, "No matter what color your eyes are, I love the man behind them. My heart belongs to you. I promise to be there forever, regardless of what comes our way." Admiring the aquamarine diamond, I commented, "The stone's color is so beautiful."

"I thought it would remind us of where we met and the travels we've experienced along the way. It resembles the water along the Whitsundays and the Blue Lagoon, too, don't you think?"

I wholeheartedly agreed with him.

After dinner, we walked along the lighted path back to the parking lot underneath a ceiling of stars.

Returning to our temporary home without incident that evening, we revisited the plans we'd made for our future while settling in around eleven. It was exciting to think of a beach wedding, a house of our own, with a white picket fence and two children playing in it.

"So, are you ready to make these dreams a reality...Mrs.?" he paused, wondering what name to use.

"Mrs. Ava Daniels," I suggested, loving the sound of his name intertwined with mine.

Falling asleep peacefully, protected, and hopeful, I knew these feelings would persevere over any obstacle that may come our way. My soulmate had found me, just as my Grandmother always said it would happen. It was something I never thought I'd ever experience, but thankfully, I was granted that treasured wish.

| 48 |

Found

63°31'55" N / 19°30'40" W
63°34'21" N / 19°27'46" W
63°33'30" N / 20°08'45" W

Two weeks of bad weather followed our engagement, leaving us confined to the house entirely. Ryan's mobility kept improving, though. Altering his physio, using the stairs, light weights, and doing gravitational movements, the rain and wind did not hamper things.

Day by day, the cloudy, dark skies reduced. Experiencing, on average, about thirteen hours of sunlight now, I watched as the idle hibernation of winter turned into the makings of a life-giving spring. With a warm cup of coffee in hand, peering out the window towards the ocean, the ice along the shoreline started showing signs of thawing as it broke into pieces, floating freely. While writing in my journal, I could hear birds chirping in the low-lying shrubs. Thankfully, the landscape surrounding us gradually introduced various shades of green.

Ryan joined me not long after. Bright-eyed, he walked into the living area to kiss me good morning and offer a heart-warming hug while our security detail looked on.

He, too, poured a cup of coffee and asked, "So, are you up for a waterfall adventure today?"

With eyebrows raised, the word adventure piqued my interest yet again. I quickly replied, "Absolutely. I'd love that."

"There are a few east of here. It may be a two-hour drive, from what I understand. They say it's going to be a pleasant day today. Not too cold, rainy, or windy."

Ryan set the tourist guidebook on the table and showed me pictures of the selected waterfall. It looked majestic. Happy, I agreed with his plans for the day; he cleared our trip with security while they set out a list of parameters and instructions. Having seen the tourists dressed in hiking gear in the photo, we gathered our outdoor layers and hiking boots after breakfast. When plotting our route, Ryan highlighted the map and showed it to the guard.

Within the hour, I followed a more agile man down the stairs to the car with exit bags in hand, excited to explore an area we had yet to see. Ready to depart, settled in the vehicle, double-checking our wristbands, now displaying a green light, Ryan started the car and pressed the garage remote. The chain pulled the door up, granting us a sense of freedom. Carefully backing out, he shifted gears, and soon, we were on our way.

It didn't take long for the mountain range we were heading for to appear in the distance. Somehow, it seemed closer than a two-hour drive.

Ryan turned on the radio and asked, "Let's try and find an English station. I'll drive. You search?"

"Sure," I agreed while turning the dial, listening for any form of English.

Suddenly, we caught the beginning of a late '80s tune as it flooded the car. Immediately, his fingers tapped the top of the steering wheel rhythmically with the beat of the music. Humming to *Electric Blue by Icehouse*, I was surprised to hear him suddenly sing along to the lyrics effortlessly. All this time, I didn't even know he could sing. Glancing over with loving eyes, he kissed the back of my hand. It was so lovely to feel a touch of normal. A point I never thought we would reach.

Turning to look at the view out the window, I knew our handlers would soon allow us to look for a place of our own in the coming weeks. Maybe even secure a job to help establish roots. That feeling of freedom was very alluring. It made me wonder if I could start designing again or if that profession needed to stay in the past. Oh, how I missed it. My museum project came to mind. Months have passed. Was the lawsuit settled by now? Was everyone back at work without me?

Merging onto the main highway, surrounded by trees taller than four feet, we maneuvered the traffic circles and headed east. The terrain gradually increased in elevation. Eagerly anticipating our arrival at the tourist landmark, we spotted a few Icelandic horses covered in plaid blankets along the way, each enjoying the newly sprouted fields of spring.

Eventually, making it over the small ridge and descending into a valley on the other side, we remarkably found ourselves in the middle of some very flat, lush farmland. It was amazing how the volcanic earth on this side of the island had flourished versus the west side, which seemed more moon-like in comparison.

Halfway through the two-hour trip, hitting hamlets boasting modern conveniences, I jotted a few notes in my journal.

"What are you writing?" Ryan asked curiously.

"Nothing, really. I'm just taking note of the places I'd like to stop at on the way home. It would be nice to pick up a few things that aren't available in town."

"Good idea. A little variety would be great," he added.

The landscape turned flat once again outside of the last community. Our destination was still quite far away. The sun had burned off the clouds nicely, spreading its light across the landscape. Approaching a long bridge built over a black volcanic riverbed, we stopped to see the sparkling ocean on the right and Eyjafjallajökull volcano to the left. The scenery was mind-blowing.

Outside the vehicle, effortlessly breathing in the freshest air imaginable, we counted five waterfalls cascading over a luscious green cliff as ribbons of sunlight accented the picture-perfect postcard.

"This seems like a vision straight out of a fairy tale book," I whimsically divulged.

"Wow. I've never seen anything like this," Ryan replied, standing behind me with his arms wrapped around my waist.

Taking mental pictures of all the beauty around us, we continued our journey alongside the massive snow-covered volcanic peak. The closer we got to our destination, it amazed me to see how many people were taking a risk building their homes at the base of a volcano.

Close to the tourist attraction, unable to find the road we needed to turn on, Ryan slowed down and tried to translate the signs. The only word we recognized was Skógafoss. Spotting a waterfall in the distance to our left, we ignored the map and followed a bus heading in the same direction.

Confident on our own and unafraid, we arrived in the middle of a field and parked the car before getting out and locking up. Mingling with other tourists, slinging our backpacks over our shoulders, we started the short hike toward the base of the falls. Having seen so many people pitching tents on the damp grassy field along the grey pebble riverbed, I could not imagine how cold it would be to spend the night in this place as beautiful as it was.

Attempting to blend in, Ryan took hold of my hand as we walked.

Smiling, he said, "I don't know about you, but I'm feeling much happier these days."

"Me too," I replied, leaning on his shoulder. Grasping hold of his arm, I was relieved he was digging out of the depression he'd been in for so long. Today, I felt like there was finally a light at the end of the tunnel.

Almost at the base, we noticed there were two ways to experience things - one was a long hike to the top, and the other was to see it from below.

"So, Ev. Which way? Want to attempt the climb or take the easy way out?"

Needing a workout, having been cooped up for too long, I exclaimed, "Let's climb."

Hesitant but in agreement, he peered up at the challenging staircase. "Alright. I'll give it a try. Guess this will be an endurance test for me."

"If you start to hurt, you make sure you tell me. No being the hero today," I sternly warned.

"Don't worry. I think you'll pick up on it before I do. You are pretty good at that."

Knowing I was so in tune with him, we started up the first section of low-rise steps, making the climb easier. Sadly, it seemed we spoke too soon since the path changed to include steel treads carved on a sharper incline, leaving the two of us humorously having to stop to take breaks, hoping we'd eventually make it to the top. Dodging people on their way back down the mountain, we stayed to the right, looking up at the vast space still ahead. Exhausted, I figured it might be the death of us. With my legs feeling like jello and my breathing labored, I turned to Ryan and found him just as miserable.

Laughing with each step we took, lungs and limbs burning, knowing we were terribly out of shape, Ryan suggested with gasps in between, "I think we need…to join…a gym…like tomorrow."

Unable to respond to him, I nodded my head, hardly able to laugh in the process.

Reaching the final step, we stopped and turned around to look out at the view.

"Wow," Ryan said, out of breath. "This - is - incredible."

With our hands clinging to the railing, leaning our weight forward, the view had to be seen to be believed. The cold, dark blue ocean glistened in the distance. The lush green, flat farmland seemed miniaturized by the towering volcano on our right and the rolling hills to our left. At the point where the water flowed over the crest and down two hundred feet to the river below, we watched the mist gracefully drift upward with the breeze.

Ryan stood beside me in amazement.

I whispered, "This was well worth the climb."

"Yes, it certainly was." Distracted by the ring sparkling on my finger, he raised my left hand and said, "I can't believe you are going to be my wife."

Peacefully turning towards me, he glanced at all the tourists around us. Despite them looking on, Ryan slowly leaned in and lovingly kissed me without reservation. Pulling back, immersed in each other, I felt like it was only us. Nobody else existed.

"Love you," I declared wholeheartedly, hugging him tightly.

That's when we heard a somewhat muffled sound. It wasn't coming from the crowd around us. Startled, recognizing the ominously familiar tone, Ryan pulled his sleeve up to find the wristband glowing a solid red. In disbelief, letting his cuff slide back into place to hide the device, not wanting to bring unwanted attention, he looked at me first and then at all those surrounding us. Unable to speak, I, too, confirmed my bracelet reflected the same color.

"Oh, my god...." I whispered, breathing erratically, my hands shaking, not knowing where to focus my attention.

Breaking from a blank stare, Ryan reassured, "It's okay, Ev. Everything's going to be okay." Without hesitation, he went into action and delivered that sense of calm.

I saw his level of concern escalate as he systematically scanned our location and analyzed the activity taking place below, looking for anything unusual.

The air in my lungs expelled abruptly, restricting my breathing. The only words I could voice were, "Do we go to the car?"

His eyes followed a trail leading further up the mountain. "No. We go up. The team will track us there and send the Airbourne unit."

Grabbing hold of my hand, we swiftly continued along the rocky, dirt path, keeping tabs on anyone trailing behind. I could tell he was in pain after climbing about a half-mile up the mountainside.

Eyes peeled, stopping to catch his breath, he questioned, "How confident are you with a gun?"

"What?" I replied, knowing I may not have a choice in the matter. Not hesitating, remembering I needed to be more instrumental in our survival, I nodded, "I'm good."

Ryan searched for a location to load our weapons without creating a scene. Moving further and further away from the passers-by, we saw Cascading Falls marked on the trail map. Breaking from the path, he found a grassy knoll to disappear behind momentarily. Both kneeling to open our exit bags, Ryan loaded both clips. Double-checking the safety on each weapon, he slipped one arm out of his jacket and put on the shoulder holster. Quickly securing his gun in that holder, mine got latched around his waist for safekeeping. He knew I didn't want to use it, but if I needed to, it was easily accessible. Immediately after, he held down the red light button on his bracelet and received one long, constant tone in return.

"They are coming for us," he confirmed with relief.

"Are you sure?" I asked, trying to recall the extraction protocols, with my head continuously moving in every direction, terrified to death, knowing we were being hunted.

"One long tone means they were dispatched. Short blips mean they are minutes out. Come on. We need to keep moving."

Standing up and scanning the area around us, we slipped our backpack straps over our shoulders before he took my hand. Swiftly making our way up the trail, careful not to fall or twist an ankle on the rocks jutting out of the ground, we arrived at a gorge with another powerful waterfall thundering into the break in the earth.

Spying two tourists coming into view, Ryan cautiously walked ahead a couple of feet, acting as a shield, prompting me to ask, "What are you doing?"

"Ev, please don't argue with me right now. Stay behind me."

His commanding voice, filled with great confidence, left me silent. That is when he let go of my hand, and I heard him rack the slide on his gun inside his coat.

Please, God, no. I pleaded in my mind. Please.

Focused on the tourists taking pictures with cameras sporting long lenses, nobody acted out of the ordinary. Then, one man looked our way. Reaching into his pocket while lowering the camera, Ryan stopped me and extended his arm behind him, making my heart race.

"Ev..." he said, stabilizing his center of gravity.

Our sights melded to the man's hand. We were unable to look away. It soon emerged from the right side of his parka in slow motion. Holding my breath, waiting to see a weapon, I prepared to grab my gun from Ryan the second we hit the ground if shots broke out. Chests pounding, watching in horror, the man unexpectedly exposed a lens cap and placed it on the end of the camera. Able to breathe, Ryan heard the beeping sound again. This time, one long tone followed by a pause and nine short tones.

Counting them, not looking at the device, he confirmed, "Still nine minutes out."

Briskly moving along the gorge, almost hitting the two-mile mark, we passed five more tourists while they casually made their way back down the trail, laughing and talking. Exhausted, with our legs burning, we walked over the next hill and found a sheltered, shallow riverbed below with a small flat island in the middle. Ryan swiftly guided us over to a volcanic rock protruding from the hillside. Removing our tracking bracelets and stuffing them under the segmented layers, he could hear the welcoming sound of the helicopter breaching the hills on the opposite side of the water. Flying stealthily low to the ground, we prepared to leave our refuge point.

"Ready?" Ryan said, trying to time our pick-up.

Pausing, he lifted his hand above us to give the pilot a visual before making our way across the river. About to step out into the open, a shot hit the ground inches from us, spraying dirt and debris on impact. Launching himself to shield me, we heard the second shot echo through the gorge. Then another. Safeguarded by the rock, with him now on top of me, he realized I'd hit my head.

"Are you alright?" he assessed urgently - his eyes moving steadily, scanning every angle.

I nodded and said, "Yes," while he shifted onto one knee, watching the inbound helicopter.

Removing the gun from his belt, he stayed on task and grabbed the hidden bracelet. He pressed the red button repeatedly to indicate that the team would be coming in hot. With his back against the rock, he tried to peer around it in the direction of the gunman, making sure he wasn't advancing towards us. Yet another muffled shot filled the air. This time, one bullet hit the upper edge of the rock above our heads, and another pierced the ground seconds later, a couple of feet away. Ryan knew what we were up against by the tone of the gunfire.

"It's a sniper rifle," he revealed, "I hope the pilot brought backup."

Thankful to see our rescuers descending in the crosswinds toward the island in the middle of the flowing water, the doors of the unstable chopper opened, and in seconds, men jumped out. Two officers emerged and bravely took point with the target in view, immediately providing cover fire as another combat-ready body hastily ran through the shallow stream. Staying low along the embankment, he reached the place where we were hiding.

"You guys alright?" he firmly asked, with eyes peeled.

Ryan confirmed, "Yeah. We're good."

Not hearing revengeful shots from the hillside, the armed officer ceased fire and issued the GO signal with sights on the ridge. In seconds, all three of us made a run for it. Unable to think through what we were doing, it seemed instinct just took over. Racing through the freezing ankle-deep water to reach the barren island, the military officer took up the rear, shielded by a thick bulletproof vest. Running, our waterlogged boots weighing us down, I shuddered at the thought of the sniper issuing the one shot he needed to make. Ryan ducked my head as we got closer to the helicopter. Mere feet from the open door, more cover fire broke out to battle the gunman.

The bullets ricocheted off the rocks around Ryan's feet, emitting a splash of mud as we jumped aboard. Seated, he got in beside me and put his weapon away.

Inching back, the men tethered themselves to the chopper with a click of a latch. Doors left open; they sat on the edge. Aiming at their target, we lifted off and rotated around.

Boldly, the assailant emerged in full view with a gun aimed in our direction.

The officers yelled, "Incoming!" before belting instructions back and forth at each other, ready to hurl a retaliatory barrage to aid our exit.

Ducking down, Ryan covered me with his body and secured us tightly since we hadn't time to buckle in. Gaining altitude, I heard one officer verify that the target dressed all in black was a 'lone wolf.'

Slipping around in our seat, I caught a glimpse of him scaling the hillside, only to see us gain distance. He did not fire on us again.

"Just another day at the office," one officer said humorously to the pilot over the radio while packing their weapons and closing the side doors.

The other looked deep in thought. "Yeah, I figured the dude would bring us down with an RPG?"

"This isn't Qatar, man." A seriousness fell upon both of them.

Terrified to hear that, I clung to Ryan as the pilot skillfully flew low altitude across the desolate landscape to hide us from sight.

"You both okay?" the officer to our right asked.

Nodding my head, unable to speak, Ryan answered, "When shots rang out, I shielded Ava. The back of her head hit a rock in the process. Can you look at it?"

The man to our left pulled out a medical kit and quickly located the gash. While cleaning the blood and disinfecting it, Ryan strapped us in and placed the headphones over our ears. Watching the pilot maneuver a receding glacier, we soon descended into a remote airport named Bakkaflugvöllur. With two white buildings and a black paved runway, only one plane was situated there. A dark-blue duel prop.

"Please tell me that is not for us," I questioned, deathly afraid of small planes.

"Yes. That's your ride," the pilot confirmed. "You'll be heading out immediately."

"What about all of our things?" I asked Ryan in desperation, re-thinking my statement and reminding myself we were lucky to get out alive.

"Don't worry," Ryan said as the helicopter touched down. Each officer scanned the perimeter to secure the premises. "They will gather our stuff from the house and bring it along at some point. We don't have much."

"Follow tight behind me. Right hand on the right shoulder of who is in front of you," the nameless man instructed.

The propellers on the plane were already moving. My heart beat out of my chest, and I found it hard to breathe. One of the men slid open the door.

Ryan attempted to shout over the loud sounds, "You walk between us!"

Shadowing the man in front of me, placing my hand on his right shoulder as instructed, and feeling Ryan's on mine, we raced quickly in a straight line to the plan's open door about twenty-five feet away. The officer stepped aside just ahead of the stairs and got me on board while Ryan followed. With everything happening so fast, I sat in the first row and watched the officer jog back to the helicopter.

We didn't even get a chance to thank them for saving us, I thought.

In an instant, the team was gone. The co-pilot on board the plane closed the door and instructed us to fasten our seatbelts. With every-thing secured, we started moving to the end of the runway for take-off. Suddenly making a sharp left turn, there was a brief pause before it loudly bolted down the straightaway. With my head pushed back tightly against the seat, holding onto the armrests with a white knuckle grip, I felt Ryan's hand rest on top of mine. Looking his way, he tried to offer encouragement.

"You're okay," he whispered. "I'm here. We're good now."

With no choice but to nod, unsure of what he said, I closed my eyes when we lifted off. My stomach did a few unwelcome flips as the turbulent crosswinds above the ocean caught the wings and shook us up a little. Leveling out and stabilizing, we flew over the Icelandic coastline towards an unknown destination.

Later, the co-pilot came to check on us. We discovered that we'd left Iceland and were bound for Nuuk International on the eastern coast of Greenland, where we would meet up with the team in three hours. Apparently, they were already en route and would be awaiting our arrival.

| 49 |

Hunted

64°11'30" N / 51°40'38" W

That day, we crossed the vast ocean between Iceland and Greenland, leaving all the plans of starting some semblance of a normal life behind. Just like that, in the blink of an eye, everything changed.

High in the air, with soaking wet feet and dirty clothes, we both stayed relatively silent. The trauma of what just happened resonated, leaving us with that same sense of dread, uncertainty, and displacement. Terrified beyond belief, I stared straight ahead, not moving a muscle. A tear drifted down my cheek. About to lift my finger to wipe it away, Ryan beat me to it. Gently sweeping the droplet away with his thumb, cradling my cheek in his hand, he took off his seatbelt and winced before kneeling in the aisle beside me. Noticeably in pain, with open arms wrapping me tightly, a flood of emotion overtook the two of us while I cried.

"It's okay, Ev. It's okay. I'm here. We made it out," he whispered.

With the shock of it resonating, I was thankful we were safe.

Leaning back, looking into my eyes, he whispered, "It doesn't matter where we go as long as we are together, right?"

"Yes," I quietly agreed, gathering the courage to be brave. Hearing the pilot say we would land in precisely two and a half hours, I asked, "Are you okay? You're hurting."

Ryan sat across the aisle and said, "Don't worry about me. I'll be fine."

While saying that, he lifted my legs and removed each boot before peeling off the sopping-wet socks from my frozen feet. Doing the same, ringing them out, he draped them over the seat behind us, hoping they'd dry a little before landing. Belted in as the trip got bumpy, he grabbed dry socks from our exit bags and handed me mine.

Reaching out his hand, giving it a few gentle squeezes, he said, "Love you," prompting me to say without hesitation, "I love you too."

Approaching Nuuk International Airport, flying over receding glaciers, the snow-laden rocky landmass reached upward through the low-lying blanket of clouds below, making it look like they were boulders floating in oblivion. Resembling a desolate alien planet, we slowly descended into the haze only to find a shortage of land and icy waters. How I missed the various shades of green found in Iceland, all of which were absent here. It seemed this part of the world lived out its days in black and white.

Circling a remote peninsula situated below the jagged fjords and rocky inlet shores, Ryan noticed a jet waiting on the tarmac.

Tightly holding my hand, we descended, bouncing and swaying in the crosswinds. The engine cut when we finally touched down. Inching closer to the end of the runway, we made a left turn and taxied back to the terminal. Slipping on our wet boots, we decided to leave the socks behind.

Met by two plain-clothed FBI agents approaching the prop aircraft when it came to a stop, they prepared to transfer the two of us to the mid-sized jet.

With little emotion, one officer said in a monotone voice, "This way, please."

Following him to the luxury plane, we immediately recognized a familiar face when we stepped aboard.

Greeted with warm hugs by Kayla, she said, "Thank God. Are you both okay?" She knew there were reports of gunfire, so she quickly scanned each of us.

Not answering her, reading a sense of fear on our faces, she got down to business and introduced the other personnel on board in a questionable tone. "Barry Raymond will no longer be your case officer, so in the interim, they have assigned USMS Officer Stan Siler."

Arrogantly elevating his rank above Kayla, Officer Siler nodded and opened his file, ready to divulge the newest Intel updates, when we took our seats across from him.

"Alright, this is what we know. Recently, six additional witnesses to Cartel murders did not make it into protective custody fast enough this month and have either been found dead or have mysteriously disappeared since you've been in Iceland. The Cartel has ramped up its mission to punish those trying to expose its operations. We're assuming Consuelos is still running his business from behind bars."

Before allowing him to continue, I boldly interrupted with immense concern. "Based on what just happened, these people know we are alive. This gunman shot at us. How did they know we were in Iceland, let alone at the waterfall? How is that possible?"

"Wait?" Ryan said, curiously looking over at the two agents. "How did you make the trip from Virginia to Greenland so quickly? It must be what, a five-hour flight?" Pausing, he realized, "You knew about this more than six hours ago, didn't you? And nobody bothered to warn us earlier? Why?"

Giving Kayla the eye, unable to answer that question for us fully, Agent Siler advised, "All I can tell you is that one of our informants alerted the team that a hitman was in Iceland. It wasn't entirely credible, so I opted to verify the threat. Unfortunately, the information came too late, but we secured you both despite that. As for how they tracked you to the remote waterfall location? I can not be certain. We are still gathering intel on this."

A questionable expression flashed across Kayla's face. We knew then something was wrong.

Intent on changing the subject, the agent interjected again. "Consuelos was incarcerated over four weeks ago within the walls of San Quentin State Prison, where they house all the death row and violent offenders. Our agency confirmed his brother vowed to avenge those responsible for his imprisonment, along with anyone closely connected to them."

Looking at my frozen feet, then over at Ryan, I realized our ordeal was not even close to being over yet, as a part of me questioned whether the new guy was really on our side, ready and willing to protect us at all costs.

Flying over the Arctic towards our scheduled refueling stop at the Elmendorf Air Force Base in Anchorage, Alaska, Agent Siler and Kayla communicated with HQ securely, trying to gather evidence of what had happened in our case and where the ball seemingly dropped.

That is when we overheard that a different long-range plane had been dispatched to both that location and the Marine Corps Air Station in Oahu for the next leg of the journey. Ryan asked Kayla for a word. Strolling down the aisle, she sat across from Ryan and me.

"So, where do things stand?" he asked, going to a faint whisper. "I don't trust that guy."

Silently extending a flat hand, requesting that he keep his voice down, she softly mouthed the words, "Don't worry. Given what's happened, they assigned another permanent Agent to your file moments ago. He'll be meeting us in Oahu. I'm familiar with him. He's good. A new cyber group has also been briefed. Their task is to determine how your location is continually compromised. Someone is still supplying your whereabouts to the Cartel. That's the only way this assassin could have tracked you to the waterfall. I promise I'll get to the bottom of this before we reach the Gulf of Alaska. Until then, hang tight. Our next transfer needs to be efficient and precisely executed."

Assured by Kayla that she was working to keep us as safe as possible, Ryan concurred. Returning to her seat, Siler sneered before turning in our direction to project a very unsettling look, not at all happy with our little conversation.

Seeing Ryan's mind reeling a mile a minute, I knew his gut feeling made him question the man's trustworthiness. With everything going on, believing it would be a long flight, thankfully, I glanced out the window to see the mainland coming up on the horizon.

| 50 |

Tracked

61°15'45" N / 149°48'11" W

Touching down after passing the vast line of tall, snowy mountain peaks, I was happy to see pockets of green emerge. The location was not your average bustling airport. Being the only plane to land in the vicinity, amidst a few fighter jets and military bombers on the tarmac, we soon took refuge within the confines of Elmendorf Air Force Base. The pilots promptly stayed on task and taxied the plane to a private hangar near the end of the runway. Waiting inside was a mid-size jet.

Announcing the time of 2:16 pm AKST, remembering it was 3:05 pm WGT when we landed in Nuuk, passing so many time zones, it seemed the world oddly stood still while flying further west.

Once the plane came to a complete stop, the FBI Agents went into action, pushing for the co-pilot to get the door open efficiently for the transfer. Securing the area, the team moved us to the waiting aircraft. Inside, I followed Ryan to the very back. Finding a VIP cabin with chairs and a sofabed and the ability to slide a door closed and separate from the rest. The team knew we needed a space.

Watching Agent Siler and Kayla set up their workstations towards the front, Ryan recalled what Kayla said. "We just need to get to Hawaii. Then, hopefully, everything will be fine when we dump this guy," Ryan whispered.

I silently agreed.

Laptops were opened before the cabin doors got secured. Each of them was working as the plane departed. Two agents sat socially facing Kayla and Agent Siler, almost as if frozen in time.

On the move, seatbelts fastened, we heard the pilot announce our intended destination - the island of Oahu, yet another six hours away. Discouraged, having already been in the air for nine hours, it felt like we were leaving this world and never coming back.

What would our life look like now? I thought while the jet raced down the runway at high speed, rocking back and forth before leaving the ground. Would we ever find that small piece of heaven called home?

Again, drifting into the unknown, there were more questions than answers. Whatever happens next, I thought, we would have to be ready for anything. Turning to Ryan, seeing him flash an uncertain smile, I was glad he was not going through this alone.

Ten minutes into the flight, Kayla distributed the food trays. Emerging from the VIP area, sitting in two seats beside each other, she set them on the table in front of us.

Quickly diving into his hot meal, famished, Ryan glanced over at me. "Why aren't you eating?"

"I don't have much of an appetite right now."

"Ev, you've got to keep your strength up - stay in optimal condition. We don't know what lies ahead. Please..." he asked with great concern. "Please eat something."

Knowing he was right, I peeled the foil off the container and tried my best to finish it. I found it hard since my head had had enough of flying for one day, and sadly, it looked like we weren't going to land anytime soon.

While clearing our trays, Kayla secretly gave us a thumbs-up sign. The gesture helped diffuse my nerves. Carrying the dishes to the front disposal cabinet, Ryan kept a close eye on Agent Siler since the FBI agents seemingly dozed off.

Sneakily peeking over the seats, I quietly whispered, "Do you have a bad feeling about him?"

Ryan rested his pointer finger over his lips. I assumed he wanted to keep that subject under wraps. Getting up, we walked into the VIP cabin in the back and slid the door closed.

Now alone, he nodded in agreement. "There is nothing we can do about it right now. We have to wait and see what happens once we land in Hawaii. I trust Kayla. It will be better to leave him behind and continue with the new guy in charge." Pausing, he said, "You get some sleep now. Don't worry. I'll watch over us."

Helping me get comfortable on the sofa, buckling me in, and covering me with a blanket, he sat in the chair across from me and reclined. Eyes closed, I tried to sleep, but happened to open them and found Ryan staring out the window, deep in thought. His words echoed through my mind. How was Kayla and Agent Siler able to get to us so quickly? We checked in with security before leaving the house to visit the waterfalls. The team cleared us around the same time they knew trouble was brewing. Why weren't we relocated as a precaution at that time? Why did they allow us to continue with our plans? My mind reeled. Countless questions circulated, making me wonder what train of thought Ryan was deciphering. That is when my hands began to shake, and fear set in. Did he think we were flying with a trader? Were we in danger?

Kayla continued to work on her computer, as did Agent Siler. We could hear the clicking of their keyboard keys through the closed door as the sound became increasingly annoying. Covering my ears with the blanket helped to block it out.

Ryan opted not to sleep. At one point, I felt him reach over and place his hand on top of mine. Caressing it the entire time, it was almost as if doing that helped him concentrate more while we flew further into the South Pacific.

| 51 |

Hawaii

21°26'38" N / 157°46'14" W

Hours passed. Knowing we were traversing the globe was unnerving, yet somehow, the trip seemed shorter than expected. Waking to the pilot announcing our approach to the Marine Corps Base Station on the Eastern Shore of Oahu, he asked us to prepare for landing and our departure from the plane.

Kayla knocked on the sliding door. When Ryan opened it, I heard her say, "Can you guys take your seats? The pilot believes we might experience some crosswinds on the way in."

With a nod, he agreed before she returned to the front of the plane.

Leaning over me, I opened my eyes.

"Ev. Wake up. We're here. They need us to move."

Still half asleep, disoriented, and in a daze, I sat up and moved from the sofa to the seats outside the VIP cabin door. We listened to the FBI agents give basic departure instructions when buckling in. My ears started giving me trouble upon descent. Gently blowing them out a few times, I felt the landing gear hit the runway. Flaps deployed, making the plane slow down. Exhausted, peering out the window, I was confused by the setting sun far in the distance to my left. That is when it hit me. My internal clock was completely off. I had no idea what time of day it was. Taking a deep breath, I knew no matter how horrible I felt, I needed to soldier through regardless. If Ryan could do it, so could I.

Thankful to have arrived safely, we found ourselves amidst the tranquil waves and sandy beaches while the plane taxied to our rendezvous point alongside military aircraft of all sizes. Coming to a stop beside a large jet in front of hangar 104, everyone on board took off their belts and stood up.

"I am going to secure the other plane first. Then, my counterpart will escort you over shortly after that. Sit tight until we are ready," the one agent said as the co-pilot opened the door to allow him out.

Kayla had packed her computer and duffel bag while Agent Siler made his way over to us.

"Well, this is where I leave you," he confirmed. "Agent D'Agostino has been assigned to you now. He is waiting on the other plane."

Offering his hand, Ryan saved face and said, "Thank you for helping us. We're grateful."

"Yes, thank you," I said softly, with ears muffled, still uncertain whether he could be trusted.

"No problem at all. That's our job. My hope is that you get through this and start your lives anew. It is my experience that people in protective custody eventually find some semblance of normal. It just takes time. You have to be patient."

In agreement, he stepped aside, allowing us to pass. We met with Kayla standing at the door, waiting for the signal to proceed to the next plane. Getting the go-ahead, we disembarked while Agent Siler looked on.

Hit by a salty, humid air mass, with feather-lite jackets now wrapped around our waists, guns secured inside our backpacks, sporting long sleeves, it only took seconds to start sweating. Stepping aboard the new plane, with more FBI agents flanking the stairs, heads on a swivel, we hoped they'd have clean clothes and a few basic necessities for us. You don't realize how much you miss brushing your teeth until you don't have the option. How I wished I had a breezy dress or workout clothes to change into. A shower would be nice, too.

Inside the new plane, rounding the corner, Kayla smiled and greeted a short, dark-haired man, cleaning his stylishly smart, black-rimmed glasses. Turning to us, she introduced him. "Bryan and Ava, I'd like you to meet Agent D'Agostino."

"Hello! Welcome aboard," he announced cheerfully, returning the glasses to their rightful spot.

Addressed by our new names, we bid him a pleasant "Hello" when he offered his hand to shake each of ours in a gentlemanly way.

"Please, please. Have a seat," he requested.

Sitting adjacent to him, with a table between us, the agent opened the file folder in front of him. Kayla sat to his left and looked on.

Now in control of our situation, he started by saying, "I had you land here because the Commanding Officer of this base is a close friend of mine. I am extremely confident that he will keep our transition off the books. From here on out, we are going dark. Nobody will know our coordinates. It is the only way to keep you both safe. I hope you'll trust my judgment. Over the years, they've brought me in on many challenging operations like these. Each has turned out favorably for those involved."

"I guess, at this point, we don't have much choice," Ryan replied with a hint of frustration.

He fully understood our position. "I know things have been difficult, but I guarantee you will be well protected. This is something I take great pride in."

Getting a good vibe from the new agent in charge, I glanced over at Ryan and placed my hand on his knee. Turning my attention back to the man, I said, "Thank you for that. We are grateful for any help you can offer. The past twenty-four hours have been tough, as you can imagine."

While taxiing down the runway for take-off, Agent D'Agostino replied, "Hey, how about we start things off a little more casually." Reaching his hand across, he said pleasantly, "Hi, my name is Frank."

Kayla looked on with a smile.

Happy to shake his hand, reintroducing ourselves as Bryan and Ava a second time, Frank exclaimed, "We are going to be spending a lot of time together, so it's better if we keep the air light."

In agreement, feeling more secure, we left the runway, floating effortlessly above the ground and into the darkening night sky. This time, though, the thickness of the air was absent. I felt calmer and much more at ease.

Glancing toward the back, Frank explained, "We have prepared a bed in the back for you both. I'm sure you are in desperate need of sleep. We will be flying for almost ten hours. I strongly advise that you get some rest."

Upon hearing that, the seatbelt signs went off. Ryan and I got up as Kayla, the two FBI agents, and Frank began reclining their chairs into single beds.

Walking toward the rear, I located the double bed in a separate room with an ensuite. Turning around, I noticed Ryan waiting to speak to Kayla quickly before joining me. With a nod, he walked down the aisle and closed the wood door.

"Is everything okay?" I asked while perusing the space, wondering if something was wrong.

"Yes. All good," he replied casually, switching the lock as a precaution.

"Ryan, look. It's our duffel bags with our things from the house. How did they get them here?"

So thankful to see something familiar, Ryan and I sat on the bed. More than ready to freshen up and change out of our dirty clothes, I was disappointed not to see a shower. Nonetheless, running water, soap, face cloths, and towels were a welcomed sight.

Gratefully going through our bags, finding everything accounted for, I got ready for bed and changed into more comfortable nightclothes. Finally, cuddled under the covers not long after, it felt heavenly. Wrapped in Ryan's arms, my head found a spot on his chest.

"Are we going to be okay?" I whispered, staring at the ceiling, clinging to him.

"I've always told you I'd be honest. My gut says something doesn't seem right with that Agent Siler. I was glad to see him go. I still don't understand why he withheld a precautionary redirect. That bothers me. They could have saved us from going through all that. Under the circumstances, I know they need to ensure the threat is credible first. But still." Taking a deep breath, he sighed, "I'm glad Frank is going dark. We need to disappear - completely. Let's try and get some sleep. We're gonna need it. Not sure what tomorrow will hold."

Barely able to respond to him, feeling excessive fatigue converging in every extremity, having flown almost fifteen hours and counting, Ryan rolled onto his side and propped up his head. Looking down at me, he gently touched my cheek and ran his thumb across it from left to right.

"Try not to worry. Leave that to me."

Staring into his eyes, I knew that would be easier said than done. He moved closer and kissed my lips. That familiar feeling of warmth wasn't far off. The love we shared could never be fathomed or understood. It energized me and made me believe I could do anything with him by my side. Quietly loving each other, flying high above the world, we detached from reality. Sharing a moment like no other, drifting farther into the unknown, a part of me was still scared of the dangers that lie ahead.

| 52 |

Palau: South Pacific

7°21'54" N / 134°31'58" E

7°21'21" N / 134°26'33" E

Somehow, finding myself back in New York, walking to work as usual, my heart ached to know Ryan wasn't there for some reason. In a panic, the pain of our apparent separation confused me. My mind wandered, trying to remember what had happened exactly. Beginning to sob, believing he had died, I soon heard a voice faintly comforting me.

"Ev?" he whispered, rubbing my arm softly. "You're dreaming, Ev. Wake up."

Opening my eyes, getting my bearings, I rolled over on my back and rested my hand on my forehead. Relieved to see him lying beside me, the tears flowed uncontrollably.

Holding me, he said, "It's okay. It's okay. I'm here."

Unable to break free and compose myself, overwhelmed beyond, I couldn't stop my body from trembling.

"It's just a dream," he said. "It's just a dream."

Amidst it all, the pilot announced our impending arrival. In need of reassurance, I looked into his eyes and found a subtle smile on his face. Suspicious, I hoped I hadn't talked in my sleep.

"Are you okay? Better now?" he whispered. "You're safe."

Nodding my head, he helped me sit up. I propped my elbows on my knees to hold up my head with both hands. Feeling the plane floating through the air, I realized we were still high above the earth and slowly descending from thirty thousand feet.

Eventually, up and moving, slipping on clean clothes, we got ready for landing. Ryan and I emerged from the private room and found our seats at the back of the plane. The darkness of night still blanketed the skies outside the cabin.

Intriguingly spotting a single airstrip below, unable to see a horizon, Ryan asked Frank, "Where are we?"

"We're approaching the Islands of Palau. It is situated east of the Philippines. This will be our layover location for the next few days," he replied.

"What time is it?" I asked.

Frank checked his phone. "It's 12:03 a.m. Palau time."

Feeling like it had not been dark for days, seemingly missing hours in between, the plane descended towards the sparsely lit Palau International Airport.

Not feeling an ounce of choppiness when we touched down, there was a sense of relief, knowing we were finally on the ground for a while. As the jet stopped, we gathered our things and prepared to move on to our temporary home.

Escorted to two shuttle vans, parked alongside the plane, with the humid air weighing us down, the FBI agents slid each door shut when we were safely inside and instructed the driver to proceed. Making our way along the winding, narrow roads, we noticed a lack of street lights, creating an eerie scene. But that said, it seemed our driver knew where he was going. The van swayed whenever he tried to avoid a pothole or obstacle on the road. Still tired, stressed, and out of sorts, I just wanted to get to our destination and sleep.

After passing over a large bridge, we entered a small village, thankfully lined by business signs and a few more lamp posts, making us feel we hadn't left civilization entirely. At the other end of town, shining night-time reflectors guided us through a narrow causeway with black water on either side. Making it through the danger zone, we reached land. A line of eerie-looking hotels made the streets resemble a ghost town. Surrounded by jungle, branches hitting the vehicle, we turned the next corner, apparently arriving at our destination.

Stopped in front of a well-lit, open-air building with a Polynesian feel, the agents slid open the doors and guided us inside the lobby. I scanned the space with cathedral wood-beamed ceilings, white stucco walls, ceiling fans, and a tiled floor. Light wicker chairs with teal cushions added a topical touch of color. Accented by orchids and palms here and there, the men led us to a boardroom on the far end. Meeting the new stealth team sitting on the left-hand side, the group of five happily introduced themselves despite being tired and jet-lagged. Agent Frank briefed them before they escorted us along a beautiful pathway to a redwood bridge leading to a charming group of over-water bungalows in the Palau Pacific Resort cove. Gazing at the dimly lit huts with grass-thatched roofs and exterior white stone and vertical wood planking, the team pointed directly across from us, saying they were staying a stone's throw away in the garden suites if we needed them. The group had already set up a command center the day before. Securing the location, they had also taken possession of a small boat with a motor, which was attached to the water access steps just below our room.

About midway along the bridge, we stopped at our hut. The aroma of beautiful tropical flora was so welcoming as the door swung open. That is when Kayla let us in on a little secret.

"So, before I say goodnight, I thought I'd let you in on some arrangements I've made during our two-day stay."

Standing beside Ryan, hand in hand, I asked, "What do you mean?"

With glistening eyes, she quietly said, "Ryan, maybe you should explain."

"Ev, to make the most of this relocation, I hoped to marry you here. On the beach. Like you wanted." Pausing, he added, "That's if you feel ready, of course."

I glanced up at him, grinning from ear to ear with happiness. There wasn't an ounce of doubt in my mind. Tightly wrapping me in his arms, my gentle smile revealed joyful tears. Seeing my reaction, Kayla received the answer to her question.

While we kept our emotional embrace, she said, "I'll finalize everything for the wedding tomorrow evening on the beach at sunset, your favorite time of the day, from what I've been told. We will arrange for wedding attire, flowers, and rings. Everything is available within the resort, so there is no need to venture out. I'll reserve the officiant as well."

Moving my attention away from my husband-to-be, I immediately asked Kayla, "Can you join in as our witness?"

Humbled by my request, Kayla confirmed, "It would be an honor. I wouldn't miss it for the world."

I was so happy to hear her say that.

"Perfect. Until tomorrow, then. Have a good night, you two," she said before awkwardly exiting the room.

Left alone, Ryan hugged me tightly. "So, are you sure you're ready?"

"Well... I am. The question is, are you?"

With a thoughtful pause, his face brightened. "I have been waiting a lifetime for this moment. You are the one I pictured in it."

Kissing me with absolute intent, he suddenly stopped. Backing away, he said, "Maybe we should shower first..."

Laughing, I told him I couldn't agree more.

| 53 |

Until Death Do Us Part

7°21'16" N / 134°26'39" E

Kayla separated us early the following day, insisting it was bad luck to see the bride before the wedding. Agent Frank requested that Ryan join him for a workout and breakfast while she and I prepared for the day.

Able to finally eat a balanced meal, I disguised myself in a hat and sunglasses to meet with a wedding coordinator on-site. Needing to arrange a few last-minute details for the simple ceremony we'd planned, with the stealth team, Kayla, and Agent Frank as our only wedding guests, I wished my family could have been here to share our special day. That said, there was comfort in the fact that my grandparents would be present in spirit - knowing they were always watching over me from heaven.

Having a list of things to do, the morning quickly transitioned into the early afternoon. Slowly crossing off each task, we selected the floral bouquets and the boutonnieres before registering the wedding certificate and booking the officiant. Ryan had already picked out his wedding band at the resort shop. I did the same, having chosen one to complement my engagement ring. After all that, in need of some pampering, Kayla and I headed to the spa for a much-needed manicure, pedicure, and hair appointment.

Returning to our hut over the water a couple of hours later, I took out the Babylon dress Ryan bought for me on Hayman Island so long ago. While fondly recalling how much he loved the beautiful colors, I decided to wear it as my wedding dress. I figured it would suffice as my *something new* because I hadn't worn it yet. Hanging it from the ceiling, steaming it out a little, I couldn't believe I was about to marry my best friend.

Kayla added a few finishing touches to my salon-sculpted up-do by inserting tiny tropical flowers with a hint of turquoise for the *something blue*. For the *something borrowed*, she graciously offered her necklace since I had nothing in the way of jewelry with me anymore. All I had left were the diamond earrings Ryan bought me months back.

Wrapped in robes, ready to get dressed shortly, Kayla and I sat on the navy blue cushioned lounge chairs on the back deck of the hut overlooking the water.

Staring at the view, she asked, "Did you ever imagine your life would turn out like this? I mean, take a turn the way it did?"

"Umm, I'm not sure how to answer that...." Giving it much thought, I replied, "You know, before my life fell apart, I figured my future was set in stone. I had my dream job, dream apartment, and a dream guy. I even acquired my parents' mindset - meaning, if I weren't successful, then I'd failed, kind of attitude. Looking back, when I think of it, maybe I wasn't meant for that life. Growing up in New York City, you're accustomed to the hectic pace, but a piece of me longed for something simpler - quieter. The time I shared with my Grand-parents in the Hamptons every summer - now that fit me more than the corporate one. I still remember my grandfather working in his study, overlooking the ocean. He always balanced business with fam-ily. Unlike my parents, who did the opposite. Don't get me wrong, I loved my job, and I'm sure I'll continue that talent in some way, hope-fully." I turned to her and said, "I certainly didn't expect my life to end and have to start anew. But being with him. That missing part of me feels complete."

Kayla nodded happily. Inspired by my speech, she looked at her watch. "Guess it's time to get dressed."

"Okay," I said nervously. Getting up from the chair, I felt a few jitters.

Ready to walk down the aisle, touching up the makeup on my face, Kayla helped me slip into the dress. Stepping back to look in the mirror, I was so happy to see the reflection staring back at me. The all-white bouquet stood out beautifully against the brilliant colors I was wearing.

Shedding happy tears at the thought of getting married, Kayla swiftly grabbed me a tissue and blotted my face. "Oh! Don't do that yet…" all the while shedding a few herself.

Bare feet, with our bouquets in hand, Kayla and I emerged from the bungalow at six o'clock to meet Ryan and Agent Frank on the pathway to the beach. Spotting them, I inhaled deeply. This was it.

Ryan was dressed in white linen, standing tall, with his hands behind his back. His face brightened with every step I took in his direction. While walking along, he watched the beautiful dress float freely in the breeze, happy that he'd chosen it many months ago.

"You look so beautiful," he said, reaching out his hands and kissing my cheek. "Are you ready?"

With nervous butterflies, I said with unquestionable certainty, "Yes."

Arm and arm, we moved toward the officiant. The stealth team was already waiting, with our two witnesses close behind. Standing at the edge of the shoreline, in front of a floral arch graced with orchids and palms, the older gentleman promptly started the ceremony with the sun setting behind him, casting an amber glow across our faces as it had so many times before.

I passed my bouquet to Kayla, feeling like this moment was a dream.

The officiant started with a traditional opening. "Dearly beloved, we are gathered here today to join this man and this woman in holy matrimony." He asked, "Do you, Bryan Daniels, take Ava Thomas to be your lawfully wedded wife, to live together, love her, honor her, comfort her, and keep her in sickness and in health, forsaking all others, for as long as you both shall live?"

Beaming with pride, Ryan squeezed my hands and answered, "I do."

"And do you, Ava Thomas, take Bryan Daniels to be your lawfully wedded husband, to live together, love him, honor him, comfort him, and keep him in sickness and in health, forsaking all others, for as long as you both shall live?"

Tearfully, I said, "I do."

The officiant requested the rings. Handed them from Agent Frank and Kayla, he said, "You will now give your vows to each other."

Ryan slipped the silver band on the third finger of my left hand and said, "Ava Thomas... I feel like every decision in my life to date has led me to you. Every minute. Every second. This morning, I realized we would never have met if I had done anything differently - if my path had changed ever so slightly. I am so thankful to be standing here before you. With this ring, I give you every ounce of my being. I promise from this day forward, you will never walk alone. I will protect and honor you all the days of my life. You will forever have my love."

With the silver band held between my fingers, his words sentimentally resonated. Placing it on his third finger, I vowed, "My Grandmother always said fairy tales never start with a happily ever after. For us, it has been no different. Bryan Daniels, on this day, I give you my heart. We have struggled and survived months of uncertainty. Through it all, you have been my rock - my protector. I promise to keep walking with you hand in hand wherever the journey leads us, no matter the circumstances. I could never imagine my life without you by my side. You will forever have my undying, everlasting love."

Hearing our promises to each other, the officiant pronounced us husband and wife. For the first time, Ryan kissed me as Mr. and Mrs. Bryan Daniels. Swinging me around, he raised my feet off the sand

and clung to me tightly. It was hard to believe this was our new reality.

The stealth team clapped, cheered, and whistled. Kayla and Agent Frank congratulated us warmly while everyone looked on with genuine celebratory delight.

Thankful for another hug and kiss from my husband, we took a stroll up the beach. The hues of the setting sun were beautiful from our vantage point.

Kayla and Agent Frank approached on the way back.

"As much as we would love to stay, we have received orders to continue to Guam Air Force Base for a briefing in two days," Kayla said regrettably.

Frank quickly added, "You'll be safe here. The stealth team will remain on site. They will brief you both on extraction protocols should a problem arise."

Hugging us one more time, Kayla said, "Congratulations, you two."

It was hard to bid her goodbye as I watched them start down the path toward their cottages to change clothes and gather their things.

At the last second, before rounding the corner, Kayla turned and shouted, "I'll see you guys soon!"

Waving to her, I felt like I was losing my best friend again. It was nice having her around.

While the clouds floated heavily in the sunset-filled sky, they reflected a hint of fire creeping through the darkness before bidding us an end to our perfect day.

Ryan took hold of my hands and said sincerely, "I am so happy to call you my wife finally."

Kissing me, I knew life was now complete. My heart's missing pieces had mended, and I felt whole again.

That night, after enjoying a romantic dinner inside our bungalow, we got ready for bed, thankfully sheltered from the outside world. He exited our ensuite while I removed the bobby pins from my hair. For some reason, I was nervous. Staring at the girl in the mirror, knowing she was now a wife, I somehow looked different. Putting on nothing but a white robe, I slid open the pocket doors and found my husband waiting for me. With one arm positioned behind his head, he smiled while I walked over. Turning off the bedside table lamp and removing the robe, I cuddled beside him, unable to believe he was mine. From then on, he had my heart and soul, and I had his - forever.

| 54 |

Peleliu: South Pacific

7°21'21" N / 134°26'33" E
7°15'20" N / 134°22'40" E
7°20'45" N / 134°27'04" E
6°59'35" N / 134°13'36" E

Cut off from the outside world, days passed. It was hard not to be distracted by the extraordinary array of natural wonders surrounding the turquoise lagoon while staying in Earth's tiniest, most scenic location. But the truth was that both of us were concerned about why we hadn't moved along as initially planned. The team had dwindled to a skeleton staff of four, which got me thinking that maybe Agent Frank and Kayla had forgotten about us.

Always keeping our bags packed and ready to depart at a moment's notice, day after day, it was nerve-racking to know that life could change in an instant and take a drastic turn. It seemed a dark cloud was steadily hanging over us - this heavy feeling weighed us down. Ryan was always looking over his shoulder, scanning our surroundings for anything out of the norm. He never let me out of his sight. We tried to keep ourselves busy to pass the time, but quickly got tired of swimming, snorkeling, and lying in the sun. Even the short kayaking trips were no longer enjoyable since we were barely an eyeshot from the beach. I recorded our experiences in my journal, always returning the notebook to my exit bag for safekeeping. The last thing I would ever want to do is forget it somewhere.

Our stay in Palau was extended by almost a month. Trying to make the most of it, I couldn't help but feel trapped, confined, and overly restricted at times.

One morning, over breakfast, Ryan said he cleared an off-island activity with our remaining stealth members. He suggested I try scuba diving since he enjoyed it and would love for us to experience that together. Agreeing, I started with lessons in the pool before graduating to the shallow ocean shoreline in front of the bungalow. Feeling somewhat confident, I hoped to gather enough courage for the giant clam fields diving excursion he had planned.

Joining a group of twelve tourists on the guided dive three days later, I was nervous about descending to depths of thirty-five to seventy feet, wondering if we would come face to face with any creatures. The thought made me shiver.

Actively taking part in the Dive Master's Q&A when he opened the floor to inquiries after leaving the docks, I asked about the chances of seeing an eel. He immediately informed us that eels were plentiful here, but the sea snakes could reach six to eight feet long. Some guests, including our team members, gasped as the Dive Master instructed us not to tempt the snakes. He advised that we steer clear or stay still to avoid provoking them, stating that they only attack if threatened first. Reassuring everyone that he had only five dive encounters with a sea snake in the past six months did not make me feel better about the danger.

Glancing over at me, Ryan knew I was scared out of my mind. Reaching for my hand, he said, "You'll be fine. I'll protect you. Always have and always will."

Kissing me on the cheek, I knew he was right. I never had to be afraid when I was with him. Settling down, I took a deep breath, smiled, and decided to enjoy every minute of this afternoon of freedom.

Close to our diving destination, the vessel slowly drifted above a beautiful turquoise reef. Carefully peering over the side of the boat into the crystal-clear waters, I could almost see the ripples in the sand along the bottom. Within minutes, we heard the anchor chains clanking before hitting the seafloor.

While suiting up in our gear, the Dive Master gave a few last-minute instructions.

"Alright, can I have everyone's attention, please? Thank You! Just a few notes! Concerning the giant clams, which local legends say are meat-eaters, I am here to confirm they are not. That said, we strictly advise that the clams be untouched and treated respectfully. We do not want them damaged in any way. Moving on, please be aware of the large Napoleon Wrasse fish that frequent this reef. You will most likely encounter a few, easily four to six feet long. But don't worry. They are very friendly and mean no harm. These fish are on the World Conservation Union Red List of Threatened Species and should be treated with the utmost care. On another note, be mindful of the shallow water above the reefs. Something I am certain you already know. So that said, I hope you enjoy this adventure under the sea! Have a safe dive, everyone!"

Knowing we swam alongside Angus at the Great Barrier Reef freed my mind from that worry. Excited to experience the beauty of the ocean here in Palau, I was intrigued to discover how this reef differed from the one in Australia.

Ryan got into the water first. I followed, jumping in shortly after. Slipping our masks on and prepping the respirators to submerge, I was nervous. Cautiously plunging two feet below the surface, Ryan waited for me to feel comfortable before descending hand in hand. I gave him a thumbs-up while passing the ten-foot mark. About to hit twelve feet, I started feeling pressure on my ears. Not having a choice, I returned to the ten-foot safety stop and waited until I could equalize before continuing.

Eventually, making it to a depth of twenty-five feet, we decided to remain in the middle of the reef versus exploring the seafloor below.

Finding a few of the giant clams was very exciting. They were as big as the Dive Master said and were beautiful, boasting mouths of patterned iridescent blue.

Over the next hour, having found so many hidden treasures within the coral croppings, we turned our attention to a few divers gathered a short distance away. Realizing the group had attracted a couple of intrigued Wrasse fish, we quickly swam over to join them, wishing we had a camera. The fish were so pretty. Each was painted in electric blue, green, and purple colors, with fleshy lips and a hump on their foreheads. Calmly gliding by us, one in particular was very friendly and approachable. Looking into his golf ball-sized eyes, we could not help but notice his intelligence and curiosity. The fish seemed to enjoy leaning against the pressure of our hands, sometimes even giving us a gentle nudge or a brush, just like a dog acts when it wants us to pet and rub its ears.

Unfortunately, the Dive Master gave our group the signal to surface. Disappointed, everyone began their ascent, hitting each safety stop. Enjoying the magical scenery along the way, I thought this was another completely different world under the sea. Appreciating every inch of it, I was sad to know we would never again return.

Floating toward the stern, Ryan helped me sit on the partially submerged platform. Sitting beside me, we both got assistance taking off our gear.

"How was that?" he asked with a glimmer in his eye.

"Loved it. Beautiful. No words."

"I knew you would."

Wrapping his arm around me, he kissed my cheek and stood up to offer his hand. I took hold and climbed onto the main deck. While pulling our wetsuits down to our waist, we humorously struggled to take them off. Finally free, he and I accepted two bottles of water before finding our spot near the bow. In need of a rest, I still found myself talking about the experience with abundant excitement. It was an amazing, memorable adventure.

"So? Do you think you would try scuba diving again?"

"Diving is not as scary as I thought it would be. I would definitely try it again. There is this unsurpassed freedom under the water, like you are in a different world, away from all the troubles plaguing the surface."

"Yes. I know what you mean," Ryan replied in total agreement.

With everyone accounted for, we spent a good part of the afternoon meandering through the Lazy Point Rock Islands - a grouping of ancient relic limestone coral reefs that violently surfaced years ago, now listed as a World Heritage Site.

The Dive Master explained, "Many islands display a mushroom-like shape with a smaller base at the intertidal notch. The indentation comes from erosion and the dense community of sponges, urchins, and other marine life that graze mostly on the algae below."

Amazed by the scenery, we discussed the many birds, super yachts, and sailboats spotted along the way.

Rounding a corner, steering past one group of islands, the boat's captain moved our attention to a secluded white sand beach amidst the turquoise sea.

"Lunch Time!" the Dive Master announced while the deckhands began anchoring us ten feet from shore.

One by one, each passenger grabbed a quick bite from the selection of wraps and sandwiches before heading back into the water. Most wanted to snorkel the reefs bordering the small islands, consisting of beautiful creatures and natural elements rarely seen. The brightly displayed marine life stood out over the muted coral hues, making you feel like you were visiting a foreign planet.

Saddened that the day went by too quickly, the group gathered to board the boat one last time. The second the deckhands raised the anchor, we were on our way back to the resort docks. Thoroughly enjoying the beginnings of the sun descending over the ocean, I found myself forgetting about our current set of circumstances. Grateful for the mental break, resting my back against Ryan, I felt rejuvenated - something my soul needed right now.

Drifting into the bay's calm waters late that afternoon, docking moments after, everyone went their separate ways. Tired, water-logged, and sun-drenched, we strolled hand in hand back to our bungalow.

Collapsing on the bed, Ryan said, "I think we should order room service and call it a day. What do you think?"

"Yes. I think that is a good idea." I was exhausted.

With just enough time to shower and change into something more comfortable, the concierge arrived with our food on a trolley within a half hour. Sitting down at the small table in the corner of the room, I sat quietly while eating dinner.

"Are you okay?" he asked, a little concerned.

"Yes. I am just drained. We did a lot today." Moving the seafood around the plate, I needed to ask, "Do you think we are stuck here now?"

Ryan shook his head. "No. I believe this is probably the safest place for us. We are a needle in a haystack. If anything, Agent Frank still has us here for a reason." Reaching across the table, he rested his hand on my forearm. "Don't worry. We will be okay. Let's continue taking one day at a time."

I nodded, knowing he was right on all accounts.

Effortlessly falling asleep that night sometime before ten, comfortably wrapped in Ryan's arms, the waves below us helped lull me to sleep. Enjoying the silence, without warning, our room door flung open. Fearfully sitting up in bed, the stealth team converged with urgency, flashlights in hand, instructing us to gather our things and get moving.

"Extraction time - two minutes!" Agent Tim shouted, surveying our surroundings and the speed of our reaction.

Panicked by the beams of light moving erratically, not questioning them, my body trembled while I got dressed and made a thorough pass through the room, taking account of everything. Ryan did the same before we darted through the trees to an unmarked cargo van waiting in the dark end of the parking lot. Getting in, Ryan held me tightly. When the doors slid shut, we were off.

Without headlights, the driver sped away, using only the moon to light his path through the resort gates. Sitting beside the guy, Tim took point with an earpiece inserted in his ear, tablet in one hand, and light in the other.

Hearing something come through the comm, Tim shouted abruptly, "Take a right here!"

Not sure why we needed to divert into a laneway and leave the main road, the driver turned the vehicle on a dime, adhering to instructions.

"Shut off the engine. Get down!"

Everyone ducked their heads out of sight. Each breathing heavily, the vehicle went deadly silent. Tim kept watching as a set of lights soon appeared and whisked by at a high rate of speed. My heart raced while I prayed. But fear and doubt infiltrated my mind.

Knowing the coast was clear, Tim again received intel and shouted, "Okay! Go! Go! Go!"

The driver started the engine and backed out onto the road, jerking us one way, then the other. Lights still turned off, we continued to our destination and eventually arrived in a desolate marina surrounded by small shacks.

Tim turned to us and said, "They are watching the Palau airport. We must get to an airstrip on another island just south of here. Everybody out. Let's move."

Ryan helped me out of the vehicle and grabbed our baggage. Rushing along the rickety dock, we heard the sound of a muffled trolling motor nearby. Spotting a forty-two-foot deep-sea fishing boat, Tim waved him in. One by one, we boarded. Ryan reached out his hands to me. Transferring to it, the stealth team loaded their gear before the driver pulled away, helping us disappear from the island undetected.

Leaving the docks, surrounded by the thickness of night, the winds picked up when hitting the open water, making the boat bounce around unsteadily. The air was damp and much cooler, making me shiver. It prompted many of us to grab an extra layer to try and stay warm since the boat only had a shelter above the driver's controls. The rest of us were subject to the elements.

Ryan questioned Tim. "Where are we headed?"

"Due south to the island of Peleliu. There is a hidden airstrip there. A plane will be awaiting our arrival. But the problem is, by my calculations, the trip will take almost two and a half hours at this rate," the agent explained.

Those who heard him flashed a look of concern.

Upon rounding the long peninsula to the left, we traveled further into the open ocean. Above, the stars sparkled overhead, flowing like a river from north to south.

Soon, the waves got rough. I was terrified that we would tip over or, worse, hit a shallow reef and sink. Ryan tried to keep me calm, explaining that the boat captain was using sonar to help guide us along and would keep us out of harm's way.

Suffering through an hour of rain when hit by a passing storm, Tim bravely sat at the bow holding a GPS device and helped the captain navigate through a dangerously narrow canal called the German Channel. Hearing the two men communicating back and forth, we had no choice but to slow to a crawl. Not receiving a consistent signal for the device to work, Tim stood up, totally frustrated, and opted to shine a flashlight into the water to thread us through the coral reef. It was hard not to be affected by the intense pressure on those aboard the vessel. Everyone was shivering, cold, and scared.

Thinking we may have gotten lost amongst the many islands, thankfully, that all changed when we saw a spotlight flickering ahead of us.

"There!" Tim shouted, pointing over the bow as the captain maneuvered the boat in that direction.

Carefully inching closer, he scanned the landing site with the flashlight to survey the tide level, wondering if it was safe to proceed to shore.

Somewhat familiar with the daily schedule, believing the tides at 1:00 a.m. were usually high, the captain was confident that the reefs along the waterfront were submerged, allowing us to proceed to the beach.

In minutes, the captain nudged us against the sandy shore while the waves crashed against the rear of the boat. Ryan jumped out first and helped me when I reached for him. Knee-deep in the water, we found Agent Frank waiting a few feet away. Now, on dry land, climbing the steep embankment, so thankful to have made it, the rest of our group appeared one by one with gear hoisted high above their heads.

"Is everyone okay?" Agent Frank asked, taking a headcount.

Tim updated him. "Yes. Everyone is here. Target was en route to the resort after we departed. Nobody followed us while proceeding to the extraction point."

"Perfect," he said, taking the lead through the trees.

Reaching the steps of the duel turboprop plane, Agent Frank allowed us to board first. "Please find your seats," he said. "We need to move! All electronics off. Shut 'em all down!"

Tim turned off his devices and placed each in a Faraday pouch. Leaning back in his chair after the stressful navigation task, he replied, "Don't have to ask me twice."

I sat across the aisle from Ryan. Worried about the small, long-range prop, I knew we had no choice. We needed to leave here and fast.

Positioned at the end of the bumpy, uneven runway, we overheard the pilot say to Agent Frank, "This runway is a bit short. Prep everyone in case there's a problem."

Not out of danger yet, Agent Frank got everyone's attention. "Okay, stow bags under the seats. Make sure all belts are securely fastened. Keep your heads down. Lean forward until we lift off."

So fearful, Ryan tried to diffuse the expression on my face. Taking hold of my hand, he squeezed it tightly. "It's alright. Keep your eyes on me. We are going to be fine," he said.

Whispering a prayer to myself, the deafening roar of the engine unexpectedly jerked us backward. Tightly grasping Ryan's hand, pressing the other against the seat in front of me, the plane bumped and violently jostled around while racing down the makeshift runway. After what seemed an eternity, we finally felt the nose of the aircraft elevate. Then, suddenly, the bumping stopped. Leaving the ground, the pilot pulled up at a sharp angle. Powerfully propelling us forward, dipping in and out of the crosswinds, I looked over at Ryan to see him timidly sit up, along with everyone else.

"Okay. We're good," Agent Frank stated with a sigh of relief. "So, listen up. We are about four and a half hours away from our next location. For this leg, we are completely on our own. Get some sleep. I know you're tired. I'll hold a briefing on things before we land."

Unsure what that meant - being on our own - I assumed he wouldn't communicate with anybody in his department. More and more, it became evident that there was nobody we could trust if they were able to find us on that remote island in the middle of the ocean.

Reaching cruising altitude, Ryan and I changed out of our wet clothes. Much more comfortable, I hung everything over the back of our seats to dry. Finding a pillow and blanket tucked in the side compartment, I curled up and prayed that we'd reach our destination, but succumbed to the fact that we might not make it through this alive.

| 55 |

Bali

8°44'46" S / 115°10'00" E
8°15'37" S / 114°28'39" E

Hit by a pocket of severe turbulence, the plane vibrated and shook. Dropping sharply, losing altitude twice, I sat fearfully in my seat, gripping the armrests tightly. Still half asleep, I looked over at Ryan. He was wide awake. Scared, nerves rattled, I was now on high alert, along with everyone else. Noticing this, Agent Frank decided to brief the team on our current status, hoping it would be a welcomed distraction.

"Maybe this is a good time to get all of you up to speed."

The group intently listened, not understanding how the Cartel figured out where we were situated yet again.

Frank quickly clarified things. "Okay. In the past few weeks, we've had surveillance on a suspected Cartel mole embedded within the USMS. This person accessed Bryan and Ava's files and many others."

"So, what is the common thread?" one agent asked.

"We found out that each file was connected to the Cartel. Primarily, Consuelos. Newly assigned to the agency, we assume this guy's been tracking these two for his boss." Agent Frank pointed directly at us. "We've proven that he's been supplying intel since they were discharged from their designated holding facilities and transferred to the Icelandic safehouse. Also, there is a strong possibility that Bryan was tracked even before that. I assume this guy's been offered a lot of money in exchange for intel. Possibly even threatened should he not comply. We caught on when he recently slipped up, which aided us in his reveal this past week. He has since been detained and refuses to cooperate when questioned."

Ryan asked, "So, who is he? How did he slip up?"

"Because it was an internal breach, the information is considered classified now. That incident aside, being honest with you here, we recently entered an offset of your Palau location in the system. By doing this, we discovered a level three clearance accessed the file shortly after. The bottom line is we believe the same Cartel hitman from Iceland was passed this information and was about to hunt you down."

Stunned at the bluntness of his words, I couldn't breathe. In my mind, I heard - I intentionally put your life in danger because...

"So, what's the plan?" Ryan inquired, shifting his weight forward, getting down to business, not missing a beat. Resting his elbows on top of his knees, he focused in and clenched his hands tightly in front of him. Grabbing hold of his arm, I leaned my cheek against his shoulder across the center aisle.

With each stealth member looking on, Agent Frank continued to explain, "We now know someone with a higher level of clearance is involved - someone with unlimited access to our database systems. That is the only way to access your classified records. There are a restricted number of agents with this level of accessibility. The agency is having difficulty tracking and deciphering the access methods used, meaning this person is an expert on backdoor computing. That said, I also want to inform you of another mission assigned to us."

Agent Frank elaborated on how we needed to be involved further.

"To expose and capture the informant supplying the Cartel information on your whereabouts, we will plant false info in your files to see who takes the bait. While we wait, I'll devise a plan to capture the hitman ID'd in Iceland and Palau. The agency now knows his identity. It's Constantine Consuelos' brother, Tomás. This man has recently conducted most of the Cartel's rather messy hits. We assumed the guy was tracking you since he outwardly vowed to avenge his brother's incarceration."

"Wait! Tomás? He's Constantine's brother? That so-called assassin? He's the guy who murdered my partner and his family a few years back?" Ryan looked stunned. Had his past life just come full circle?

"Yes, the same, unfortunately."

"If his work is so gruesome, why has he not been successful in my case?" Ryan questioned.

Stunned by his question, I said, "What are you saying?"

"I mean, he's had many occasions to knock me off, but hasn't. Why?"

Handed a file, Frank said, "We know this man is highly unstable. Profilers believe he likes to play cat-and-mouse games. He prefers the thrill of the hunt. In Iceland, he didn't want to kill you. If he did, the game would be over."

I couldn't fathom how he could say that so casually.

"Look, Bryan, we know you have specialized law enforcement training, and you're no stranger to this type of thing. The top six agencies worldwide are coordinating to orchestrate a highly covert operation to bring down Tomás and his newest global affiliates. This campaign will inevitably end an extensive ten-year rap sheet of horrific crimes he has participated in across the globe and will hopefully create a gap in the Cartel's reviving hierarchy. We know Tomás is obsessed with his quest for power. Since his brother isn't at the helm to keep him in check, we assume his notoriously careless behavior could play to our benefit. We need to stop him from becoming an international threat, and we are requesting your help to do so."

Calmly waiting for a response before explaining the intricate details, Ryan looked at me with a sense of sadness, then anger. "This guy killed my partner and his family. If I do this, maybe we'll finally be able to live a normal life, and he won't harm anyone else ever again." Pausing for a second, seeing me nod, he replied, "I'm in."

"Just to clarify, we need both of you to make this operation work. Bryan, you've been listed as Tomás' number one mark on his revenge list, and sadly, by association, Ava, Tomás will probably target you to get to Bryan," he blatantly explained.

The weight of that statement sent an element of absolute terror right through to my core. Driven to kill, this man wanted us both dead. The ancient rhetoric, eye for an eye, was still a coveted part of this dark, hidden, criminal world.

"What do you need us to do?" Ryan prompted.

Deep in the South Pacific, partway through the four-hour flight to the island of Bali, everyone listened as Agent Frank explained the basic details of the mission thus far. Not having a choice, Ryan and I agreed to the plan's terms, even though the situation for me was beyond frightening.

Before landing in Bali, we made a fuel stop in Manado in North Sulawesi, which extended our trip by almost an hour. Without wasting any more time, we were back up in the air, as my head and stomach could barely manage.

Two and a half hours later, the pilot announced our descent into Bali Ngurah Rai International Airport. Thankful to soon be on the ground again, I suddenly felt more nauseous, believing the flight had caused a bout of dreaded motion sickness. Keeping it to myself, I thought how nice it would be to rest my head on a pillow tonight.

Touching down early that morning, with barely a soul on the tarmac, the team disembarked, leaving us on board with Frank. Sadly, I discovered there was one more flight to take. The group had arranged a floatplane to escort us to our final location - Agent Frank's friend's villas along the far western shore.

The floatplane maneuvered to our turboprop parked a few yards from the terminal. The team boarded with their baggage in tow. Settled on the single-engine aircraft, we took off not long after with engines roaring. The sound reverberated through our bodies until we got into the air.

The last twenty minutes were excruciating for me since my nausea got worse. Finally landing on the water in front of two secluded white buildings, noticing it was the only sign of life we could see for miles, we stepped from the pontoon onto a long, weathered dock. Quite queasy, I focused on the first hint of dawn appearing on the horizon behind the white structures. Exhausted beyond measure, we followed Agent Frank to the back door of the one safe house and were immediately met by five more agents, who had already set up shop on the ground floor. Surrounded by computer systems and screens everywhere, a table in the middle of the room had piles of drawings, plans, and maps. I got the feeling each person knew who we were and why we were there as each looked up the moment Ryan and I walked through the door.

With a laptop briefcase and black tactical duffel bag in hand, Frank said, "The team is staying in both villas. The place on the left is our tactical situation room, and this villa is our command center. Try and get some sleep. Over the next few hours, we will start planting information in your files announcing your impending relocation in exactly two weeks, orchestrating the outcome we've discussed. That should reveal the mole and give him enough time to pass along the info to Tomás, who we suspect will immediately travel with an army of men to ambush you upon arrival at the new location. Your room is upstairs. Agent G will show you where. We'll meet up later, and oh, by the way, nobody else outside these walls knows you are here. I handpicked this team for a reason. I trust them. So, don't worry. Nobody will track us."

Shown upstairs by the straight-faced Agent G, we settled into the small blue room with a king-sized platform bed, a private bath with twin stone sinks, and a glass-encased rain shower. Unable to ignore the sick feeling as I surveyed our strange new surroundings, I got changed and quickly splashed some water on my face, desperately needing to lie down. Under the covers, utterly drained, we both fell asleep quickly, unable to stay up a minute longer.

| 56 |

Unwell

8°15'37" S / 114°28'39" E

Seeing the early afternoon sun flicker and illuminate our room, I rolled over. Feeling disoriented, I found Ryan lying on his back, deep in thought. I didn't have to ask what was on his mind. I'm sure we both knew this latest extraction was not a dream but rather a piece of an ongoing nightmare. Someone was hunting us. Once again, we were the target.

Ryan suddenly broke his silence and bypassed our morning small talk while staring at the ceiling. Glancing my way for a split second, he said. "We don't have to do this, you know. I've dealt with this Tomás guy before. The things he's done. I can't even..." Shaking his head, he added, "Above all that, he is notoriously unpredictable. Going ahead with this will mean significant risk."

Sighing, not sure how to respond to that, I noticed the sick feeling I was dealing with yesterday hadn't seemed to subside at all. Being mindful of the impending doom hovering over us probably didn't help matters.

"Can you please do me a favor?" I desperately asked.

"Sure. Anything."

"Can you grab me something bland to eat? Like toast or a bagel? My stomach's off. I had a lot of motion sickness on the plane yesterday. Now, I think it's just nerves."

Without giving it a second thought, he pulled back the covers and sat on the edge for a moment. Slowly slipping on a pair of shorts and a shirt, he left the room and headed downstairs, leaving me on my own.

The second he stepped out the door, I ran to the bathroom as my stomach turned. Staying there for a few minutes, feeling dreadful, I haphazardly stumbled back to bed, hoping I'd feel better once I could lie back down again. Sadly, that was not the case.

Minutes later, Ryan returned with two pieces of plain buttered toast in hand and a bottle of water. I slowly sat up and rested my back against the low headboard. It was hard to ignore the nauseously heavy sensation in my head. Taking a bite of my toast, Ryan sat beside me - his mind noticeably reeling.

In a different mindset, he looked overly distracted by his train of thought. I could tell he hadn't noticed that I was sick.

"I don't like the idea of placing you in danger," he said firmly, "They need me there so Tomás gets a positive ID, but what if we send in a decoy for you? They wouldn't know the difference if the woman had dark hair, sunglasses, and a hat or hood. As long as they see me, that would be all that matters. I think you should stay out of it."

Bothered by his theory, hating the fact of him being in harm's way and having to be separated for any given amount of time, all seemed too much for me. "I don't want to be away from you, though."

Ryan looked me straight in the eye. "What I mean is…I don't think I can do this job with you by my side. You are my number one priority, and my main focus would be on your protection and not the task at hand," he clarified. "Please don't take offense."

Understanding what he was saying, I knew I might have to stay away for us to both come out of this alive. If I were absent, then he could focus on his safety and nothing else.

"Well, are you going to pitch that to Frank?" I asked.

Serious, he paused a second, still pondering things. "Yeah, think so." Kissing me on the forehead, he said, "I'll be right back, okay."

When he left the room, the door closed behind him. I got out of bed with my toast in hand and walked over to the double-louvered doors. Flipping each open revealed the calming view of the ocean and pool below. I stepped onto the balcony and saw no sign of life except for the activity on the ground directly below me. There wasn't even a boat on the horizon. It was apparent we were in a very remote part of the island, making me feel so far away from civilization. In absolute disbelief, it was hard to comprehend how my life had taken such a drastic turn in the past year, going from exceedingly calculated and controlled to extremely unpredictable and unprecedented. Believing this could be the end for us, I interrupted all the negativity with a simple image of Ryan in my head.

"You must remain focused on the happiness you've found with him. Nothing else," I said to myself, adjusting my frame of mind. While peering down at the rings on my finger, I had faith, knowing as long as we stayed together, we could make it through anything.

Feeling slightly faint, I quickly sat on a lounge chair a couple of feet away. Not knowing what was wrong with me, I chalked it up to stress and extreme fatigue. Unsteadily heading back inside to lie down for a while, I wrapped my head with a pillow, trying to drown out the noise of all the commotion taking place downstairs.

Sometime later, I heard a sound and assumed the door opened. While lifting my head off the pillow, my eyes found the love of my life hovering above me.

"Ev, are you alright? What's wrong?"

Rolling over, not feeling as poorly as I did earlier, I admitted, "I'm not sure, just not feeling well today. Maybe I picked up a bug along the way? I felt worse earlier. What time is it?"

Hugging me with an abundance of empathy, looking over at the clock on his side table, he added, "It's ten after five. Can I get you any-thing?"

"No, I'm good. So, did you talk to Agent Frank? What did he say?" I inquired, holding my breath.

"Because I don't want to separate from you, we will travel to our intended destination together, and on the last leg of the journey, they will switch you out with a decoy. The team will hold you back in a different location about an hour from the mission site. Again, when Tomás sees me, he'll assume the woman with me is you."

Terrified, thinking the worst, and trying to keep my mind positive, I figured after everything was said and done, I hoped we could disappear for good and start a new life elsewhere.

Ryan noticed how pale I was. "You don't look good."

"I'll be okay - just need to sleep it off. Don't worry. I'm fine."

He tucked me in. "Alright. I'll let you rest, and I'll check on you in an hour."

Nodding my head, I closed my eyes and quickly fell asleep again.

| 57 |

Unexpected

8°15'37" S / 114°28'39" E

With each passing day, Ryan spent most afternoons with Agent Frank and the team when they gathered for multiple meetings to discuss the mission.

By day six, I started feeling worse and wondered if the bottled water with unfiltered ice was making me sick or if I had picked up a flu virus somehow along the way. My head was dizzy, and my stomach felt very queasy. Surviving on toast and juice, sitting quietly about the property, I felt drained and awful most of the time. Worried, the team requested a doctor to drop by since I couldn't even fathom getting on a plane feeling like I did.

Two days passed in a blink. The stealth group told us they cleared a female, former military, American doctor to visit. Lying in bed that afternoon, having lost weight, unable to eat much, I waited for them to escort her to our room.

Ryan led the doctor upstairs, making small talk along the way.

Entering the room, the woman made eye contact with me. "Hello, I am Dr. Rashi. I hear you are feeling under the weather."

I nodded and explained my symptoms to her in great detail.

She, in turn, took my blood pressure, temperature, and pulse.

Breaking her silence, she asked without hesitation, "Is there any way you could be pregnant?"

Ryan's eyes immediately bounced back and forth between the doctor and me. Thinking for a second, I realized that never really crossed my mind.

"Well, if you want, we can do a rapid test quickly to find out. If it is negative, we'll test further to see what might be ailing you."

Pulling out a sealed package, she asked for a sample, which I supplied. After returning from the bathroom, I sat beside Ryan on the edge of the bed. He refrained from rubbing my back, knowing it made me feel worse. While we waited, the suspense made it hard for me to breathe since my heart was racing. My palms were sweating profusely, trying to recall the cycle of things with all the weeks jumbled up in my head. I wasn't sure what to think.

The doctor emerged minutes later and smiled. "Ma'am, the test is positive. You are pregnant. Congratulations."

Unable to respond, the air expelled from my lungs, and I felt a subtle hint of joy amidst the shock. But the thought of our current situation quickly replaced that happiness, knowing this was undoubtedly a less-than-perfect place in time for this to happen. With a mix of emotions, Ryan's face went blank.

While the news settled in, he lovingly put his arms around me, but I couldn't tell if he was thrilled.

"Well, you're going to be a Dad," I whispered, flashing a nervous, uncertain smile.

Slowly separating from our embrace, a serious expression came over him. Mindful of what he was about to say in front of the doctor, he whispered, "Ava, this changes things. In exactly five days, we are supposed to travel to the UK. It's almost a sixteen-hour flight. How are you going to do that? I think you should stay here where it's safe."

Wholeheartedly disagreeing, not having to think it over, I lowered my voice so the woman wouldn't hear what I was about to say. "Absolutely not. We have to travel together. It'll be fine. Once we get there, I'll wait at the alternate location."

The doctor kindly interrupted our conversation. "I can give you something to help with nausea, but I can't do much about the overall symptoms - you'll have to ride those out. Usually, they subside at around the three-month mark."

"Alright," I nodded, acknowledging her.

Collecting some blood to see how far along we were in the pregnancy, she said, "I'll be back tomorrow with the results and your medication. Until then, get some sleep and eat regularly. You may see a slight difference if you have something every hour."

Exiting our room, the doctor shook Ryan's hand. We both thanked her for her help. Reiterating that she'd be back, he closed the door behind her and returned to where I was sitting.

"Can I get you anything? She said to keep having little snacks - not let your stomach go empty."

I agreed to have a piece of toast and some fruit. Going out the door, he left me by myself for a moment. Sitting in bed, glancing down at my stomach with thoughts of a little person growing inside me, suddenly changed my thought process. That fear I once had turned to more of a protective instinct. Rubbing my hand along my waist from left to right, I wondered when we could lead a quiet life without running, fear, or violence. A life with friends, and maybe, eventually, our families involved in some capacity. How I wish I could have called my sister to share the happy news. Knowing I couldn't communicate with her brought about feelings of sadness, making me homesick.

Getting out of bed, I walked onto the balcony to look out over the ocean, trying to distract any harmful thoughts from invading my mind. Content to soak up a little of the sun's warmth, I convinced myself that nothing else mattered in life now but the baby and my husband.

Moments later, Ryan returned with my snack. He sat on the lounge chair beside me. "I can't believe we are having a baby." Noticing that I was not as thrilled as he was, knowing what I was probably thinking, he said, "I know this isn't exactly an ideal situation, but Ev, this is amazing news. We are going to be parents. This is a gift." Placing his hand gently on my stomach, he peered into my eyes. His face brightened with much joy and love. "I'll be here for you every step of the way. Both of you are my only family." Kissing my lips, always being so sure about everything, I felt his strength flow through me.

That evening, we quietly fell asleep in each other's arms, knowing that within a few days, we would leave the peacefulness of this place and be thrown into harm's way, God willing, for the last time. That night, I prayed that all three of us would be kept safe, whatever comes.

| 58 |

New Life Emerges

8°15'37" S / 114°28'39" E

Faintly hearing the waves crashing against the volcanic black sand beach outside the villa, I opened my eyes, deciding to lie there silently and listen to the tranquil sounds around us. The wind joined in from time to time, bringing subtle gusts that created a constant hum in the air. For the first time in almost a week, I heard nothing from the situation room below and assumed many were trying to get a little extra sleep before departing for our next destination in the coming days. Pulling the white sheet closer to my chin, I turned to Ryan, still sleeping, unable to believe the grim reality we faced despite the glimmer of happiness now mixed in.

You've drifted far from what you dreamed your life would be, I thought.

Exhaling, wondering how I would survive the next nine months, Ryan happened to roll over and face me. His peacefulness drained every ounce of doubt from my mind.

"Good morning," he smiled. "How are you doing this morning?"

I wanted to keep calm and not make him worry. "I'm doing okay," I answered, hoping he bought it.

Rubbing my shoulder, he asked, "Need some breakfast?"

"If you don't mind. That would be wonderful."

Kissing me, he said, "I do not mind at all. I'll be back in a minute."

Ryan returned minutes later with fruit, toast, and bottled water. Setting the tray on the table on the balcony, I walked over and sat in the chair he had pulled out. Sitting beside me, we watched the waves rolling in along the shore.

Seeing him glance over from time to time, smiling, I asked, "What? What is it?"

"You are going to be a Mom." Beaming with pride, he said, "Me? A Dad? I still can't believe it. You've got a little person growing in there." He placed his hand on my tummy. "Being a parent is something I've dreamed of but never…"

"I know what you mean. I never thought this would happen, either. I mean, I always wished to be a mom one day, but I guess when you are with the right person, fate finds a way." I tapped his arm lovingly.

Overwhelmed, he reached with both arms and hugged me so tightly. Kissing me, it felt different. "You are going to make an amazing Mother," he said in the most sincere tone.

"Well, you will be the best Dad ever."

| 59 |

Results

8°15'37" S / 114°28'39" E

Late that afternoon, as expected, the doctor arrived. She presented the bloodwork results and passed along my medication. She told us we were about three weeks along, meaning it must have happened while in Palau, which made sense in hindsight. Still trying to grasp hold of this news, still very much in shock, she gave me instructions on how to take the meds meant to reduce nausea.

Continuing to eat something small every hour, I started getting used to the brain fog and dizziness. Keeping a close eye on me, Ryan tracked when I ate last and brought me food often. We spent the time thinking of baby names and discussing what kind of parents we would be. Sadly, everyone around us was not married, nor did they have children of their own, including Agent Frank, who referred to himself as unattached. Needless to say, they weren't much help to us. Regardless of the confusion and newness ahead, Ryan said if we could outrun an assassin, then chances are, we could survive parenthood. I hoped he was right.

| 60 |

The Plan

8°15'37" S / 114°28'39" E

The day before our scheduled departure, Agent Frank called a final strategic meeting with the team at eleven in the morning. Ryan included. While quietly sitting at the desk in our room, updating my journal while he had a shower, I decided to walk downstairs with him when he was ready. For me, the only thing on my agenda was to float weightlessly in the pool for a while. Hand in hand, we stopped beside a lounge chair.

He hugged me tightly. "I'll be back soon," he said, kissing me on the forehead. "Enjoy your swim."

Seeing him walk away and disappear into the tactical room villa, part of me desperately wanted to join in and listen to the discussion, hoping to learn more about his role in the whole thing. Not wanting to risk putting undue stress on myself and the baby, I opted to linger in the water instead.

Two hours later, Ryan found me on the balcony upstairs. Resting on a chaise lounge wrapped in a beach towel still in my swimsuit, I immediately noticed the intense expression on his face.

"What is it? What's wrong?"

Looking out over the ocean, with the waves rolling in gently along the shoreline, he placed both hands on the railing and confided, "They traced Tomás' goons. They've already taken the bait and have set up a base camp about a mile from the sting location. No sign of Tomás yet. The drones have made multiple surveillance rounds and have reported extensive activity in an abandoned farmhouse where they've illegally taken up residence. Our allies have systematically entered the region, disguised as tourists. Everything is proceeding according to plan. They have agents surrounding every angle of the projected zone, also making sure to detour civilians from the site, claiming work is to proceed on one of the main bridges there."

"So, what is going to happen then? What do they need us to do?"

"The plan is we land at Luton Airport in London, England. During a short layover, before I continue to East Midlands Airport, you will enter the washroom, just inside the terminal, and quickly change clothes with the decoy, who will then accompany me to the central zone. They are certain the cartel informants will be watching our arrival at the airport, so we must stick to the plan down to the second. Since we'll be landing around 8:30 a.m. U.K. time, the airport may be busy, offering a bit of a distraction and additional security. After I've left, another female agent will find you and escort you to a safe house an hour from the extraction point. You will wait there, and I'll join you once everything is said and done."

Scared to hear the rest of the details, I debated whether to ask anything further, but I needed to know... "So, what do you have to do?"

Not wanting to scare me, he walked over, sat down, and said, "Let me worry about that. The only thing I want you to focus on right now is our little person in here." Rubbing my tummy again, hoping to nurture his connection to the miracle we made, he confidently shared, "I promise you. I'll be fine. Please don't worry about me. I've had extensive training for situations like these. It's not as if I'm going in blind. Years ago, this was my life. Besides, I'll be surrounded by the best of the best."

Ryan pulled me in close. I knew this would be the last day we would have to be alone together for a while.

We spent most of the afternoon and evening just enjoying the scenery, the sun's warmth, and the caressing breeze.

That night, partially packed and ready to depart for the airport the following evening, I tried to get some sleep but kept tossing and turning.

Waking around three in the morning, feeling an empty spot next to me, I wondered where Ryan had gone. Turning on the side table light, I found him on the balcony. Upon seeing the glow transcend from our room, he quickly returned to me after closing the louvered doors behind him.

Slipping under the covers, he asked, "What's wrong? How are you feeling?"

"I was about to ask you the same thing."

"Yeah, umm, just going over things in my head, nothing major. Come on, let's go back to sleep," he suggested while settling in, hoping I wouldn't ask any more questions.

My gut feeling told me he was just as worried as I was.

| 61 |

UK Bound

8°15'37" S / 114°28'39" E

On day fourteen, we decided to sleep in for a bit longer, making sure to get ample rest. Being about a three-hour drive from the airport, they told us our flight was leaving at eleven-forty that evening, and our departure time from the villa had to be no later than eight o'clock. It would be a long, exhausting day, even though we would have the luxury of napping on the plane. With everything going on, I figured the chances of that were almost slim to none.

Trying to keep up my routine of snacking every hour, I kind of felt worse with the stress of the trip looming. All the details made it difficult to muster an appetite. Most of my time was spent lying on the couch, praying the dizziness would stop as my unbearable nausea began to subside with the meds.

That evening, the final few hours went by at a snail's pace while listening to the team packing up on the lower level. Doing the same, gathering what little we had, I placed our bags on the chair in the corner of the room, ready to go.

Around twenty after seven, the vehicles arrived out front to take us to the airport. The team filled the designated cargo vehicle to the brim. It was interesting to see how quickly they could dismantle and compactly parcel all the equipment.

While waiting downstairs for the convoy to leave, Ryan kept a close eye on my condition, fully aware that I was not feeling the best. When it was time to go, he carefully helped me into the van and slid the side door shut as everyone else followed suit simultaneously. We stayed quiet most of the way en route to the airport, unsure how this would end. Feeling unsettled during the long three-hour drive through the darkness, unable to see any scenery, we soon entered the main gates of the airport and passed through without incident. The caravan proceeded to the far side of the terminal and stopped in front of a Global 7500 charter jet waiting in a private hangar.

The team swiftly got us to exit the van when they secured the perimeter. One by one, cargo in tow, our group boarded and found a seat while Agent Frank handled the passport particulars with absolute ease. Back in familiar territory, the crew secured the doors for departure to move on to our next destination halfway across the globe.

As expected, we left Bali on time and prepared for the nine-hour flight to our fuel stop at a private FBO in Dubai. Requesting some bland crackers and a bottle of juice, I made sure my stomach was full before trying to get some sleep. Cuddling up beside Ryan in the VIP bedroom in the back, a flight attendant graciously offered us extra blankets and pillows.

Eyelids heavy, I dozed off quickly. I could feel Ryan cover me up and position his pillow just right, assuming he was watching me sleep. It would be a long haul to our destination. But there was no turning back now. Thinking of this operation as our Everest - this mountain we needed to climb up and over - I hoped, God willing, we would reach the other side and find a paradise that would allow us to live our new life in peace. Saying a silent prayer, I knew HE would keep us safe through it all.

| 62 |

Crossroads

24°52'56" N / 55°10'07" E

Hours later, hearing the pilot announce our descent in the United Arab Emirates, everyone was asked to prepare for landing just south of Dubai. The crew returned their seats to their upright position while Ryan and I got up to join the others in the main cabin. Once everyone was belted in, we began our approach into a country filled with wealth and beauty, power and prestige. Unfortunately, we couldn't enjoy the many attractions and culture. This time, we were only passing through. Limited to the view of the city boundaries, it was an endless blank canvas of desolate desert sand.

Smoothly drifting through the air, the landing gear touched down on the runway, and the flaps deployed. Slowing down in record time, it took ten minutes to maneuver the many winding taxiways to reach our assigned refueling apron outside the hangar. We waited on board during the procedure, noticing it was about twenty-five minutes past five, Dubai time. Seeing the subtle brightness of dawn approaching the flat landscape, I took some time to freshen up slightly, stretch my legs, and grab a much-needed salted cracker snack from the pantry for breakfast. Thankfully, the plane not only got refueled but also re-stocked. After passing the FBI Agents' thorough security checks, the catering company brought hot meals aboard.

Agent Frank kept checking his watch, knowing we were falling behind schedule. The short layover took much longer than expected. On the ground for almost an hour, the pilot finally confirmed our clearance for take-off, asking everyone to return to their seats promptly. Sitting beside Ryan, I could see a look of concern on his face. It seemed he knew we were that much closer to our final destination now. In his mind, that included a confrontation with the man who killed his partner and his family. The burden he was carrying was heavy. Reaching out for his hand, giving it a few gentle squeezes to break him from his thoughts, he turned to me and forced a smile.

Lifting off for the last leg of the journey, the plane ascended into the air with a bird's eye view of the city center, boasting tall skyscrapers, The Palms, and The World barely visible through the desert haze. The pilot mentioned that we were headed towards London's Luton Airport, over seven hours away. Wide awake, Ryan aimlessly looked out the window, resting his elbow on the armrest, stabilizing his chin with his thumb. His index finger moved tactfully from side to side across his lips, deep in thought. Even though he was beside me, I knew he was a million miles away.

"Are you doing okay?" I asked with great concern.

"Me? I'm good," he said, attempting to convince me that everything was fine.

"I seem to recall you saying, *Yeah, I'm good* on the yacht at Whitehaven just before we had to make a run for it. So, what are you thinking?" I blatantly asked, wondering if he would share the *straight-up* version as he often referred to it.

"I am going through things in my mind - making certain the plan's ingrained. It's been a long time since I've done anything like this. I suppose instinct will kick in when the time comes." Hesitating a moment, not looking my way, he calmly advised, "Ev, if they tell you to leave without me, please do what they say and go. I need to know you will do that to keep you and the baby safe."

Staying silent, looking forward, focusing on the empty seat across from me, I didn't know how to respond.

In that split second, Ryan got up and moved into the VIP cabin. Following him, I slid the door shut as everyone on board took notice.

He lowered his head with his back to me, arms outstretched and hands resting on the ceiling. "Ev? Promise me. Promise me you will leave if things don't go as planned."

Not wanting to fight, I reluctantly agreed, hoping to settle his mind. "I promise," I said while wrapping my arms around his waist.

"Thank you," he replied, turning to grab hold of me.

"But..." Before I could continue, he placed his finger over my lips and shook his head back and forth.

"No buts. You promised." Kissing me on the forehead, he held me tighter.

Deciding to spend this time together, quietly falling asleep in bed, Ryan moved his hand over my stomach. His mood filled my heart with worry as reality hit hard. I knew his mind was going there. His thoughts had already drifted to the possibility of him not surviving this, and me having to leave without him. Was there more to this mission than he was letting on? I was afraid to ask. All I knew was that if I stayed strong, he wouldn't be as concerned about me. This would allow him to focus more energy and attention on himself and his survival. I promised myself the rest of the flight I would stay positive and reflect an overall resilient façade, hoping to reassure him that I'd be fine. While lying there, I said so many silent prayers and had faith that each would be heard by the heavenly angels sent to protect the love of my life.

| 63 |

Decoy

51°52'41" N / 0°22'51" W

Beginning our descent, running almost an hour and a half behind schedule, we approached the outskirts of London. While Agent Frank recapped the details of how the next phase of the plan would transpire, I visualized entering the private terminal lounge and knew this was it - this was where I needed to leave him.

Sitting in on our last briefing, understanding my part, knowing I would meet the decoy in the washroom marked with a red dot, Frank reminded me that the next step had to be quick. I only had five minutes to exchange clothing with that person and make things seem believable. Even though the instructions were simple, the whole thing made me extremely anxious.

Minutes later, the wheels safely touched the ground. Applying the powerful reverse thrust, we quickly slowed down. Taxiing to a spot on the tarmac about twenty yards from the main building, we eventually came to a complete stop and unbuckled our seat belts, ready to get moving. Ryan stood up in the middle aisle and offered his hand. He looked my way. Eyes filled with love, he reached out with both arms. Wrapping them around my shoulders, he held my head against his chest with one hand.

Arms encircling his waist, I tried to stop the negative train of thought infiltrating my mind, casting doubt and fear. Was this the last embrace I would ever receive? Clutching tightly, I smiled and tried to put on a brave face. "You be safe and come back to us."

"I will…" he replied without hesitation, not wanting to let go.

Flashbacks of the Hamilton Island extraction resurfaced. Heart aching, I wished I hadn't agreed to stay at a distance. I wanted to be with him, not separated. Trying my best to exude positivity, I said, "I promise I'll be fine. You concentrate on what you have to do."

"Don't worry," Ryan reassured.

Tears developing, not wanting him to see me cry, I whispered, "I love you."

Calmly kissing me, he looked into my eyes and said confidently, "Love you more. Take care of our baby. This will all be over soon."

We kept our embrace for as long as he could before saying our last goodbyes. This had to be done here since we couldn't show emotion inside the terminal. The last thing we wanted was to tip off Tomas' informants and make them question whether something was amiss.

With my heart racing, filled with anxiety, I shivered even though I wasn't cold. It took every ounce of my being to manage a smile.

Reluctantly letting go of Ryan and taking a seat, Agent Frank said, "Hang tight, everyone. We got customs inbound. Stay quiet. I'll deal with them."

The co-pilot opened the aircraft door seconds before the immigration officer arrived. Stepping aboard, not looking very friendly, Agent Frank poured on the charm. The man looked over our documents and made eye contact with everyone to cross-reference their identity. We could have heard a pin drop in the process; it was so quiet.

In an instant, returning our passports and paperwork, the man said in a monotone voice, "Welcome to England," before descending the stairs and departing.

Relieved to pass that inspection, we refocused our attention on the mission.

Turning to us, Agent Frank said with a clap of his hands, "Okay, you two. You're on."

Not given time to contemplate what was happening, we quickly gathered our things together and made our way down the aisle hand in hand.

"Remember, Bryan," Frank quietly reminded, "You meet the decoy minutes after Ava leaves you. She will be dressed in Ava's clothes, so it will be easy to spot her. Don't skip a beat. Stay on task. Make it look real. Continue to the refreshment bar, grab something small, then return to the plane like nothing happened."

Legs weakening, my backpack slung across one shoulder, we flung our jacket hoods over our heads and left the plane to walk into the Signature Elite hub. While descending the steps, the place looked busy. Inside, wealthy business travelers prepared for their morning flights. Breaching the doors as they slid open, an attendant directed us into the arrivals lounge after we presented our passports and documentation to him. It did not take me long to locate the washroom entrance right after. Afraid to let go of Ryan, glancing back at him, he gave me a reassuring look. I offered him a smile and held his hand until the last minute before having to let go and walk away.

Pushing open the main door, I found a string of private washrooms in the inner hallway. Meticulously inspecting each, I discovered the one marked with a small, round, red sticker at the very end. Entering, locking it behind me, the lights automatically illuminated the room, revealing a woman hidden inside. Startled beyond belief, prepared to defend myself and fight, she raised her hands between us as a buffer.

"It's okay! So sorry! Sorry!" she said. Pausing, she asked, "Mrs. Daniels?"

Realizing that meant me, I whispered, "Yes?"

"I only have a short window to change and be on my way," she explained, opening the zipper on the bag on the floor beside her.

Not having a choice, I swiftly changed into the clothes she provided and handed her my outfit piece by piece.

I watched her fix her hair in the mirror and flip the hood over her head the way I had it. Before departing, she instructed, "Stay in this stall. You will hear someone knock three times. Open the door. Let the woman in." Eyeing my backpack, she added, "I need your bag. Place your things in this one."

After emptying the contents into the duffel, within seconds, she left. That is when I realized how much the decoy resembled me. Soon, she would be meeting up with Ryan and acting as though she were his wife. Feeling somewhat insecure that my husband was now with another woman, per se, made feelings of betrayal surface, reminding me of the night I caught Scott cheating. Uncomfortable with the situation, convinced Ryan would never do that to me, I diffused those thoughts, knowing the woman was just doing her job.

Listening to many people coming and going, using the other washrooms, I figured at least twenty minutes had gone by, if not more. Believing they had forgotten about me brought a level of panic. Then, I heard it. Someone gently knocked on the door three times. Opening it a crack, I found a mature woman standing there.

"Mrs. Daniels?"

Silently nodding, I swung the door open. The energetic woman, armed with a suitcase filled with supplies, did not waste any time. Washing my hands at the sink, she immediately started to tie my long hair up with bobby pins and placed a dark bobbed wig on my head with a stylish black hat on top of that.

"It's Ava, correct?" Nodding my head, she added, "Nice to meet you, Lovey. My name is Deniz."

"Nice to meet you," I replied, detecting a staunch English accent while shaking her hand.

Somewhat casual but task-oriented, Deniz was dressed in relaxed tourist attire, sporting long reddish spiral curls parted to one side. Initially sounding bubbly, she instantly flipped and got a bit intense.

"Here, Lovey. Put your things in this." Giving me a smaller suitcase she had secretly embedded inside her larger one, she zipped hers shut. It was now lighter than a feather. Psyched and ready to proceed according to plan, her tone changed again.

All business, she said, "Okay, Lovey, we are going to walk out of the loo. Along the way, carry on with some friendly banter about the trip and the weather. We must chivvy along to the front of the terminal, where agents are waiting for us in a black Land Rover. Act happy to see them. Be joyful and pretend like they are family. After all the pleasantries, we will give them our bags to place in the boot and be on our way. Do you understand?"

I caught most of what she was trying to say, but wanted clarification. "Loo? Banter? Boot?" I asked.

Seeing me look at her, slightly confused, she laughed. "Oh, you, Americans," she stated quite concretely before attempting to reiterate what she meant in plain English. "I'm sorry. Let's try this again. Umm, yes, we are going to walk out of the washroom. We are going to chivvy, umm, hurry along, to the front of the terminal, meet friends joyfully, and put our bags in the boot, or, how do you Yankees say it? The rear? No. No. No. That's not it. Wait. Let me think."

"The trunk?" I suggested.

"Yes! Trunk. That's it." Giving me a thumbs up, she said, "Got it, Lovey?"

With the instructions somewhat clear, I decided to follow her lead. Double-checking everything, we left the washroom hall and stuck to the plan.

Striking up a conversation through the passenger lounge, Deniz asked, "So, have you ever been to London?"

Walking to the left of the welcome desk, I replied, "No, never. This is my first time here. Too bad it's under these types of circumstances." Not feeling the best, I believed the adrenaline I once had was dissipating as we walked outside. It was good to get some fresh air, though.

Beneath the covered breezeway, we were on the lookout for the Land Rover. The deep rumble of a powerful engine caught our attention as it drove up along the curb. Inside was a middle-aged couple who got out and greeted us enthusiastically. Given heart-warming hugs and crying false tears of joy, the couple placed our empty luggage in the back while we got into the backseat.

Seconds later, we were pulling away from the terminal. I watched the driver place an earbud in his ear.

"Confirm. This is Elder - One - Nine - Six. Rapunzel has joined the family."

Thinking, who the hell is Rapunzel, I quickly realized they meant me. Huh? I thought. The only code name they came up with was a blonde cartoon character. Really? It was disappointing that it wasn't something a bit cooler, but then again, the people driving us were as old as my Grandparents once were, so it was to be expected. Clever, too, because no one would ever suspect they were undercover agents.

Taking note of our surroundings, reading the compass displayed on the rearview mirror, showing that we were headed north, I paid attention as best I could. Connecting to highway M1, resembling every other freeway in the States, I sat silently, wondering what Ryan was doing, as my stomach started up.

Concerned for his safety and desperate for updates, I turned to Deniz. "Do you know if they will keep me informed while the operation unfolds? How will I know if Ryan is alright?"

With eyes straight ahead, not flinching, she said, "Who is Ryan? Aren't you married to Bryan, Lovey?"

"Oh, yes," I hesitated, quickly backtracking, lowering my sights to the floor. "I call him Ryan or Ry for short. It's our thing, a nickname, you know...." I added while trying to correct my mistake, hoping she bought it.

Not missing a beat, giving me a tilt of the head with an eagle eye, knowing I'd slipped up his name, she said, "Yes, don't worry. Your secret is safe with me. One word of advice, though. Leave your old identities behind and become the person on paper. It makes it much easier that way and less confusing. It could one day mean the difference between life and death - if you know what I mean." Lowering my head, Deniz tapped my knee and said, "We are all good. Don't worry. Once we arrive at the safe house, you will find a stealth team monitoring the operation. If you wish to sit in the tactical room and take a gander, you must ask the Officer in charge for permission."

Determined, I took a moment to think about how I might do that. Not saying much the rest of the way, I began feeling sick and somewhat restless since my last bite to eat was over two hours ago.

"Excuse me. Do you have any snacks? I need to have something every hour, and it's been a while already."

The older woman sitting in the front seat opened a cooler bag on her lap and passed back a chilled ham and cheese croissant sandwich and a bottle of water to us in a gentle, grandmotherly way. "Yes, I was informed you are eating for two, Ma'am. I also brought some crackers and a couple of bland snacks, in case you fancy those instead."

Thanking her, I opened the sandwich as the countryside passed by in a blink.

Finally, after two hours and many interchanges, we branched off the highway into Nottingham. Quickly maneuvering through the traffic circles connecting the narrow streets, I began feeling overly queasy with the truck weaving in and out.

"How much longer?" I questioned, barely able to speak. "Are we close?"

"We will be there in exactly five minutes, Ma'am," the older gentleman said.

Scared, unsure if I could hold on that long, I closed my eyes and put my head back. Crossing my arms over my stomach, I focused on not tossing my croissant. Thoughts of Hamilton Island played through my mind. With it were feelings of helplessness and dread. I didn't want the vehicle to stop, knowing it would take even longer to get to the house, where I hoped they would give me an update on Ryan's progress.

Speedily turning down a deserted alleyway, arriving in front of a commercial building with a sign that read Steel Supplies, situated on an unnamed street, I wondered if we were in the right place. Approaching a tandem silver garage door at the rear of the red brick structure, we waited as it slowly retracted, allowing us to drive in and come to a stop.

"Here we are," the older man said, throwing the vehicle in park as the door closed behind us.

The woman in the front seat got out and swung open my door. "This way, Ma'am. How are you doing? You look a little ropey, dear."

Finally, stepping out onto the concrete floor, I didn't know what ropey meant and, at that point, didn't care.

Waiting for a second, wanting my head to stop spinning before we did anything further, I drank some water, praying it would stay down.

Deniz said, "Follow me. I will show you to your room so you can lie down. Don't worry; I'll take care of you, Lovey. So that you know, I am also a registered nurse."

On the way up the stairs, Deniz decided to walk behind me in case I got dizzy and fell. When we arrived on the upper floor, we came to another door, which unexpectedly opened when I got close.

There, we were met by a young, lanky English guy who said with a thick accent, "Welcome, Ma'am. Hi Deniz! How was the journey?"

"Oh, the bee's knees it was," she stated pretty sarcastically, paying more attention to my paleness while escorting me along.

Entering the large room, I counted at least ten other agents in the crowded command center. The windows were completely blacked out. The only light was from a multi-split-screen image projected onto the twelve-foot cathedral wall facing the desks. Quickly taking note of all the drone imagery on the screen, I found a seat and began surveying the seriousness of what was unfolding. From what I could gather on the one map, Ryan and the other agents were en route to a place dubbed 'the District.' The aerial view displayed was broken up in a grid pattern, labeled with real-time moving images of personnel marked in orange. Spotting the live feed on many other cameras, the crew seemed to be near a lake with a dam or bridge.

Analyzing my reaction to everything, Deniz stood beside me as a stern-looking man approached.

"Mrs. Daniels, I'd like you to meet Commanding Officer Ben Ainsworth. He is in charge of this tactical group," Deniz introduced.

I put my hand out to shake his hand politely, hoping to make a good impression and break the ice. "Pleased to meet you, Sir."

"Pleasure, Ma'am," he stated coldly, going about his business, ignoring the handshake.

Deniz stepped forward bravely. "Mrs. Daniels is requesting permission to stay in the room and quietly observe, Sir."

To my dismay, he looked at me with icy eyes and firmly stated, "I will not authorize that request. Please show Mrs. Daniels to her room."

Shocked by the rejection, I frowned in anger. Deniz sensed I was about to say something. Interfering, she sternly shook her head, suggesting I not make a peep.

"This way, Mrs. Daniels," she directed, giving me the eye.

Reluctant to follow her, with an enormous amount of rage looming, we walked down the corridor and entered another room.

Now alone, she pointed her finger at me. "Don't say anything to that man to make him angry. I hope to drop in on things now and again while going to the kitchen for you. That is the only way I'll be able to gather information when things proceed. The last thing we want is for both of us to be confined to this room. Anyway, I think it might not be wise for you to have stayed and watched. I mean, it will be stressful and might get…umm…difficult. I'm trying to be as straightforward and honest with you as possible. I think it is best that I relay information as we go."

Processing what she said, knowing she was right, my main focus had to be on the health of the baby and me. I calmed down and replied, "Yes, I understand. Thank you. Any help you can offer, I will certainly appreciate."

"I know, Lovey. Let's just play along with what Officer Ainsworth expects, and we will work around his parameters. I will get you through this if we cooperate. Deal?"

"Deal," I agreed, offering a truce.

Throughout the afternoon, Deniz frequented the kitchen almost every hour and kept returning with nothing new to report. Overly tired, around four o'clock, I told her I wanted to rest. Left on my own, I curled up on the bed, feeling helplessly anxious about everything, on top of suffering from fatigue, nausea, and dizziness. Taking a moment, I closed my eyes and tried to fall asleep, even if the nap would be short-lived.

| 64 |

The Battle

52°57'24" N / 1°04'51" W
53°21'56" N / 1°42'05" W
53°21'49" N / 1°41'54" W

Not knowing how long I had slept, my eyes opened upon hearing the sound of a door creaking. Urgently sitting up, the room spun in circles, causing me to fall back into bed. Unaware of my surroundings, with vision blurred, I saw a figure rushed over. It was Deniz.

"Sorry, I frightened you, Lovey. How are you feeling? Can I get you anything? You haven't eaten in about four hours."

Slowly sliding my body over to rest against the headboard, the nausea got worse. "Crackers and a Ginger Ale would be wonderful."

"Right away. I'll be back in a moment."

Deniz left the room and closed the door behind her. I tried to wake up in her absence. Struggling to get my bearings, I sensed a heaviness. Our situation felt very real all of a sudden. It wasn't a nightmare. Chased by an invisible enemy and violently attacked, we had a target on our backs. Now, having flown halfway across the globe, I was hiding in an undisclosed location. At the same time, my husband was about to participate in a dangerous mission involving the Cartel and was hours away from me. Not knowing how this would end, time passed at a snail's pace.

Returning with a tray of bland snacks, Deniz set everything on the floor beside the doorway. Taking a seat, she promptly waved me over. Upon joining her, we heard Officer Ainsworth instruct the team in a loud, commanding voice, "This is Jag-One-Two-Five. Let's get ready, people. Strike teams sound off."

One by one, every team leader checked in and confirmed their status, causing Officer Ainsworth to spout unknown commands quite intensely.

"Confirm. Jag-One-Two-Five. This is Slash-Four-Niner. Strike Team Alpha checking in."

"Roger that, Slash-Four-Niner," he confirmed over the radio.

We could barely distinguish what a few were saying between the static and commotion on the communications floor. It sounded like they were breaking up at times.

"Confirm. Jag-***-TWO-five. This is Mac-One-Two. Strike Team Bravo. Checkin' in."

"Copy. Jag-One-***-Five. This is Bam-Six-***. Perimeter Team. Watching over LADY-BD."

"Roger that. Mac-One-Two. Bam-Six-One."

There was dead air on the comm for a moment. All we could hear was the clicking of computer keys under the fingertips of the control center agents.

"This is JAG-One-Two-Five. Confirm Reaper standing by?" the officer requested.

A fussy voice announced over the radio.

"Roger. This is Kirk-Nine-Seven. Confirm. Pilot ready. ETA eight mikes."

"Jag-One-Two-Five. This is Signal-Two-Four. Sensor Pilot ready."

"Roger. Kirk and Signal. Conduct surveillance. November 532231 Whisky 14223. Need eyes on the compound."

Officer Ainsworth sounded calm.

"Roger JAG-One-***-Five. Standby FOR visual."

Deniz leaned against the wall and whispered, "Okay, let me get you up to speed with what I've gathered while you were sleeping. Your Bryan is en route to the Peak District. He is approaching the Ladybower Reservoir, where the perimeter team sounded off. A safe house bunker is located under what was once the old dam's pump house. It has mostly been converted into luxury apartments on the upper levels. Two weeks ago, agents were covertly embedded in this location. When the Cartel moved into the farmhouse across the lake, the rest of the teams systematically converged, disguised as tourists. Intel has been running satellite surveillance, keeping track of how many men he has with him, noting movement at any time, and recently, the weaponry he's acquired and from whom. Initially, this campaign aimed to capture Tomás and his men and incarcerate them on multiple murder charges. Since receiving a confirmation on the array of illegal weapons supplied to him, it seems the plan has changed. This is now a combat mission. They have tracked each delivery truck coming and going for the past few days, investigating their place of origin. When this goes down, known arms dealers stationed within the UK and surrounding countries that had contact with Tomás will be raided simultaneously. This operation could possibly be the largest, multi-agency Cartel weapons takedown in history."

Terrified, realizing they planted Ryan in the middle of a war zone, I felt numb with an overwhelming sense of helplessness, knowing there was absolutely nothing I could do. With sights lowered to the floor, my stress level heightened. Trying to keep my emotions in check, I found it helpful to clench my hands intermittently to ward off crying.

Unable to offer comfort, Deniz asked, "Should I continue sharing the rest, dear?"

With a nod, desperate to know more, I gave her the okay.

"The safe house Bryan will be in is surrounded by the same classified agents and special operations assault teams who have been on-site this whole time. This drastically reduces the chance of a security breach. In addition, every agent's communications are being secretly monitored, given the nature of Bryan's file history thus far. As for Tomás, he will be looking for your husband and the decoy to enter the complex. If he doesn't see them, it will tip him off that something is wrong. The plan is to beat Tomás to the punch. Upon receiving orders, agents and strike teams will move in on the farmhouse, arrest them, and contain the mess behind the curtain. Based on intel, the team has gathered enough evidence to put this guy away for a long time, solely on the illegal arms in his possession. Add in several murders, and he will be given nothing short of a life sentence, if not the death penalty, depending on extradition. Hopefully, this whole thing will go down peacefully, but they've given the field orders to use deadly force if necessary."

Too sick to speak, I overheard Officer Ainsworth go through several more checks, prepping everyone involved.

While listening, my attention returned to Deniz as she continued to explain, "I heard Bryan is armed and wants to be more involved in the operation. They have sternly declined his request, given that he is not an active agent, regardless of his specialized training. So, when the time comes, your husband will be escorted to a series of historic tunnels far below the pump house. They lead through the interior walls of the dam to the extraction location on the opposite side of the lake. From there, he will be taken to a clearing beyond the densely wooded forest when it is safe. The special ops team has confirmed the details of his extraction via helicopter. The timing of this part must happen with great precision. These agents have done this many times, so I feel everything will go well."

Fully understanding the specifics, I knew all we could do was sit and wait.

"Magnify camera one," a voice announced urgently within the room next to us.

"Control. This is Kirk-Nine-Seven. Got A visual of the compound. Count of seven heavily armed vehicles. RM-31s, with 120mm SRAMS, one with VDV 30mm cannon, and Twelve RZR-ATVs."

"Copy that. Kirk," the agent replied.

"Control. This is Signal-Two-Four. Confirming counts of Kirk-Nine-Seven."

"Copy that. Signal."

Listening further, Deniz confirmed that the convoy of Land Rovers was still en route and would reach the front gates of the pump house apartment complex shortly, with Ryan amongst them. Worried, she also shared an observation. "If they have not arrived there by now, they must have stopped somewhere along the way. Perhaps they used side roads instead of the main highways. Hopefully, they didn't run into any trouble." Stopping, she wished she could take that last sentence back after seeing the expression on my face. "Sorry…" she said as I nodded to acknowledge her apology. "I don't mean to worry you."

"I know."

Officer Ainsworth brought attention to the camera images supplied by the drone. "Jag-One-Two-Five to Kirk-Nine-Seven. Do you have a headcount on the compound? What are we looking at? Do we have a final number?"

Turning to me, Deniz said, "Our remote location is responsible for perimeter site operations, including personnel, cameras, and drone surveillance. Other locations are monitoring different aspects of the mission."

"Kirk-Nine-SevEN to Jag-ONE-Two-Five. Looks like 83. Repeat. That's headcount Eight-Three."

"Jag-One-Two-Five. This is Signal-Two-Four. Confirm headcount Eight-Three."

"Roger that. Kirk-Nine-Seven. Signal-Two-Four. Standby," Officer Ainsworth said. "We move at 23:00."

Realizing how many military personnel were involved to rid the world of this dangerous man and his affiliates, the thought struck me. If Tomás went through this much trouble to avenge his brother, can you imagine how much damage he could cause if left to take over his family's empire? The guy loved power. He needed to be stopped.

Quickly diverting my attention to the situation at hand, we heard more information coming from the room.

"Jag-One-TWo-Five. This is Perimeter Bam-Six-ONE, covering Lady-BD—Rovers home. Repeat - Rover is home."

"Perimeter Bam-Six-One. Copy. Confirm embedding phase," an agent requested on behalf of Officer Ainsworth.

"Roger that. Embedding confirmed."

Deniz deciphered what was said, "Okay, Lovey. Your husband just arrived and is safe inside the pumphouse complex."

With each agent spouting off so much information, it was hard to decipher what was going on. It sounded like the group was looking for anything, indicating Tomás and his men were about to move.

Unable to eat, with my stomach in knots, praying Ryan would make it out, my mind turned to those men and women in the field, placing themselves in harm's way, knowing most would have families. I asked for their safe return and promptly included them in my prayers.

By nine-forty-five, still nauseous and tired, I knew I had to try and stay awake. Surrendering from the floor to the bed with eyelids fluttering heavily, I asked Deniz to tell me when something happened. Even though I knew she was on high alert, I still couldn't settle my nerves. Lying on my back, changing positions often, I half-listened to everything going on and ended up resting my eyes.

Then, seconds later, an agent in the control room shouted, "Sir! Signal-Two-Four confirming movement outside the compound."

Quickly waking, sitting up straight, Deniz must have thought I rose from the dead.

"Tomás' men are moving," she whispered.

"Targets *Oscar Tango Mike*," an agent urgently beckoned, indicating they were *ON THE MOVE.* "Two vehicles headed north on a service road just east of the farm. Pax count ten. That's pax count one-zero. Possible mortar. Possible RPGs. Stand by."

Breathing erratically, a man's voice on the control floor said, "Five trucks departing the compound! Caravan demonstrating hostile formation based on chatter on the wire."

"This is Signal-Two-Four. Confirming two more RG-31 carriers just uncovered, fitted with 120mm SRAMS on north service road ridge," the Reaper Signal Pilot belted out. "Confirming ten pax and mortar. Standby for weapons identification."

"Mac-One-Two! Secure the area," Officer Ainsworth ordered, firmly questioning in a monotone voice, "How many are en route to the bridge?"

"This is Kirk-Nine-Seven. Thermal shows five moving inside the compound. Count of Twelve on the ridge. Forty pax in trucks headed east on A57. Along with twenty-six - that's two-six - on ATVs flanking trucks and hillside trails. ETA to bridge – three mikes."

"This is Control," the communications operator stated. "All Strike Teams. Heads up. Targets are mobile."

Each officer on the ground confirmed in succession following protocol.

"Roger Control. Strike Team Alpha. Copy."

"This is Strike Team Bravo. Copy that Control."

"Roger. Roger. Perimeter Lady-BD. Copy that."

"Why do they keep saying PAX? What does that mean?" I asked.

Deniz chimed in. "Pax means passengers in the vehicles. They are trying to determine the headcount. The strike team had them surrounded. Unfortunately, they scattered before we could move in and contain this to one location. Seems like he got a jump on us. I wonder if someone tipped him off?"

Chaos erupted down the hall. With commands spouted internally and from field personnel on the ground, I swiftly sat with Deniz on the floor to listen by the door.

"Caravan approaching bridge. That's Targets on bridge heading south. A6013. Over."

Heeding every word, trying to figure out what was happening, the room again unexpectedly burst with a surge of dialogue. My heart pounded inside my chest so hard my body uncontrollably rocked back and forth on its own.

"Vehicles one, two, and three heading south. A6013. Towards Lady-BD. Vehicles four and five are holding position on bridge."

"This is Signal-Two-Four. Count Sixteen on bridge. That is one-six pax and holding. Over."

"Confirm. Ready to Engage, Strike Team Bravo. Snipers offer cover. Keep eyes on RG-31s hillside and tangos on the bridge." Officer Ainsworth sounded so calm.

"This is Mac-One-Two. Strike Team Bravo. Copy."

Within seconds of that response, the communications floor went into battle mode.

"Deniz. What is happening?" I asked with concern.

Focused on the commentary, she replied, "Tomas wants a fight. He beat us to it. He's got men on the bridge and some en route to the pump house."

"All Targets dismounting. Repeat. Targets dismounting. Engaging fire on the bridge! Repeat, engaging fire Killbox-Bravo! Heads up! Narcos has NVGs! They have eyes!"

Immediately, my hands moved into a praying position. Resting them against my lips, hearing everything unfolding, I hoped they had gotten Ryan to that tunnel-holding area. With a sense of horror, we waited, listening to the rest of the agents concurrently belting out Intel on what was happening in the different zones. Most of it was in code, so it was hard to translate what they were saying amidst multiple blasts and gunfire loudly spreading down the hall toward us.

"What does that mean?"

"NVGs are night vision goggles," Deniz clarified. "They can see in the dark just like us."

A voice counted down calmly after an order was given. We could hear a loud explosion engulfing the Comm-Link seconds later, before getting confirmation.

"This is Mac-One-Two. Ridge RG-31s. Tango down. Over."

"They just took out the weaponized trucks on the ridge," Deniz clarified.

"Caravan 1 and 2 attempting to breach perimeter. Repeat, Narcos crossing Lady-BD boundary. Truck 3 is holding position by the docks. Multiple targets engaging fire!"

Realizing that there was a full-scale assault taking place, with many locations battling the Cartel, Deniz and I were shell-shocked by how this escalated so quickly.

"Sir. Trucks one and two are carrying heavy weaponry. Visual confirms Elbit RMS combat vehicle—headcount - eight. Vehicle two is fitted with 120mm SPEAR. Eight pax."

Receiving a radio transmission with orders from another Commander, Officer Ainsworth belted out with authority, "This is Jag-One-Two-Five. Snipers take out all targets. Strike teams, Alpha. Bravo. Perimeter. Clear the field."

"Copy Jag-One-Two-Five. Clearing the field!"

Lowering her head, Deniz knew what they were doing. Unsure whether she should elaborate, it was the most hated part of the job. Taking the life of another was not something they ever took lightly. In such cases, she understood that those in battle were not given a choice when the threat level was high. Waiting for me to ask for clarification, she hoped I wouldn't.

"What? What does that mean?"

With slight hesitation, Deniz said with a heavy heart, "Clear the field means to dispose of all targets."

Unable to breathe, I realized several men were about to lose their lives because of their loyalty to Tomás. Moments later, multiple confirmations came through from personnel, with gunfire and destructive blasts echoing through the command center as the speaker system made the floor vibrate beneath us. Unsure of what had systematically blown up, I knew by the calmness of the men in the room it must have been successful.

"Chameleon in Storm Room. Cover Chameleon in Storm Room!" Officer Ainsworth demanded.

Deniz sat up straight and looked over at me. "I think they've already moved Bryan to the bunker. This is it."

"Ready Helo for EVAC. Repeat. Helo for EVAC," Officer Ainsworth boldly ordered.

"They are sending in the helicopter to pick him up." Hanging on every word from the command center, she gathered what information she could.

"Affirmative. Helo inbound for EVAC."

I could not decipher anything more, but Deniz said, "They wouldn't move him out unless the coast were clear."

"Helo approaching EVAC ZONE - two mikes! ETA on Chameleon? Over..."

"Roger that. Chameleon arrival - four mikes. Confirm..." an agent stated.

"Roger. Helo, standing by."

We heard the pilot respond in a monotone voice without a hint of emotion.

Praying harder than ever, I hoped God would bring Ryan out of this safely, along with every other agent in the field. Heeding the chaotic jargon going back and forth on the Comm, we completely lost track of what was transpiring. Then, out of nowhere, we caught the words,

"Storm room under fire! Repeat! Storm room HOT."

"Positive ID. Tomas in Storm Room. Four flanking him."

Deniz looked up at the ceiling in desperation, suspecting Ryan's group was ambushed. Backing away, grabbing the pillow I was sitting on, I wrapped it around my head to block my ears, hoping not to hear the words, *Chameleon down.*

With her ear angled toward the hallway, Deniz listened intently and raised her index finger to silently signal me to wait as she gathered what information she could.

Giving me a thumbs-up, I removed the pillow and heard the helicopter pilot confirm -

"This is Helo… Got visual on Chameleon."

Finding out Ryan was going to the helicopter, we took note of anything more that had to do with him. I curled up on the edge of the bed and sat gently, clenching my hands around my knees, making sure I wasn't squishing baby, and waited, rocking myself back and forth.

Five minutes passed…

"Affirm. Chameleon on board. Ready for EVAC. Over…"

Officer Ainsworth replied, "Roger that, Helo. Stand by…"

"They've got 'em, Ava. They've got him." Deniz sighed with fists clenched.

The room went into a frenzy. Every agent simultaneously shouted countless instructions, comments, and commands.

Crying, I looked up and thanked God for watching over him, but knew he was not out of danger yet. He still needed to make it safely out of the zone.

"Helo. Affirm. EVAC Chameleon. Over…" Officer Ainsworth authorized.

"Roger that."

"Slash-one-four-nine to control! RPG on ridge! Repeat! Ghost RPG tango on the ridge! Abort Helo!"

"Kirk-Nine-Seven! Take out target!" Officer Ainsworth shouted, authorizing the hit.

"Copy Jag-One-Two-Five. Launch confirmed!"

Amid gunfire echoing down the hallway, Deniz's face flashed elements of fear. The only thing I could decipher was the word *ABORT*.

"Oh, my God!" she said with a look of shock, "They have sights on the chopper."

Holding my breath, we heard a massive explosion over the Comm… Was it the helicopter that exploded, or someone taking out the gunman? Deniz wasn't sure.

"No. No. No," I shouted, covering my ears once again! "No. Please, God. No." Losing hope, I thought that was it. Unable to control my emotions, I began sobbing.

Deniz suddenly stood straight and quickly made her way over to where I was sitting on the bed.

In seconds, a man entered the room and instructed, "Deniz? We have orders to move Mrs. Daniels to the extraction site. Please follow me."

Expressing a look of dire concern, she helped gather my things. While leading me back down the hall, holding me up by my arm, passing the situation room, with tears flooding my cheeks, barely able to focus, I heard in a somewhat daze-filled moment…

"Control. This is Mac-One-Two! RPG down! But missile away! Repeat missile away!"

"Helo! Helo! DIVERT! Evasive action! Missile away!" Officer Ainsworth barked, not taking one second to acknowledge us at all.

Descending the stairs to the garage below, we returned to the Land Rover.

"Welcome back, my dears!" the lady agent joyfully said, sitting alongside her husband in the driver's seat.

Unaware of what was happening, Deniz sternly shook her head at her, causing the woman to turn around and skip the pleasantries.

Backing out of the garage, we pulled away from the building.

I sobbed while they adhered to the GPS coordinates, maneuvering through the narrow streets of whatever small town it was. The compass inset in the rearview mirror showed we were driving in a northeasterly direction.

"Where are we going?" I asked grimly.

The woman confirmed, "We are heading for Syerston Airfield base about thirty minutes out."

Worried beyond words, I feared the worst. Staring out the window, forcing myself to think positively while driving cross-country in complete darkness, we rarely passed a vehicle along the route. I kept my hands melded together for the entire trip, listening to the rhythmic hum of the tires moving over the cracks in the road. Constantly praying, believing Ryan was alive and we would make it through, I closed my eyes.

Just before one in the morning, the driver told Deniz we were about two minutes away from our destination. Anxious, I could hardly sit up. I was so exhausted.

Entering the gates of the deserted airfield was eerie. No one else was in sight. We passed two buildings before pulling up to a large steel hangar, where a mid-size jet sat waiting with two pilots finishing their safety checks. Hit by a burst of adrenaline, I flung open the door when the truck stopped and rushed to the plane. Deniz raced behind me. Climbing the steps of the small aircraft and walking inside, I instantly looked around and realized - it was empty.

In disbelief, I saw the somber expression on Deniz's face.

"He's not here! Oh, God, Deniz. Ryan's not... He's..."

Confirming something terrible had happened, overcome with emotion, my knees went weak in the aisle. Deniz reached out and caught me. Lowering my body to the floor, unable to breathe, the tears flowed. With my heart racing, a feeling of helplessness and sorrow engulfed every inch of my body and soul. Gasping for bits of air, Deniz did her best to offer comfort, fully aware her efforts were in vain. Sinking into darkness again, I clung to her, mindful that I was being extracted alone. Caressing my tummy with my hand sparked thoughts of our baby growing up without a father. Not knowing what to do, a sense of devastating grief took over.

"How could this happen?" I gravely whispered between sobs.

Unable to stop the crushing torrent flooding through me, I had flashbacks of them removing Ryan from the helicopter many months ago. Forcefully separating us at the time, the feeling was blood-curdling. It was then the familiar searing pain in my chest returned.

Deniz kept a tight hold of me. Concerned for the baby's health and well-being, she rapidly reviewed medical protocol should things go very wrong. Trying to keep me calm, I could hear her speaking. In a muffled state, nothing she said made sense. Amidst it all, her attention suddenly gravitated elsewhere. Turning from me, not moving a muscle, concentrating on a few loud bangs outside the plane, Deniz placed her finger over her lips and whispered, "Shhh…Stay down…"

Immediately slipping a gun from her hidden holster, she moved me to the back. Instructed to get on the floor and hide in the last row of seats, shaking in fear, I did what she asked. Placing herself in harm's way, Deniz racked the slide on the gun and aimed at the only entrance to the aircraft. Lacking a clear view out the side windows, we waited. There was nowhere to go. Keeping the doorway in her sights and her finger on the trigger, we heard someone climb the steps. With hands over my ears, bracing for shots to ring out, Deniz watched a shadow round the corner in the dimness of the cabin. Noticing baggage awkwardly in tow, hitting the interior walls along the way, she quickly lowered her weapon. It was Agent Frank. Returning her gun to its holster, checking on me, thankful we were not in danger, I got off the floor and sat in the seat.

Not even noticing Deniz had him in her crosshairs, Agent Frank stumbled about and stashed his things into an empty spot before finally making eye contact with us, quickly detecting that I was distraught.

"Oh my god, what's wrong? Is she okay?" he asked, moving in our direction, overly concerned.

Finding me with tearful eyes, unable to speak, he realized what was happening.

He took a knee and placed his hand on my shoulder. With a hint of arrogance, he said, "What? Did you think I would actually leave without him?"

Standing up, moving aside, he looked towards the door as my eyes gravitated in that direction. There, I found Ryan on board, frantically searching for me.

"Ev?" he said in desperation while scanning the plane.

Marked by bloody scrapes and bruises, dirty clothes and all, Ryan's protective instincts surfaced as he urgently made his way over, pushing D'Agostino out of the way. The rest of the crew boarded the second Ryan wrapped his arms around my shoulders and held me tightly in the most loving embrace, realizing full well I thought he'd died. Tucked against his chest, I could feel his heart pounding.

Unable to stop trembling, crying a mix of emotions, he kept whispering, "It's okay, it's okay. I'm here. I got you, Ev. I got you." Kissing my forehead, he knew all I needed was to hear him repeat those words.

Deniz backed off to give us a moment. Standing there, she dramatically collapsed into an adjacent seat to gather herself, relieved that Ryan had survived. Seemingly a little pale herself, taking multiple deep breaths, she soon got up and went out to collect my things from the truck before returning with them, working up the nerve to say goodbye.

"Thank you for protecting Ava for me."

"Oh, you're so welcome. It was a pretty emotional assignment, to say the least, but everything worked out for you both," she said sentimentally while we each descended the steps of the aircraft.

Walked with her to the truck, Deniz turned around. With open arms, I immediately hugged her and expressed my gratitude.

"Thank you for helping me through this. I couldn't have done it without you. Maybe we will see each other again someday, under happier circumstances?"

"Yes, maybe someday. Until then, take care of yourself and this wee one in there," she smiled, placing her hand on my tummy. "I'm so glad I could help. All the best to you, Lovey. You are going to make a great Mum."

Lost for words, all I could do was nod.

Through the tears streaming down my face, Ryan put his arm around me.

Deniz got back into the SUV. Closing the door, she rolled down the window and waved before departing the airfield.

Lovingly escorted by my husband to the plane, the co-pilot emerged from the cockpit and said, "We just received departure clearance. Please take your seats."

Settled in, watching them prepare for take-off, Agent Frank disclosed, "Unbelievable few weeks...huh?" He took a deep breath and continued with a heavy heart. "Tomás' violent nature was to his detriment since he decided to fight until the very end."

Ryan lowered his head upon hearing that statement.

Exhaling, Frank added, "Most of his men did the same, unfortunately. Only a few were able to think for themselves and surrender. The rest, well." He paused in a moment of silence. "The main thing is, we got you both out safely and discovered the mole in the process."

"Who was it?" Ryan asked as we taxied to the end of the airstrip.

"Officer Barry Raymond, the guy assigned to both your cases. From what we know, the Cartel threatened his family if he didn't supply info on anyone within the program slotted to testify against Consuelos. Four weeks ago, the agency received a call from his wife. She seemed very concerned for their safety since she suspected her husband was involved with *some evil people.* Thinking the accusation wasn't entirely credible, knowing Raymond's stellar record, the call was noted and left at that. Unbeknownst to us, Raymond mysteriously disappeared that day. Also, his wife fled their home and went into hiding with the children. When they were reported missing by close family members, we investigated their disappearance. Safely locating their whereabouts, we placed them in protective custody, suspecting

Raymond may be involved with Consuelos based on the wife's findings. Searching Raymond's house, the agency confiscated his computers and any electronics. The Cyber unit accessed his files and found information transferred directly to an unnamed IP address, where we discovered a connection to a rogue Consuelos affiliate. Once we confirmed who it was, the bureau issued a warrant for Raymond's arrest and tracked him down at a remote family cottage in upstate New York. Long story short, it looks as though you two might get that opportunity to disappear permanently. We cleared you from the system. Here are your new IDs. As requested, we're moving you to another safe house built to your specifications, Bryan. I think you'll feel secure in this new location."

Reaching cruising altitude, I reclined my chair after Ryan grabbed us a couple of blankets and pillows. Noticing that I wasn't doing well, he also went through the cabinets at the front of the plane to find chilled water and some packaged salted crackers to nibble on.

An hour into the flight, Agent Frank and the team kept typing on their laptops. I assumed they had numerous reports to submit.

Eventually, Ryan and I surrendered to sleep while the trip dragged into the late morning hours.

| 65 |

Safe

46°16'48" N / 63°07'58" W
46°22'07" N / 62°08'27" W

With the faintness of daylight hitting the Atlantic Ocean, my eyes opened when the plane made a turn and cast a beam of light across my face. Carefully moving, mindful not to wake Ryan, I stretched a little, feeling the dizziness and nausea return with a vengeance. Quickly heading to the washroom to splash water on my face and change into the last of my clean clothes, I scrounged for more bland crackers and water.

Hearing the landing gear deploy, the pilot announced, "Good morning. We are beginning our descent into beautiful Charlottetown, Prince Edward Island, Canada. Please place your chairs in the upright position to prepare for landing. Secure all baggage. We will be on the ground shortly."

Relieved that our journey was almost over, I felt somewhat rested but still sickly, not to mention in desperate need of a shower and real comfort food. On the way back to my seat, I found Ryan alert and moving about freely without pain despite the blood-stained, dirty clothing he had changed out of hours earlier. Ready to disembark and continue to our new destination, Agent Frank came over to give us final instructions.

"Everything you will need is in this envelope. We linked the credit and debit cards to your new names and accounts. Your driver's licenses, passports, cell phones, and the deed to your home are there. I also included some cash to get you through the first few months. Should you ever require my assistance, the information you need is listed inside. The US Government thanks you for your service. It was a pleasure working with you both."

Shaking our hands, Ryan said, "Thank you for getting us through this."

Humble, he responded, "That's my job. Happy to do it. Your life will be a little quieter now, but if, heaven forbid, that changes, you know where to find me."

Touching down on the runway in the smoothest landing ever, the pilot confirmed in a monotone voice, "Welcome to Charlottetown, Prince Edward Island, Canada. The time is 6:15 AM Atlantic Daylight Time. We are just going to taxi to the Brackley hangar, where I believe you have another vehicle waiting. I hope you enjoyed your flight."

Once the plane stopped, the co-pilot opened the door for Agent Frank to deal with immigration before we could disembark. With the formalities out of the way, we left the plane after bidding the team goodbye. Frank waved before the door was once again secured. They were now en route to Virginia.

With our bags in hand, two security officers standing beside the silver Suburban SUV greeted us on approach.

"Hello, Sir," the burly man said to Ryan while opening the back door for us.

"Hi," Ryan remarked, knowing these guys had no idea what we had just suffered.

Knowing I looked a little worse for wear, probably not in the mood for casual conversation, the man addressed me with a nod. "Hello, Ma'am."

Taking a seat beside me once I got settled, Ryan cast a look of concern. "Av, you don't look good. What do you need? Just tell me, and we'll get it for you."

The security guards offered some water and a protein bar. Ryan passed it over to me.

"I just really need to get to wherever we are going," I confirmed, hoping the trip wouldn't take too long. Taking a drink from the bottle and a few bites of the bar, I reclined my seat. Thankfully, the sick feeling started to subside slightly. Grateful to be resting in Ryan's arms, I thanked God for returning him to me safely, knowing how indebted I was to Him for protecting the love of my life once again. Content and relaxed, I dozed off.

After almost an hour on the road, the driver slowed and turned off the highway.

Wishing for me to share the view, looking down at the ocean and our new home, Ryan whispered, "Av? We're here. Look. You have to see this."

While waking up, trying to focus, I saw this quaint, gray-cedar-shingled house nestled alongside an awe-inspiring cove. It immediately reminded me of my grandparents' Southampton home. Sitting up, I felt a bit better. Within minutes, the driver stopped in front of the place and officially announced our arrival.

Scanning the area before getting out, I noticed there wasn't a soul around except for another cottage, similarly built to ours, about three hundred yards away.

"Where are we?" I asked, wondering if it had a name.

"We are on the outskirts of Souris," Ryan revealed. "We'll visit the town once we've settled in. Come on. Let's go check out the house."

In an instant, we got out and inched our way around the deck attached to the home, taking in the peaceful view and listening to the sounds of the Atlantic Ocean rolling in. The first thing I felt was a sense of tranquility, similar to what Hamilton Island offered before we had to escape.

This was where our new life was about to begin, I thought. In a few short months, we'll be starting a family and hopefully be able to experience a sense of stability for once.

Standing outside the main entrance, about to walk inside, Ryan suddenly stopped me, saying, "Ev, wait!"

Startled, terrified to ask why I needed to stop, he suddenly scooped me up in his arms after opening the door.

"I have to carry you through. Isn't that tradition?"

With great care, he stepped inside. Carrying me over the threshold, we explored the beautiful space, noticing the grand floor-to-ceiling fieldstone fireplace, spacious modern kitchen, and professionally decorated rooms we'd call home for a while.

On the counter, Ryan found the operations manual left behind by their contractor, Paul. Locating the security control panel, he started testing out all the extras installed in the house. Showing me the retractable steel shields, bulletproof windows, and a few unique upgrades, he said, "Follow me. I have something cool to show you."

Both of us passed through the living room. Following Ryan down the hall, he stopped at a bookcase built under the upper staircase landing.

"Watch this," he said with anticipation.

Quickly referring to the manual, he pulled back a title-less book from the shelf. Instantly, the cabinet slowly slid forward, revealing a secret room behind it. Hand in hand, he guided me down the long, enclosed spiral staircase as each step illuminated. Finally reaching the bottom, our feet hit the floor, and a state-of-the-art security room came to life automatically. Countless computer screens displayed an abundance of detailed information on anything we needed. The middle monitor above the control area had crisp camera images that scanned the perimeter and interior with video and audio. To the right was a stocked weapons cabinet, and to the left of the bunker was a storage area with food, water, and supplies to get us through any emergency. To the south of the desk area was a tunnel leading to a split underground pathway.

Pointing to the left, Ryan said, "This access leads to the ocean and has a boat, and the path to the right leads to a car parked inside an underground garage about 50 feet in that direction. Both have completely undetectable departure doors."

Proud of what he had designed, divulging it took almost a year to complete, I was thankful to stay in one place finally.

"I hope and pray we never have to use any of this - but I'm glad it's here if we do," I said, seeing him smiling at me, knowing he was too.

Upon returning upstairs, the entire security room shut when we left, and the bookcase moved back into place. Curious, I decided to continue climbing the stairs to the second floor to find our room. Entering the primary suite, captivated by the view from the bed overlooking the ocean, I rounded the next corner to find the walk-in closet. With a selection of clothing hanging there, I knew who had shopped for us. Thinking it must have been Kayla, thoughts of her made me smile. "You are now our only friend."

Journeying into the hallway to see the other bedrooms, I was excited to transform one into a nursery, knowing it would be a nice project to work on for the time being.

When I joined Ryan downstairs, I found him setting up the new alarm system. Opening the envelope from Agent Frank, I was curious about our new names and hoped this was the last time they would be changed. Optimistic, turning to the photo page of each passport, I read them out loud. "So, your name is Evan Hamilton, and your wife's is...Elle O'Connor, AKA Mrs. Elle Hamilton. Hmm... How long will it take to get used to those?"

Chuckling and putting the manual on the counter, he said, "I don't know. It will probably take a while. They're different. Hamilton, huh? How fitting. No matter what it says on those, you will always be Eva to me. My life began when I met you, so it doesn't matter what it says there. We are still the same people who found each other months ago. The only difference is I love you more than ever now." Strolling up to me, he wrapped his arms around my waist as mine found a home around his neck. "I love you, Eva Thompson."

"Love you too, Ryan Davis," I said while smothered by his precious kisses.

Rubbing my belly, he quickly added, "Love you too, little man."

"How do you know it's a boy?" I asked, quite skeptical.

"I don't know. Just a feeling, I suppose."

Slowly separating, he concentrated on making the security system fully operational.

Peering out the side window, I noticed the other house not far from ours. It seemed another couple was living there.

"Hey, look, I think we have neighbors?"

Questioning whether they were friendly, I walked out the back door. Focused on the two people sitting on the deck, both reading books quietly, with brimmed Tilly hats shielding them from the sun, the woman suddenly looked up and saw me. Waving frantically in our direction, she quickly nudged the man beside her. He calmly closed his book. The two began making their way hand in hand down a grassy path. Getting closer, I couldn't believe my eyes! It was Kayla and Captain White. Confused by the couple thing, wondering if it was part of an undercover operation, I couldn't wait to talk to them.

Bursting with excitement, I said, "Kayla! Captain White! What are you doing here?"

Ryan emerged from the house when he heard me call out their names.

"Hi, you two!" Kayla greeted us with absolute joy, offering heartfelt hugs.

Captain White and Ryan shook hands before pulling each other in for a manly pat on the back.

"Hi, Sir," Ryan said respectfully.

Immediately catching up on what was new, we revealed we were pregnant, and she informed us that our ordeal brought them even closer together. So much so that after working together for ten years, they eloped two weeks ago and have since semi-retired. Like sharing special moments with a sister, she and I seemed to have this deep-rooted connection. Knowing we had *family* nearby to spend time with made this place feel more like home.

| 66 |

Hiding in Plain Sight

46°22'07" N / 62°08'27" W

Writing what could be the last entry in this journal, having run out of space, I opened it to the final pages remaining and recorded the date. Staring out over the Atlantic, the water sparkled with the sun beating down upon it. The sound of the waves roared while crashing against the beach below.

Six months have passed since settling in this picturesque town of Souris, Prince Edward Island. We don't live in fear as much anymore. We know the stealth team is never far. Always ready to take us out of harm's way, I hoped we would never need them again.

For now, we are enjoying a somewhat ordinary married life. Ryan launched another home security system business, this time offering international elite clients the ability to create the perfect safe house for their families. Lucky for him, his wife is qualified to design the blueprints. Our clients only see the faces of Kayla and Captain White at the helm since we've decided to stay hidden from sight because you never know who is lurking in the shadows, and honestly, I rather like it that way.

Coincidentally, I came across a news article featuring my Los Angeles museum this week. Construction had just now resumed after all this time. The article paid homage to the talented architect, the late Eva Thompson, and included a quote from George Gavin.

She was the most talented young woman I have ever had the privilege of working alongside. Everyone at the firm misses her terribly. Well beyond her years, she was an inspiration to so many. A plaque will be unveiled in her honor upon completion of the project. May she rest in peace.

I teared up while reading it. Now a treasured piece of my past, I look forward to seeing the finished product in the coming months.

As for the new house, I feel like it has become a home, especially after adding little touches to make it more ours. Even though it has a few unorthodox technologies secretly concealed, it still feels very cozy and warm, especially when our wonderful neighbors come by for a visit. They have seen us through the best and worst times, but now live a stone's throw away, proud to join us as members of our little family.

We finally finished the nursery a couple of days ago and are eagerly awaiting the arrival of our new addition, scheduled to make his appearance early in the New Year. Ryan was right; it's a boy! Life could not get any better than it is at this moment in time. I have everything I could have ever dreamed of having. I found my Prince, most unconventionally, I might add, just as my sweet Grandmother once said I would. The only thing missing was the closeness of the families we left behind. Maybe one day, if the universe allows, we will have an opportunity to see all of them again. Until then, we still have each other.

Throughout this journey, I learned life is about timing. You can't force something that is not meant to be. If two hearts have a future, no matter how many years go by, how far they need to travel, and even how many obstacles stand in their way, fate will get them to where they need to be so they can experience a love like no other.

Escaping Whitsunday was horrifying. Fondly looking through my journal, our time together blended many memorable moments amongst all the bad. Months filled with experiences most only dream of and others you wouldn't wish on your worst enemy. It is not the life I expected, but I'd go through it all over again if I knew it led me to a future with my husband, my soul mate and protector.

So many times, I looked to the sky in desperation and prayer, hoping for that one person to show up with a smile that gave me butterflies. Little did I know, he, too, was wishing the same.

Sitting at my new drafting table, having placed the computer screen to the right of my desk to marvel at the unobstructed view of the ocean, I now work alongside the love of my life.

Yes, the love of my life. After all this time, I finally found him.

The End

Visit
EAStarkBooks.com
for stories that take you away!

9 781777 112400